TWISTED THROTTLE

Satan's Devils MC - Next Generation Book #3

COPYRIGHT

PRODUCTION ACKNOWLEDGMENTS

Cover Design by Wicked Smart Designs

Edited and formatted by Maggie Kern @ Ms.K Edits

Proof reading by Melanie Darrow

Photographer: Golden Czermak of Furious Fotog

Model: Dylan Horsch

CAST OF CHARACTERS

Officers

Wizard – President

Drummer (ex-Prez) – Vice President

Hound – Sergeant at Arms

Throttle – Enforcer

Heart – Secretary

Dollar – Treasurer

Joker – Road Captain

Mouse – Computer Expert

Patched Members

Wraith (ex-VP)

Peg (ex-Sergeant at Arms)

Blade (ex-enforcer)

Bullet

Cast

Drifter

Hawk

Jekyll

Lady

Marvel

Roadkill
Rock
Shooter
Truck

Prospects
Butcher
Nathan
Rascal
Tommy - Honorary Prospect

Old Lady's and Children
Amy (Wizard's)
Olivia (Hawk's): Layla
Sam (Drummer's): Eli (Hawk) and Zane
Sophie (Wraith's): Olivia, Zoey, Eliza and Hilda
Tash (Blade's): Sabrina and Mason
Darcy (Peg's): Noah (Throttle) and Lisa
Marcia (Heart): Amy, Jacob, Isabel and Alexis
Maya (adopted daughter of Joker and Lady)
Mariana (Mouse): Yiska, Maria and Tanya
Becca (Rock's): Rose and Aidan
Ella (Slick's): Faith
Allie (Truck's): Hope
Carmen (Bullet's)
Sandy (Viper's)

Sweet Butts
Clover
Pussy
Sable

Members who've moved on
Hyde – left the club
Dart – transferred

Beef – transferred
Road - transferred

Deceased Members

Adam
Buster
Tongue
Hank
Viper
Slick
Kidder
Shortass

SATAN'S DEVILS MC

CHAPTER ONE

*T*hrottle…

"I've got a sighting of the prospect's bike." Striding up, Mouse brusquely interrupts the conversation I'm having with Hound.

Both of us stand immediately and my heart starts racing. "Where?" I could do with dishing out a good ass kicking.

Flicking his long grey streaked hair over his shoulders, Mouse grins, having gotten the response he wanted. "It's not gone far. It's hidden in a junkyard to the south of Tucson."

"Cast?" Hound yells at the brother standing by the bar. "Throttle and I are headed out. Wanna come?"

I grin. He hasn't even asked me, but he knows I won't turn this shit down. Nathan might just be a prospect, but he and his belong to the Satan's Devils, and stealing a man's ride is one of the worst crimes possible to commit. Flexing my knuckles, making them crack, I know I'm going to enjoy teaching the culprit a lesson he won't forget once we get our hands on him.

As our phones ping with the location, the three of us waste no time.

Nathan's rightly proud of his ride and had tricked it out. While it might be broken for parts, shipping it out of state and selling it would bring in far more dollars. We can't waste time if we want to get it back and hopefully catch whoever stole it red-handed as well.

Since our previous enemy, Archangel, was put into the ground, life has been quiet. While I wouldn't wish trouble on the club, I could do with some excitement. My adrenaline rises as I head for my bike.

"Want company?" Drifter asks as I'm throwing my leg astride the seat.

News has obviously got around, and brothers are flooding down to the clubhouse.

"Nah, we've got this," Hound calls. I show my agreement with a raise of my chin.

"I want to come." Swinging around, I see Nathan standing there with a petulant look on his face.

"You were the one who lost it in the first place," I round on him. "If I were you, Prospect, I wouldn't be reminding us of that fuckin' fact. No ride, no place in the Satan's Devils."

He pales and takes a step back. Sure, I can yank his chain, but the way his bike had been stolen from under our fucking noses had been slick. It could have been mine if I'd left it without it being padlocked up, which I might have done had I expected to only be gone for a minute. Who locks their bike when stopping just for a moment to drop something off?

"Hey, Prospect! Yeah, you, Razza." I point to Rascal, another one of our prospects and, if he keeps his nose clean, one who'll soon be patching in. "Get your fuckin' bike. You're coming with."

He's sharp and eager, and doesn't waste a minute to run to his own two-wheeler.

"Go get 'em, Brothers," Joker calls out, walking down toward us with his arm over Lady's shoulders.

Hound, the club's sergeant-at-arms is waiting for me. As enforcer, I'll head the ride alongside him. With just a check over our shoulders that Cast and the prospect are ready to go, we twist our throttles and ride down to the gates, which our third prospect, Butcher, has already opened. Then, once carefully down the track that always seems it could do with some maintenance, we hit the highway, increase our speed, and head toward town.

Nathan's bike is red-hot property. Unless it was stolen by a blind man, no one could have missed the prospect leaving it unattended outside Angels for fuck's sake, the strip club the Satan's Devils own. He'd only parked there to take Butcher the phone he'd left behind, but those few minutes proved more than sufficient for it to be hot-wired and driven off.

Two days it's been gone. Two fucking days that Mouse has spent pouring over the CCTV footage and tracking it across the city. The thief had been clever though, detouring through residential areas where security cameras didn't exist or were less accessible. How Mouse found it in the end, I hadn't bothered to ask. I just assumed he'd done what the computer guru always does best and worked his magic on his keyboard.

Of course, our burning question was whether the bike was deliberately taken by someone wanting to fuck with us, or if it was just an opportunistic crime. The danger is the more time passes, the more likely it would be stripped or moved on. It's a matter of pride to all who wear our patch that we get it back. No one fucks with the Satan's Devils. The recovery is a question of our honour, and the punishment of the culprit needs to send a message. As enforcer, it's my job to emphasise the stupidity of messing with the club.

My anticipation grows each mile we cover as we ride through Tucson. When Hound pulls us over before the place comes into sight, I understand, but am frustrated with the delay.

As we stand around him, he places a call to Mouse.

"Got eyes, Brother?"

"Of course I fuckin' have." There's a snick, then an indrawn breath, and we wait for Mouse to take an inhale of his inevitable joint. "I've tapped into their security. I've seen only two men—one in the office, one operating the crusher."

"The prospect's bike?"

"Back of the yard, near the rear boundary. I only spotted it because of the flames painted on the tank. It's hidden in with a heap of others."

"Stolen or wrecked?" If there are more intact motorcycles, we could have stumbled into a bigger operation, and not just one where it's only our club that's the target.

"Hard to tell from the view I've got."

I raise my chin toward Hound. He nods, clearly thinking the same as I.

"So, do we just walk in the front door?" Cast asks.

An idea occurs to me. The bike of the prospect who's come with us is a proper rat, something he'd cobbled together himself —a bit of this, a bit of that. We tolerate it as it's as fast as shit. But it's ugly as hell, doesn't even have a proper paint job, though he promises one day he'll get around to it.

"Hey, Razza. You looking to scrap that heap of shit?"

His eyes go wide, but, like I reminded myself earlier, he's not far off patching in, and catches on immediately. "Could do with the cash," he replies with a wink.

"And we're just friends along for the ride."

Hound grins widely and starts removing his cut. Cast and I do likewise, and Rascal follows our lead. With our cuts safely stowed in our saddlebags, we get back on the bikes and head off down the road again.

From there it goes like a dream. Our story gets us in. We overpower the man in the office and have him tied up in under a minute. Then, we meet the same man again, causing me to do a double take before I realise he has to be the first man's twin. Two down, and one prospect's bike quickly found.

Hound calls for the crash truck to take two breathing bodies and one reclaimed bike back to the compound, while I connect my own call to Mouse.

It doesn't take me long to sum up the situation. "Looks like a trade in stolen bikes," I tell him, having seen sight of a number of perfect bikes hidden in a heap of wrecks. "And there's a computer here." When he asks me to switch it on, I do and henceforth follow his instructions. Within moments, his exhaled *Bingo!* tells me he's in and already downloading their secrets.

An hour later, we're back on the compound along with Nathan's bike and the two thieves trussed like chickens.

"Hear you brought me a present, Brother." Blade, our ex-enforcer, grins widely as he falls into step beside me. "Been quiet lately."

"Mine," I growl possessively. Well, fuck. I did all the work bringing them in.

"Hey, I can watch, can't I?" he whines.

"Fuckin' ol' guys," I grumble.

The prospects jump into action, Nathan being particularly rough, but who could blame him? In no time at all, both culprits are strung up in our storage-come-torture room. Plastic sheeting has already been spread out, luckily. As it happens, one has already pissed himself.

Other brothers follow in after us, all wanting to see justice served. No man should touch another man's ride, let alone steal it. It's a cardinal sin in our eyes.

As I step closer, I throw Blade a warning glance. Sure, I respect the fuck out of him, but ill health meant he had to step down, and as much as he doesn't like it, this is my role now. As he raises his chin toward me while simultaneously rubbing at one of his hands, I know he understands and wouldn't disrespect me in front of my brothers.

Glancing around, I see the room has filled and is standing room only. Now it's my turn to shine.

Finally, I get the sign I was waiting for. A nod from our prez, Wizard.

"This can go one of two ways," I drawl lazily as I grab hold of a stool and position it in front of the men. Sitting, I stretch out my legs, crossing them at the ankles, and fold my arms, purposefully relaxing my body. It's a direct contrast to the way their arms will already be feeling the strain. "This can go easy or fuckin' hard. Which will it be, boys?"

The thieves are so similar it's hard to tell them apart. I suppose working where they do you couldn't expect them to be spotless, but they're scruffy and not particularly clean. From where I am, I can smell a bad case of body odour. Maybe I'd accept it easier if I thought they'd shed sweat as a result of an honest day's work.

When they don't answer my question, well, I discount the faint whimper from one, I lift my chin and bark, "Names. You first." I point to the one on the right.

Still, they make no move to cooperate, but a deep voice booms out behind me.

"The Dray twins. Cedar and Oak."

"Cedar and fuckin' Oak?" I half-turn to check Mouse isn't joking.

He gives me a chin lift, then continues, "Their Pa owns the scrapyard, but is more of a silent partner nowadays." Thank fuck Mouse has done his work.

"So," I face front again, "is Pa someone we should bring in?"

The men look at each other in horror. "No. It has nothing to do with him," the one on the right calls out.

Are they protecting the old man—his sons must be at least forty—or are they doing something he wouldn't approve of? Well, that's for me to discover.

"Cedar?" I try, and yeah, one pair of eyes shoots to mine. "Was it you who stole a Satan's Devils' bike?"

His mouth slams shut.

I sigh, unfold my arms and straighten my legs, then I get to my feet slowly. "Hard it is." I pick up the baseball bat.

A few broken ribs, two broken noses, and at least one broken leg later—the injuries split equally between the pair—I find out precisely what racket they're running. They run a gang who steal then bring them the bikes. They, as expected, either strip them, or ship them to California where they've got a friendly dealer.

I step back, put down the baseball bat, then approach them again. "You going to shut your operation down?"

"Man, how d'you expect us to earn a living?"

"Going fuckin' straight," I toss back at Cedar. "You've got a legit business."

"We'll go straight," Oak cries out. "We promise."

"Shut it, Oak."

"One sure way of making sure they permanently end their operation is to finish them here and now," Wizard says coldly, his tone making even me shiver.

Shrugging, I take my gun out of my cut.

"We'll stop." Cedar's got the hang of this now. "We'll break up the gang. Go straight, just like you suggested."

Blade's eyes are fixed on me. His brow is creased. Does he think I'm going to let them get away with it? I throw a grin in his direction.

"See," I turn back to the twins, "you may not think it, but I was brought up right. I even know some of the scriptures. You know what happens to thieves?" I pause for a moment, enjoying their confusion before I tell them. "They get a hand cut off. I seem to think that's a good punishment."

"It was him," Cedar shouts. "I just went along with it. Oak told me what to do. I've got a family, man. I can't work if I lose a hand."

"Cedar?" Oak's expression makes me sure—far from being the ringleader—he was the one coerced into the game. He's shaking like a fucking leaf. Seems like Cedar got the backbone which he lost out on.

"A word, Brother?"

Blade's got a gleam in his eyes. It's a sign he's got something to say that might well be worth my while to listen to. When he jerks his head, I follow him to a corner. As I listen to what he has to say, I start to grin, then my expression becomes a full-on smirk.

The ex-enforcer is a working example of while much of life can be taken away when your hands no longer fully function, there's nothing wrong with his brain. And on this occasion, he does have the answer. I'm also keen on trying his experiment. I mean, I've heard and even read about it, but empirical evidence always helps.

Screams, pleas and begging go completely unheeded as first Oak, then Cedar, is taken down and forced over to the vice.

Their eyes flick in horror as I casually ask, "Now, who's going to be first?" I decide for them. "Cedar it is."

"He's Cedar!"

"Fuckin' not."

"Nah," I break up the familial betrayal, "Oak was the one who pissed himself. Get him in place, brothers."

Shooter and Marvel jump forward, anticipation sparkling in their eyes. At my signal, they take a tight grip and force Cedar's right hand down.

Now, following Blade's helpful suggestion, I turn the vice, crushing the bones and severely damaging the tendons.

Beside me, Oak screams in pain and wrenches his hand away from the prospects, cradling it in his left. I exchange glances with Blade and grin. He owes me five dollars that he'll have to pay me later. Seems that identical twins do indeed feel each other's pain.

Being convinced Cedar's the ringleader, I catch Prez's eye, jerk my head toward Oak, and give a negative shake. Prez nods, sealing Oak's reprieve for now. If they go back to stealing, he will know what's coming for him.

As a verbal warning I add, raising my voice to be heard over Cedar's continuing sobs of anguish, "Next time it will be your dick in the vice. You fuckin' hear me?"

When Oak pukes, luckily on the plastic, it's time to get them out of here. The two men are loaded into the truck, and Butcher takes the driver's seat. The other prospects, Nathan now back on his bike, and Rascal, I instruct to provide an escort. Then, waving at Blade, I invite him to come along for the ride. The ex-enforcer and I follow the procession into Tucson to complete the final stages of our plan.

I know a junkyard is full of dangerous machinery, and vehicles of all shapes and types just waiting to go into the crusher. A blow to the back of each of the twins' heads renders them unconscious as soon as we arrive and gives us time to work out how to pose them.

It takes only a few minutes to decide which of the toys we have at our disposal we'll play with. Then we put our plan into action. When it's done to our satisfaction, we drive away, relishing the image of the two men trapped how we left them. A block and tackle will be thought to have given way, trapping both their right hands under a heavy truck engine. Cedar's clearly is crushed, possibly beyond repair. Oak's? Well, it depends on how loudly they can scream for attention, and how long it takes for rescue to arrive.

How long will it be? Fuck knows. I don't give a damn. If they die, so be it. If they're found, well, a surgeon will be earning his money.

Any story about Satan's Devils' involvement? Very unlikely. Before knocking them unconscious, I'd issued some threats should they point a finger in our direction or ever steal a motorcycle again.

When Mouse discovers they have no health insurance, I grin.

Don't touch a man's ride. It's not fuckin' worth it. Bikers don't take shit from anyone.

CHAPTER TWO

*T*hrottle…

"Walk with me?" Though he's voiced it as a question, I'm only too well aware that coming from my dad, it's more of an instruction.

Draining my remaining beer in two swallows, I leave the empty bottle on the bar and follow in his footsteps, something I feel I've been doing for the whole twenty-four years of my life. Some habits are hard to break.

"What's on your mind, Peg?" I still sometimes refer to him as my parent, but more often I use his club name. I'd prospected as soon as I'd turned eighteen, and for the last five years I've been a patched member. So as well as father and child, we're both club brothers. Since he stepped down from the sergeant-at-arms role and I became the enforcer, I outrank him. I think that's taking us both time to adjust to.

"It's a nice day, let's walk."

Suppressing my instinct to roll my eyes, I just follow him out. Except during the summer months when a monsoon's lashing down and no sensible person would go out at all, it's always a nice day in Tucson. Even rain brings the benefit that water from the heavens has, the effect of cooling the air, so it's not all bad, though born and bred in Arizona I can deal with the heat.

Having nothing better to do, no other place I need to be, I follow him up the track that leads to the houses situated at the top of the compound, then continue as he carries on through the gate at the rear boundary. Peg walks in silence. Though curious as to what's on his mind, I say nothing to prompt him. With my old man, he'll get around to whatever he wants in his own time.

With me easily matching his long strides, we don't take long to cross the all-important firebreak that's saved us a few times, and on into the Coronado forest that backs onto the compound. It's cooler here, shaded. Whether he knows it or not, he leads me to the fallen tree trunk where a few months back I'd found Hawk brooding alone.

It makes me cast my mind back to how we'd all missed the signs that Hawk had been heading for a mental breakdown. He's doing better now. With his blood and club family supporting him, he's well on the way to once again being the man he was.

When Peg sits, I perch beside him. As I've done many times during my life, I run through anything I could have done wrong, which would cause a parent's lecture to come from his mouth. But I come up blank. It's not like he can give me the talk about being respectful to the girls. I grew out of pulling their pigtails more than a few years back.

I wasn't lonely growing up on the compound. The other chapters had always joked there must be something in Tucson's water, as our club had become overrun with rug rats. Being one of them at the time, I couldn't see anything wrong in it. I'd had the biker version of an idyllic childhood, growing up with a whole tribe I regarded as brothers and sisters, just as much as Lisa, the sibling of my blood. I'd been a typical boy, I admit it, teasing the fuck out of the younger kids until I matured, when my desire for fun had become overridden by an innate desire to be a protector. As that began to show, I'd had a clear path to first becoming a member, and subsequently, the enforcer for the club.

Sure, that had happened years earlier than I expected. At least I hadn't stepped into a dead man's shoes. Blade and the other old guard had abdicated their positions for one reason or another, including Peg who used to be the sergeant-at-arms.

While Peg continues to stare into the distance, I begin to get bored with the history running through my head and prompt him.

"What's on your mind, ol' man?"

"Less of the fuckin' old," he growls, turning his head toward me. He grimaces, breathes in and out, then starts in on what he's brought me here for. "Your mom and I are worried about you."

The fuck? What have they got to worry about? I'm twenty-four years old with an officer role in the club I was born into. I thought I'd been doing alright. As is my way, I often resort to gestures instead of words, so I raise one quizzical eyebrow toward him. Being economical with words often prompts the other party to start talking. It's one of the traits which makes me a natural in my role.

He shifts uneasily as I put him in the position of being the one to communicate. "That business with the twins—"

"That's my fuckin' job, Peg. I knew what I was getting into when I stepped up to be the enforcer."

"I know it's your job," he snarls back. "But after Hawk…"

Just those words, and it makes sense.

"I'm not Hawk," I tell him firmly.

He grimaces again. "I know. But it makes me wonder. You're even younger than him, and you've taken on so much responsibility for the club."

I'd thought he was proud of me. Is he not? "Peg, you know things were heading this way for years. Blade took me under his wing years back. Maybe I didn't expect to get the title until I had a few more miles under my belt, but with Blade's hands…" My voice trails off. It's as sad as fuck to see the previously proud man's hands gnarled by arthritis. "You know Blade's there alongside me more often than not."

I don't mind the ex-enforcer insisting on being present when I have to do the less pleasant parts of my job. I'm mindful he misses it, and on my part, I'm not going to turn down good advice. I like helping him still feel useful. It's payback for the support he's given me in the past. Thank fuck he can still ride a bike, leaving the club would destroy him.

"You're so young," Peg tells me with a shake of his head.

"For fuck's sake, Dad." It's time to get personal. "What were you doing when you were my age?" I continue without giving him space to answer, "I'll tell you what. You joined the Marines at the age of eighteen and had already done numerous tours. You'd killed more people than you can probably remember. And you think I'm too young?" I scoff. "Age ain't nothing but a fuckin' number."

"You know I didn't want you to follow in my footsteps."

I do. I'd been brought up with that message. He and Mom had thought the sacrifice of his leg was more than enough for any family. I had wanted to go, like Mason, Blade's son, and Jacob who's Heart's, but I'd stayed back out of respect for my parents. Wars kill and maim and go on without end. The location might be different to back in Peg's day, but every day people are being sacrificed for things which aren't most people's business or concern with no seeming benefits except for those pulling the strings. It's a never-ending cycle.

"Fact is, Peg, if I had signed up, I'd be subjected to far worse than I am being here."

"You'd have grown up fast."

That makes me brittle. "You trying to say I'm fuckin' immature?" My hands form fists. He might be my dad, but if I, as enforcer, feel the need to lay down the law, the club would be on my side. Only thing is, one-legged as he might be, and in his sixties now, he keeps himself fit. I wouldn't necessarily come out the winner.

As if knowing he's pushed me too far, Peg holds up his hands. "Whoa, down boy. I didn't mean any disrespect." His eyes seem to gaze straight ahead at nothing. "You're right. Being a Marine taught me the facts of life, forced me to grow up fast. Made me realise what I wanted from life. The important shit, a family."

"Fuck, Dad." I have an idea where this is going now. "You're right in one thing, I am young. Too fucking young to have a family."

He shrugs. "Your mom and I are worried about you, that's all. What would be wrong in having a woman in your life? Mom would love for you to bring a girl home, but all you seem to do is fuck whores."

I can't see anything wrong with that. "Maybe it was the example you set. It took years for you to get together with Mom. You must have been forty or close to it when you met her."

His eyes firmly fix on mine. "I wasn't sowing my wild oats everywhere while I waited. I knew a woman like Darcy would be worth holding out for. I spent that time searching, not fuckin' around."

I breathe an exasperated sigh. I can't see what's wrong with how I choose to live my life. My focus is on the club which is right where it should be. I've no time for female distractions, so what's the problem with me going to indiscriminate women for casual hookups when I get fed up with my hand? Which, admittedly, is quite a lot. *It's not possible to have too much sex, is it?* I make sure they all go into it with their eyes open so no one gets hurt or has expectations.

"Mom says she'd be able to get you into the fire service if you wanted to do something different with your life."

I sigh, trying to put the point calmly and suppressing the instinctive roll of my eyes. "You didn't want me to become a Marine because it was dangerous." I pause for emphasis. "Now you want me to be a firefighter? I've seen you, Peg. You get worried as shit when Mom goes to work." Even though her promotion ties her up with bureaucratic shit which keeps her away from the front line, she'd still prefer to be in the thick of things when we have a major incident, and, occasionally, to Peg's absolute horror, is. My temper starts to flare once again. "Is this it, Peg? Are my *fuckin'* habits all you wanted to talk about? 'Cause I ain't got time for this shit."

"I'm worried about you, Son, and so's your mom."

"I worry about you, *Brother*," I retort. "I think you're losing your fuckin' mind." I breathe deeply, in through my nose and out through my mouth. "I'm a Satan's Devil, just like I was always meant to be. I'm not going to do a Hawk on you. Hell, that was a lesson for all of us. So if I think I'm falling, I'll ask for a hand to help me back up. Stop with trying to hook me up with a woman—can't you see that was Hawk's problem? He couldn't cope with the VP role *and* having an ol' lady to lose. You should be pleased I'm concentrating on just one thing, and that's being the best fuckin' enforcer this club has ever had." I get to my feet, needing to leave before I say something I regret.

"Throttle, Noah…"

Shaking my head, I stride away. I need to get on my bike and clear my head with a long ride, or better still, find an anonymous woman to fuck.

Peg sometimes says looking at me is like seeing a reflection of his younger self. *We've both got the same desire to protect the club, but that's where our similarities end,* I think to myself, as I stride back down to the compound, bypassing the clubhouse and heading straight for my bike. One line he hadn't used today when referring to my preference for variety when it comes to women was about how he'd brought me up to respect them. My usual retort, I grin to myself as I approach my motorcycle, is that I sure am respectful, always making sure they come first.

It's early evening and I decide to head down into Tucson to the Wheel Inn, the restaurant and bar which the Satan's Devils have owned forever in my view, going back long before I was born. Over the years, the place has changed and modernised. Sandy had retired years back, and Martha had taken over. A few months back, despite Martha's declaration she'd work until they carried her out in a coffin, she'd sadly suffered a minor stroke and had reluctantly decided to give up.

It had been Tash who'd shown an interest in taking over the job. For years, Tash had had a successful career writing books for children, with Blade, who'd shown a hitherto hidden talent, providing the illustrations. As Blade's hands worsened, he'd sadly had to give it up. Tash hadn't wanted to work with anyone else, so the children's series came to an end. But she hasn't given up writing completely. She's turned her hand to romance novels, and had thought working at the Wheel Inn would help her research, considering the gambit of characters she'd meet there.

Knowing and respecting Tash as we do, no one had objected to her becoming manager, although it was rather ironic. Blade's first introduction to her had been when he'd found her digging for scraps from the food bins. Being Blade, he'd chased her off.

One thing that hasn't altered is that brothers are usually here, firstly to grab a delicious dinner, and secondly to make sure any rowdy element is kept out.

The Wheel Inn is divided into two halves, one a table service restaurant, the other a bar area for patrons who just want to wet their throats and/or order a bar snack. Only needing a drink, I make my way to the latter. Cast is already there waiting to be served. As I walk up to him, he waves forward a paying customer so they can be dealt with first.

"Sup, Brother?" He follows his greeting with, "Anything up with your ol' man? Saw you walk off with him."

I shrug. "That business with Hawk has got him scared. He seems to think he should do check-ins to make sure I'm not heading for a breakdown."

Cast snorts. "You? Nah. Mind you, I'd have said that about Hawk. Guess it could happen to any of us. You don't see that shit coming."

That's true, I suppose. "I'm right where I want to be, Brother. I've got nothing going on inside." I tap my head, as if to emphasise my point.

Cast raises his eyebrow and grins. "You're just twisted, Throttle. You have to be after spending all that time with Blade."

"You using my ol' man's name in vain?"

I startle. Seems I wasn't the only one to learn lessons from Blade. Tash has crept up every bit as quietly as her old man would have done.

Cast smirks. "Yeah, I was saying he's twisted. Just like Throttle here."

Tash laughs, then shakes her head, but doesn't dispute his choice of word. "What can I get you boys?"

"Beer," Cast and I say at the same time, then look at each other and chuckle.

Tash gets us two beers, then turns to the next paying customer.

"Noah?" A hesitant feminine voice sounds. It's vaguely familiar. Cautiously I turn, thinking one of my old conquests might be around, and prepare to let them down gently. It's very rare, if ever, that I go back for seconds.

It takes me a moment to place the woman in front of me, partly because my brain has to translate her transition from a girl. It must be six years since I've seen her. Placing her though, I give a genuine smile.

"Gwen!" When I hold out my arms, she walks into them. We hug, then I hold her at arm's length, taking a good look at her. "Well, look at you. You're all grown up." *And in all the right places.* "What the fuck you doing here?" Noticing the tray she's just put down on the bar, I supply my own answer. "You working here?"

Smiling, she tells me, "Yeah, I have been for a week now. I've finished college and I've got to find some way to pay off my student debt."

I know what we pay our waitstaff—slightly above average, but not enough to make someone rich. "You won't do that fast, working here."

She shrugs in agreement. "I've got a day job as well, kind of."

Raising my eyebrow encourages more. "I just finished my four-year degree this summer. I'm interning at a legal firm now. I'm hoping to be a paralegal."

As an intern, the wages would suck. Needing a second job is understandable, especially when drowning in debt. Little Gwen, as I still refer to her in my mind, seems to have her head on straight.

"Law? What are you specialising in?" It's actually a relief to talk to a woman without expending effort trying to work out whether there's a chance of taking her to bed. Gwen's out of bounds, just as she always has been. Her vibrancy, her spark, shows none of my original reasons have changed.

"What I want to specialise in is family law: divorces, child custody, that kind of shit. But I'm getting all-round experience at the moment."

There were so many Satan's Devils' kids at school that we formed a close-knit unit. Only a few outsiders had managed to worm their way in, but somehow Gwen had been successful when she'd formed a friendship with my sister Lisa. Quiet, innocent, and undeniably naïve, there had been something about Gwen that made the girls befriend her and the boys want to protect her. From time to time we'd had to step in, as Gwen had been the victim of bullies. Of course, her close relationship with the Devils' kids hadn't always helped her, but at least it stopped the physical abuse.

Gwen had never come to the compound, however. We'd figured out early on what a *nice* girl she was, with citizen foster parents who'd be horrified if she associated with bikers. But at school, we'd all done our bit to make her life easier. While I hadn't given her a thought over the years, it's nice to catch up on what's happened to her. I'm happy she's found a direction in life that seems to suit her.

While she still looks much the same, she's filled out a bit—got tits now at least—but still has got that wholesome, girl-next-door look that doesn't get my cock particularly excited, screaming, *off-limits*. It won't though, I decide, be a hardship to see her around more. I also sense a work ethic, meaning she'll be an asset to her employers, and in this case, my club will benefit.

"Gwen?" Tash calls and pointedly jerks her head toward a table which is full of empties.

"On it, boss," she throws over the bar with an easy smile. To me, she says, "See you around, Noah." Going on tiptoes she places a kiss to the side of my cheek, like the one that used to reward any Devil kid that helped her, and one which could have been given by my sister.

"Sure you will. I come here a lot."

"Nice-looking girl." Cast looks after her appreciatively.

My eyes narrow as I notice his eyes glued to her, admittedly, shapely ass. I slap his back hard. "Not for us," I tell him. "She's not for a Satan's Devil."

Cast raises his eyebrows, sees I'm serious, then shrugs as he accepts it. He takes to scanning the bar. "What about her?" He subtly shifts his eyes, and I glance quickly in the direction he's pointed out.

Yeah, this one looks like she might know the score. She's about five foot four, or would be when she's not in those stripper heels she's wearing—a bit short for my liking. I get my height from my dad and stand six-and-a-half-feet tall. Still, I'm not looking for an old lady, and at least I wouldn't strain my muscles when fucking her against a wall. Assessing her as quick fuck material, I notice her short blond hair that looks like it's come out of a bottle, unlike Gwen whose rich chestnut locks are the same colour and just as long as she wore them in high school.

As this girl's hair is as fake as hell, it makes me wonder whether her tits are as well. Even from here, they look too perfect. Gwen's are natural of course. I can remember back when she hadn't had any, but tonight I'd seen they'd developed quite nicely. Inwardly I laugh at myself, *I shouldn't have noticed.* But what's that saying Sophie uses? A cat can look at a king? Just because I could appreciate her, didn't necessarily mean I'd make a move on her. *She's out of bounds.* Just as I'd told Cast.

The other woman catches me staring, returning my gaze with a hint of speculation. Hmm. I wouldn't be surprised that if I beckoned my finger, she'd bring those slim-looking legs my way.

She's brassy, not a woman you'd put on the back of your bike, but definitely one I'd be happy to give my cock to.

"Excuse me."

I jerk, having been lost in making mental plans for the rest of the evening. "Oh, sure, Tash. Sorry."

I move aside so she can get out from behind the bar. Automatically my eyes follow Blade's woman as she crosses the room and goes straight to the person who'd just caught my eye. I'm interested to see them talking together. *Friend of Tash's?* Nah, looks more like business.

I drink beer and talk bikes with Cast, noticing, like me, his eyes land now and then on the woman who Tash is deep in discussion with. Then, clearly giving up on approaching her tonight, he slaps my back and tells me he'll see me back at the compound. Once he's gone, I realise that it's gotten late without me noticing, and the place is closing up around me.

I frown, then realise I've calmed sufficiently from my altercation with Peg and I might as well get home too. I'm finishing up my last drink when Tash returns. Her face is flushed, as though she's been in a heated discussion.

"Who was that?" My eyes narrow, seeing she's agitated.

"That? Oh," she waves her hand in dismissal, "nothing I can't handle. That woman I was talking to has arranged a bachelorette party for one of her friends. It's being held here tomorrow. We were discussing the final details." Tash casts a glance behind me, then rolls her eyes. "She was hard to convince that male strippers weren't allowed." Drawing in a deep breath, she confirms the problem. "They're holding it in the restaurant—"

"Which is a family space," I finish for her.

She nods, seeing I get it, then her eyes sharpen. "It's

tomorrow night, Throttle. Any chance you'd be an angel and come to make sure it goes alright? I get the impression no one tells her no very often, especially when she brings flattery into play. I'd rather have someone here who can handle whatever goes down, and I don't want to ask Blade."

That I can understand. Blade's got a short fuse, and is liable to get out his fucking knife, especially if there's any backtalk toward his woman. A prospect may not be able to handle a situation with women with the tact and diplomacy our business requires, but it would be no problem for an enforcer.

"I can do that, Tash. No worries. What time does it start?"

As Tash tells me the details, I notice the woman has now left. Oh well, there's my chance gone for tonight. But tomorrow? Well, if she tries to cause trouble, I know one good way of shutting her up.

CHAPTER THREE

*T*hrottle…

"Your mom and I just want what's best for you, Throttle." Peg starts almost as soon as he walks in. "We worry about you."

Peg might be getting on in years, but the gym, originally put in when he came back from war missing half his leg, is still his domain. He works out himself and is always on hand to help anyone who needs it with some spotting, or advice on their form. If I wanted to avoid him, the gym's the last place I should have come. But that wasn't what I'd wanted. I'm here on purpose, needing to clear the air between us.

"I know that, Peg. But you've got to accept I'm a grown man." To get him to admit it, I've got to watch how I act, and keep a tight rein on my temper.

Peg idly checks the weights have been put back to his liking. After a few seconds pass, he replies, "I know that, Son."

It's as much as an apology as I'll get from him.

It's not that I don't have sympathy. He's had the front-row seat watching my transition from baby to boy, then from man to enforcer. As a kid, he'd help me up when I fell, but now he's got to just let me get on with it. Will I make mistakes? Of course, who doesn't? But I need to be allowed to make them and learn whatever lesson that results for myself.

Sure, Hawk's breakdown made us all question ourselves—the FOGs, or fuckin' old guys—more than us younger generation, perhaps. Had Drummer and Sam missed the signs when their son had been suffering so badly? That they must have has made the other parents on the compound, and there are many of them, re-examine themselves and keep a closer watch on their offspring no matter their age.

"I'm happy, Peg. I've got my life just how I want it. I know you hate me fuckin' around, but I make sure no one gets hurt. You and Mom have got to let loose the apron strings." I pause, then toss him a bone. "I promise you, if I do have problems, you'll be the first I'll come to."

He nods, his frown lines easing as he takes me at my word, then looks down at my hands as I remove the boxing gloves, having beaten on the punching bag enough for today. "Not chasing you off, am I?"

"Nah, I've finished. Was here long before you rolled out of your bed, *old man*."

Peg's hefty thump to my shoulder belies his age, I stagger, but laugh. "Could still take you down, whippersnapper."

Even if I wanted to challenge that, I wouldn't try. I've too much respect for him, both as my father, and as the former sergeant-at-arms. We may have words, may spar in the ring, but I'll never raise my hand to him in anger.

"You got a busy day?" He walks around eyeing the equipment as he normally does, adjusting this here, and that there.

"I'll put in some hours at the shop, then Tash has asked me to go back to the Wheel Inn. There's a bachelorette party later that might get rowdy."

He snorts, knowing full well, like I do, that while bachelor and bachelorette parties pull in the dollars, they're almost more trouble than they're worth. Then he chuckles. "Take care. Those bitches have claws, Throttle."

"Only too well aware. I'll watch out." I wink. "Ain't any of those bitches getting their hooks into me." I slap his back, then leave.

The morning workout has got my blood pumping. Returning to my suite, I shower, get into some fresh clothes and am ready to start my day.

Most days if I'm not needed elsewhere, I work in the auto-shop conveniently located at the entrance to the compound. I enjoy using my hands, and today put them to use tuning a bike to perfection. I then move on to servicing a car. About mid-morning, Blade appears. Back in the day he ran the auto-shop, doing a lot of the work himself. But now his hands are too gnarled. Most days he's either here, or down at our tattoo parlour, focusing on paperwork.

He slaps my back. "Throttle. Hear you're watching out for my ol' lady tonight."

I tense slightly, hoping he won't offer to come with me. Blade can be a loose cannon if things get out of hand, which at times is not a bad thing. If it had been a bachelor party, I might have invited him as extra back up. But women? Fuck, I can handle that with one hand tied behind my back.

"No need to worry, I'll take good care of her, Blade."

"Sure you will, Brother," he responds confidently. "I trust you to have my woman's back."

Strong words from a strong man. I might have taken over his position in the club, but I still feel a sense of pride when my worth is acknowledged. I just wish my own father would do that. Blade doesn't doubt me, so why does Peg?

Once Blade leaves, I continue alongside my brothers doing anything required and getting Drifter's help when a clutch replacement proves awkward.

When the day draws to a close, I clock off early, shower again to wash off the oil and dirt, then dress in clean jeans and a clean Henley as the nights are getting a little cooler—cooler but not cold. Autumn's never cold in Tucson. I complete the ensemble with my cut. I do the familiar journey on autopilot and walk into the Wheel Inn just after six o'clock.

The place is already busy with families and couples ordering specials and shit, many of which still come from Ma's cookbook she left to the club more than twenty years back. *Twenty-five*, I mentally correct. I wasn't even born at the time which shows how long ago it was. Her legacy is legendary, and part of the success of the restaurant is down to the recipes she'd left. She was a whiz at knowing just what herb or spice would turn an everyday meal into a gourmet experience. The secrets she left are a closely guarded secret.

Entering, I immediately spot where the bachelorette party will be seated. My cock twitches when I spy the girl from last night already there, along with a couple of giggling friends who are decorating the chairs with balloons and banners. In the middle of the table, there's a heap of things for the bride-to-be to unwrap. This not being my first rodeo, so to speak, I wouldn't mind betting a lot of that shit will be penis shaped. My ears already hurt in expectation of the squealing.

Hopefully the other patrons won't be offended. The noise and bawdy gifts are par for the course when a woman is about to settle down for some reason. Probably to remind her what she'll be missing. *Why would one person give their forever to another?* To me it sounds like a fuckin' life sentence.

It's certainly not the first time that I've been a spectator at one of these events. If I were to choose, I much prefer bachelor parties. If men get out of hand, I've no qualms in threatening or actually using my fists to settle them down. Women break far easier, and a big fucker like me needs to take care where he puts his hands if he wants to avoid being accused of sexual abuse.

When the girl who's the organiser beams at me, I give her a chin lift in return, turn away and go to where Tash is keeping an eagle eye on proceedings.

She seems to breathe easier when she sees me. "Throttle, thanks for coming down. Can I get you a beer?"

"Sure." She waves at Gwen who's obviously working tonight–maybe she's been pulled in especially to help with the bachelorette party—and tells her what I want. I order my usual beer, knowing I'll need to drink it slowly. I'm working, and I'll be needing my wits about me tonight.

"We meet again." Gwen winks at me as she hands me the bottle with the top taken off. "Something tells me tonight's going to be… interesting."

I chuckle. "You worked a bachelorette party before?"

"No." The corners of her mouth turn up, and her eyes sparkle. "But I've been to a couple. I hope you're not easily embarrassed."

"Me?" I full on laugh now. "Darlin', it takes more than a bunch of hormonal women swooning over candy dicks to get me rattled."

Grinning, she nods at the beer in my hand. "Want me to keep those coming?"

I tell her no. "I'll need all my faculties tonight, Gwen." I hear the street door open, and turning, narrow my eyes. A bunch of giggling women enter. One, presumably the bride-to-be as she's wearing a mock bridal veil, staggers slightly, suggesting she's been pregaming.

Tash notices and rolls her eyes. "Guess I better keep a close eye on the restrooms tonight."

Gwen gives her a shrewd look. "I'm pleased I'll just be waiting tables." Then she sighs. "So I best get started now."

Showing me that delectable ass I noticed yesterday, she walks off, skirting around the bachelorette party table, approaching a family who's just been seated. She has a tablet in her hand so she can take orders and have them go direct to the kitchen or bar, depending whether they're for food or drink. Our service is slick nowadays, and something we've got a good rep for.

If I were here on normal duties, I'd be sitting on a stool at the bar. But given the task of babysitting the bachelorette party, I'm on the restaurant side where there's nowhere to perch myself.

Instead, I go to take up position at the door, acting the part of exactly what I'm here for, a bouncer to keep undesirables out, and patrons within on their best behaviour.

I stand with legs apart and arms folded, surveying the room. Music is playing quietly in the background—old rock tunes I can just make out. It makes me smile to myself, wondering if Peg had anything to do with the playlist.

Apart from the bachelorette party, the customers fall into two camps—those eating without saying a word which points to their enjoyment of the restaurant's offerings, and those chatting amicably, while waiting to be served. A few eyes come my way, but with interest, not apprehension. Everyone who eats here knows it belongs to the Satan's Devils, and being able to take a walk on the wild side and get close to the bikers is part of the attraction, secure in the knowledge we've got too much invested to start trouble here. We're far more likely to end it. In fact, it's one of the safest places in Tucson.

In the thirty or so years we've owned the place, we've worked hard to maintain that reputation, which is why there's always one of us hanging around.

Ah, I spy another brother putting his head around the doorway that leads to the bar area. It's Marvel. As I give a sharp nod to show I've got it all under control, he raises his chin, signalling he's here if I need him.

The table with the bachelorette party starts to fill up, quickly becoming the noisiest corner of the room by far. Presents that had sat on the table are now being opened with great glee, a lot of laughter and girlish giggles, and the bride-to-be seems to be enjoying herself immensely. As I expected, penis lollipops, dildos and other paraphernalia are littering the table now, some items being passed around by the women in various stages of hysterics.

I have to feel sorry for the bride. If a dick made out of candy is so welcomed, what does it say about the cock of her future old man? Is he lacking in that area? Bored, I consider the uses for a chocolate dick, and grin at the possibilities. It would certainly sweeten a pussy. *Hmm.*

My thoughts might be rambling, but my eyes and body though, remain vigilant. Missing nothing, I see the petite blonde approach out of the corner of my eye.

"Hey, handsome. Why don't you come join us? We can put an extra chair at the table."

"Can't," I reply pleasantly. "I'm working." I soften my eyes. "Got to make sure you're all behaving yourselves."

She pouts. "It's a party, we're allowed to have fun." Then, narrowing her eyes and fluttering her eyelids, which honestly makes her look like she's got something in them, adds, "You could keep a better eye on us if you sit with us."

"Nah, the boss wouldn't like it."

Her head tilts to the side. "Don't you own this place?"

"The Devils own it," I agree, amicably enough. "But here the manager is in charge. And this is where she wants me."

She's so short compared to me, I have to bend to have a conversation, and when I look down, I'm staring right into her cleavage. Fake it might be, but hell, I wouldn't be male if I didn't see the possibilities of sliding my cock between those ample breasts.

"I'm Hattie by the way." She holds out her hand. It's small, with brightly painted long fingernails. Either she doesn't work, or those aren't real either.

"Throttle," I respond, seeing no harm in exchanging names. I touch her hand, then drop mine immediately.

"Can I get you another beer?" She spies my bottle already half empty.

"No, I'm fine. Thank you, sweetheart." I add the endearment without thinking.

The door opens behind me, and the final two guests of her party walk in. There are hugs, air kisses and the usual shit that goes on when women meet. Then Hattie, as she'd introduced herself, leads the newcomers to the table.

For that first hour, I sip my beer. The door behind me keeps opening and closing with the change of clientele. Customers who finished their meals are replaced by those that have come in hungry. Each time fresh air intrudes from the outside, I turn to check who's entering.

I'm grateful for my positioning when a man dressed as a cop crosses the threshold, his intention revealed when my rapid inspection shows his pants aren't standard issue, but one's made to come apart at the seams. My hand on his chest pushes him outside immediately.

He huffs and demands, "Let me in. I'm booked for a bachelorette party."

"Not here you're not."

Now I'm subjected to a glare. "This is the Wheel Inn. I'm in the right place. Look, man, I don't get paid unless I perform."

"Nope." I pop the 'p' deliberately. "There are kids in there." I don't want to argue or cause a fuss, so I enquire, "How much are they paying you?"

When he tells me his price, I take out my wallet and pull out some bills. I hold them just out of his reach. "Easy money if you go quietly. You don't even need to show your junk."

"You for real?" He eyes the bills eagerly. "I'll take it, man." He gives me a conspiratorial wink. "Sometimes those bitches, man…" Shuddering, he doesn't need to complete his sentence.

Passing him the money, I wait until he walks off. On re-entering, I find Hattie standing with her hands on her hips.

"We paid a deposit for him." She glances around me as if to see if the stripper is still in the vicinity.

Uncontrite, I point out the facts of life. "You were told no strippers in here as a condition of your booking. Losing the deposit is down to you."

"You… you…" She can't seem to think of a word bad enough. Tossing her head, she stomps back to her party.

Gwen, I see, is being run ragged, taking empties off the table and returning with trays laden with drinks. The bachelorette party is fast getting louder and rowdier.

"Hey, pretty boy! You lost us our stripper, why don't you take your clothes off?" one of the party shouts at me.

The whole table dissolves in giggles, then someone starts a chant, "Off, off, off…"

When I approach, they start to cheer, but I lean on the table, resting my weight on my hands, and say in my most menacing enforcer voice, "Calm it the fuck down. If you don't, I'll chuck you all out."

"You and who's—"

I don't even need to turn around. I sense Marvel at my back.

"Oh."

"I bet you'd look good naked." The girl who first spoken is not only drunk, but persistent.

"Yeah, take them off." There's obviously safety in numbers as another chimes in.

"Nah." It's Marvel's voice. "I've seen his body a thousand times. Even changed his goddamn diaper once. Christ, what a fuckin' mess. Think you've had a lucky escape, ladies."

I was a kid. What did he expect? Still, my cheek twitches as I try to hold in my laughter.

My amusement slides a little when he adds, "And he's got a tiny dick. Nothing worth seeing."

Turning, I glare toward the man at my back, while the women at the table erupt with more giggles, this time at my expense, and not a few glances down at my crotch. "I'll take it from here, Marvel." My eyes promise retribution.

"Hey, Brother. Just helping you out." Failing at an innocent look, Marvel grins widely and steps back.

I turn back to the ladies. "Now simmer down," I warn. "Any trouble and I will kick you out." Groans follow me as I return to my station.

Fucking bachelorette parties. Did I say I hate them?

CHAPTER FOUR

*T*hrottle…

Although there were no more taunts and suggestions about me stripping—maybe I should be grateful to Marvel for downplaying my attractions—when Gwen starts bringing out the desserts, I'm pleased it signals the end of the evening is approaching. They'll be on their way soon.

I'm watching both their table and the effect they're having on the other customers when Hattie gets to her feet and comes over.

"This has been a great night," she confides cheerily. "Bella is so happy." She stares at the bride who's beaming. And drunk. Very drunk.

"When's the wedding?" I'm not that interested, I just hope for the girl's sake it's not tomorrow. She'll be hungover as fuck.

"Next week. You married?"

I bark a laugh. "No, I'm not." I point at the bride-to-be. "You going to get her home okay after this?"

"What?" She shakes her head. "We're going to Angels. They've got male strippers tonight."

That makes sense. We own the Satan's Angels and from time to time, have visiting strippers in—ones with dicks rather than tits and pussies. I hadn't remembered there was one tonight.

Why should I? Guys strutting their stuff means nothing to me, but I wouldn't be surprised if Joker and Lady weren't in attendance. I make a note to shoot Heart a text in warning.

Drunk bachelorette party incoming. I grin, then to Hattie, say, "Well, you have fun." I widen my stance and look away from her.

When she takes the hint and returns to her table, I slide out my phone and shoot a text to Heart.

Throttle: Got a bachelorette party heading your way. Drunk off their asses.

Heart: …

Heart: …

Heart: Fuck. I'm shorthanded. You up for helping out?

Fuck. That's the right word. But I go where I'm needed.

Throttle: Joker and Lady not there?

Heart: Nah. Having an early night. (roll eyes emoji)

I thought I'd finished for the night. While wondering what sin I'm being paid back for, I respond.

Throttle: Sure I'll be there.

Heart: Owe you one, Brother.

You certainly do, Brother. And I'll be calling it in.

"They're leaving now, Throttle." Gwen speaks quietly as she passes, adding, "Guess you're glad the night's almost over." Then, huffing out a breath which makes her bangs rise delightfully, she confides, "I can't be a liar and say that I'm not."

I smile down at her, but don't tell her my night's only just starting. I've another few hours of watching women ogling men with their junk swinging. Fuck.

I only just realise she's continuing talking, "And as for what Marvel was saying, I don't believe him for a minute." She chuckles.

What exactly has Marvel been saying? I cock an eyebrow at her.

She shrugs and gives a girly giggle. "I suspect you're quite well endowed."

Throwing back my head, I snort. I hadn't realised she'd been around to overhear. It crosses my mind that I could ask her if she wants to find out, but she's a nice girl, and I don't want to upset her, so I swallow my comment.

Instead, I incline my head. "Best get them their bill if you want a tip, sweetheart." I've indicated the women are starting to gather the presents up, and a couple are getting into their jackets.

"Yeah, I better." Then she's gone, approaching the table.

Of course, settling up doesn't go fast, most wanting to pay for themselves and split the soon-to-be bride's portion between them, some wanting to pay for a friend. After what seems a tortuously long time, they're soon getting their shit together, and heading out the door.

When I reach the bar, I lean my elbows on it, and rub my hands over my face. *Thank fuck that's over.* Hopefully at Angels I can leave them to the bouncers and stay in the background. Maybe have a moment to shoot the shit with Heart.

"Thanks, Throttle. You going to relax with another beer now?" Tash eyes me sympathetically.

I wish I could. "Nah, Tash. Heart needs me at Angels."

Her eyes widen. "This lot going there?"

My huffed in breath gives her the answer.

She laughs softly. "Rather you than me."

"More suited to you, Tash. It's male stripper night."

She belly laughs. "Oh, no. Blade's more than sufficient for me."

After twenty years? My brow furrows. *Surely she must be a little interested in what another man's got to offer?* But the expression on her face suggests she's not.

She winks when she tells me, "Well, you have a good night."

"You too, darlin'."

She touches my arm lightly as I turn, mouthing her thanks again. I raise my hand in a wave toward Gwen, then head out to my bike.

Three hours later, I've had enough of watching guys cavorting and swinging their barely concealed dicks in their thongs. I've gone from mildly interested to wondering how they can demean themselves, rolling their hips and enticing women to stuff dollars in their miniscule underwear.

Surely there are better ways to earn a living? But hell, if they were female, I wouldn't be having such thoughts. Men dancing, I find, are boring. Now with females I could spend the time imagining whether their pussies are tight and how they'd feel around my dick. Men? I have absolutely no intention of thinking about their asses.

My view is certainly not the prevalent one in Angels, the air is tainted by the scent of a hundred or more aroused pussies. It's beginning to get to me. My cock could do with some relief. I start to eye the audience, wondering if I could be of aid to any of the women who've been turned on.

"You work a lot of jobs."

Having been lost in my thoughts, I hadn't seen her approaching. *Now here's a pussy I might be able to use.* I grin at Hattie. "I go where my club needs me."

She's staring at my cut. "What does *enforcer* mean?"

Draw her in. I'm not just a biker, I'm a club officer. From experience I know the fact makes panties drop faster. "It means I enforce the rules of my club."

"Ooh." She touches my arm, feeling my muscles. "I bet you keep everyone in line."

Chuckling, *she's on my hook.* I reply, "I try." And succeed. I'm not known for failure.

She gives me a sly look. "How about you and I get together later? I'd like to find out if what your friend says is true. I've got a bet going that he's lying."

I haven't had to lift a finger to reel her in. Bingo, I could high five myself.

I've had a boring evening just hanging around, and this atmosphere is taunting my dick. I need a woman badly. Her? Why the fuck not? As long as she knows there's a limit to what I'm after. "My brother was all talk," I defend myself. "I'm in proportion, babe, I assure you of that." The question is more whether she can take me. *I* know I won't disappoint. Then there's that other similarity between me and my father, I, too, have a Jacob's Ladder and a dick big enough to show it off—and there's a story to go along with that. "But... Hattie, wasn't it?" I exaggerate my bad memory on purpose. It never hurts to let a woman know you weren't making up poems about her in your head. "I fuck. I leave. You want a good time, then I'm your man. You looking to get hitched like your friend there?" I nod my head toward the woman in the now very eschew mock bridal veil who looks almost comatose. "Then I've nothing to offer."

She stares back shrewdly. "You're offering a good time though, right? That's all I want."

I stare down at her, right into that cleavage which I swear shows more than it did before. Am I making a mistake? I've been upfront with her. I try one more time. "One night, that's all. No repeats."

"Just how I like it," she purrs, now touching my chest. "What time do you get off?"

I'd expected she was the type to know the score. Some women search for a happily ever after, some are just after a good time for the night. She's spoken to me, sure, has demonstrated her interest, but hasn't monopolised my time tonight. She's only talking to me now that the dancers are having a break. I've no doubts when they return, they'll garner her attention once more. And if they've got her riled up with an itch that needs a scratch, who am I to argue?

"When the club closes," I answer. She's been drinking, yes, but she seems levelheaded. "You got a place we can go?"

"What about yours?"

Nope. Not taking a woman I don't know back to the compound. Never have, never will. Not even a club whore has slept in my bed. "No can do, darlin'. Can't take a woman like you back there. I live at the club."

I wait to see what she's going to do with that information.

Call me out on my bluff, or take it as a compliment that she's too good for the Satan's Devils?

The corners of her lips turn up. "Your parents waiting up or something?"

Snorting, I respond, "Something like that." The day I bring a woman onto the compound is the day I'll hand over my balls. Hell's more likely to freeze over.

"Yeah. I got a place." She leans close, and I swear she sniffs in my scent as her nostrils flare. I've been working all day, and the interior of Angels is hot. I won't apologise for my BO. But she's not distracted by that, probably smelling pheromones instead. "It's your lucky day. I'm close."

Not as close as you will be. Down boy, I instruct my cock, making my head focus on the fact she lives nearby. "You driving?"

"Yeah, unless I can go on your bike." She looks up through her eyelashes, hopefully.

My eyes go to the ceiling and then back down. "That's hell to the no, sweetheart. I don't have bitches riding behind me."

"Why not?" she pouts. "It would be fun."

"No one's riding behind me unless I find a woman to be my ol' lady." And that will be never. I like variety, and plenty of it. I don't see me changing.

I wait a beat for her to suggest that she might have a chance to become permanent with me. If she even hints at it, I'm off.

She mock shudders. "I'm not looking for an old man. So no riding up behind you." She winks. "I'll be here when the show's finished. You can follow me home."

My evening has started to look up. By coming on to me, she's saved me the bother of searching for someone to ease my dick. I lean back against the wall once again. My cock jerks as I watch her walk off.

Maybe she's too short and a lot of her is fake, but hell, I don't give a damn. A hole's a hole, and I've no doubt hers will suffice. *I wonder what she can do with her mouth?*

"Thanks, Throttle." Heart walks over as the lights above the stage go off. "Your party wasn't as bad as I feared."

I grin. "I think they were too drunk to do much. Only one actually made it onto the stage."

"Billy Boy was speaking in an octave higher after she grabbed his dick." Heart chuckles, then slaps my back. "Well, we've just got the stragglers to kick out, then I'm off to a warm waiting woman." He steps away, then turns back. "Oh, I meant to tell you, I was offered good money to put you on the stage."

"Fuck that," I respond with feeling. "And it couldn't have been the bachelorette party. Marvel told them I had a tiny dick."

Heart bellows. "Well you do, Brother. I've seen it, remember? That phase when Darcy couldn't get you to wear clothes."

"I was three," I round on him, but lose my ire when I see he's yanking my chain. There are disadvantages growing up with a fuckton of uncles in the club. They never forget...anything.

"Get out of here, Throttle. Take your tiny dick home." Heart laughs loudly. "We've got it from here."

But I've a reason to help, it will bring forward the highly anticipated end to my night. I walk over to the bachelorette party. "Club's closing up, ladies. You ready to leave?"

Hattie's helping the bride out of her seat. I wince as her charge slips from her hands and slides to the floor. *Guess I'm going to be hanging around for a while.* I could go over and help, but I've a feeling I might get puked on, which would not be a great start to putting my plans into action.

Hattie's talking, pointing at me and the girl prone on the floor. As she continues gesticulating wildly, at one point putting her hands together in prayer, the girl she's talking to glances at me. After shaking her head, her shoulders slump and she nods. Within moments, Hattie trots over.

"We can go."

My eyes narrow. "What about your friend?" I nod over to the bride-to-be who at least seems to be on her feet now, if swaying dangerously.

"She'll be fine. The others said they'd get her home."

Hmm. If that was one of my brothers, I wouldn't be leaving his side. But hell, who am I to complain? My cock tells my brain to shut up.

I open the door for Hattie and usher her out, then walk her around to the parking lot. After I've seen her into her car, I point to my bike.

"Wait for me to get behind you, then pull out. I'll follow you home."

"You got it, lover." Her hand finds my cut and tries to pull me down. "Any chance of a taste to keep me going?"

Recoiling, I remove her hand from my leather. I'm not a fan of kissing. I've got nothing in particular against it, but there's a time and a place, and normally it's in the throes of passion. But if it's going to move this along, I suppose I won't object.

Lowering my lips, I brush mine against hers, ignoring when her mouth opens. After only a second, I draw back, tap the roof of her car, tell her this is going to be continued shortly, then I close her door.

She lives in an apartment block in town. It's in a decent enough area, and not one where I'm too concerned about leaving my bike, but when I pull up behind her car, I lock it with a heavy chain and activate the alarm, knowing you can't be too careful however safe you think it is. At least Oak and Cedar's gang won't touch another Satan's Devils bike. Or if they do, they'll be dead men for certain.

Hattie, wasting not a minute, is already out of her car by the time I've secured my bike, then she curls her finger, beckoning me as if I'm a dog. My mouth quirks, not unhappy with the analogy as I'm going to make her my bitch, for tonight. One night only. That really should be my middle name.

"You know how this is going to go, don't you, darlin'?" As she fumbles to get her key into the lock, I brace my hand against the wall and lean over her, warning her once again. "Meant what I said, Hattie. When I'm gone, I'm gone. However magical your pussy is, I won't be coming back. You got doubts you can handle that? Let me know now, and I'll go." I offer a smile. "No harm, no foul."

When she swivels her head on her neck and turns up her face, I stare into her eyes, my set expression showing there'll be no discussion, no room for pleading or her harbouring hopes I'll change my mind.

"You going to hurt me? Do things I don't like?"

Rearing back a little, I reassure her, "Fuck no. I've never hurt a woman in my life. You don't enjoy what I'm doing, just tell me to stop and I will. But I'm here to fuck, babe. Just making sure you know there's nothing else on offer."

"I'm down with that." She grins. "What makes you so sure that I'd want a repeat, anyway? I mean, after I've seen your tiny dick, once might be more than enough."

I growl when finally she gets the door open. Giving her just enough time to slip out of her jacket and hang it, and her purse, on a hook by the door, I crowd her, pulling her back against me, and biting her neck at the pulse point. Demonstrating my desire to get straight down to business avoids the refusal of a drink, or her offer to *slip into something more comfortable*. I'm here for one thing only. If she doesn't want that, she can kick my ass to the door.

My action has the desired effect—her breathing speeds up, her skin flushes, and a slow moan comes from her lips.

"Where's your bedroom?"

A shaky hand lifts and points. Sweeping her light frame up into my arms, I go in the direction indicated. When I enter her domain, I slide her down my body until she's steady on her feet.

She raises her face, her lips pouted as though expecting a kiss. I oblige, pressing mine against hers while multitasking and finding the zip of her cute little dress. Pulling away, I slip the straps off her shoulders allowing the material to pool at her feet. There had been support in the dress, she's braless, and those tits fall free. Well, drop, slightly. There's so much silicon there they basically stay in place where they are.

She's wearing stockings and fuck that does something to my cock, making it pound in my jeans. Feeling like a child unwrapping a Christmas present, I sink to my knees and stare. Then, leaving the garter and stockings in place, I ease down her panties.

She's bare, and briefly I'm disappointed I can't prove my theory that the carpet doesn't match her hair, but at least I won't get pubes mixed up in my beard.

The bed's right behind her. Raising my hands, I push her gently until the mattress meets the back of her knees, then I'm more forceful and she drops down, giggling as I'd taken her by surprise.

Leaving the rest of my clothes on, I slip off my boots, then return my attention to her.

She comes first. Whoever I'm with, I always make sure the woman gets her release before taking care of my own. So, wanting to get onto the main event, I slide my fingers through her labia, pleased that she's already slick.

"Put your mouth on me," she instructs. But I don't do that, not with bitches I don't know. She'll get my fingers and a condom-covered cock, but saliva is the only body fluid we'll share, and even that I'm wary about.

"I'll make it good," I promise her.

Back in the day, there'd been many a night when the teenage boys on the compound had shared an illicit beer and conversation had centred on some of the many times one of us had snuck out from behind the bar and seen things we shouldn't technically have—brothers fucking the sweet butts. Of course, we weren't supposed to be around, but all of us had, one time or another, either accidentally or on purpose, walked in on a scene and got an eyeful. We'd discuss their techniques, especially those that seemed to cause the most pleasure. When we were eighteen, the sweet butts themselves were fair game—supposedly out of bounds, but hell, if they wanted to break in us young studs, we knew to keep that shit quiet. Now we were allowed to physically demonstrate what we'd thought we'd learned. I'm not ashamed to admit I'd perfected my skills with a club girl. It had been a lot of fun for us both, and it means I know exactly how to find a G-spot, and the quickest way to make a woman scream.

Practice makes perfect, and I've certainly had a lot of that.

Planting a kiss on Hattie's mound I use the fingers of one hand to curl up inside her, and my thumb to rotate on her clit. With the other, I pinch one of her nipples, then moving my body up, use my mouth on the other.

She likes what I'm doing, there's no fucking doubt about that. Her head's thrown back against the comforter, and her fingers curl into her hands. Her eyes are closed, her mouth is open.

Fuck, I love it when a woman comes. Their faces are transcended to beautiful just at that moment in time. Hattie's pleasant enough to look at, but right now? She's exquisite.

"Yes, oh God, yes, right there."

I let her down gently, then make her come again. While her breaths are still coming in pants, I reach into the pocket of my jeans and extract a condom I always keep there. I push down my pants, freeing my cock and start to cover it using only one hand.

"What the fuck?" I hadn't noticed her eyes opening.

Grinning broadly, I tell her, "That's your surprise."

Her eyes gleam. "I've never—"

"Never had a pierced cock before?"

She bites her lip. "I want to feel it. You don't need a condom, I'm on the pill."

Yeah. Like no man's ever been caught out with that statement. "Condom or no fuck." I roll the rest of the latex so it covers my dick, but hold back for now.

"Fuck." She decides fast as I knew she would, then a gleam comes into her eyes which go almost impossibly wide as they focus on my groin. "Your friend lied. You're fucking huge."

Despite living in close proximity to a compound of bikers,

many of whom weren't shy about fucking in public, I've never had any desire to compare the size of my dick. All I know is it's large enough to provide pleasure, and, as long as I'm careful, not so long it hurts the woman I'm with. Ideal to my way of reckoning, but it doesn't do my ego any harm for her to be impressed.

Raising her legs and hoisting them over my elbows, I start to press in. She's not too tight, and, as a result of my earlier administrations, is sopping wet. I slide in easily, pause for a moment, then when she clenches in encouragement, I start to hammer in.

The only finesse is that I make the most of the piercing to get both her clit and her G-spot on each thrust, another manoeuvre I've perfected. I wait until her muscles start to contract, then thrust in again a couple of times. Her squeezing down hard on my cock has me shooting my load into the condom.

I bow my head. That hadn't taken long, but she's got off three times, and I feel my own relief. My job here is done.

Carefully holding the condom, I pull out. "Bathroom?"

"Down the hall, first door on the right."

When I reach the small room, I notice a man's shaving kit on the side of the counter. Curiosity getting the better of me, I open the cabinet and see more men's shit there, including a three-in-one shampoo that I doubt Hattie uses. *Married?* I frown, I don't like cheaters. But that's on her, not me. *Could be a roommate.*

Whatever. It's none of my business. I'll never be here again.

Knowing my conscience can be clear unlike hers, I deal with my shit, carefully flushing the condom away and washing my hands. I rinse my dick, then tuck it into my pants.

When I return to the bedroom, she's under the sheets, one side pulled back invitingly.

"Why don't you get undressed?" I think she's trying to sound like a seductive siren, but to me it sounds like a demon's hiss.

"Nah, I gotta run." Starting to pull on my boots, I don't tell her while I was going anyway, the speed with which I'll leave has increased. I've no desire to be caught by a furious boyfriend.

Her eyes narrow. "How about I give you a blow job?"

"Nah, I'm good." I'm anxious to be on my way.

I could ask her, I suppose. There could be an innocent answer. But her invitation makes me nervous. *Will I have to remind her she agreed to my terms?* Fuck, I hope not. It wouldn't be the first time a bitch thought her cunt would entice me to abandon my nature. I'd told her what was going to go down, and she'd signed up for it.

"You sure, Throttle?" Throwing back the sheet, she thrusts those expensive titties up as if I won't be able to resist.

If there's a man in the mix, he must be away for the night. Or is she setting me up? I decide to challenge her.

"There's a man's shit in the bathroom."

She snorts, then roars with laughter. "That's my brother's. He lives here. But," she tries a seductive look again, "he's away for the night."

I find I don't doubt her. I can usually tell when people aren't telling the truth, but in any event, it doesn't matter. Inwardly sighing, I remind her, "Told you how this was going to go, don't make it more than it is. I enjoyed myself, and you did too." She can't deny that, I'd brought my A game tonight. There's no way she was faking those orgasms.

I get a calculating look, but she must realise she has nothing more to offer. "Will I see you around?"

Not if I see you first.

"Maybe." Yeah, there's a chance our paths will cross, but I need to make sure she knows where she stands. "But, Hattie, I never go back. I explained that. We did this," I wave at the tousled bed, "and it was good. But that's all it is."

There's nothing more to say, so I turn, checking my pocket for my bike key, wallet and phone, then get out of there.

Am I a bastard? Possibly, but I'd been clear from the start. Hattie and I were a one-night thing. I'd gotten off, though it hadn't been remarkable—plenty of other cunts out there which would feel much the same.

If some of my brothers are to be believed, maybe one day I'd find one I'll be unable to resist, but I'm not optimistic and definitely not actively looking. Why should I? One-night stands have always been my thing. No complications and no recriminations, no promises made and none broken.

As I throw my leg over the saddle of my bike, Hattie's already the last thing on my mind.

CHAPTER FIVE

*T*hrottle…

"Hey, Brother. How's the kid?" Placing my hand on Hawk's shoulder, I lean around him and tickle the chin of the baby that he's rocking in his arms.

"Fuck, Throttle, don't wake her. I've just got her off to sleep," Hawk hisses at low volume.

Lowering my voice, I ask, quietly, "Where's Liv?"

"Getting some down time. Never realised how loud babies can be, or that they're nocturnal. What I wouldn't give for a good night's sleep." He turns away as he yawns widely.

Rather him than me. "Layla's only a month old, Brother. You can't expect her to do much else." Or so I think. What would I know? I know nothing about kids. "She's a cutie though." Well, asleep she is.

"I can't wait for her to start smiling," my brother starts. "All she does is scream, sleep or eat. I can't even tell if she likes me. Even a dog would show more emotion."

I'd thought I'd already seen her smiling, but perhaps it was gas. "When do they do that?" I'm not really interested, but think I need to say something.

"According to Liv, maybe in another week." I squeeze my

fingers into his shoulder. "You're doing great, Hawk. She's gonna love having you as a dad." I think for a second, then add a qualification, "Until she's old enough to date."

He huffs. "Already dreading it, Brother. And did you hear it's official? Prez and Amy are having a fuckin' boy."

Up to a few months ago, before we knew Hawk was having a mental health crisis, he was the VP. In my view, now his problems are out in the open and we can recognise the signs if we need to take the pressure off him, he'll soon be back to where he was. He's certainly better able to cope nowadays and there's no one I'd like better at the right hand of my prez.

Of course, Drummer does a great job as a stand-in VP, but then he would. He'd been our prez for more than three decades, stepping back nearly a year ago to let younger blood take over. When Hawk walked away from the club, Drummer was brought out of retirement. He'd been a good fucking choice. Not only had he had the experience in spades, but he had no desire to step permanently into the shoes of his son. Having enjoyed the time being free from his responsibilities, he'll be happier when Hawk takes his rightful place again.

Like Hawk being the son of our ex-prez, Liv, or Ollie, or Olivia to give her her full name, was Wraith, the previous VP's kid. Drummer and Wraith had had kids only a couple of months apart. Hawk had been put in Liv's crib as soon as he was born. From that moment, they'd formed a lifelong bond and had ended up married.

Now the cycle seems set to repeat. There's already a book going at the clubhouse about whether Wizard's, the current prez, unborn son and Layla will end up together.

Knowing Hawk as well as I do, my vote is no. He's already vowed to keep them apart. I'll watch on with amusement to see how that plays out.

As for me, I've no thoughts about procreating. If the FOGs are anything to go by, a new generation of babies will be provided without my input. Liv, herself, is one of four kids.

My nose twitches and my face twists as Hawk takes a shallow breath, saying despondently, "Fuck." He frowns at the baby in his arms and then jerks his head. "Pass me that bag, will you, Brother?"

The bag he's indicated is one that in a million years I wouldn't have expected him to carry around. It's white and decorated with colourful unicorns. Hiding my smirk, I go to pass it to him, but his gesture suggests he wants me to set it on the couch.

"I'm out of here," I say fast. That smell's getting worse by the second. At least you can train a dog to crap outside, not so with kids it would seem.

"Coward," Hawk hisses with feeling. Holding the baby in one arm, he opens the bag which transforms into a changing mat while still retaining a pocket for the baby paraphernalia parents have to carry around.

Fuck that. I'm not having children. Never, no way.

With a *good luck* tossed over my shoulder, I make my way back out, almost bumping into Blade in my haste to get away from the stench.

Steadying him with my hands, I shoot him a look of warning. "Take a deep breath of fresh air if you're heading inside."

"What?" He peers around me. "Oh shit. What I came for can wait."

"Hey, you've had kids. Thought you'd be offering assistance." I smirk.

"Little kids are long in my rearview, thank fuck. Mine are grown. If I never see another ass needing to be wiped, it will be too soon."

I chuckle and follow him as he turns away. He takes two steps then stops. "Got a message for you, Throttle." When I raise my eyebrow, he expands, "Tash was grateful for you helping her out with that bachelorette party the other night. Wants you to stop by so she can thank you herself, give you a good meal on the house. One where you can sit, take your time and enjoy it."

Usually we grab a plate and eat in the kitchen, leaving the tables to paying customers. Tash's offer is welcome, if totally unneeded. "It weren't no bother." My shoulders rise and fall. "Just required me standing looking pretty and keeping the peace with a couple of frowns."

"Heard they were offering good dollars for a striptease. I think she's demonstrating how grateful she was you kept your clothes on." His delivery is dry.

Snorting, I slap his back. "I don't think Tucson is ready for me to be a stripper. I'd put the rest out of business." I roll my hips suggestively.

He chortles. "Nah, it's your pencil dick she wouldn't have wanted anyone to see. Women don't need to be disappointed like that."

Yeah, Marvel had been unable to keep his mouth shut, thinking he'd said something hilarious.

"I've still got to get the asshole back for that." Shaking my head, I wonder how to get one up on the motherfucker.

Blade winks. "Talking about getting revenge, fancy some practice?" Blade pats his hand against the sheath he wears to show me what he's got in mind.

"Sure." I was going to stop by the shop and catch up on some work, but improving my knife throwing skills under Blade's instruction is what I'd prefer.

The ex-enforcer's hands aren't able to follow his brain's commands as well as they once did, but he's still got an expert eye, and is a good teacher, though his way of keeping me sharp is a few hints of exactly where one of his blades will go if I don't pull my finger out. We spend an hour at target practice, then when I see him shaking out his hand and the pain lining his forehead, I tell him I've got shit to do.

"Don't forget Tash is expecting you when you've got a moment. Hey, Tommy?" Blade's caught the sight of our oldest and longest serving prospect who'd come in a package deal with his old lady more than two decades ago. When Tommy brings his motorcycle-shaped mobility scooter to a halt in front of him, Blade pinches his nose, and gives an exaggerated shudder. "Give it a moment before you go inside. Layla shit her pants."

Tommy's eyes widen comically. "Uh-uh." He shakes his head vigorously. "Tommy's got somewhere else to be." With practised moves, he turns his 'bike' and heads back in the direction he'd come from.

Laughing loudly, I share the moment of mirth with Blade, then salute in acknowledgement and walk off. Before I have my fun, I'll put in a few hours at the auto-shop.

It ends up being a full day. I'd brushed up my knife skills with Blade, and after that I'd gotten a good deal of work completed while sharing jokes with my brothers. The offer from Tash remains on my mind. While I believe she's got nothing to be grateful to me for, the woman is kind, and if she needs to repay the favour, I don't want to upset her by declining.

Being free and single, I have no one else to consider. I can do what I want, when I want. As my stomach rumbles, I decide some good grub would be welcome, and tonight might be a good time to go. Today it's Thursday and tomorrow night will be church followed by our customary party, then it will be the weekend. I wouldn't go to the Wheel Inn on a Saturday, unless I was working, as the restaurant will be packed and the staff rushed off their feet.

When the sergeant-at-arms approaches, I call him over. "Hey, Hound. Know who's going to the Wheel Inn tonight?"

"I am, as it happens. Want to come along for the ride?" The sergeant-at-arms chuckles, then adds, "Not sure if there are any bachelorette parties tonight if you were thinking of earning yourself a few dollars." Grabbing his crotch and thrusting his hips, he sniggers.

"Fuck off." I've had enough of them joking about my potential career as a stripper to last me for a while, but I can't complain how last Saturday had ended. I'd gotten my rocks off, what more could I ask for? *What was her name again?* I shake my head, she had gotten the job done, but it hadn't been remarkable. I'm not surprised I can't remember.

"Meet back up in an hour?"

That gives me just enough time to get the grime out of my hair and skin and dig out fresh clothes. I raise my chin in agreement.

A couple of hours later, Hound diverts to the bar, and I continue walking into the restaurant. As Tash is by the hostess station I don't need to go searching for her. Her face lights up when she sees me.

"You taking me up on my offer?"

I put my arm around her waist, pulling her close and kissing her cheek like I would any of my 'aunties'. "You've nothing to thank me for, you know that. I was just doing my job."

When she glances up, her eyes are twinkling and I note, not for the first time, that while she's in her late forties, she's still an attractive woman. Blade's a lucky fucker if you're the kind of man to want just one woman for yourself.

"I wanted to thank you properly." She brushes off my denial.

I give in. "If it makes you happy, show me to a fuckin' table, woman."

Immediately Tash pulls away from me, first checking the list on the screen at the hostess station, then turning, surveys the room. She raises her hand and beckons when she catches a waitress's eye. When she comes over, I'm more than happy to see it's Gwen who will be seating me, Tash whispers into her ear. Gwen nods, turns to me, and gifts me a beaming smile.

"Follow me."

I do. She leads me to a corner table. Choosing the seat that has my back against the wall and my front facing the door, I sit down.

When she hands me a menu, I ask, "How's it going?"

"Good." She grins. "I'm getting the hang of it now. Tash is a great boss. She adjusts my hours to suit me. I'm also getting the hang of keeping my ass tucked in and away from roaming hands."

I narrow my eyes at that statement. Sure, I've noticed she's got a very touchable ass, but she shouldn't need to put up with that shit. "Anyone tries to lay a hand on you tonight, just let me know and I'll break it off."

"Look at you going all macho on me." She laughs. "Now, what can I get you? Need to see the menu?"

Not really. I know it by heart. "Just the T-Bone, rare, baked potato and a salad. And I'd love it if you could bring a beer."

"You got it." There's a spring in her step as she walks off. Watching as she lithely skirts around the tables, grinning at other waitstaff and offering a smile to customers she's clearly served before, I can see she told me the truth—she does seem to enjoy working here. She'll be a good asset to the club. I hope we can keep her.

The food as always is spectacular, and eating at a table like a customer is a different experience, meaning I can take my time and properly savour the food. When I finally push away my empty plate, I rub my very full feeling stomach. The chef's obviously made an extra-large portion suitable for a man of my size.

Demonstrating she's already developed an eye for seeing what needs doing, Gwen's back at my side shortly after I put down my silverware. "Want another beer?"

"Yeah, I do. But don't worry, I'll get it myself. I need to go catch up with Hound."

"Your biker brother? He's in the bar." Efficiently, she lifts the empty plate. "Catch you later," she throws over her shoulder as she walks away, her rear view drawing my eyes for a moment.

I might not have to pay, but that won't stop me from leaving a generous tip. I take out a fifty and tuck it under the napkin holder. Then I stand, shift my cut so it sits comfortably on my shoulders, then head through the archway into the bar.

"Hound!" I slap his back when I come alongside him.

"Enjoy your meal?" He doesn't tack on his thought that I was a lucky bastard, but it shows in his expression.

"Too damn right I did." I pat my satisfied stomach to rub it in.

Hound grins. "The scenery wasn't bad either. Saw that pretty waitress laughing with you." There's a gleam in his eyes I don't like. Just as I'd told Cast last week, I tell him now, "She's hands off for the likes of us, Brother. She's a citizen through and through, kick-starting her career in law and working off her student debt."

His eyes widen. "You get all that just from talking to her while you ate?"

"Fuck no. She was Lisa's best buddy for a while back in high school, but she never came to the compound so you wouldn't remember her. I used to pull her pigtails." I grin at the memory. "We caught up when I came in a week back. I hadn't seen her for years before then."

The woman in question comes walking past to get an order of drinks filled from the bar. I wait for her to list what she needs, then whip my arm around her, pulling her into my side. Her hair's still long and tonight it's pulled up tightly in a bun, but she's got bangs hanging loose. I tug on those instead.

"Get off, Noah," she exclaims, grabbing hold of my hand. "What was that for?"

"For old times." I grin. "I've been telling Hound I used to torment you and my sis."

"Seems like you haven't grown out of the habit." But she's smiling and also giving Hound a speculative glance. She leans into me and stage whispers, "Who's the hottie?"

Hound snorts beer out of his mouth.

"No one a nice girl like you needs to know," I reply sharply. But when her eyebrow rises, I relent, "Gwen meet Hound, Hound, Gwen."

Hound places his hand over his heart. "The pleasure is all mine, sweetheart."

"You know?" she begins drily. "There are rumours in town that the Satan's Devils MC are tough. But you two are just like sweet cuddly pussycats."

That's not the kind of thing you can say to the enforcer and sergeant-at-arms of a one-percenter MC that takes itself very seriously, so I punish her just as I would have done years ago, digging my fingers into that sensitive spot under her ribs and tickling her mercilessly.

She tries to get loose while laughing uncontrollably. "Stop, Noah. Unhand me now!"

"Drinks up, Gwen," the bartender interrupts.

"I have to go," she insists, squirming and giggling.

I stop tormenting her immediately, appreciating she has to work, and knowing Tash won't like me hogging one of her waitresses. I hug her briefly and plant a kiss to the side of her face, "Saved just in time."

"You're a bully." She's grinning.

I can't resist, as she walks past carrying a heavy tray with both hands, I reach out my hand and pat her ass, being rewarded by an over-the-shoulder glare.

"Nice girl," Hound remarks.

"Yeah." I pull my attention back to him, thinking about warning him off with a glare, but content myself with changing the subject. "So, you going to get that new bike you were looking at?"

While we talk, my eyes automatically scan the room. I might not be here on duty tonight, but that doesn't make me kick the habit of checking what's going down. As Hound commences giving me a rundown of the model he's thinking about, my surveillance comes to a dead halt. Across the room, scowling at me, is the woman who's name I'd forgotten earlier. *Hattie.* That was it.

Why the frown? Had she expected me to call her? Hell, she hadn't offered her number, and if she had, I'd have already lost it. Inwardly grimacing, I hope she isn't coming over. I told her I wouldn't go back, and I hadn't, but what other explanation is there for that look on her face? Did she think I used her? Well, she's right, I had. But I hadn't led her on to expect more.

I turn back to Hound. "What's the horsepower?"

As I continue to listen to my brother, I risk another glance in Hattie's direction. This time, she catches my eye, and fuck me, she raises her hand and gives one of those girly finger waves and smiles at me.

What's with that? A glare, then all sunshine and light? Maybe the frown had just been her resting bitch face.

She's a woman, why bother to try to read her?

As Hound gets more and more enthusiastic about his expected purchase, I get swept along. Soon we're discussing the best places to ride when he eventually buys it, and I completely forget the woman who'd glared at me earlier.

I stay until closing time to keep Hound company on the ride home. I fuck a sweet butt when I return to the compound, then go back to my suite alone.

What better life could I possibly have?

CHAPTER SIX

hrottle…

The Satan's Devils MC has only seven single members including myself, and of that number, I'm pretty sure Drifter is seeing a woman in town. He rarely spends long at our parties, and doesn't involve himself with the hangarounds who come along, nor is ever seen with a sweet butt.

While in some ways it's sad to say, there's never a lack of women attracted to the life of living with bikers and having a roof and food provided for them. In exchange, they make themselves available to any member who wants to use their services. Once, I'd overheard Allie, a sweet butt from way back in the day, explain what attracts them. *It's better than waiting on a street corner, never knowing who's going to come along, or whether your next trick is going to be your last, and you'll end up trafficked or dead.*

Sweet butts come with dreams they could become an old lady, but in our club at least, Allie was the only one. That was twenty years back when she saved Truck from desolation. Truck had been a firefighter, he'd worked on the same crew as my mom. He went to fight a wildfire in California and received life-changing injuries for his pains. He'd been on a downward spiral when Allie had stepped in. There's no denying the pair were made for each other, but as far as club women go, Allie's very much the exception.

Sweet butts are here of their own volition. Some stay for years, some move on quickly. There are just two living at the club now, Clover, who's a more recent addition, and Sable. Us unattached members wouldn't turn down a few more, but Drummer and Wraith's old ladies, Sam and Sophie, now vet them. Any hint they're encouraging the men who are already attached, and they get the feminine version of a beatdown using sharp tongues instead of fists. After that, the club girls tend to move on.

Of course, if in the unlikely event the old ladies can't dissuade them, their next line of offence is Pussy. Pussy's an odd one. Way back, she was a sweet butt herself, and technically one of their number now. But who'd want to dip their wick into a sixty-year-old pussy? Not me, for sure.

Even she doesn't want to work anymore, but she stays on in the original house built to house the sweet butts, keeping the girls in line. Having never succeeded in getting her own biker—hell, I'm not even sure she wanted one—she keeps the younger sweet butts from getting ideas above their station.

And if Pussy isn't enough, well, Sam brings in the ultimate weapon. Drummer would do anything to keep Sam happy, so if a girl attracted Sam's displeasure, she wouldn't last long. Now Drummer's stepped away from sitting at the head of the table and Sam's not our queen anymore, Amy has found similar ways to influence Wizard.

Of course, I hadn't been born at the time, but the story of Sam's introduction to the club is legendary. She'd come to find her father and found him with his dick in a sweet butt's mouth. Viper, rest his soul, was never again found with his pants down.

But having only two women to service six willing men means getting in fast, or know your brothers had already used them earlier in the night. It's frowned upon to hog a girl for the whole evening, which suits me. Girls are for fucking, not for company or conversation.

I like to think, being young, virile and with stamina, and a few tricks up my sleeve, I'm a favourite with the club women. Not wanting either to start getting ideas beyond her station, I alternate between them.

I tend to get in early, trying to be the first on any night. This past week I haven't gone wanting, and as Thursday comes around again, I've already had my satisfaction via a long session with Sable before I return to the clubroom where I see some of my brothers settling down to play cards.

Body relaxed and mind sharpened, I approach the table. "Deal me in."

Rock smirks widely.

Christ, I'm an idiot. I'm not alone, but somehow we all keep trying to beat our resident card shark. *This time,* I think to myself, *I'll watch him carefully, see how he does it.* Maybe I'll get lucky and he'll have an off night. Maybe the state of relaxation I'm in will help me concentrate.

"Don't know why the fuck we bother," Marvel grumbles. "All the fuckin' years we've been playing, I never beat you."

"It's because we're stupid fucks and eternal optimists," Wraith observes, setting his beer down on the table and pulling up a seat. "I keep hoping he'll show signs of Alzheimer's."

Rock shakes his head showing he doesn't give a damn but blows a kiss toward his ol' lady. "You gonna wish me luck, Becca?"

The woman in question comes across. She glances at the pack held in his hand, then each of us in turn. "Will you do me a favour? Someone beat him, else he'll be bragging all night."

"Hey," Rock puts his arm around her waist, pulling her to him, "just think how we'll celebrate my winnings." He waggles his eyebrows, and she flicks her hand and gets him in the shoulder. "And you have got your eye on a new ride," he reminds her.

She tilts her head to one side. "True. Time to start playing, lover." She giggles as she walks off.

I chuckle. "Sam's ol' lady's riding club's still going strong I see."

"Tell me about it, Brother. Becca's already got one bike, now she wants another." Rock shuffles the pack and starts to deal.

"Not so fucking fast," Wraith growls, putting his hand over the cards and pulling them to him. "I'll deal. I don't trust you, fucker."

I laugh and watch Wraith expertly cutting the pack. I'm reaching for the hand I've just been dealt when a shout comes from behind me.

"Throttle!"

"Yeah, Prez?" Looking around, I see him beckoning me over. Sighing, I gesture toward Cast, then hand him my cards. "Play this hand for me, will you? And try not to fuckin' lose."

Cast's eyes go to Rock, then he mumbles, "You've gotta be kidding me."

Patting his shoulder, knowing all he can do is his best, I cross the room to Wizard.

"Whatcha need?" It's then I notice Drummer is standing next to him.

Wizard frowns. "Just got a call from Tash. One of the waitresses at the Wheel Inn was jumped when she went to her car. Was hurt pretty badly. She's been taken to the hospital. Got cops on the scene, and I need someone to go down there."

"No brothers around?"

"Shooter and Jekyll were there, but they left with the last of the customers." He winces. "There was a prospect, but he stayed with Tash while she cashed out."

Leaving the waitresses to walk alone to their cars. I frown, but don't hesitate. "Sure, I'll go." I start turning away, then look back. "Which waitress?"

"The new girl..." Wizard scratches his head. "Jean?"

Jean? I don't recall anyone of that name. Hang on… my gut tightens. "Gwen?" I suggest, hoping to fuck I'm wrong.

Unaware he's dropping a bombshell, Prez nods. "Yeah, that's her."

Fuck.

"I know her, Prez. I'll check on her at the hospital once I've cleared the cops, okay?" I swing on my heels to get going as fast as possible.

"Ride safe, Brother," Wizard calls after me.

"Always fuckin' do," is my parting comment.

As I mount my bike, I'm wondering why the fuck something like this has to happen to a nice girl like Gwen. She doesn't deserve this. I only hope she wasn't hurt too badly, and they've only taken her to the hospital as a precaution.

Fuck.

As fast as I can I get to the Wheel Inn, I'm not surprised to find Blade has beaten me, surmising his old lady must have called him. He's raking his hands through his hair and cursing.

"Why the fuck didn't Shooter and/or Jekyll stay?" His eyes blaze at Tash, though it's not his old lady he's exasperated with.

I take it the conversation I've stepped into has been going on for a while. Tash looks frustrated. "We don't have trouble here, Blade. You know that. The parking lot is well lit—"

"Not where the employees park."

Tash sees me, but turns to her man. "People working late all know to park close to the rear entrance."

I step in. "How did they get to Gwen then?"

Now Tash looks down. "It's my fault. She thought she'd be leaving earlier. I asked her to stay an extra couple of hours. I didn't think about her car, or that she should move it."

"Not your fault, Tash," Blade snaps. "The fuckin' prospect should have walked her out."

"For heaven's sake, Blade. He had instructions to stay with me until I left. You were the one who told him. I didn't think, okay?"

I step in front of Blade and put my hand to his chest. "Leave it, Brother. We'll make sure all brothers stay until everyone's left the premises from now on." I lean in closer. "You're upsetting Tash, it wasn't her fault." I watch as the wild look slowly leaves his eyes. "Now tell me what the fuck happened. How's Gwen? And who the fuck got to her?"

A shuddering breath leaves his body. While none of us like that a woman was hurt, I know what's got to him is it could have been his old lady. He glances toward her, reaching out and touching her arm as though to convince himself she's safe, leaving it to Tash to enlighten me.

"Gwen was the last staff member out. I couldn't get the receipts to balance, and she helped me. Then," she pauses and grimaces, "we found the discrepancy. I told her I could do the rest, and she left. Butcher and I left about ten minutes later. Luckily, I'd backed into my spot so when I flicked on the headlights they illuminated the back of the lot and I saw her lying there. No one was with her, no one around. I ran across, then called an ambulance, then Blade, then Wizard... The cops got here fast."

"Cops find anything?" Glancing around, I see they've already left. I'd thought I'd gotten here before them.

"Of course they fuckin' didn't," Blade snarls. "We're an MC, aren't we? Doubt they even looked. Probably just thought it was someone getting back at us."

Tash nods. "They didn't seem particularly interested. Just said they'd speak to Gwen as soon as she's stable."

"What about Mouse? Have you asked him?"

Blade shoots me a *what do you think I am* look, but provides the information. "Security camera didn't catch shit. It was facing the wrong direction."

"Aren't they on an arc? Or did it happen that fast?"

"Someone fuckin' jammed it."

Which means it could have been premeditated. But had it been set up specifically for Gwen? Gwen's car must have been the only one left parked there. They might have just been waiting for the owner to come out and then mug whoever it was.

"You go outside?" I ask Blade.

"Butcher did. Said there was fuck all to find. Guess we won't find anything out until we speak to Gwen."

"I'm going to see her now," Tash states.

I notice how pale she's looking, her hands wringing together. She's clearly had a shock and while it wasn't she who was hurt, she needs looking after. "No, I'll go. You go home with Blade."

"I have to go. She's got no family and I don't know any friends I could contact. She needs someone and won't want a stranger—"

"I'm not a fuckin' stranger," I snarl.

"She one of your fuck buddies?" Blade asks.

"No, she's fuckin' not," I tell him firmly. "I know her from way back. She was one of Lisa's friends at school. If anything, she looks on me like a big brother."

"That's settled then." When Tash opens her mouth to object, Blade takes hold of her arm and pulls her away. "We'll leave Gwen to you. Thanks, Brother."

After Blade and I exchange chin lifts, I decide there's not much point hanging around. But before I leave, I go outside where I find the prospect, Butcher. He's got a flashlight and is examining the ground all around a car sitting forlorn and abandoned. In the beam of his light, I see blood on the ground. *Fuck.*

"Find anything?" I ask through a tight jaw.

"Fuck all. Oh, this was by the car." He tosses a car key to me. "It's hers, I checked."

"Did you find her purse?"

His brow furrows. "Nah. But the paramedics took over. Maybe they took it with her, or maybe the cops picked it up?"

Or maybe that's what her attacker was after. Just a mugging as I'd half-expected. That makes more sense than anything else. While I don't know much about her, Gwen certainly doesn't seem the type to have made enemies.

"I'll ask her. I'm off to see her now." I wave my hand, leaving the prospect and head for my bike.

I've got a strong stomach but seeing what was obviously Gwen's blood on the ground makes me feel sick. Even if she wasn't my sister's old school friend, she's an employee of the club, and therefore, of mine. How dare someone do this to her?

I'm still angry when I draw up at the hospital and park in a designated motorcycle parking bay.

Stomping toward the emergency room entrance, I suddenly realise that I can't remember her surname. I shoot a quick text to Blade, then have to wait a moment for him to respond. When he does, I recognise it. Boseman, of course. Gwendoline Boseman.

I go inside where I impatiently wait my turn to get the information I need from the reception desk.

"Are you a relative, sir?" The receptionist eyes me as if I might be her assailant come to finish the job.

"I'm a close friend, very close, if you know what I mean." I add a wink.

She shakes her head. "Then I can't give you any information."

I count to ten silently. "She doesn't have family." Or that I know of who I can contact. "Don't you think she deserves to see a friendly face?"

That seems to get through to her. "I can get a nurse to ask if she wants to see you. What's your name?"

"Throt..." I start to say, then wonder if she's so hurt, will she remember what I go by now? I give my government name, the one she best knows me by instead, "Noah Rinter."

I'm directed to take a seat which I do, my glare clearing a space where a man has put his bag. You'd think I'd come in with the plague from the way people in close proximity soon decide there are other places they need to be, clearing the space around me.

One minute, two. It's closer to ten that pass when fucking

finally someone calls my name. I leap out of my seat and am halfway across the room before the last syllable is pronounced.

"I'm glad she's got someone," the nurse says as he leads me down a corridor with curtained-off cubicles left and right. "Ms Boseman's in a lot of pain and is quite shocked and distressed about what happened to her. Understandable, of course. She's in here."

As he says the last, he slides a curtain back. I come to an abrupt halt, trying to school my features. I clearly fail.

"That bad, huh?" Gwen's voice sounds weak.

Her nose is so swollen I suspect it's broken, and one eye is completely closed. She's got a bandage wrapped around her head, and a huge Band-Aid running down one side of her face. Her left arm is in a sling.

Again, I find myself counting under my breath, gaining some time to come up with something that could comfort her.

"I've seen worse," I settle for at last. I go closer to her and pull up the chair. Placing it at the side of the bed, I sit down, and reach for the hand which isn't injured. "Do you remember what happened?"

When she tries to smile, it draws my attention to her mouth. I hadn't noticed that was also swollen. She winces as she tries to talk. "Shouldn't you ask how I'm feeling, first?"

"Like shit, I expect." I dismiss it. "I didn't think it was worth making you waste the words, or trying to kid me you were fine."

"I have felt better," she admits softly.

I'm sure she has. I doubt she's felt worse. Shit like this doesn't happen to a nice girl like her. It was one of the reasons Lisa was never allowed to bring her to the club. Violence is part of our life. Even seeing brothers fucking around, trading punches would upset someone like her.

"So, what happened?" I try again. Getting the fucker that did this is the only way I can think to make this right for her.

She tries to sit up. When she flinches, I offer my arm for support. "I don't really know," she begins when she's made herself more comfortable. "It was all so fast. One minute, I was opening my car door, the next, I was flat on my face. They must have hit the back of my head with something. Then, they wrenched my hand behind my back." She nods down toward the sling. "My wrist is badly twisted and sprained, but not broken." Tears come to her eyes. "My purse was wrenched off my shoulder." A mugging, as I expected. But then I have to revise my opinion as she continues, her voice dropping to a whisper. "But they didn't stop. They punched me in the back, grabbed my hair, lifted my head and smashed my face into the ground again. That's when my nose broke, I think."

"Oh, darlin'." I want to pull her into my arms and comfort her.

But she hasn't finished yet. Her voice catches. "They didn't stop. They turned me back over and slashed a knife across my forehead and down my face. Then I was hit again, and that's all I remember."

"Man or woman?"

Her good eye finds my face. "I don't know, I didn't see them, and they said nothing. I assume a man, a woman wouldn't do this, would she?"

A junkie trying to get money for their fix could be either sex. But one thing doesn't make sense—once they had her purse, why not leave her? Why continue a brutal attack?

"Can you remember anything about them at all? Tall, short, thin, fat?" Any description might help. If she has nothing, hopefully Mouse has already got the security footage, and though the camera wasn't working properly, he might be able to pick up the assailant entering the parking lot or leaving. "Anything about them you recognised?"

Her swollen lips press together, the pain she'd forgotten about making her frown. "They came at me from behind. I was on the ground before I knew what was happening. I'm sorry, I've tried to remember, but there's nothing I can tell you that would help."

"Don't sweat it." Gently I squeeze her hand, then come at it from a different angle. "This could have been just to get your purse."

"But they could have just yanked it and run off."

Yeah, that's what's confusing me. The attack was vicious. Of course, it could have been someone so high they got carried away, but it could also be personal. I have to ask her.

"Have you any enemies? Is there someone you crossed?" I pause before continuing, feeling the question isn't appropriate for her, but what do I know of her circumstances or what's happened to her since I last saw her in school? I have to ask, "Do you owe money to anyone?"

"No, no and no," she replies without hesitation.

Part of me is relieved she hasn't upset anyone, but in some ways I wish it had been simple. A *yeah, I had a beef with so and so* would mean I could clear this up quickly.

"The cops asked the same questions."

I'm not surprised. "You tell them the same as you told me?"

"I couldn't tell them more." She sounds disappointed, and there's something else, she's scared. "If it were random, well, I'll have to be more careful in the future, but what if it wasn't? What if I have upset someone that I don't realise? Throttle, what—"

"We'll sort it." Again, I tighten my fingers around hers. "We'll make sure you've got nothing to worry about."

"We?"

"Me, my club. You'll have the Satan's Devils on your side. Once we find who it is, he won't get away with it, or be able to come after you again." Strong words, and I can only hope I'll be able to keep my vow.

"But why?" She sounds surprised. "Why should your club get involved?"

"You're my friend, aren't you? And, you work for us. Once you signed that contract, you came under the protection of the club. It happened on club premises where our security should have kept you safe. That it didn't means we fucked up. We'll settle that score, babe."

"Ah, Ms Boseman." The nurse who'd shown me where she was appears now. "The doctor's happy to discharge you. You may have a mild concussion, but as long as someone will be able to be with you, there's no need to keep you in. The x-rays showed your nose isn't broken, just swollen. You'll be in pain for a while. Here's a script you can get filled for painkillers."

"I just want to go home," she replies, her voice weary and drained. I suspect she's only taken in half of what's just been told to her.

As the nurse gives her one final check, I stand. "I'll be back in a moment."

Going out into the corridor, I take out my phone. One call later and it's all arranged. A prospect will bring one of the club's SUVs, and I'll use that to take her home. It's only after I press the red button that I realise he'll have to ride my bike back to the club—the one thing I own that I'm ultra-possessive about.

I'll just have to suck it up. I'm doing this for the club. I hadn't blown smoke up her ass when I told her we'd all feel some responsibility toward her and were to be blamed because her attack happened on our watch. Prez would want to make sure she was being cared for. We'll also need to make sure something like this never happens to any of our employees again.

CHAPTER SEVEN

Gwen…

Noah hasn't yet returned, though I've no doubt he will. He promised, after all, and from what I know of him, once he gives his word he means it. Hopefully he can get me a cab, and I'll return home and lick my wounds in private. I ignore that the nurse said I shouldn't be alone, I've been looking after myself for a long time.

Noah. God, he's grown into an attractive man, even better than he'd been at eighteen.

At school, Lisa and her friends had taken me under their wing and saved me from the kids who bullied me. I rarely saw them outside, only on a couple of occasions when I'd risked going to the mall with Lisa. The security of my life with my foster parents was tenuous, and I knew they wouldn't be happy with the company I was keeping. To retain my home, I had to get straight As and not step out of line. Hence the previous bullying, I was a student who listened to everything, and who turned in every piece of work on time. Strangely it was bikers' kids who stepped up to protect the nerd I'd been. The other students who'd taunted me for wearing conservative clothes and, as they put it, sucking up to the teachers, had soon faded away when I'd gained their protection.

When I'd graduated from high school, I never expected to see Noah again. I'd only known him through Lisa, and our shared meals at lunchtime. I knew they all lived on a place which had become mystical in my mind when they'd talked about it, the Satan's Devils' compound. Lisa knew I wouldn't be able to visit her there, so I was never invited to see the place for myself. Neither did I take her home. No friend, and certainly not one with a connection to the Satan's Devils, would ever get over the threshold in my foster parents' home.

The Satan's Devils Brat Pack as they were known in the school yard tended to stick close, there were enough of them that they could form tight friendships between themselves. Everyone knew if you hurt one of them, you'd have to take on the whole pack. Which meant they were untouchable, as were any lucky enough to become affiliated with them. It was thanks to them my high school days had been bearable.

At fourteen, I'd gone through another change. A new foster family, a new city to live in. As a new girl, shy, not particularly outgoing and very studious, I'd been a target and unable to stand up for myself. Lisa had seen what was happening, and from then on I was left alone. Of course, my association with the Brat Pack meant I wasn't well liked in the general school population. Other kids had stayed clear, and no other friendships had developed. But with them at my back, I was safe.

I still got teased, but it was by Lisa's connections, and all done without malice. Noah, Lisa's brother, had treated me much like his sister, pulling my hair and stealing my books, and putting all kinds of shit in my locker.

My school days had been fun. Thanks to them.

My friendship with them had endured until I was eighteen when we went our separate ways. Noah, two years ahead, had left before I did, but I'd still seen him around, often appearing on his bike to collect Lisa.

Noah, tall, devastatingly handsome, had had an effect on an impressionable and affection starved girl. Yeah, I'd had a crush on him, but I don't think he'd known that, or, if he had, he'd ignored it.

Now I'm older and wiser, and recognise my attraction for what it was. I can smile at the memory of my heart beating faster when he was in the vicinity, remembering how I used to hang onto every word out of Lisa's mouth, hoping she'd drop his name into the conversation. It was akin to any young girl's yearning for a pop or film star, someone who'd forever be out of their reach.

He'd lived in my daydreams. I'd even dreamed about him at night.

Until the real world had intruded and I grew up fast. Their duty done, my foster parents had turned me out the day I turned eighteen. I was on my own from then on.

I started college, my efforts now to please only myself, and to secure my future. Without the Satan's Devils Brats I'd been forced to make new friends. But my maturity together with a harder skin gained thanks to the Devils, I managed. Lisa and I had lost touch, and if I ever thought about it, it was to look back with amusement on my teenage crush. Only occasionally would I find myself thinking, *I wonder what Noah is doing now?*

I knew the Satan's Devils technically owned the Wheel Inn, but thankful just to get a job where I could earn much needed cash, I took it without thinking twice. I truly hadn't considered I might bump into any of my old friends there. If I had, it wouldn't have deterred me. There's no one to criticise my friendship with bikers now, and, bringing home money was my priority.

I'm twenty-two, far removed from the schoolgirl I once was, and Noah? Well, he's a man, no longer a boy. It had been good to see him when I'd been working a shift. And if he again had made my heart beat faster, I recognise it for what it is, a reminder of pleasant memories of my childhood, and heaven help me, there weren't many I could treasure.

As I wait for him to return, I wonder why he's here tonight. As a friend? No, my true connection had been with his sister. It's only because as, he belatedly admitted himself, the Satan's Devils feel responsible that what happened to me had taken place on their turf.

I don't want pity. *I've been attacked.* I shouldn't have been. I know better.

None of my foster parents had been much, but none had physically punished me. I'd been shocked to become the target for bullies when I started that school. The Satan's Devils might have played pranks on me, but the other kids, well they'd do things that would physically hurt or cause mental scars like locking me in a broom closet. The lesson had been learned. When I no longer had friends to protect me, I made damn sure I was able to protect myself.

Attending self-defence training, I soaked up everything. I know how to get out of a strangle hold, I know to watch my surroundings. I know to walk out with my keys in my hand. I know what to do theoretically, and should have been able to defend myself.

Except, I hadn't been paying attention. All the steps I'd taken to make sure something like this would never happen to me have come to nothing. That's why the attack has left me in shock. My assailant had come at me from behind, so silently and without warning, I hadn't a chance to defend myself.

Why?

It has to have been a druggie who just wanted my purse, which, unfortunately had all my tips in it. Shouldn't that have satisfied them? Why keep on punching when they'd got what they wanted? That's what I can't understand. Maybe a meth addicted addict didn't know when to stop. I shudder, *I'm lucky to be alive.*

"How you doing?"

I startle having been lost in my thoughts. "I hurt," I admit, but unable to put a brave face on it. It's the truth. Automatically I touch the bandages covering my forehead and cheek, wondering if I'll end up looking like Frankenstein's monster.

"Scars will fade." Noah seems to read my mind. His voice is firm, and his expression suggests he's making a promise. When I shrug, he continues, "It's all arranged, the club's sending an SUV so we'll get you home."

My eyebrows try to draw down, making me wince as they pull at the stitches. "You don't need to do that. I can get a cab. Or…" *am I up to driving? I'll just have to try.* "Can you give me a lift back to my car?"

He draws something out of his pocket and shows it to me. "I've got your car key. We'll get it back to you tomorrow. You can't drive tonight."

I want to argue with him, but my head is pounding. "Then it's a cab."

"No. We'll get you home." He takes the decision away from me.

Suddenly my brain kicks into gear, something I've seen breaks through the fog in my aching brain. "Show me that again?" When he looks perplexed, I elaborate, impatiently, "The car key?"

He does, still looking confused.

The hand I can move covers my mouth. "Where are my house keys?"

His eyes sharpen. "This is all the prospect found."

"They were on the same ring." They had been, but the car key did have a habit of working loose.

Visibly he stiffens, then snaps, "Was your driver's license in your purse?"

I rack my brains. *Shit!* It was. Along with a bill I'd gotten in the mail this morning and brought it with me so I could remember to pay it. I gulp, then reply, "Yes."

"Fuck," he breathes, then his eyes close and reopen. "Okay,

we got this. Until we know why you were attacked, we'll have someone on you, okay?"

Someone on me?

He sees my confusion. "I'll stay tonight with you. No, don't argue, I was going to do that anyway, you've got a possible concussion and shouldn't be left alone.."

I'm stunned into silence for a second. "You can't do that. There's no need. I'll get the locks changed." I try to ignore that the person who attacked me now knows where I live. "I'll get onto a twenty-four-hour service once I'm home."

He chuckles though I don't see the reason for any amusement. "Gwen, we'll take care of all that. We'll be there to make sure you're safe. There's nothing for you to worry about."

Instead of comforting me, it worries me further. "But there's no reason to think they'll come after me again, is there? They got all the cash I had."

"Gwen." He moves closer, and for the first time I wish he wasn't so damn tall as he looms over me. "Until we know who hurt you tonight, we're won't be taking risks with your safety. You need to rest, and you might have a concussion so will need someone with you tonight. I'll do that, and I'll speak to Wizard and get him to assign a prospect to watch your house for a while."

"There's no point. I already said I'll change the locks."

"Fuck, Gwen." His eyes flare. "Even if it was a junkie who attacked you, they may think you've money or something to steal in your place. They've got your address. We'll keep an eye out, just for a few days, to make sure they don't come calling."

I hadn't thought of that. The idea this might not be over makes me whimper.

"As for the locks, prospects will change them tomorrow."

I bristle and insist, "I can do that. There's no need for you to do anything."

His lips press together. "I don't like the idea that someone who shouldn't knows where you live. Nah, we'll be watching out for you." He remembers something about me, that I'm stubborn as he follows that up with a stern, "No argument, Gwen. Whether you think you need us to protect you or not, we've got your back. Now, are you ready to escape this joint?"

As much as I can with my painful face, I glare. But his face is set. I'm more than ready to go home, so I decide to leave arguing for my independence for when I feel more like myself.

Moving is painful. I groan as I go to slide my legs off the bed. Everything hurts, even those parts which I'd thought had been spared.

Seeing me struggling, hearing the groans I can't suppress, Noah's there. Not only is he big in height, he's also muscular, one push from him and I'd probably topple, but his gentleness belies his strength as he gently puts his arm around my shoulder to steady me then pull me up. He keeps his arm there until I stop wobbling.

"I'm sorry, I feel so weak."

He frowns. "No need to fuckin' apologise. You're hurt, sore as shit, and suffering from shock, babe. I'm not going to blame you for that. Lean on me, let me help."

If it had been anyone else, maybe I wouldn't be so accommodating, insisting I can do it all myself, but he's my old friend's brother. He was there when I did my awkward growing up. Nothing I could do now would alter his impression of me. His help I can accept without embarrassment.

Lisa used to wax and wane, one minute calling him an utter pest, the next admitting he was the best brother she could hope for. I'd seen all of that, and now something tells me he's grown into the good man I'd always expected he would. Sure, he might need to enforce the rules of his club and I'm not so naïve as to believe that wouldn't include using his fists. But I've only ever known him to be gentle and caring, unless getting a noogie counts. If I'd asked for someone to help me, no one could be better than him. So trusting him completely, I do what he says, and lean on him.

His support doesn't falter, he doesn't let go of me for even a second as he weaves me through the people in the waiting room, his scowl making them step back a pace. Then we're out into the night air. I notice the darkness is already being split by a bright line of light above the horizon.

"It's late," I breathe, only just realising how long I've been in the building behind me.

"Early," he corrects. "But you need your bed. Here's us. Let me help you in."

Having seated me in the SUV, he leans over and fastens my seat belt. I rest my head back and sigh with relief as he goes around to the driver's side.

"We'll stop off at the pharmacy and get your script filled. Then you can have a painkiller before you try to sleep." It's said conversationally as he adjusts the seat, then starts the engine and the SUV moves off.

I close my eyes, suddenly so tired I feel I could sleep for weeks, then, just as quickly bolt fully awake. *I was attacked.* I suppress the cry that wants to escape from my throat. *Why me? Why couldn't they have picked on someone else?*

I'd been careless. Once I'd seen how dark it was I should have used the light on my phone, or have gone back inside and asked for someone to walk me out. But I hadn't, I'd walked to my car oblivious to the danger I might be in. *It could have been worse.* I could have been molested, or killed.

Tears leak from my eyes as it all catches up with me.

As if Noah knows, he reaches out his hand and squeezes my thigh. No words, but that simple touch reassures me I'm not in this alone. Suddenly I'm glad his club are going to be watching out for me. Even if there's no need, it might be the comfort necessary to ensure I can close my eyes at night. I feel like a victim, and that doesn't settle well with me.

He pulls up outside a pharmacy. After telling me to stay

where I am, he locks the doors as he goes to collect my medication. Sooner than I would have been, he's back, and passing a paper bag to me.

"That was quick."

He snorts. "This cut does wonders, Gwen. They couldn't wait to see the back of me."

I smile in the darkness. The Tucson citizens fear the Satan's Devils, but I don't think they need to. If they're going to protect a no one like me, they're good people.

I'd given him my address and he drives there unerringly, he must know the streets of Tucson like the back of his hand. I relax as my house comes into sight, it's not much, just a two-bedroom single storey that I rent, but it's my base. Having only lived in shared student apartments before, this is the first place I've ever been able to call my own. I've only lived here a few months, but gradually I'm personalising it and making it mine. It's home, a safe haven. I begin to feel better the nearer we draw to it and I direct him to park on the driveway.

He takes off his seat belt and then reaches out his hand and takes a small pouch from the glove compartment. "Wait here a minute."

"Why?"

The dawn light reveals he's rolling his eyes. "Because you don't have your keys, Gwen. I'll need to pick your lock."

My eyes widen. *Should I be worried he knows how to do it?* "And you've got a lock picking kit in your car?"

He winks at me. "Yeah, we're boy scouts, what can I say? We're always prepared in case someone locks themselves out."

"But you don't need to." At his raised eyebrow, I inform him, "There's a spare key in the plant pot by the door."

"Gwen!" he exclaims as though disappointed in me. He opens his mouth as if to say more, but at that moment I try to undo my seatbelt, but one handed I wince. Whatever he was going to say he changes it to, "Nevermind, let's get you inside." He undoes my seatbelt himself.

During the short journey, I've stiffened up, so when he tells me to wait so he can help me out, I don't argue. He lifts me and, like he had in the hospital, waits until I'm steady on my feet. Then, wrapping a supportive arm around me leads me forward, only letting me go when he needs to get the key, He humphs when he finds it easily.

Then the front door opens and I step inside before he can stop me, automatically reaching for the light switch and flicking it on.

"Gwen, wait…" But he's a moment too late.

Oh shit. My gut rolls as the devastation comes into sight.

Immediately, Noah pushes me behind him and reaching into his cut takes out a damn gun. *A gun.* It's not the weapon that unnerves me, but that he thinks he needs it.

"Get back to the car, Gwen. Lock yourself in," he hisses, then without waiting to see if I obey, he steps forward, moving so quietly I'd have thought it impossible for such a big man. He checks everything, even behind the curtains, first peering over the counter in the small kitchenette before checking behind it. Then he moves onto the bedrooms.

Within moments he's back, his gun now back in its holster or wherever he keeps it, and his hands are raking through his hair.

"There's no one here." Then he realises I'm still here and his face hardens. "I told you to get back to the car and wait."

"Walking wounded, remember?" My voice is shakier than I mean it to be. "It was kind of easier to stay where I was."

He shakes his head. "If someone were here, they could have run toward you, hurt you, taken you…"

I'm scared enough without him telling me that. "But they weren't. Oh, Noah, this place is a mess." My words come out in an embarrassing wail, but the damage here has finished me.

His face gentles. "I'm sorry, Gwen. The bedrooms are no better." He leaves me and starts looking around, noting as I do my television on the wall, my laptop open on the table. He swears under his breath, then takes his phone out of his pocket.

"Prez?... Yeah, I know what fuckin' time it is. Yeah... I just got Gwen back to her place. It's been fuckin' ransacked... No, not a burglary, they've left expensive gear. But it's a fuckin' mess." He turns away, speaking quietly but my ears still pick up, "Someone fuckin' pissed in her bed."

My exhaled exclamation gets his attention. He turns, focusing his eyes on me as though trying to give me his strength.

"Yeah. That's what I was thinking... Yeah, that would be great if she doesn't mind."

During the last part of the conversation, his eyes have remained fixed on mine. When he ends the call, he steps closer, "You're coming back to the compound."

In another life those words would have been a dream come true. But right now? No, I'm not going to be chased out of my house. As anger takes over from fear, summoning what strength I have left, I ignore him. Instead I take a step into the room.

"No, Gwen." His hand closes around my arm, and he shakes his head. "You don't want to see that."

But I do. I want to know exactly how they've defiled my living space and my bed. I pull away and go to see for myself.

When I come to the door, I peer inside, and gasp.

I didn't have much growing up, but one thing I'd managed to keep was a teddy bear and a stuffed toy dog that my parents had given me the Christmas before they'd died. I'd never been parted from them. Even though the odour is gross, and I'd been warned about the mess on my bed, what's a hundred times worse is the sight of my childhood treasures in shreds.

I'd kept it together in the hospital, I'd kept it together when I was speaking to the cops. Hell, I was distressed when I'd heard Noah say how they'd desecrated the place where I'd slept, but now I lose it and wail, sinking to my knees at the extent of the damage.

"Jesus. Gwen, I got you. I got you, okay? Let it out, let it all out." Noah's voice mumbles against my ear. "You're safe, I got you."

I clutch at him, unable to speak, unable to scream, *I don't understand*. This isn't a burglary, this is something driven by hate.

But I have no enemies.

Or, up until now, that's what I thought.

CHAPTER EIGHT

*T*hrottle…

As I haven't yet been to bed, I count it as still late rather than early, so I gratefully take the whisky Wizard's just poured me.

"Christ, what a mess," I tell him, staring into the amber liquid.

Wizard's head moves up and down in agreement. "And there's no one she can think of who might have a grudge against her?"

"Nah." I'd brought him up to date, so would just be repeating myself to expand. "Mouse got anything?"

"No. I checked the parking lot security footage as well. One unit was out as you know. Whoever it was had been clever enough to evade the other cameras. Shooter's getting his crew to go there first thing, set up new lights. Mouse is going to install new equipment." He sighs and sips his coffee. "There were any number of people in the bar last night, it will take a while to check all of them. Even then, it could be someone who hadn't even entered the premises and was waiting for her out back."

"I thought it was random. But after seeing her house? I mean, fuck it, who'd want to hurt a sweet thing like her?"

Again he nods. "Yeah, that was my gut feel. But pissing in her bed, Brother? That smacks of being fuckin' personal."

Hearing footsteps behind I turn my head, smiling as Amy, Prez's heavily pregnant wife comes into sight. "Gwen's sleeping. I made her take her painkillers and slipped her a sedative." I'd worry about the latter if I didn't know Amy's an experienced nurse and knows what she's doing. "She needed to switch off."

"Where did you put her?"

Amy's brow furrows. "In your bed, of course."

Uh-uh. They've got the wrong idea. "That's not her place," I tell her fast. "Should have put her in one of the empty rooms. She's nothing to me other than she's the friend of my sister."

"Oh, well, from what Drew said…"

Drew, or as he's better known nowadays, Wizard, looks unrepentant. "Well you can't move her tonight, and she can't be on her own. Poor girl will have nightmares and needs to be watched in case she's got a concussion. Sort something out with Lisa tomorrow, maybe she can stay with her in town. But wait until morning. Or," he takes out his phone and glances at it, "whenever she wakes up." As my face darkens, he shrugs. "You did bring her here, Brother."

"I did, she's an employee who needs our protection."

Another shrug. "I'm sure you can cope for one night. Or morning, whatever." He stands and holds out his hand to Amy who takes it. "Now I'm going to take my wife to bed."

Amy chuckles softly. "But I'm not sleepy, Drew."

"Thank fuck." Wrapping his arm around her, they leave the clubhouse.

Jeez. This is fucked up. I've never had a bitch sleep in my bed, my room's my personal space. Even if I go with a sweet butt, I use one of the crash rooms. Maybe I can get Dad and Mom to take her in, or drop her off at Lisa's if she's got space. Or, maybe she could stay with Blade and Tash if she'd prefer to be on the compound.

I could use a crash room tonight. Though I can't. Fuck it. She's supposed to have someone with her, and how will Gwen feel when she wakes up alone in a strange bed? She was so upset when I'd driven her here, I'm not one hundred percent that she'll remember she's on the compound, particularly if she wakes hazy from whatever Amy's given her. And even if she does, that won't help her, she won't recognise anything as she's never been here before. There'll be nothing familiar.

Fuck.

Helping myself to another whisky, I drink that back, then decide to man the fuck up. Okay, while I'm particular about my bed being mine and mine only, under the circumstances I can suck it up. It's not like she's a complete stranger.

When my glass is empty, I walk up to the bloc where my suite is housed. There are two suites in each bloc, Marvel being in the adjacent one. I've my privacy, room for the shit I feel is important, a bed, television, closet and desk as well as a private bathroom. What more does a man need?

"Mornin'."

I exchange chin lifts with Shooter who's on his way to work. He's an early riser as he runs our construction company with Bullet and more recently, Drummer's second son, Zane. Luckily, he doesn't stop or ask me questions. I reach the bloc, then pause to rub my hand over my eyes before entering my room. *Christ, I'm tired.* Not only haven't I had any sleep for almost twenty-four hours, it's been as stressful as fuck. All I want to do is crash and get my head down for a few hours. But I can't, there's a girl in my bed.

Fuck it.

Opening the door as quietly as I can, I peer inside. She's there, just as I'd been told. Instead of hogging the bed, she's carefully positioned on just one side, her long hair, now loose from its bun, spread out over my pillows. As I watch she whimpers a little. *Bad dream?* Or, is she hurting?

The sight of her looking so forlorn touches my cold fucking heart.

She didn't deserve to be attacked, nor have her house invaded, smashed up and defiled.

She looks right in my bed.

What the fuck? Where did that thought come from? Then I laugh at myself, of course she does. She's not a sweet butt, nor a one-night stand, she's just a friend who I'm giving shelter to for the night. Tomorrow I'll sort out something else. Dad and Mom have a spare room. That's the best place for her. Mom will be all over having a pseudo daughter to stay, I know she misses Lisa since she moved out.

For now I'll just have to suck up my discomfort and sleep on the uncomfortable chair. I'm tired as fuck, so it shouldn't be hard.

Sitting by my desk, I stretch out my legs. When I lean back to rest my head, I find only air, so let it drop forward. Damn, that pulls on my neck. I shuffle down further, raising my arm and trying to make a rest for my chin out of my fingers. But it's only a wooden chair, without arms, and there's nothing to rest my elbow on.

Deciding the floor is probably the best option, I slide off the chair to lie myself down. I reach out my hand, but before it makes contact with the floor, there's movement from the bed. Gwen's thrashing, and her hands are trying to ward something off.

In one swift movement I'm at her side. *What do I do? Wake her, or...* Fuck it, in seconds I'm around the bed and on the side which is free, easing myself on and moving behind her.

"Shush," I murmur, taking her into my arms. "It's over. No one's going to hurt you while I'm here."

Without waking, she stills, snuggles back, and then her breathing deepens.

I shouldn't be doing this. I'm all but a stranger. I shouldn't be holding her in my arms. But when I try to pull away, she becomes agitated. *Fuck.*

Lying still, hardly daring to draw in a breath, I lie awake

thinking. Would it hurt just to hold her to help her rest? God knows, she needs it.

Feeling awkward and on edge, I myself remain unable to drop off, however many fucking sheep I try to count.

Every time I breathe in, her scent fills my nostrils. Amy must have got her showered in my bathroom and used some of my shower gel. Gwen smells exactly like me, tinged with her own perfume and the faint aroma of hospital disinfectant that still lingers. However I try to think of other things and tell myself she's my sister's friend, having a female in my arms results in my cock hardening. It's so damn wrong, this woman means nothing to me. There couldn't be a worse person to bring into the club, she's sweet, naïve, and nothing like the type of woman I use for relief.

She's working to be a paralegal for fuck's sake. Our lifestyle would corrupt her.

I inch away, putting space between us. She whimpers again. Reaching out my hand I let it rest on her shoulder, and thank fuck, that seems to be all the reassurance she needs as her breathing evens out and she settles.

Giving up on trying to sleep, in my head I run over shit to do the next morning, or, rather later today. First off, unless Wizard's already put it in motion, I'll send the prospects to clean and salvage what they can of her house and get a decent security system installed. I'll also need to find somewhere for her to stay until we decide it's safe for her to return.

Eventually I must doze, as I'm jerked awake by a gentle knock at my door. Before Gwen becomes conscious enough to realise I've slept next to her, I slide off the bed. When I open up to see who's there, I'm pleased that I'm still fully dressed because it's my mom and my sister. I step outside, pulling the door to behind me.

"How's Gwen?" Mom asks, sounding concerned. "I've just heard what happened. Who did it, Throttle?"

"We don't know, that's why's she's here."

"Have you been hiding something, Noah?" Lisa's glaring at me. "Why's she in your room? Gwen's not a sweet butt—"

"Lisa!" I snap, while trying to keep my voice down. "There's nothing between me and Gwen. I went to the hospital as the club are her employers, I thought she'd appreciate seeing someone she knew. And why the fuck are you here anyway? Shouldn't you be in college?"

"Mom rang me." Lisa glares at me. "I had to come."

"You've not seen her for years," I throw back, trying to keep my voice low. "You're just nosy as fuck, admit it."

"Stop it, you two," Mom hisses sharply. "It's no time for one of your sibling spats. And you should have brought her up to us, Noah."

"Yeah, Mom. Like you'd have wanted to be woken in the small hours." I calm down and try to approach this rationally. I love my sister but sometimes she riles me. "It was the quickest solution to put her here. But it would be useful if she could stay with you and Dad if you wouldn't mind. Until we know her place is safe. I don't think she's got anyone else, no one came to the hospital. Her house is a fuckin' mess. We can clean it up, but—"

"Of course she can stay," Mom replies quickly, her eyebrow rising as if challenging I'd think anything different. "From what Amy said Gwen needs time and a place to heal. Going back to her house after a home invasion is the last thing she needs."

"I want to see her." Lisa tries to push past me.

I place my hand on her shoulder, holding her in place. "She looks and feels like shit, okay? And she's probably not up to a hundred questions."

"I know that," Lisa snipes back. She takes a breath as if, like me, she's realised she's been too combative, and says more reasonably, "I know we've lost touch, but I've often wondered where she was and how she was doing. I'm still her friend, nothing will change that."

"Just let us in, Noah," Mom adds. "She probably needs to see someone other than your ugly face."

Jeez, thanks Mom. Outnumbered, I move aside, pushing the door open, and wave them in.

Our voices must have disturbed her as Gwen wincing and pulling herself up into a sitting position. If anything she looks worse this morning. Both eyes are black, and the rest of her face which isn't bandaged is red and swollen.

"Gwen." Lisa runs forward with her arms stretched out, but pulls them back as she notes the condition her old school friend is in.

"Oh, sweetheart," my mom says, shaking her head.

"I'll get showered." Perhaps Lisa being here is a blessing. I can leave the women to sort Gwen out. My job here done, I pause only to select some fresh clothes to take in with me.

I'm a man, I don't take long in the shower, but by the time I'm out, Lisa's walking in with a bundle of clean clothes in her arms, while Mom's fussing about helping Gwen to stand.

Leaning in, I ask, "You got this, Mom?"

"We've got this," she confirms, waving her hand to dismiss me.

Placing a grateful kiss to her cheek, I direct a chin lift toward Gwen. "Mom and Lisa will look after you, okay?"

Her gaze holds mine, and her mouth attempts a smile, it's not very successful, one side being so swollen. "Thanks for every-thing, Noah."

My dismissive shrug tries to convey she's no need to thank me, then I leave my sanctuary which has been invaded by women, and head down to the club house.

It's mid-afternoon, so most of the brothers are absent as I walk in on what at first glance appears to be a woman's meeting. Sam's talking to Amy, Sophie's sitting with Olivia oohing and ahhing over baby Layla, Charlotte, Shooter's old lady, is by the bar talking to Carmen who's recently given up her hairdressing business. In the corner, Becca and Mariana are having a heated discussion.

Little Rose, well, not so little now, is openly making eyes at the only man in the room, Mason, Blade and Tash's son. Knowing Rock would have something to say about Rose's fixation if he was present, I head for the other male with my hand outstretched.

"Mason. You on leave?"

"Yeah. Just for a few days."

"How's it going?" If my dad hadn't been so set on me not joining up, I might have gone with him when he'd signed up.

"Shipping back out to the sandpit next week," he explains. "Just wanted to touch base with everyone before I go again."

I'd like to ask more about his career, he's done fuckin' well and is now a Marine. But the women have other ideas, demonstrating they're far more interested in things closer to home.

"How's Gwen, Throttle?"

"About how you'd expect," I call back to Amy, though it dawns on me, in my hurry to abdicate my responsibilities, I hadn't actually asked her. "Mom and Lisa are with her now. She's moving in with Mom and Peg."

Mason frowns. "Not yours, Cuz? I was kinda given that impression."

I slap his shoulder. "Since when do you think I'd have a woman, man?"

He chuckles. "Yeah, I did think that was strange." He glances around, then lowers his voice. "I hear there's a new sweet butt. Any good?"

"Not for you to find out, she's for patched members," I tell him, earning myself a thump in my ribs. "So hands off." Inwardly I'm laughing, like them being out of bounds would put him off. Same as me, he's a Satan's Devils kid, and we'd always found ways around the rules and knew how to discreetly break them.

But he's put Clover in my mind. Being new and not yet

jaded, she loves sex and lots of it. Originally employed as a stripper at Angels, we had to call it a day when her exuberant lap dances had risked us losing our licence. Problem solved, she could get all the sex she wanted, as well as a roof over her head, but only dancing for Satan's Devils members. Maybe I'll get a personal lap dance later. My cock's reminded me I went all night lying next to a woman being unable to touch her.

A movement out of the corner of my eye brings Rose back to my attention. She has her hands on her hips and is watching us with a pout.

Speaking quietly, I give my advice, "If I were you, I wouldn't encourage it." I jerk my head toward her. "Rock's very protective of his daughter."

Mason snorts. "I might have been away, but I haven't forgotten. Nah, I'm not doing anything to further her interest. She's a nice kid, but not for me, Cuz. I'm like you, Throttle. Can't see me settling down anytime soon, and I'd be dead if I had other intentions toward Rock's daughter."

It's hard for me to imagine what the clubhouse was like before I was born. The Satan's Devils MC at one time had more sweet butts than old ladies. Only a few members had settled down, Viper—may he rest in peace—had been married to Sandy, Bullet was, and still is, with Carmen, and Heart with his first love of his life, Crystal. Those were the only three encumbered with old ladies until Wraith met Sophie and started something off. Drummer, a man who no one thought would ever be tamed, followed soon after when he found Sam. Then, like dominos falling, a large proportion of the club had settled down.

Kids had come along, kids had grown, the dynamics of the club had changed.

Though I'd never experienced them, I miss the days the old guys talk about. I've always wondered what it would have been like to live in a club where men rode motorcycles and had no worries except which whore was going to fill their bed tonight.

If the club wasn't so family oriented, maybe Mom and Peg wouldn't be trying to marry me off.

Perhaps Mason—when he leaves the Marines and joins the club—and I will be the start of a return to the good old days and restart the trend. One where variety was accepted as being the spice of life.

CHAPTER NINE

---

*G*wen…

"So, you and Throttle?" Lisa nudges me with her elbow, then leans back again.

I gaze at the sun dancing on the pool and think back to that morning three days ago.

Distant voices had invaded my sleep. Slowly trying to fight through the fog in my mind, it had been hard to distinguish actual words and had taken a while to realise I hadn't fallen asleep in my room with the television still blaring. I'd startled, unable to think where I was, until I tried to move and the pain brought all that had happened to me into focus. I was mortified I'd spent the night in someone else's bed, with no idea of whose room I was in, except it had to be somewhere on the Satan's Devils' compound.

When the door opened and two women had accompanied Noah in, I was beyond pleased to recognise one of them. While we may have lost touch, Lisa was probably the best person I could see at that moment.

I'd been introduced to their mom, Darcy, a strong no-nonsense woman who quickly took charge of everything, directing Lisa to bring me some clothes. Almost before I could blink, I was taken to a house at the top of the compound, and settled into Lisa's old room. Neither Peg, Noah's father, or Darcy could have been kinder to me.

Lisa has spent most of the weekend on the compound, and we've easily stepped back into our friendship as if no time had passed. I love her company, as long as she stays away from those probing questions about why she'd originally found me in what was apparently, Noah's room.

Sighing, I explain. Again. "I've told you, there's nothing between Noah and me. I hadn't seen him for years until I bumped into him at the Wheel Inn."

"You had a crush on him back in the day." That she'd been able to tell, doesn't surprise me.

"Sure, I did." I chuckle. "Along with almost every other female, present company excepted, of course."

Lisa smiles and rolls her eyes. "It was the bane of my life. Girls wanting to be friends with me just so I'd introduce them to the bad boy. Hey," her eyes narrow at me, "was that why you became my friend?"

"As I remember, it was you who approached me," I remind her, placing my hand gently on her arm. "And I'll always be grateful. Without you and the brat pack's support, my school days would have been very different."

Tossing her long hair over her shoulder, she shudders. "I hated bullies then, and I hate them now."

"I'm not surprised with a father like Peg." I've only been here two days, but I've picked up a lot about Noah and Lisa's dad. His attitude over my beating for one thing, his face had darkened and he was almost frighteningly horrified on my behalf. Darcy, too, is a no-nonsense woman who'd probably have given her kids hell if they'd picked on someone because they were different or socially awkward.

"True, dat." Lisa grins. "Dad would have given me hell if I'd been a bully myself." She shifts herself on her sun lounger.

I think I missed out, not being able to come to the compound when I was younger. Here I am, lying beside a glorious pool, kept clean by the prospects, apparently. It might be autumn, but it's a lovely day, warm, without the scorching heat of summer. Lisa had never invited me, and I understood why. For one thing, the Satan's Devils kids had stuck closely together, rarely inviting outsiders back to their home. And for another, even if she had I'd have had to turn her down. My foster parents would have disowned me.

"How are you two doing?" Darcy appears and plonks herself down on a vacant lounger.

"Everything okay?" Lisa counters in return. Darcy had run off earlier when her work phone had pinged.

"Yeah, it's fine. They had the fire under control by the time I got there. No casualties."

"Do you still have to attend in person?" I ask, having learned she's a fire chief.

"Not really." Darcy grins. "Unless it's a particularly bad one, I do mostly paperwork nowadays." Her expression turns wistful.

"Thank goodness," Lisa sighs. "Dad can't afford to get many more grey hairs."

"Have you ditched the idea of going back to work on Monday?" Darcy turns the conversation back to me.

She's spent the weekend trying to persuade me I needed to take time off, and I'd been protesting.

"I have to go in tomorrow. I don't get sick leave."

Darcy's concerned eyes examine my face. "You might not be able to, honey. You're pretty banged up."

I will, I'll have to. I can't afford to lose this internship. "I'll be fine. And I have to get back to my house and start sorting it out."

"Noah says the prospects have done a good job, and Mouse has installed a security system."

Darcy's words don't comfort me. Fiercely independent, those are things I should have been doing myself.

Now I have to live with the knowledge I could never afford

the system like the one that the Satan's Devils have apparently installed for me, complete with cameras which Mouse himself has promised to monitor when I first go home. I offered to pay them back, though I've no idea how I'd do so, but they said it was recompense for what had happened to me on their premises where I should have been safe. They insisted it was their fault as I should have had a prospect escorting me, when I know the blame sits with me. I'd been careless.

Trying to get comfortable, I wince. It doesn't go unnoticed.

"Why don't we get you back to the house? You could do with more painkillers."

There's no reason to pretend they're wrong. Feeling stiff, I get to my feet. I want to push myself to do things, but know the more I rest, the quicker I'll heal.

Though I'm sore and hurting, the day is a pleasant interlude for me, my only regret is that I haven't seen Noah again. I'd wanted to thank him for all he'd done that night, and to do it when I'm not doped up and half out of it.

Shortly after we'd got back to Peg and Darcy's house, Amy had appeared to redo my bandages and check my stitches, then, her man, the prez, Wizard had turned up.

"I'm so fuckin' sorry this happened, Gwen." Wizard's mouth purses as he takes responsibility for what happened on the club. "We'd understand if you don't want to come back and work for us."

I still have a job? I was only a casual employee and know how busy the Wheel Inn is. They can't afford to keep a place open for me, and I know I'll be pushing it just to get back to my day job. Working evenings as well will be too much for me until I'm healed better than I am now.

But Wizard is insistent, going so far as to press a weeks' wages into my hand. When I'd tried to refuse, he'd showed me why he was the prez. His face had changed and had become that of a man with whom sensible people didn't argue.

Darcy and Peg are great, but nice as they are, they're

strangers, and I don't feel at home. Sunday I make up my mind to return to my own. I'm ambulatory, not confined to bed, and I've been looking after myself long enough to know I'll be able to cope.

While the prospect's driving me home, I grit my teeth and try to prepare myself mentally for the mess I'm going to enter. *Did my clothes survive?* I hadn't checked my closets, while much of that night was hazy, that much I remember.

But I walk into a place unfamiliar, yet tidy and clean. The destroyed furniture has been removed and replaced. When I pause before entering the bedroom, I find nothing to concern me had been left. My bed is spotless with a new mattress and new comforter, and brand-new sheets. And there, nestling against the pillows is a new teddy bear, and beside that, a toy dog.

The sight had brought tears to my eyes. Of course, it couldn't replace the lost memories, but the idea there were people who cared enough to make the gesture that was huge in my eyes, was almost overwhelming.

As was the fact that whatever argument I brought against the suggestion, Butcher was adamant he was planning on staying.

I'd argued until I was blue in the face, but he'd had his orders.

That night, when I went to bed, I was grateful he hadn't listened to me. Instead of being scared, I'd been able to sleep, and woke up refreshed, determined and ready to take up the reins of my life once again.

CHAPTER TEN

*T*hrottle…

I'd stayed away from Gwen, getting updates from Mom while she was staying with them, and then from the prospects who'd been assigned to guard her house. Brothers can be as bad as fucking women for the way they gossip, and any ideas they'd got from her sleeping in my bed had to be knocked on the head. In keeping my distance I'd made plain she was nothing to me, except as a childhood acquaintance, and an employee of the club.

I've thrown myself into work this week, which means before I know it, the days have gone by and it's Friday again. As I head down to the clubhouse for church, I'm early on purpose, as I've the intention of grabbing a bite to eat first. Exiting the suite I grin at Marvel, who's come out of his side at exactly the same time. We share chin lifts acknowledging we're probably on the same mission.

As we continue past the other blocs, we're joined by Jekyll, Hound and Cast who are all heading the same way.

"Hope there's something fuckin' good on the menu." Cast rubs his stomach.

Yeah, as I thought. We've all got the same thing on our minds.

Outside the clubhouse Joker's standing looking on concerned, while Lady's on his knees peering under his bike.

While the others walk on in, I pause. "Problems?"

"Fuckin' oil leak," Lady replies. "Can't see where the fuck it's coming from."

I'm too hungry to investigate now. "Bring it into the shop tomorrow, I'll take a look."

"Thanks, Brother. I might well do that." Lady takes the hand that Joker offers him. Once he's standing, the pair follow me inside.

"Throttle! C'mere." Blade points to the bar. As I approach, he gestures excitedly to the prospect on bartending duty. "He's here now, pass it across."

"Yeah, I'm here. Whadya want?"

Blade grins that rictus smile of his, and taps his teeth with the blade of his knife. "Package for you, Brother."

Nathan gives an exasperated smile as he lifts a box. "He's been dying to find out what it is."

"I ain't ordered nothing," I say, as Nathan places it in front of me. Staring at it, I'm confused, bike parts would go straight to the shop.

"Let me!" Blade's there, his knife ready. After giving an amused shake of my head, I nod. Blade can be like an overexcited child at times. It doesn't hurt to occasionally indulge him.

His claw-like hands slide the box closer, and while he might be disabled, his movements are sure and he slices the tape holding it together. When he makes to reach in, I push him aside and take over for myself.

"I'm Throttle," I tell him, tapping the address label on the top. "Doesn't fuckin' say Blade here, does it?"

He pouts. "You're no fuckin' fun. Should let an old man enjoy himself."

Yeah, and if I called him old, he'd let me have it. I glare, then delve my hands into the box, having to brush aside tissue paper.

What? My brow furrows.

"What you got, Brother?" Blade's bouncing on his feet.

Still not totally sure myself, I reach in, and extract a pair of exquisite and expensive top branded boots.

"Oooh," Blade exclaims. "You been spoiling yourself?"

No, I have not. My boots might be old and don't come with a fancy ass label, but they're serviceable and comfy. These, well, they're the bees knees as Sophie would say. Or the dog's bollocks. In other words, top of the range and the best. My problem is? I'd never waste good money on something like them. Seems a damn shame to get them scuffed on the bike.

"It must be a mistake," I muse aloud, tilting the box so I can read the name on the label once again. *Throttle, Satan's Devils Compound*, followed by the rest of our address.

"Hey, Peg. You get your son an early birthday present?" Blade shouts out.

"Not me, Brother. Hey Throttle," a hefty hand lands on my back, "whatcha got... oooh, fuckin' nice."

"They're not for me," I tell Blade again, half turning to include Peg in the dismissal. "There's a mix-up, gotta be."

"What size are they?"

I check. They're my size as luck would fucking have it.

Blade does the same, then groans. "Why d'you have to have such great fuckin' feet, Throt? I wouldn't have minded taking them off your hands if you've got no use for them."

Beside me, Peg snorts. "You going to look a gift horse in the mouth, Son? They're mighty fine." He reaches out and takes one. "Not for show either, quality shit. Good tread too."

"You got a secret admirer?"

Swinging around, I see Prez whose face is split with a grin.

"No I've fuckin' don't."

Prez shrugs. "Well, someone sent these to you. Any message in the box?"

Narrowing my eyes, I start to pull out reams of tissue paper, but there's nothing at all. Zilch.

"Local postmark. This must have come from the store in Tucson. Why not go down and ask them?"

Peg's made a good suggestion. I replace the boots in the box. Not knowing who sent them means I'm unwilling to accept them.

"Not even going to try them on, Brother?"

"Nah, Blade. I don't like strange gifts." Not when it could end up with me obligated to someone unknown.

"Said like a true one-percenter… not." Marvel, sticking his nose in where it's not wanted, chuckles loudly. "Who the fuck cares who they've come from? Keep quiet if it's a mistake. That's what I'd fuckin' do."

It seems I do care who's sent them.

"What about that Gwen woman?" Drummer's appeared behind Peg. "She might have been grateful for you sorting out her house for her."

"That was the club, not me."

"Does she know that?" Now Hawk's arrived and is getting into it.

Christ you'd think no one had ever received an anonymous gift before. Though, come to think of it, I don't think they have. Maybe they have an excuse to be curious.

Could Hawk be right? Possibly. I did tell her what we were doing, and she might have thought her new security and the replacement furnishings in her house were all down to me, when the fact is they were not. "Whatever. I don't need her thanks, and anyway, she's working at the Wheel Inn as she needs money. She'd never have been able to afford these." *Or shouldn't have, if she did,* I add in my head.

Wizard growls. "I gave her a week's money, she had cash, Brother."

I hope she didn't waste it on a present for me. Still, I've got two places to start if I want to solve this mystery. The store and

Gwen. I'm determined I'll track the sender down and then return the gift. It's not that I don't like them, I just don't want to feel I owe anyone.

"Okay, fuckers! Show's over. Church." When he bellows, Wizard's just as loud as Drummer ever was.

Fuck. All this fuss over the package had meant I'd lost my chance to get food. Glaring at Hound who's stuffing the last piece of pizza into his mouth, I hope my stomach growls loud enough to interrupt the meeting.

We take our seats in church, Drummer, sits in the VP seat placed to Wizard's left, and me next to him. Hound sits to the prez's right, and next to him is Dollar. I try to get my mind to focus as Dollar gives his report of our financial situation, but there's nothing much different to usual, and half my mind is still on the mystery present I'd received.

While I can't put my finger on why, I'm uneasy. If Gwen has sent it, I'll feel awful about her wasting her money. If so, I'll need to explain why I'd done nothing to deserve it.

"Any fallback from the fucker's who stole the bike from us?"

When silence falls, I belatedly realise Prez is looking at me for an update. Sitting straighter, I give my report. "I've had the prospects doing drive-bys. The scrap yard was closed for a week, but has reopened now. Seems like the old man has stepped up with Cedar out of commission. Rascal had a friend who was about to scrap his car, he got him to take it there, and it was the old guy who spoke to him and didn't hold much back. Told him there'd been an accident and both his sons were hurt, one quite badly. The dad was grumbling about having to employ temporary new staff, and what he's got aren't up to scratch." I tap my fingers on the table. "Razza's friend also asked whether they had any motorcycles that were worthy of doing up. Old man Dray was definitely flustered and said they didn't deal in bikes."

"Truth?" Drifter wonders aloud.

Prez nods. "Mouse and I have been keeping an eye on their security feed. That pile of bikes has been shifted. Could mean they're waiting for the gang to replenish their supply, or hopefully, they've taken our advice and got out of that business."

Peg sits forward, clasping his hands. "What about Dray's injury? Any sign of cop involvement?"

Mouse takes this one. "No. It was logged as an industrial accident at the hospital. And, as well as watching their feed, I've been keeping my nose to the ground. Reports of stolen bikes have tailed off. "

"So that's finished with." Wizard nods in satisfaction. "Hopefully the lesson is learned. But we shouldn't let down our guard. Keep your eyes and ears open. I doubt they'd come after us for revenge, but I don't want to be blindsided."

"You got it." My response is echoed around the table.

Mouse hasn't finished. He waggles his fingers to get our attention. "I've been looking at their financials." He pauses and looks up to make sure he's caught our interest. "You know the drill, people scrap cars and the Dray's pay for them. No fuckin' money transfers for them though, every transaction is cash only."

Whoa. That is interesting, especially in the cashless society we're heading for nowadays. "Money laundering?"

The half Native American's face splits in a grin. "Yeah, Throttle. And I traced back the money trail. You wanna know where it led me?"

Of course I fucking do, like every man at this table now hanging onto every word coming out of the computer guru's mouth.

Fucker makes us wait for the punchline. "The Wretched Soulz," he finally announces, with more than a touch of dramatic flare.

There's silence. I break it. "You've got to be fuckin' kidding me." Rage rises as I wonder whether the Satan's Devils need to go to war. "The Wretched Soulz knew about the stolen bikes? Fuckin' condoned stealing one of ours?"

As multiple growls accompany my words, Mouse hurriedly

corrects me. "No evidence of that. I reckon the Drays are greedy fucks with their own sideline."

Prez bangs his hand on the table. "Everyone simmer down. The Soulz are the dominant club. Us, and every MC in the locality exist with their permission. They've no beef with us. They'd never condone motorcycle thefts. Just think of the damage it would do to their reputation."

He's right. If news got around that the Wretched Soulz were tolerating the stealing of bikes from their MC partners, they'd be facing a war with not just one, but all sub-dominant MCs. While with their vast number of chapters they've got the numbers, if every other club joined together and rose up against them they'd be in for an all out bloody war. Unimaginable, but not inconceivable given a serious reason like this. Every man's bike is his most treasured property. Thefts of rides could be something that would unite everyone against them.

"Assuming they don't know what the Drays are doing, we gonna enlighten them?" Drummer raises his eyebrow toward Prez. For a moment I wonder what he'd have done were he still in position to take the decision. Does it irk him that he now has to defer to someone years younger?

Prez's lips narrow and he rubs his temples. "We keep this hand close to our chest," he decides at last. "If we turn in the Drays, the Wretched Soulz would need to look elsewhere to get their money through the system. If they've stopped their trade in bikes, then we've stirred a hornet's nest for nothing. Let sleeping dogs lie for now. The Drays don't know we've discovered their connection. I see more benefit in keeping the knowledge in our back pocket, to take out and use should we have need."

I agree with him, and notice Drummer's lips curling, a sign it was a decision he himself would have made.

We proceed to any other business.

"We've got prospects on Gwen, do we need to keep them on her? There's been nothing that concerned them this week." Wizard focuses his eyes on me.

"It's leaving us low on manpower," Shooter observes. "Sometimes no one's free to man the gate."

I honestly can't think of an argument. Sure, we still don't know who attacked Gwen or who invaded her house, but for a week there's been no further sign of them. The most likely answer is that it's a junkie who's moved on. His meth befuddled head might already have forgotten her.

Begrudgingly, I admit, "I can't justify the manpower, Prez."

He nods. "Mouse, you monitoring her security?" When he gets an up and down of Mouse's head, he continues, "She's due back at work on Monday. We'll keep the prospects on her this weekend, then leave her alone. If anything was going to happen, I'd have expected a move before now." Again his eyes find mine, and I raise my head to show I agree. "Right, who's got anything else?"

Hound raised the topic of whether it's time to patch Rascal in.

Knowing it will need a long and serious discussion before we proceed to a vote, I groan. Simultaneously my stomach growls loudly. "Can't we leave it to another fuckin' day, Brother?"

"Yeah, Throttle wants to go try on his new boots," Marvel quips.

"Fuckin' shut up, Marvel," I snarl.

Shaking his head, Wizard bangs the gavel. "Meeting adjourned. We'll discuss Razza next week."

Thank fuck.

Immediately we're out I divert to the kitchen where I raid the fridge. Snagging half a cold pizza, I eat it fast, then decide I need to wash it down with a drink.

"Hey, Throttle. Where are these new boots?" Lady shouts out as I'm approaching the bar.

"Yeah, you going to model them?" Joker turns around, his eyes lighting up at the scowl on my face. "I've heard they look fancy."

I've had more than enough of this. "Gimme." I gesture to the prospect to pass me the offending box, then, bundling it under my arm, I toss a glare at anyone who looks like they're about to open their mouth and march out of the clubhouse.

Out of sight, out of mind might work. Or, so I'm thinking, maybe a bit optimistically, as I stride up the track to the place I call home.

It's embarrassing as fuck to be sent new boots, even if I knew who they were from. I don't make a bad living as a member of the club, if I want something or need it, I can buy it myself. I glance down, *hmm*. Sure, my boots are worn, but I've broken them in and they're comfortable as fuck. Mom's commented on how scruffy they look a couple of times…

Depositing the box in my room, I make an abrupt change of plan. I had intended to return to the clubhouse and have a few drinks, then, later when the old ladies and girls go home, maybe see if a sweet butt's available. After that I might play a game of pool or get dealt into a card game, as long as Rock's not playing of course.

Instead I go up the compound, rather than walking back down.

The sun has disappeared and the moon is rising in the sky. Breathing in the fresh air, I think, not for the first time, there could be far worse places to call home. I was brought here a day after I'd been born, and I can't see me ever wanting to leave. Some people might get tired of being constantly surrounded by family as well as living and working in the same location, but that man's not me.

Life in a citizen world? I'd consider that torture.

Marching up to the front door of my parent's house, I knock twice in quick succession. Without waiting for an answer, I push open the door. Any thief would think twice about coming onto the Satan's Devils compound. Most who live here don't worry about locking up.

"That you, Noah?" Mom calls out.

Locating her by her voice, I enter the kitchen. "Hi, Mom." Approaching her, I place a kiss on her cheek.

She swings around, her face lit with a smile, and hugs me to her. "How's my favourite son?"

"I'm your only son." I roll my eyes.

Her eyes narrow slightly now the greeting is over. "What's up?" She can read me like one of her books she so much enjoys.

Reaching over, I wipe my finger through a mixture she's got in the bowl, then grimace. I'd expected cookie dough, but it's far blander, and I hate to think what it actually is. "Why should anything be wrong?"

Staring at my offending digit, she swipes at my hand. "How many times have I told you that's unhygienic? And it's Friday. Party night. Didn't expect you to come around."

I rest my elbows on the countertop. "Well, there's a reason for that, Mom. I got a strange parcel today. I wondered if you had anything to do with it."

Her brow furrows. "Parcel? I haven't sent anything to you. Noah, you only live down the way, I'd have just brought it on down. What was in it?"

"Boots. Good ones." As I tell her, I examine her face. She's as straight as a die, and if she knows anything about them, I'll easily catch her out in a lie.

With a glance down at my feet, she smirks. "Not denying you need a new pair, but why would you think that's something I would buy? It's personal stuff."

To a biker, it is. It's not so much about style, it's the grip and the feel. Mom would know, some years back she got her own bike and joined Sam's Old Ladies' Riding Club. She'd said it replaced some of the adrenaline rush she'd lost when she was no longer on the firefighting front line.

"If you didn't, then someone else bought them and sent them to me."

Her brow furrows. "Wrong address, perhaps?"

Now my hand strays toward the ever-filled cookie jar. Taking one, I bite a chunk out of it. "It was addressed to me, and the boots were my size."

"Expensive or cheap?"

"Expensive," I confirm. "Could be I might even use them if I knew who to thank." *And who to pay back.*

She taps her fingers against her teeth. "Could it be Gwen? She was really grateful for all that you'd done."

"She doesn't owe me a thing, Mom. It was the club who helped her. I just gave her a little of my time." *And held her in my arms all night.* I shake the thought of how I now miss the scent of her on my sheets out of my head. "I'm going to ask her tomorrow, but she's not got spare cash." I frown. "If it's from her they're going back for a refund."

After going quiet for a moment, she finally shrugs. "Well, I can't think of anyone else. I know it wasn't Peg. He can't keep a secret from me to save his life. It's not Christmas nor your birthday."

I muse on that for a moment. "Well, I just thought I'd check."

As I turn to go, she places her hand on my arm. "Let me know how Gwen is doing. I like that girl. She's the sort I'd like to see you with."

I huff out a breath. "She's a citizen, Mom. She knows shit all about the club and what we get up to, and she's a really nice girl. Even if I were inclined to think of her in that way, and I'm not, she isn't someone to bring into this life."

Her hands go to her hips. "And wasn't I a nice civilian girl when Peg brought me into the club?"

Grimacing, I try to avoid the minefield that's just opened up. "You were a firefighter, Mom. Gwen's more innocent, naïve. You embraced danger, she'd run a mile."

Shrewd eyes meet mine. "You don't think she's strong enough to be an old lady?"

I suppose that's summed it up. But she's overlooking one

thing. "Whether she is or is not, there's no spark there." I tell my cock it doesn't get a say in this. "Which means I'm not going to be finding out."

"That's a shame, Noah." As if losing interest, Mom turns away and gets back to doing what she was when I had come in.

CHAPTER ELEVEN

Throttle...

It was bad enough when Dad started lecturing me about finding a woman and settling down, but I hadn't realised Mom was equally intent. I've got years ahead of me before I need to think about that. Need? Why should I even bother? Marvel and Dollar have never got hitched, so why should I? My bike and the use of a sweet butt or the occasional hookup in town are more than enough to keep me content.

My thoughts are endorsed as my path away from my parents' house leads me past Hawk and Olivia's. My feet speed up as the sound of screaming all but shatters my eardrums. Hawk loves his kid, but how he can put up with that, I've no idea. Spending my weekends knee deep in diapers and trying to comfort a child that seems to do nothing but cry is not my definition of fun. Hawk's got responsibilities, he can't just head out on his bike whenever he feels like it.

Nah, I'm going to enjoy my life exactly how it is. Being able to ride whenever I want is something I'd never want to give up, The thought of having to explain myself to anyone is an anathema. As for having a kid and being tied down, hell to the no for that. Maybe I'll change as I grow older, who knows? But now's far too soon to be saddled with a wife and kid.

How could I give my all to the club if I'd other priorities waiting for me at home? That was the added complication which had contributed to sending Hawk off the rails. He'd been neck deep in club business while trying to keep his then pregnant wife safe. Couldn't Mom and Peg see that trying to corral me could lead to me doing the same?

This is the life. I pause before entering the clubroom. The room is filled with men drinking, playing cards, or milling around the pool table. As the last of the old ladies leaves, and the room empties of my cousins, both male and female as club nights are parties for members only, the sweet butts venture out.

Glancing around I see Blade holding up a beer bottle and waggling it. Taking it the drink's for me, I head his way.

"I never expected we'd hear from those thieving assholes again." I realise he's looped back to what Wizard had asked in church.

"Me neither. We taught them a lesson they'll never forget." I grin at Blade, who gives his version of the expression back at me. "You hanging around tonight?"

"Nah. Tash is finishing early tonight, she's got her deputy closing up. I think she's got some new lingerie she wants to model for me."

"In other words, what you bought for her." I chuckle, knowing him well.

I've known Blade all my life. For years he was like an eccentric uncle, then our relationship changed when I prospected for the club. I was given no favours or leeway and soon learned he was a fuckin' asshole where prospects were concerned. But once I'd gotten my patch, I grew to know him as an equal. His view of me, and mine of him, had undergone a transformation.

To give him and the rest of the club their due, those twelve months being at everyone's beck and call, given anything to do from menial make-work tasks to digging graves, transitioned the change between nephew and club brother. Gradually a mutual respect had grown and we'd become friends. Enough so that if I ask him a question, he won't consider it as one from a kid.

"You ever regret it, Blade?" When his face scrunches up, I elaborate. "Having just one pussy in your life?"

He barks an incredulous laugh. "Like fuck. Hell, why look for something else when you've got the best at home?" He points to Clover and Sable, "Take them. You've fucked them enough, Throt. Ever feel there was something missing?"

It's my turn to be confused. "Like what? They've both got tits and asses, and holes there to be used. The only thing I can see as a negative is that I've been there and done that. There's no mystery there anymore, you know? That's why I like finding a woman in town, some are good, some better, but none of them bad. I get off, they have a good time, isn't that all that matters?" I raise the bottle to my mouth and take a long drink. "Never found one that was worth going back for a repeat."

"You've been with the sweet butts more than once."

I shrug. "Sure, but they're convenient." Shaking my head, I tell him, "I don't know how you fuckin' do it. I like variety too much."

His face softens, and for a moment I think his mind is elsewhere. "One day, Throttle, you'll find a pussy that fits you just right, but not only that, you'll find what's been missing, that illusive emotion that binds you more than just physically." His eyes glaze. "I was once like you, but when I found Tash, well, it might not have been the easiest journey for us to get through, but hell, now I've got her, I'm never going to fuck that up." He turns intense eyes on me. "I won't fuck that up by looking elsewhere 'cause I fuckin' *know* no one's better. She's my other half."

Could he be right? Is there something I haven't yet found? A someone who's out there waiting just for me? I can't imagine it. I think it's more likely in time my parents will wear me down and I'll settle for what I can get, just because it's expected. For a second, I envy him.

"You'll find her." Blade slaps my back. "There's someone for you, Throttle. Someone you don't expect." He winks. "But for now wrap it up and take care. You don't want a paternity suit."

Snorting, I reassure him. "Always do, Brother, always fuckin' do." I've never forgotten yet.

He finishes his drink and places the empty on the bar, then raises his chin. "Well, I've got a dick that needs some attention, and an old lady to give it. See you around."

My reply is a wave of my hand.

"Want company, Throttle?"

Sable's my age, pretty blond hair cut short to frame her pixie features. Her mouth is full, and, I know from experience, looks good around my cock. It's not hard to imagine it being that way very soon, if only as a welcome relief from using my hand. I eye her for a moment, then find myself raising my chin up and down. I drain the rest of my beer, and slide off the stool.

Grinning broadly, Sable struts off, her hips exaggeratedly swaying as she leads the way to the crash rooms. She gave up asking to come to my suite ages ago, and now wouldn't think to ask. My bed is mine, and only I sleep there. *Except for Gwen*, I think with a frown.

My cock's semi-hard when she leads me into the crash room which smells of sex, and the furnishings are little more than a bed.

"What can I do for you tonight?" Sable approaches, her hands running down my chest. She licks her lips, again drawing my attention to her mouth.

Running my fingers through her stubbly hair, I tilt her head up so she can look into my eyes. "I want you to suck my cock," I tell her gruffly. "That okay with you, doll?"

A grin covers her face showing her confidence in her skills. Her response is to fold gracefully to her knees, hoisting her short skirt up and around her thighs. Reaching out, she expertly undoes the buttons on my fly, freeing my cock. Despite that I've got an attractive woman on her knees, it's still half flaccid.

Sable's not deterred, as my head rolls back on my neck, she uses her mouth, hollowing her cheeks and sucking me in. Those administrations of her tongue make my previously disinterested member stir. Once she gets me hard, she really goes to town. This is where her experience shows, using the repertoire of tricks she's learned from fucking the single men in the club and from wherever she'd been before.

If one thing doesn't work, she tries another. Soon she has me bracing myself with a hand against the wall. But I make the mistake of looking downward to see her short haired head bobbing up and down. For a second it's a turn off, so I close my eyes, but not before I clock her working her clit at the same time as she's sucking me off.

Good for her. I'm going to be selfish tonight. The thing about sweet butts is they never complain if you don't get them off.

She hums and moans, the vibrations going straight to my cock. She swallows around me, the pressure getting me close. When she deep throats me, she doesn't complain when I place a hand around the back of her head, holding her still so I can fuck her mouth.

"I'm going to fuckin' come," I warn her, releasing my hold and giving her a chance to pull back.

She doesn't. Her movements intensify, and seconds later I'm flooding her mouth. A few pumps and I've given her all that I've got.

When I pull out and look down, her face is flushed, my cum running down her chin, and her hands are busy as she takes care of herself, coming quickly with a satisfied sigh.

There's no cuddling required and no after care. Tucking myself away, I button my jeans back up.

"Thanks." Inadequate perhaps, but it's all I can muster.

Still on her knees, she looks up with a cheeky grin. "My pleasure."

A sharp nod, then I leave her to go clean myself up.

As I leave the crash room, Dollar's leaning against the wall just outside. "Sable in there?"

Guessing his intention, I hold the door open and gesture him in. "She's all yours."

Soon, I'm standing at the bar with another beer in my hand, thinking to myself, *Blade was wrong.* If I had a woman of my own, I couldn't be as casual about sex. I'd have to think of her, check if she was in the mood, and if not, see what I could do to encourage her into it. I haven't got time nor inclination for all that shit. However good the pussy is, it's not worth the bother of working for it.

But a voice in the back of my head asks, *was what I just had really any different from jerking off?* I scoff at myself. Of course, it was.

While I was otherwise occupied with Sable, some hangarounds from Tucson have appeared. A few men who've hopes of becoming prospects at some point, and there are several girls and young women who've all come with one thing on their mind, the desire to experience biker loving, if only for one night.

Idly, I scan them, not really interested in further wetting my dick. Unlike the sweet butts, any of these would need conversation before getting down to the deed, and a full explanation of what's on offer, and what's not.

Interested, though, just in case any stand out, my eyes move from one to the next, finding nothing to delay them. Until... I snap my gaze back. *Why's she here?*

Unfortunately, our eyes have locked, and she waves her hand in recognition, then comes straight over.

Fuck.

I was brought up to be polite, so however much I'd prefer to snub her and walk out, I stay fixed to the spot, wondering how long it will take to dissuade her.

I remember her name just as she gets to me. "Hattie." I nod. "Didn't know this was your scene."

Her hand reaches out and touches my chest. "I thought I could come and see you. We were good together, Throttle."

Removing her hand only this side of gently, I push it back down to her side. "I made myself clear, no repeats. No second times."

She pouts and repeats, "But we were good together, Throttle. We clicked."

Blade's words come to my mind. What was it he said? That sex was best when there was emotion attached to it. There's certainly none here. Disinterest at most. I wouldn't care less if Hattie's and my path never crossed again. His statement echoes in my head, "*I won't fuck that up by looking elsewhere 'cause I fuckin' know no one's better. She's my other half.*" If I live until I'm a hundred, I already know Hattie would never be my missing fifty percent, there's not one part of me that would miss her.

Is she getting ideas? Fuck, that she's here tonight suggests she is. Quickly I look around, at last spying a single unoccupied brother. But before I can open my mouth, she's speaking again.

"I'd love to see where you live, Throttle. Why don't you show me?"

Fuck no to that. "Hound's free." I point to the sergeant-at arms, while part of me feels guilty I'm siccing her on a brother. "He looks like he could do with some company."

Her cheeks go red. "I want you, not another biker."

What we want we don't always get. I decide I need to be firmer. "You and me aren't happening, Hattie." Hurriedly I drink the rest of my beer, leaving the empty bottle on the bar. "You're welcome to stay and party, but I'm off." Without giving her a chance to respond, I head for the door, not even pausing when Marvel shouts out an offer to deal me in on a card game that's just started.

I do check to make sure she's not following me. Luckily, in that at least, she shows sense.

CHAPTER TWELVE

*T*hrottle…

In one way Hattie did me a favour, I muse, as I wake bright and alert. She'd saved me from having a normal after-Friday-night-party hangover. Instead of wincing and running back out when I enter the clubhouse to the sound of Layla's angry screaming, I actually go over.

"She alright?"

Hawk, busy shifting her from arm to arm and bouncing her as he does so, looks up with bleary eyes. "She's hungry. Liv's gone to make a bottle for her."

"I thought she was breastfeeding?"

He shrugs. "Either she's not getting enough, or this one is an extra hungry bugger. We've taken to supplementing her with formula."

I nod seriously as if I'm interested, then make my exit and enter the kitchen.

"Hey, Maya. I didn't know you were back." I lean in to give Joker and Lady's adopted daughter a peck on the cheek.

"Got in last night," she says, cheerily. "How are you, Throttle?"

"I'm good," I tell her. "How you finding Vegas?"

"It's good."

Maya had wanted to spread her wings, and to Lady and Joker's horror, had gone into hotel management, landing herself a job in one of the just off strip hotels in Vegas. She'd only been gone a couple of months.

"Red looking after you?" Of course we wouldn't let a Satan's Devils brat off compound unless she was going to be watched out for. In this case asking the favour of Red, who's still hanging on to the title of prez in the Vegas chapter, despite him staring sixty in the face.

She grins. "Red's great, if not a little overbearing. If I'm working late, he insists I let him know and he puts a prospect on me."

As he should. I jerk my chin in approval, then gesture at the stove. "You on breakfast duty?"

"It was me and Isabel, or the prospects would do what they normally do." *Burn everything,* mentally I complete her sentence.

Chuckling, I turn and gesture my thanks toward Heart's daughter. I'm just in time to take a loaded plate from her.

"Isabel's been catching me up with the gossip." Maya switches off the stove and sits down beside me.

"Not too much been going on," I tell her.

"Except for the mystery of who sent you boots."

What? My brow furrows until the penny drops. Mom must have told Lisa, and Lisa can't keep her mouth shut.

"I'm going to sort that out," I tell her.

She frowns. "Sounds like you've got a secret admirer."

Hmm. I hope not.

"Or maybe someone appreciated the work you did in the shop."

That hadn't occurred to me. I do custom work at times, but I can't think of anyone who stands out, hell, most of the time they don't even tip me.

Maya's still thinking aloud. "Or maybe not, they knew your size. Or could that have been a lucky guess?"

Maybe. I'm a big man, it follows I'd have big feet.

"Right." Breakfast finished I pick up my plate, rinse it off and place it in the dishwasher. "Nice seeing you, Maya, but I've got things to do and places to be." Passing her, I ruffle her hair.

"Get off, Noah!" She pulls away indignantly, patting her hairstyle back into place.

Yeah, I grin as I walk out, some things never change.

Today's first stop is Gwen's house. I park behind her car and walk to the door. I ring the bell and it's opened quickly.

"Noah!"

"Hi." I look at her face. Both eyes are open, and the swelling has gone down, but her face is mottled in yellow. Across her forehead and down her cheek angry red lines show where the knife had sliced her. The stitches, though, have been taken out, though the marks they left are still there. "You look better."

"Better?" Her voice sounds so small, I wish there was some way I could comfort her.

"I don't think the scarring will be too bad," I tell her, raising my hand to place it under her chin and turning her head one way and then the other. "It looks like they've done a good job."

"They might have done, but the scars won't completely fade. Especially the one on my forehead."

Anger grows inside me. I hate this. Hate it on her behalf. Hate that because she was working at our restaurant, her beauty has been marred. "You'll still be beautiful," I try to impress on her.

She shrugs off my comment. "Have you just come to check up on me?"

"Kind of."

"Want to come in?" She steps aside in an invitation which I accept. When she's closed the door behind me, she glances around her. "I owe thanks to you and your club. For tidying up, for the prospects always coming around. They've done all my shopping, followed me to the hospital when I had the stitches taken out. They've been passing by keeping an eye on me."

"It was our fault, Gwen," I reply, tersely. "We fucked up. You should never have been put in that position."

"The cops think it was random, just wrong place, wrong time."

I didn't expect them to come up with anything. If we don't have a clue who her attacker was, they'd have been unlikely to do better.

"You want a coffee or anything?"

I won't be staying that long, so I turn her offer down. "You been back to work, yet?"

"I wanted to, but I keep getting headaches. But they're improving now, so I'm going back on Monday." She frowns again, clearly not relishing being seen in public, but she seems to shake her despondency off. "I meant it, I owe you a debt, Noah. That night, you took over everything, from bringing me home and then taking me to the compound. I know it was you that got your club involved."

This is my in, the excuse I've been waiting for. "There's no need to thank me, Gwen, I'm just fuckin' annoyed it happened."

"Nevertheless, I feel I have to."

I let my eyes land on her face, watching her expression carefully. "You didn't have to send me a gift, Gwen. I don't want you to spend your money on me."

"Gift?" Her eyes open wide. "What on earth are you talking about? Oh, don't get me wrong, I'd love to have got you something, but I wouldn't know where to start on what you'd like. As for money, I haven't been paid from work, I've gotten by on what Wizard gave me. I could buy you a beer, but that's about the extent of it."

There's no twitch, nothing that would betray she's lying to me. But why should she? If she'd sent me the boots, why wouldn't she own it? What's the point of giving a thank you present to someone and not admitting it.

"Fuck," I breathe out. "Then that hasn't solved the mystery."

As her head tilts to the side, I find I'm explaining everything.

"The boots sound expensive," she offers when I've finished. "I'm sorry, Throttle, I'd love to say it was me, but it wasn't. It must have been someone else."

But who? I prefer to think of another explanation. "Or a mistake. When I leave here, I'm off to the store to see if I can find who ordered them, or whether they were sent to the wrong address."

She chuckles softly. "There could be worse things for a biker to get."

She's right, there are. Maybe Marvel's right and I shouldn't look a gift horse in the mouth. But I'm not built that way. I'm too suspicious by nature.

Now that that conversation's over, I start feeling awkward. When she was hurt, there were things I could do for her. But now she's well on the mend, I don't know what I'm doing here. Once I leave, I'll have no excuse to return, but then, I don't know why I would want to. Part of me wants to stay, but for what reason? We weren't close friends back in the day.

There's no reason for me to delay. "I best be off. See if the store's got answers for me."

Her head dips up and down, and she steps back to the door. "I mustn't keep you. Thanks again, Noah, I wish I could have sent you such a thoughtful gift, but I couldn't. I expect I'll see you at the Wheel Inn sometime."

I start to raise my chin, then stop. "You're going back?"

She startles. "Of course. I need the work."

Gwen must be stronger than I took her for. I thought she'd never return to where her attack took place. My surprise must show on my face.

"Tash called, she told me they've upped the security, installed more lights, and will never again let me walk to my car alone." She shrugs. "Probably safer working there now than anywhere else. And don't they say, lightning never strikes twice in the same place?"

"When's your first shift?"

"I go back to the legal firm on Monday. I thought I'd give myself that day to see how I cope. But all being well, I'll be there Tuesday night."

As will I, I decide. If only to make sure someone's not taking an unhealthy interest in her and make sure she gets safely to her car. After that, I'll follow her home, just to be sure. She's an employee of ours, I need to watch out for her.

I brush her cheek with my lips as I leave the house, tossing behind me a wish for her recovery to continue, and then go to my bike. I take one last glance at the now closed door. *She's going back to the Wheel Inn.* I'd thought there was a good chance she would not.

Checking behind me, I pull out into the street, heading into the city. A glance in my mirror shows me a car has just pulled out about fifty yards back. Not surprisingly, this is a residential area, and cars come and go all the time. But I'm not a Satan's Devil for no reason, and so I keep a close watch on the vehicle behind.

I turn, it follows. At a junction, another car gets between us, but still the first one is there. It stays there for another few minutes. But I'm heading into town, I've no monopoly on that journey.

The hairs on the back of my neck rise, making me act cautiously. Taking a detour, I turn into another residential area, and that darn car follows me.

It's definitely on my trail. *Game on.*

However hard I look I can't see who's driving, the windows are tinted and the sun visor pulled down. *Is there a passenger?* I can't see. An apprehensive tingle runs up my spine. A lone rider is vulnerable, however much of a Devil he may be. Discretion is the best part of valour today. I twist the throttle, hoping there are no cops close by, then take turnings almost horizontally both left and right, ducking into a parking lot when I momentarily lose the vehicle behind me, then doubling back when it passes by, disappearing out of sight.

My heart's beating fast, but gradually slows as I take a roundabout route to my destination. Once there, I place a call.

"Hound? You busy?"

"Just shooting the shit. Whatcha need, Brother?"

"I picked up a tail when I left Gwen's. I've lost it now."

Hound's voice, all easiness gone, snaps, "Where are you?"

"At the Harley store."

"You sure you lost him?"

"For now, yeah."

"Licence plate?"

"Couldn't see. It was a black Ford Explorer, that's all I saw."

"Stay put, Brother, we're on our way. We'll give you an escort back."

It's safer travelling in pairs, but since we'd dealt with Archangel, we're aware of no other threats, so have relaxed that rule. It may now be time to resurrect that. I'll be glad of the company. I'm not a pussy, just careful. Sure, I'm armed, but it's not as easy as movies make it look riding a motorcycle flat out while firing at a vehicle behind. Added to that bikes are always at a disadvantage, not only do bikers have a healthy respect for guns, but cars and trucks themselves are more than adequate weapons.

While I'm waiting for backup to arrive, I do exactly what I came here for. Unhooking the bungees which fastened the box containing the boots to my pillion seat, I carry it inside.

Pushing my way through the weekend warriors dressed head to toe in branded gear, I stride up the sales desk and ask to speak to a manager. I expect to be brushed off, and I am, but I'm insistent.

When at last I'm faced with a well rounded woman in her fifties, I'm surprised when her first reaction is to laugh. "You got a pair of our most expensive boots and you're complaining?"

Grumpily, I explain, "Not complaining as such, but I've no idea who would send them and I was wondering if you could help. I obviously owe someone and would like to thank them." I think for a moment, then add, "It's also possible that I couldn't accept them, so may want to return them for a refund and I'll get the money back into the proper hands."

"I'm not sure if I could give you the identity of the purchaser." She's phrased it as if it's an option, but from the way her face is set, I take it she will not.

Maybe I should have asked Wizard or Mouse to hack into their database and take a look. But going by the numbers of bodies in the store, it's highly possible they sell these boots all the time, and sifting through buyers would take far too long.

She doesn't dismiss me though, taking a moment to check the boots, and then going through her stock list. After a moment of clicking a mouse and staring at a computer screen, she shakes her head. "We've sold a pair for cash recently. We don't keep details for those."

"What about the other purchasers you do record?"

"I'm sorry, I can't share those details." She studies the box once again. "It's also possible they didn't come from here, we'd have put a delivery note inside. It could be they were mail ordered, then repackaged to send on to you." Picking the boots out of the box, she examines them. "The best I can do is offer a store credit, seeing as they've never been worn, but they might not have come from this store at all."

I knew that, this was my first stop, other stores sell the same goods in Tucson, but from her words, even going to those would probably be a waste of my time. I thank her for her trouble, but refuse the offer of the credit. On the outlandish premise there's a good reason someone bought them for me, getting a store credit or cash for them could turn out to be churlish.

She grins as I walk off, calling after me, "You could be a lucky man. Invite me to the wedding when you find out who it was."

I'm assuming she thinks the buyer is female, which makes me frown. Could she have seen something but not told me? Smelt perfume on the box? Or is it just an assumption? Then, again, she might think I could be gay. Being bearded and muscular doesn't mean anything, Joker's as far from hetero as you could get, but you'd never know to look at him. Lady, well, he's slight but should never be underestimated. Even at his advanced years I hesitate before taking him on in the ring.

But now I'm stumped. It's worth asking Mouse to hack into their records just in case the manager was being ultra-discreet, but it would probably be like looking for a needle in a fucking haystack.

A roar of pipes that I recognise as well as a mom knows her own baby's cry, tells me my escort home has arrived.

Hound dismounts and comes over to me. We slap each other's backs. Behind him I can see Peg, Drummer, Marvel, Heart and Shooter.

Hound leans in. "Spotted a black Ford Explorer waiting down the road with obscured number plates. Couldn't get a bead on who's inside, windows were too dark. Sound familiar?"

Too fucking familiar. I give a sharp nod. "Where?"

He shakes his head. "Gone now. As soon as I speeded up to get past him, he zoomed off."

"I lost him, Hound."

He waits a bit as the implication of my words sink in. *Who'd know I was coming to this store?* Mom, yes. Gwen, but who else apart my brothers and myself.

The sergeant-at-arms crosses his arms over his chest. "You come here a lot?"

"Not lately." Most parts I need, I order in at cost. I frown as I realise the implications. "There's gotta be a connection with whoever sent me those boots." I eye the box I'm carrying as though it holds a poisonous snake.

"It's a bit far-fetched, Brother. I reckon it's coincidence. There must be hundreds of black Explorers in Tucson."

Or it might not be. The sender could have guessed where my investigations would lead me, especially as I'd been riding around carrying those fucking boots. "Could they have been waiting for me to come out? Do they want to get me alone?" If so, I'm lucky they didn't get the chance. Then another thought occurs to me. "Fuck it, Hound, they picked me up when I left Gwen's. They had to be waiting for me."

"Which could mean they know you have a thing going on with her."

I snort. "What thing? There's nothing between us."

Hound shakes his head as if he too doubts it, but adds, "She was the first person you went to when you got that present. They might have assumed you'd think she'd sent them."

She wasn't actually the first, I'd asked my mom. And it was a pretty expensive way to get my attention. But I can see his point. The implications are scary.

There's a chill in my voice as I lay it out for him. "To know that, they'd have to know what happened to Gwen, and how I was there that night. Maybe, because I gave her a lift to her house. Which could mean they were behind her attack." It seems too bizarre, especially if I follow my thought through. "Who's the target here, Hound? Me or Gwen?"

He scratches his head. "I'd go out on a limb and say both of you. Or it's an elaborate plan to get you alone, which was why they attacked Gwen in the first place."

My brow scrunches up. "But that means they'd have reason to think I care for her." I shrug. "Fuck, Brother, if they think that, they know more than I do. I haven't seen her for years, I didn't even know she was working at the Wheel Inn until she turned up. And, until the night of her attack, I'd spent no time alone with her."

His hand again lands on my back. "Fuck knows, Throttle." He glances behind him where our companions are sitting on their bikes. "But the natives are getting restless, we better head back."

CHAPTER THIRTEEN

*G*wen...

A few times over the weekend I wondered whether Noah had ever found out who sent him the boots. He hadn't come back, so my questions went unanswered, but it didn't stop them going around my head. Had he a secret admirer? It wouldn't surprise me, he's a strikingly handsome man, caring and protective as well. Any girl would be lucky to have him.

I'm still being watched by the Satan's Devils, if anything, the security has been amped up. Not only do bikes go past my house regularly, but one often stops and parks up.

Yesterday I'd gone out and approached the man sitting on his bike. A drizzle had been falling, and I tried to get him to move on.

"You don't have to watch me," I'd told him. "Once I'm inside, I lock up, and the security you installed is top notch."

He'd shrugged. "I got my instructions."

"To sit here and get wet?" My eyes had rolled.

"To keep an eye on what's going on."

"Why?"

Again his shoulders had risen and fallen. "Not my job to know or to ask. I just do what I'm told to."

All the time I was speaking to him, his eyes weren't on me, but on the street, looking sideways and forward, then glancing in the rearview mirror to see behind.

"Want to wait inside?"

"Nah. I'll stay here."

The way his jaw is clenched made me realise I wouldn't be able to persuade him to leave, nor come in out of the rain. I threw up my hands and walked away, turning for a moment before I walked through my front door. He'd turned away from me, and I noticed his cut bears a single patch reading Prospect.

Yesterday the prospect left and hadn't been replaced. I'd woken up in the middle of the night, peered out the curtain and saw no one was there. I'd felt relieved. After all, I've got an expensive security system, and that should be enough to keep me safe. *My attacker was a mugger, a junkie who's long since moved on.*

While I'd successfully convinced myself I'd been a random victim, the prospects following me put doubts in my head. Their presence didn't comfort me, it had worried me and made me wonder, do the Devils know more than I do myself? That they've now ceased their vigilance is a weight off of me.

Now it's Monday morning and I've got more important things to worry about, like how I can hide the damage to my face. I know in time the scarring will fade, but for now it's raised, red and ugly. A man might wear scars with pride and make jokes about how the other guy looks worse, a woman is held to a higher standard. While being mugged might gender some sympathy, I also know that I'll be getting sideways glances about whether I'm telling the truth.

There's always the risk I'm going to scare the clients, some of which have been abused themselves. While only an intern, I sometimes conduct the first interview to get basic details about the case, but I doubt they'd want me to do that today. I look more like I need a lawyer myself.

The wound down my cheek isn't as deep or as angry as the one on my forehead which luckily my bangs cover. While both are still healing, I'm loathe to smother too much concealer on.

When I've hidden as much as possible of the bruises, I dress in a smart pant suit with a white blouse, then find my purse and keys. After a breath to fortify myself, I'm as ready as I can be to face the world.

Once I arrive at the office I have to go through my story more times than I'd like. In the end I get expert at the simplest of explanations. *Mugger. Jumped from behind.* As anticipated, I'm hidden in a back office restricted to doing run-of-the-mill paperwork. The only bright side is the investigative digging that I'm asked to do for a solicitor, delving into the finer points of law to help with a case he's working on. It's not in the area I'm specialising in, but in criminal law, and I find it interesting.

My headaches, my face feels sore, when I talk my jaw pulls at the split in my lip. All in all I'm relieved when going home time comes, more than ready to collapse and veg out in front of the television.

The next day begins much the same. There's a slight improvement in my appearance, but I'm still kept away from public eyes. At least I only now have to go through my story with those not already in the know. I try to pace myself, tonight I'll be going to the Wheel Inn.

There's a part of me that's scared they might give my job to anyone else, if only because they might think like Noah, that I don't intend to go back. I do enjoy the job, working for Tash is fun, but even if I didn't, I need this work, I'm scared of the hospital bill that's bound to come. With the debts I've already got hanging over me, I don't want any more.

I feel a pang of fear as I drive around the back of the Wheel Inn, making sure to park as close as I can to the entrance. Before getting out of the car, I take in a deep breath. *I got this,* I lecture myself firmly.

What happened to me was my fault for not being vigilant. I'm sure if I'd been aware that someone was coming behind me I'd be enough to take a strung out desperate junkie on, or, at least have time to get pepper spray out of my purse, or speed up and run to my car.

The incident had scared, but I should look on it positively. It had been a lesson in being aware of my surroundings, and the need to always have a plan to extricate myself. Something I should have known, but apparently it hadn't been ingrained in me. I'll know better from now on.

One last breath and I'm out of the car and heading in.

"Gwen!" Tash sounds half concerned and half delighted when she spies me entering. "You really shouldn't have come in. Not that I'm not happy to see you, but you look like you needed more time."

Grimacing, I agree. "I'm sorry. Look, if you think I'm going to scare the customers, then maybe I can help in the kitchen—"

"I'm not worried about that," she interrupts, not letting me finish. "I'm more concerned about you. You've already had a full day at work, are you really up for this? If it's money you're worried about, Wizard has authorised me to continue to pay you full wages until you're fully fit."

"The club's already done too much for me," I protest. "If I'd had more sense, I'd have been more careful and wouldn't have got mugged."

"Nonsense!" Tash glares. "Don't you go blaming yourself. If it had happened elsewhere, maybe that would be different, but it happened here, and the Satan's Devils take that seriously."

It's an argument I won't be able to win. Around us, tables are filling up, and I can spot more than one which requires the presence of a waitress. I gesture around. "So where do you want me? If it's in front of the house, I'll better start now."

Tash seems to know when to give up. She sighs, throws me a

look that shows she's not entirely happy, but says, "Sure, start taking orders. I doubt we'll be too busy tonight. Oh, and if anyone says anything," she points to my face, "just send them my way."

For the next hour I'm busy, taking orders, delivering food, getting drinks and distributing them to the diners. It's the third time I go through the archway leading to the bar that I notice Noah's in attendance.

As I pass, he stops me with a hand to my arm, examining me carefully. "You've covered most of it up well."

Making a mock curtsey I tell him, "Thank you, kind sir."

Catching the bartender's eye, I start to move forward, but Noah stops me again. When I glance at him, he's looking concerned. "You feeling okay? You sure you're well enough to work?"

I sigh, fed up with people asking. "I'm fine, Noah. It's doing me good to get back to normal again. Sitting around feeling sorry for myself isn't really my style."

His jaw clenches. "I just want you to be well, Gwen."

"Well I am." I stand my ground. I wait for his signal he's going to stop hassling me, which he gives as a chin lift. It's then I remember why he came over on Saturday and take the opportunity to change the subject. "You ever find out who was your mystery benefactor?"

His face hardens. "Nah."

"What can I get for you, Gwen?"

I tell the bartender the bottle I need and ask for four glasses. As I step to the side to wait, Noah catches my eye. "You don't go out to your car tonight without an escort, Gwen."

Too sensible to argue, and knowing I'd be stupid to disagree, I just nod.

Carrying the laden tray, weaving through the customers, I'm about to go back through the arch to the restaurant when a woman steps in front of me, sneering.

"Excuse me," I tell her politely.

"Well, I'm not sure I will. They letting abused women work here now? Fuck, you look ugly as sin. I'm glad I'm not eating, you'd put me right off my food."

It was what I'd been worried about, though I didn't expect such rudeness. The customers I'd served had been kind, asking compassionately what had happened to me, and accepting my explanation I'd been mugged with sympathy. Of course, I've been careful not to mention it had happened on these premises, I wouldn't want to put anyone off. But this direct approach? What should my response be? Apologise to her for upsetting her sensitive stomach? If so, I can't force those words out of my mouth.

In the end, it seems I don't have to. "What's up, Gwen?" Noah, it seems, has noticed I've not progressed very far.

"I'm just going." I take a firmer hold on the tray and start moving into the restaurant.

He lets me go, but behind me I hear him say, "What the fuck did you say to her, Hattie?"

Slowing my step, I strain my ears for her response.

"I was offering my sympathies." The woman I now know is called Hattie, and who's clearly a friend of his responds, "It's a shame she's in an abusive relationship."

Hell no, I'm not. I turn to put her right, but Noah holds up his hands and gets in before me.

"It's no business of yours, but for your information, she isn't."

I linger for a moment wanting to hear her response, but she gets onto another topic instead. "Throttle, I've missed you. Why don't you come back to my place tonight? We had such fun last time."

They did, huh? Marching briskly away to deliver the wine to the table who, by now, probably think I'd forgotten them, I realise of course someone like Noah would be taken, but I don't want to hear whether he's going to take the spiteful girls' offer up or not. *Surely he's got better taste?*

She'd looked trashy to me, made up to the gills, fake boobs if I'm not mistaken. If that's his taste, he'd never look at me as a sexual partner. *And why should that thought have come into my head?*

"Sorry about the wait. The bar was busy." It's only a small lie, and one which seems to be accepted without question as the diners, two couples if I'm not mistaken, only pause their animated conversation long enough for me to pour a taster. When that's accepted, I half-fill four glasses. "Your starter won't be long," I tell them, with the kind of smile that I've learned earns tips. Well, before my face was ravaged that was.

The rest of the evening goes by fast. We might not be that busy, but it's enough to not give me a moment's respite. I'm glad when closing time comes around, my feet are aching, and my face extra sore, all that smiling pulled at the healing scars. I'm pleasantly surprised I've made good tips, probably sympathy value.

Noah, to my surprise, is still here. I'd expected him to take Hattie up on her offer, but she'd left an hour ago, for some reason giving me an intense glare as she'd passed me. Wow, it's as if my face had personally injured her. Some people, huh?

As I remove the apron I wear around my waist, put my tablet on its charger ready for the next day, and open my locker to get out my purse, a deep voice behind me makes me jump.

"You ready to go?"

Placing my hand over my fast beating heart, I chuckle. "You move quietly for a big man."

"Fuck, Gwen. I didn't mean to sneak up. I'm sorry, after—"

"You stop right there, Noah. Nothing to do with what happened last week. You just made me startle, that's all. And yes, I'm done here. Is the prospect around? I know you don't want me to go out there alone."

"Too right I fuckin' don't. But I'm your escort for tonight. You got everything?"

He's leaning over me, one hand braced on a locker. As I breathe in I can smell leather and man, an intoxicating combination. As I look up, he's staring down. Just a movement from each of us would have our lips meeting.

He's probably seeing me off, then going to see that bitch Hattie. The thought makes me turn away fast.

"I'm ready." The locker door slams shut with a bang, and I take out the key and put it in my purse.

He places his hand to the small of my back, and herds me toward the back door. Leaning past me, he opens it, then waits for me to go through first, emerging only a split second behind me. Then his hand rises, resting on my shoulder and holding me back as he scans the mostly empty parking lot.

As I've parked closer to the door tonight, it only takes a couple of moments to get to my car. I open it and slip inside. To be honest, I'm feeling far more confident with him by my side than I would if I were alone.

I appraise him of that fact. "Thank you, Noah. I would have been nervous coming out by myself."

"Never walk a-fuckin'-lone to your car again, Gwen. None of the staff are. Either a member or prospect will stay until the last of you go."

That's nice to be reassured. The Satan's Devils look after all their employees well. "Thanks again. And goodnight. I'll be fine now."

His face tightens. "Wait for me to get my bike, I'll follow you home."

What? "Noah, there's no need."

"There's need." He stares at me. "Don't forget the fuckers got into your house last week. They might be waiting for you to return. Can't take the chance on your first night back."

Jeez. Thanks. I hadn't thought of that. Now my hands are shaking as I put the key into the ignition and turn it on. Like the obedient girl that I am, I wait until a single headlight appears. It's only then I pull out.

Not only does he follow me home, but he insists on checking out my house before I go inside. When he gives the all clear, he accompanies it with a salute which doubles as a wave goodbye. Before I can ask if he wants something, he's gone.

CHAPTER FOURTEEN

*T*hrottle…

Something inside me wishes I could stay with Gwen. She's so damn brave, coming back to the scene of the crime and behaving as though nothing had ever happened in the first place. How had I ever thought she was weak? She's not, she's strong. She didn't have to turn up for her shift tonight. Hell, Wizard would have paid her whether she was there or not.

As I sit on my bike, telling myself I'm only waiting to make sure she locks up, I allow myself to wonder what it would be like to sink my cock into her sweet depths. Could I go there? Before I've dismissed her as someone to be kept well away from the likes of myself, but now she's shown a backbone and guts I had no idea had existed.

What's holding me back is the knowledge that however strong I now think her, she's not cut out for a one-night stand, particularly given our history and her friendship with my sister. If I started anything, I'd have to hang on for the ride.

I'm not built to have one woman and to be faithful. One day, maybe, but right now, I couldn't commit to that. It's not only that I'm unwilling to give up my love of a variety of pussy, it's that I'm still finding my way being the enforcer of the club. I can't risk fracturing my loyalty. If I ever take a woman of my own, she'd come first in my life. What would happen if that caused conflict with the club, what if my priorities changed and I dropped everything at the drop of a hat because she needed me to keep her safe?

My instinct though tells me if I show an interest in Gwen, it would be reciprocated. It's kinder to stay away, I couldn't be the man she would need. I'd soon be looking for greener pastures and possibly leave a broken heart behind me.

No, despite my cock twitching and telling me he's interested, despite my desire to put my hands on her, and despite my head suggesting she might not be a woman I'd become bored with, any thoughts of taking this attraction further must be pushed out of my mind. I'm not ready for commitment.

She'll be fine. Someone else will come along and claim her.

Someone else? I'm stunned at the rage that rises at the thought.

My hand had pulled in the clutch ready to shift into first, but now I release it. I fuck women never giving a thought as to who will be next, or whether they'd leave time for the warmth to cool in the bed I've just left. But another sleeping with Gwen? Holding her close like I had?

The green monster inside me doesn't like it, not one bit. I eye the door to her house, my brow creased. Do I like Gwen more than a friend? I certainly don't like the thought of seeing her in another man's arms.

Should I take her first for myself instead and put this jealousy to bed?

No, she's not the type of woman any man should love and leave. Maybe she'll wait until I'm ready to settle down. Yeah, she'll wait for me.

Why the fuck do I want her to wait? And what right have I to expect her too?

I've not been upfront with my intentions. Intentions? Even I don't know what they are. The most I could offer is exclusive fucking for maybe a few weeks, and that would be a huge step forward. I can't promise commitment beyond that, I don't see kids or a wife in my future.

I'm too young, I've years ahead of me before I'll attach a ball and chain.

But still I'm hesitant to leave.

I could get off this bike, knock on her door, see if she's of the same inclination and spend the night wrapped around her. Then explain I've nothing to offer her and leave. Yeah, sure, she'd love that, wouldn't she?

Or, I could drive away, take the risk someone else will see what a gem of a woman she is. I can't ask her to wait for an uncertain future.

Starting the engine this time, my fingers again tighten on the clutch again, this time pulling it all the way in. Automatically my foot taps down into first, and my right hand applies the power. Waiting only for a lone truck to come up and pass me, almost without conscious thought, I pull away and start riding.

Part of me thinks I'm a fool, but more of me believes I'm doing the right thing. There's no room for a relationship in my life, and without trying her, how do I know she could interest me for more than one night? Maybe she wouldn't have the famed golden pussy that would make me want to go back for more. Then I'd be pressured to do so just to keep the peace.

Fuck knows what Mom or Lisa would say if I started something with a nice girl like Gwen and screwed it up.

As I ride through the darkened streets of Tucson, I become hardened in my resolve. There'd be far too many issues if I succumbed to that ass, those tits, and that unexpected spunk of the girl that I'd dismissed as a weakling before.

Stopping at a red light, I'm conscious of a vehicle behind me. In the glow of the streetlights it resembles the car that had passed me when I rode away from Gwen's house. *Plenty of Fords like that on the road.* Nevertheless, when I pull away, I hang a right at the next junction—it never hurts to be overcautious—but quickly see in my rearview that the car has, once again, stayed with me.

Adrenaline starts to rise. There's no one after the club as far as I know, but there's always an edge of danger when riding alone. I wasn't born a Devil without having that drummed into me.

I try to lose him again, but with no success. Speeding up, I think rapidly, going through a mental map of the city where I was born, plotting a route that would give me a chance to lose him.

The road I'm now on will take me past the mall that the Satan's Devils had built, a place I know like the back of my hand. I dive in, shoot across the customer's parking lot, around the rear of the stores, and through to an alley which is wide enough for a motorcycle but not for anything larger.

The lights which have followed me come to a halt as what for them is a dead end. I zoom off, taking a turn that will lead me to the I-10 and thence direct to the compound, pushing the speed limit which will keep my advantage as the car will take time to turn and retrace its route through the mall.

Again headlights appear behind me, but as they stay at a distance and don't speed up, that it's the same car I think is unlikely. When the track to the compound comes into sight, I breathe easier, and take the turn fast, checking to my rear, but nothing turns in behind me.

I ride through the gates and park outside the clubhouse. I might not have been the enforcer very long, but I know when I've picked up a tail. The law? Could be. Satan's Devils don't often stray over the line, but we're still known as an outlaw club. Someone out to get me personally? If so, I've no fucking idea why.

There may be no discernible reason, but I won't let this drop. As I dismount my bike, I make a mental note to ask Wizard or Mouse to check the security feed at the mall in the morning. Our control of the security cameras just one of the reasons I chose that place to get lost.

Both our technical gurus will be in bed by now. Mouse lives off compound with Mariana and his family, and Wizard will be curled up around his very pregnant wife. Nowadays, he barely leaves her side.

Opening the clubroom door, I step inside. Nathan's on bar duty, Rock is playing pool with Marvel, while Hound and Cast are deep in discussion. They seem to be the only ones around, oh, except for Sable who's sitting in the corner nursing a drink and looking bored. Her eyes lighten as they settle on me.

I head for the bar and indicate that I want a beer, unsurprised when out of the corner of my eye I see Sable approach me. For a moment, I'm tempted, then know I'll make do with my hand tonight. Without knowing who was following me, I feel unsettled, and these strange unhealthy thoughts about Gwen are still in my head.

On the other hand, maybe losing myself in another woman's cunt would satisfy me, and get me back on the even keel which Gwen seems to have knocked me off.

My eyes examine the sweet butt, but she comes up wanting. Grimacing, I realise Sable's not who I want. My cock doesn't even twitch, instead, getting a whiff of that cheap perfume she drowns herself in, it seems to shrink.

Gently I remove her hand from my arm. "Not tonight, sweetheart." Nodding toward Hound, I add, "Got things to discuss." I reach for the beer the prospect is handing me, then turn around. I grin, seeing Hound's already walking toward me.

"Whatcha need?" His head jerk of dismissal toward the sweet butt is immediately obeyed.

"I'm not sure." I frown. "I was followed again. Tonight. I lost him."

Hound's face hardens. "Where? How did they pick you up?"

"Whoa, Brother." I hold up my hands. "If I had the answers to that I wouldn't be worrying."

"Or more concerned," Hound retorts. "Tell me what you do know."

Sighing, I take a sip of my beer, then comply. "I followed Gwen home from the Wheel Inn, just to make sure she was safe. Checked out her house, all seemed okay, so I left." I run back over what I had and hadn't noticed in my head. "Waited outside to make sure she locked up, then started my bike. Before I pulled out, a car went past, an SUV like last time. When I got to some lights, I noticed the same car behind me. I lost it in the mall."

Hound's brow creases. "Outside Gwen's, had it been parked, or just happened to be passing?"

Shrugging, I admit, "I couldn't tell you. I was kinda lost in my thoughts."

For a second Hound just stares at me. "Fuck, Throttle. Gwen was attacked, her house broken into. Weren't you keeping an eye out for anything wrong?"

Sheepishly I concede he's got a point. "Apparently not." Now he's said it, I'm annoyed at myself.

He growls. "Has she got an ex who might like to follow her new lover?"

"Ain't her lover," I retort.

"Perhaps someone thinks that you are." He stares me down for a moment, then signals for another beer. I hold my empty bottle up indicating I could do with one more myself. When two new bottles are set in front of us, he continues, his expression thoughtful. "Who could it be, Throttle? I can think of four options. Cops? Well, we're always on their radar, but why pick you up on a residential street?" My head shake is unnecessary. "Someone looking for you personally, or tracking the club?" This time I shrug. "Or, Gwen's attack was planned and she's the target."

The latter is something I don't want to think about. Gwen being at risk? "Why do you think her attack was deliberate? She never suggested anything like that. And why follow me?" Once again I shake my head. "It can't be, Hound. She's not that type of woman to have an envious ex."

His eyes widen incredulously. "Not the type? What fuckin' type does it take, Throttle? Even nice girls can choose a partner who turns out to be a jealous asshole. Nice girls get fuckin' abused every day."

His suggestion makes me go cold. Slamming my fist down on the bar top, I round on him. "I left her a fuckin-lone, Hound. What if the asshole went back?" My hand goes to the pocket of my cut, but when I take out my key, Hound wraps his hand around my fist.

"You can't go."

"Get off me, Hound. I've gotta go see she's okay."

But his hand tightens instead. "What if it's you they're after, Throttle?"

I can take care of myself. "Hound," I warn, trying to shake him off.

"Prospect?" When Nathan runs up, Hound snaps at him. "Get to Gwen's house. Take the SUV and park yourself some-where close for the night. Make sure there's no one hanging around, you got me?"

Nathan's chin lift says yes. He pauses only to grab his phone off of the bar.

It's a solution. Not the one I'd prefer, the one where I'd end up getting up close and personal to make sure Gwen is safe. But under the circumstances, probably the best one. If I've picked up a tail and they catch me again, I could lead them straight to her door. Or, if it's a jealous ex watching to make sure she behaves, me turning up could make them irate.

"You call me," I yell after the retreating prospect. "You see so much as a hair out of place, your fuckin' call me!"

"Got you, man!"

CHAPTER FIFTEEN

*G*wen...

Yesterday's shift at the Wheel Inn was gruelling, coming as it had after a long day at work. For once exhaustion quieted my thoughts. As soon as my head hit the pillow, I went out like a light. I slept well, but today I awake feeling just as tired as when I went to bed.

Ideally I'd have liked to rest longer, but work calls. Dragging myself to the shower I let the water refresh me, then dress in another smart pantsuit and white blouse. A glance in the mirror shows I'll probably not be public facing again, but I still like to look professional. By the time I'm ready to leave, the prescription of hot water and movement has helped the worst of the aches to leave my muscles.

I'm at the door getting my keys when my phone rings.

"Hey, how you looking?"

It's Lisa. I replace my purse on the hook, glance at the time and realise I can spare a couple of minutes. Chuckling, I reply, "Shouldn't you ask how I'm feeling?"

"Girlfriend, you wouldn't admit you feel like shit, but you can't disguise your appearance, well not by much. You okay to be seen in public? I mean, I don't want to be seen out with a freak."

I giggle, loving her for joking with me and not coming over too sympathetic. "Nice shades of fading purple, yellow and green, so it depends what public you're talking about and whether that's going to offend your tender sensibilities."

"I've got a break today around midday. Wanna meet for lunch?"

Lisa and I had lost contact when we'd left school, both going on different paths. My focus had been my law course and, of course, setting out on my own. Hers was also college, but a different one. Connecting last week when for the first time I was allowed to visit the compound had rekindled our friendship. I love the fact she's gotten in touch and seems to intend to keep doing so.

"I won't be seeing clients, so can take my lunch anytime. When and where?"

She names a place that's quite close to where I work, and we agree to meet just after twelve. Knowing we'll have more chance to talk later, she doesn't keep me on the line. This time when I take my purse down and open my door, I'm feeling brighter, and looking forward to catching up with her, when the conversation hopefully won't revolve around my injuries and how I obtained them. I'm eagerly anticipating hearing more about her life.

The morning drags as it always does when you've something to look forward to. When midday comes around, I'm out of there and heading for the restaurant where we've agreed to meet.

Lisa pulls up just as I'm getting out of my car, and we laugh at our excellent timing. Then, as though the years have fallen away, she links her arm through mine as we go to the entrance, a gesture which shoots me back in time.

We find a table and seat ourselves, then order drinks while we peruse the menu.

"We've a lot to catch up on," Lisa starts. "But considering the position at the legal firm you've got now, it all worked out as you planned."

She's my friend so I'll give her the uncensored version. "You know my foster parents washed their hands of me when I aged out of the system?"

Her brow furrows. "I was hoping they'd let you stay on. Do you ever see them?"

Shaking my head, I explain, "No, that wasn't our agreement. I knew the score from the time they took me in. They wanted the money without the bother. As long as I kept my head down, gave them good grades to boast about and otherwise never reminded them I was around, they'd give me a roof over my head and feed me. The word 'parent' never applied to them. When the payments stopped, I was no longer required. Once I moved out, they took another girl on."

For a second she looks savage, but it's history and no point rehashing now. "But you got help from the state?"

"I got college room and board and a grant, so I was fine. Just ended up with a huge student debt."

She bites her lip. "I'm sorry we lost touch."

I reach over and cover her hand with my own. "Hey, don't worry about it. You tried, it was me who couldn't spare the time. I was working whatever jobs I could to keep my head above water, I had no time to do anything other than work or study. I stopped returning your texts as I hadn't time for a social life. I wanted to contact you, but felt awkward when time had passed. Now, enough about me, what have you been doing?"

She pouts a little. "I've had it easy compared to you. I've both my parents, my asshole brother, and never had to worry about where I was going to lay my head. I'm doing my Bachelor's in psychology now, I've got my Associate's and am continuing. I moved out of home last year and live with another student now." Her mouth quirks. "It was the only way of me getting a taste of this social life you're talking about."

I chuckle, understanding that while being surrounded by family, uncles and cousins galore growing up must have been fun, it had probably been restrictive when Lisa had wanted to strike out on her own.

"What do you want to do when you've got your degree?"

"I'm majoring in child psychology."

The waitress arrives and takes our order, both of us choosing salads. When she walks off, Lisa takes over the conversation again.

"So, you've been talking to Throttle,." She waggles her eyebrows and offers a lopsided grin. "You sure there's nothing I should know about?"

Snorting, I respond, "Nothing at all. I've only seen him a couple of times, and one of those was while I was working at the Wheel Inn. He's being all protective as he still thinks of me as his little sister's friend."

Lisa breathes out a long breath, and her amusement fades. "Don't take this the wrong way, Gwen, but I'm relieved. I thought that maybe something was blossoming between the two of you."

My lips press together. "Relieved?"

"Sure." She looks down at the salad that's just arrived as though it offends her. "Don't misunderstand me, there's no one I'd like better as a sister-in-law, but if you had feelings for him, I'd have had to warn you off." *She would?* Leaning forward I give her a *tell-me-more* gesture. She doesn't disappoint. "I know he's my brother, and I love him to pieces, but he's a real manwhore. I don't know if he's got it in him to be faithful. He goes from one girl to the next and never looks back, never dates, and as far as I can tell, never sees the same girl twice."

He's obviously worse than I thought. I try to keep my face impassive. "You know this?" Does he boast about all his conquests? If so he's not the man I thought he was.

"Well, he might not mention names, but he's not shy about

what he does. Dad and him have arguments all the time. Dad thinks he should find a girl and settle down. Throttle's view is that there's far too many fish in the sea for him to ever want to do that."

I feel like I've been slapped on the wrist. Sure, Noah had never responded to my teenage attempts at flirting, and hasn't given me any encouragement now I've grown up. However it's true that I've been thinking *what if?* and what I might say if he ever asked me out. Lisa's warning is timely. I've far too much self-respect to be just another notch on a bedpost.

I try to school my features, hearing about Noah's proclivities hurts more than it should. Though I'd tried to deny it, I had thought he'd shown an interest in me which I might be persuaded to explore. Now I know if I let him in, he'd break my heart. It's best for me never to know what it would be like to be held in his arms, it would destroy me to be loved and left, all in the same night.

Maybe it would be different with me.

Hell, no. Isn't that what all women have thought since the dawn of time, that they could be the one who'd change a man? Who'd get him to give up being the proverbial rake and settle down.

Suddenly noticing Lisa's staring at me quizzically, I'm worried she's able to read my mind. Quickly, I turn the tables. "So, what about you? What's your love life like?"

Her eyes widen, then she looks around before whispering conspiratorially, "Well, there's a man…"

I lean forward, gesturing with my fingers. "Tell me more."

She giggles like the schoolgirl I remember. "You mustn't tell Throttle, but there's this guy in my class. He's so dreamy." Her face reddens slightly. "We've been out a few times, and yes, we've done the dirty, and that's all I'm going to say about that." A pause during which she looks at me sternly. "We're planning on renting an apartment together next semester."

That sounds serious. "Do your parents know? What do they think?" I ask, before remembering she's said not to tell Noah.

"Hell no. Not about moving in. But Mom has met him and she likes him. I didn't mean for it to happen, but she came around the apartment unexpectedly and he was there—"

"Fully clothed, I hope," I butt in, winking.

"Thank fuck, yes."

"And Peg?"

She takes a deep breath. "Dad and Throttle don't know about him, or not yet. I told Mom we'd just started dating and I didn't know how it was going to work out. Luckily, she agreed to let me give him a chance, before the calvary sweeps in and destroys everything."

They'd do that? "What exactly would your dad and Noah do?"

Lisa frowns. "Dig into his background, investigate him, pull his life apart. If they knew he had 'defiled' me, they'd get the shotguns out and give him the talk about harming their little girl."

I make a mock shudder, but having someone to look out for me if something I can only dream about. "Surely knowing there's nothing in his closet would be a good thing?" It's hard for me to understand. Maybe it would be intrusive, but to have someone who'd cared like that would be nice.

She shrugs. "When we decide to take the leap to serious, when our idea to move in together becomes an actual plan, sure. I'm not stupid. Getting Mouse to make sure he's been straight with me would be good, but now Dad and Throttle would try to chase him off. As far as Dad's concerned, no one is good enough for his baby girl."

I push my finished plate away from me, sit back and fold my arms. "Your dad seems a bit contrary. He wants Noah settled, but keep you locked down?"

"Kind of. But it's more he wants Noah to stop fucking around and make a choice, and me not to even start looking. Double standard, huh?"

I'm just formulating an answer when I'm shoved hard from behind. Instinctively, my arms shoot out to stop me falling face first into my plate. With all my focus on saving my dignity, it's only then I feel the icy cold on my back.

"What the fuck?" I swing around.

"Whoops!" A petite dark-haired woman stands there holding an empty paper cup in her hand. "I'm so sorry, I tripped."

Accidents happen, I suppose, but there's insincerity in her tone, and something about her seems familiar. I don't though spend too much time looking at her face as I'm more bothered with grabbing for a handful of napkins to try to get the worst of the liquid, I fast identify as coke, off. However, giving a quick glance back, I narrow my eyes and ask, "Do I know you?"

"Don't think we've met," she throws back. Then, without further apology, walks off.

"Hey!" Lisa's on her feet. "What about my friend's..." But she's talking to an uninterested back. A back that quickly exits the restaurant. Lisa eases her way out from the booth and gives chase.

"Ma'am. Let me help." Our waitress runs up and tries to help mop up the pint of coca cola that's soaking into my shirt. It's also drenched my suit jacket I had hanging on the back of my chair.

Lisa returns, shaking her head. "A car picked her up. I didn't get the license plate." She walks around me, taking in the damage. "She did that on purpose."

Why would she do that? I shake my head, conveying to Lisa that I think she's wrong. Trips can happen at any time, the woman's only fault was not trying to make up for the damage she'd done.

Turning, I thank the waitress, motion her away, then open my purse and pull out sufficient notes to cover the cost of my meal. Then I stand and say with a sigh, "I've got to go home and change before I get back to work." I'll be late. Hell, I'm still on probation, hopefully they won't decide I'm too much of a liability having taken time off last week and now am the victim of an accident.

"Yeah, you go." Lisa pushes my money back at me. "I got this. I invited you remember?" As I attempt to put on my jacket, then give up as it's a sodden mess, she asks, "Did you recognise her?"

"I thought she looked familiar, but I can't remember where from. She's not someone I know." I frown. I'm pretty certain I've seen her before. She'd been fairly nondescript from what I saw. Dark hair, wearing next to no makeup, and an unremarkable pair of jeans and a top. I had noticed her boobs looked oversized for the rest of her, but that's about all. *Maybe I've seen her in a store?*

Lisa can't be right, she couldn't have soaked me deliberately, could she? But I'm too worried about getting home, getting changed and returning to work to discuss it right now.

"If you remember anything about her, let me know," Lisa demands. Her face becomes chilling, reminding me of Noah when she adds, "I've got brothers who'll teach her better manners."

I wave and make a hasty, and as I notice I've become the centre of attention, embarrassed, exit toward the door. When I'm out of sight of the prying eyes, once again I'm hit by the thought of how nice it must be to be Lisa and to have people who'd take up the fight on your behalf.

I pull out of the parking lot vaguely noticing there's a car directly behind me, it turns in the same direction as I when I ease out onto the street. Thinking nothing of it, I shift myself forward so my wet back doesn't dampen the seat, and concentrate on the road ahead. It's only when I turn into my road that I notice the damn SUV is still there. It must be following me.

After the events of today I'm more angry than scared, and also not surprised when I turn into my driveway and it stops down the street. Cutting my engine I get out, slam the door, and stride back down toward the offending vehicle, more than half expecting the driver to be the woman who's responsible for me needing to change my clothes. Without hesitation I stride up to the driver's door, coming to a halt when I see a young man sitting there staring at me.

I would have backtracked were it not that the look on his face is one of surprise, but also of fear. It's that that makes me wrench the door open.

"You fucking following me?" He gets the full burst of the rage I've been suppressing since the restaurant.

"Er…"

"Well?" I stand with my hands on my hips. "You have, haven't you? Why?"

He starts to reach into his pocket.

"What are you doing?" Belatedly I realise that confronting him might not have been the wisest thing. *What if he's reaching for a gun?*

"Easy!" He raises his hands again. "I'm getting my phone. I need to make a call."

Relieved, I snap, "No call. Were you following me or not?" Bravely, I move a little closer. As if I'm a threat to him, he pushes himself back into the seat. My eyes narrow. "Hang on, do I recognise you?"

"Er… no?"

Suddenly his face falls into place. "You're one of the prospects for the Satan's Devils. I've seen you at the Wheel Inn."

He slumps. "Yeah, I'm Razza." He mumbles something about never getting his patch.

I thought the Devils had stopped following me around. Sneaky bastards, the bikes had gone, yes, but they've taken to cars instead. *Does that mean I'm in danger?* "So why were you following me?" My voice isn't as certain as it was before.

He throws up his hands, knowing the games up. "I don't

know. Throttle asked us to keep tabs on you, make sure you were safe."

Two things occur to me simultaneously. The first, where was he when I was getting a drink thrown over me? And the second, hadn't I just been regretting no one cared enough to watch out for me? I can't have it all ways.

But along with the slight warmth the latter thought brings, I'm worried as hell.

"Does Noah think I'm in danger?" He hadn't said anything about it last night, and I thought he'd agreed to remove the prospects.

He shrugs, but looks unconcerned. "Prospects don't get told fuck, but if it makes you feel better, I got the feeling that following you is just a precaution. I wasn't warned to look for anything or anyone in particular."

Damn that I'm already late to get back for work, and damn that I still need to sort out fresh clothes. I haven't time to ring Noah and get to the bottom of this.

"Consider yourself dismissed," I tell him, waspishly. "I've got to get cleaned up and get back to work. After that I'm coming home."

"You can't dismiss me, but I'll try to be discreet." As I open my mouth to argue, he continues. "And what's with that?" He waves toward my sopping clothes.

"Bitch threw a drink over me."

My comment makes him sit up straight. "Yeah?"

Realising he thinks I've been attacked, I shake my head. "It was an accident. I was having lunch with Lisa, Noah's sister, and this woman tripped."

"Uh-huh." But he doesn't sound convinced. I reckon Noah will soon find out all about it.

But why should he care?

I'm late. I haven't got time for this. "Well, follow me if you feel you must, but don't ram my bumper."

He rolls his eyes, and knowing I'm wasting time, I stride off.

Going back to my house I quickly realise not only do I need a change of clothes, I also need a shower, some of the drink had got into my hair and as it's drying, it's sticking together. Without taking the time to blow it dry it, I pull it into a bun, grab a fresh blouse and cardigan, then put my soiled jacket into a bag to drop off at the cleaners on the way home.

On my way back to work, the prospect is right behind me. I make a mental reminder to try to get in touch with Noah tonight. Lisa will have to give me his number.

Back at the office, I try to sneak in unnoticed, but of course don't.

"You're late." One of the attorneys I'm working for stops me on my way in. "I was hoping you'd have finished that research for me by now."

"I'm halfway through," I puff, out of breath after my run from the parking lot. "I'll get right back onto it."

His hand lightly touches my arm. "Hey, there's no fire. And weren't you wearing different clothes earlier?"

Noticing he's observant for a man, I huff out, "Some bi-woman, dropped a full cup of coke over me at lunch."

His eyes land on my face, he grimaces slightly when his gaze settles on my bruises and sewn up cheek. "You really do attract the wrong type of person. You going to need a lawyer?" His mouth curves up in a grin.

I giggle. "Maybe." *Why hadn't I noticed before how attractive he is when he smiles?* My eyes soak him in. He's clean shaven, blond with fair unblemished skin, hair worn short and everything about him screams professional. The polar opposite of Noah. Perhaps this is the kind of man I should go for.

He winks, reaches into his pocket and extracts a card. Handing it to me, he tells me, "That's my personal number on there. While liability claims aren't my forte, if you need advice, just call me. Or," he hesitates, "perhaps once you're bruises have healed, we could go for a coffee?"

What he means is once I'm more presentable in public. Still, who can blame him? I look like an abused wife, and who would want to be seen with me? "Thank you, Mr Fontaine."

"Oh, Everest, please."

"Everest." I try it out with a nod.

As he turns to leave, the devil on my shoulder whispers to me, *Noah didn't care what I looked like.*

Huh, I think to myself as I pocket the card and walk off, *if Lisa's right about Noah, the last thing he was thinking about was my face..*

Then I remember the prospect wasting his day following me everywhere.

Noah cares.

That thought I really don't know what to do with.

My parents died when I was six, innocent bystanders involved in a drive-by shooting. With no living relatives I was put into the system. I was too old to be adopted by people wanting a baby and was not a particularly cute child. Unable to understand how one day my parents were there, the next they were gone, I ranted and raged at the world.

It hadn't been easy to place me. Mistakenly thinking I needed control more than love, the foster parents I was handed to were all cut from the same mould, strict and domineering. I wasn't stupid, as I grew to accept no amount of anger could bring back the people I'd loved, I started to toe the line. My way to survive was to suppress my natural exuberance and throw myself into becoming a loveable child. I'd left it too late, or had grown too old.

I was fed, watered and given shelter, but my reputation preceded me, and I was always watched so I didn't step over the line. I gave up on love, trying to earn trust instead.

Sure the various fosters had cared that I didn't come in late, and that all my school work was done on time, but they didn't care about me.

I became the obedient and diligent child Lisa and Noah had

previously known, but deep down I remained the lost little girl starved of affection.

No one had ever cared.

Noah does. Enough to send men to watch over me.

I'll take that caring even if just given as a friend to a friend.

In the end, I don't ring him and complain.

CHAPTER SIXTEEN

Throttle…

I'm down at the clubhouse early, waiting on Mouse or the prez to appear.

The clubroom door opens and closes behind me, and automatically I turn. I frown as I see the prospect walking in. He heads straight for me.

"Razza's just taken over from me. I followed her to work and he's going to hang around for the rest of the day."

At his words I make a mental note to clear with Prez that I'm again taking up the prospects' time and dismiss Nathan with a chin lift—no verbal thanks are necessary, prospects do anything to get patched in—then get myself a coffee.

"You look like you've got the world on your shoulder, Brother. Wanna talk?"

So deep in thought I hadn't heard Wizard enter. "Prez, yeah. I do."

"My office?"

After I raise and dip my chin he leads the way, going to sit behind the desk. Taking the chair in front, I place my elbows on my knees and steeple my hands. Wizard gives me a moment to gather my thoughts, then gestures for me to start.

"Prez, I think Gwen's got a problem."

"The waitress who was jumped?"

I nod. "Don't forget her house was invaded as well. Nothing taken, but they made a hell of a mess."

Wizard grimaces as I remind him. "We haven't been able to find who it was."

Gritting my teeth I add, "There could be more. I followed her home from the Wheel Inn last night. When I left hers, I picked up a tail. Lost it at the mall."

Instead of commenting, Wizard opens his laptop. "Time?" When I give him the information he starts tapping the keys. Showing he can dual task, he focuses both on the screen and simultaneously starts to interrogate me. "Doesn't it seem more likely that the focus was on you? Why do you think this had something to do with Gwen?"

"Because there was no one behind me when I followed her home, but it looked like he was waiting outside. I can't see it was me he was waiting for, why the fuck look for me there?"

Wizard looks up for a moment, his eyes meeting mine. "Unless he followed you from the Wheel Inn?"

I shake my head rapidly. "After the other incident, I was on high alert. I'd have noticed, Prez."

He accepts that with a raise of his chin, but his brow furrows. "If the person or persons unknown were after Gwen, wouldn't it be more likely they were waiting for her visitor to leave, and then pay her a visit? If she's the target, why come after you?"

That's the bit that's been puzzling me. How the fuck has Gwen got anyone out to harm her? Because that's the only place my mind can go. "Maybe he's a jealous ex and wanted to find out more about the man who saw her home?" That's the only thing that makes sense.

"Did he make any move to run you off the road?"

My eyes crease. "No," I reply honestly. "He was up my ass at the lights and could have passed and side-swiped me." Now I think about it, it was unnerving rather than a real threat. Being followed twice kind of has that effect on a man.

Suddenly Wizard sits back, his hands no longer on the keyboard but locked behind his head. His eyes stare upwards, for a moment he's still, only a tic in his jaw muscles give away that he's deep in thought. My patience is rewarded when at last he sits forward again, now staring at the screen.

"Mud on the plates. All I can get is the make and model, and hell there's enough of those. No clear shot of the driver." Fuck. He's got nothing at all. "While there are questions about whether their after you or Gwen, she's an employee of ours, and by extent our property. I want her under protection."

"Yeah, about that, Prez. I've already got the prospects back on a rotation keeping an eye on her."

His eyes twinkle. "Now why does that not surprise me? Yeah, you got my approval, Throttle. Nothing happens to Gwen on our watch." He thinks for a moment. "So the question is, is it you, her, or possibly you both?" As I widen my eyes, he continues, "Is there anything going on between you?"

"Absolutely not." I don't tell him there's a certain part of me that, despite my best intentions, has become very interested in the girl for whom a few years growth has turned into a desirable woman. "Never has been, never will. You know me, Prez."

"I also know what Peg thinks. He know you're interested in Gwen?"

Had my face given me away? "I'm not interested," I refute. "Well, not in that way."

He raises an eyebrow but luckily drops it. "So, we've got you being followed, you receiving a strange gift out of the blue. Gwen getting beaten up, her home ransacked, then someone else tailing you. Anything you haven't told me?"

I shake my head but wonder whether I'm missing anything. "I can't see a link, Prez."

"Right now, neither can I." Wizard rubs his temples. "You've got prospects on Gwen, keep them there. Whether or not we'll continue, we'll discuss at church on Friday. In the meantime, you take care of yourself too. No riding alone, and we'll tell everyone to keep their eyes out for anything or anyone who looks wrong —" He breaks off when there's a buzzing sound, and takes out his phone.

Abruptly he stands, his eyes going wild. "Amy's gone into labour. Anything else you need, take it to the VP."

I stand, am just about to wish him good luck and to tell him I'll have no problems speaking to Drummer when I'm almost knocked over with the speed Wizard goes past.

Okay then. I grin. While a kid's not something I want or see in my future, it's clear to see the emotions in Wiz war between elation the wait to meet his child is almost over, and fear for the next few hours. In my head I wish them both well.

The news has got around with almost as much speed as Wizard's SUV has flying past the clubhouse heading to the gates of the compound. As I exit there's a commotion when Heart jumps on his bike only to find he's forgotten his key. Marvel steps in to hot-wire it with a promise he'll bring the key to the hospital, and Marcia, half-laughing, half-annoyed calls out he can ride pillion with her. Other brothers are running down and jumping on their rides.

I don't know much about the birthing process, *thank fuck*, but sufficient to realise there's probably no need to hurry. Enough of the brothers are heading down to the hospital that I don't need to add my presence. If I went, I'll just be hanging around waiting, so I stay at the clubhouse. While I wish Wizard and Amy well, I really can't get excited about a new baby.

My view is not the pre-dominant one. Once the front of the clubhouse is emptied of all but a few bikes, cars start to flood past me full of old ladies and their offspring who still live at home. I stand and wave them away.

Going back into the clubroom I notice it's little more than

Butcher and me. Instead of sitting around, I decide to go to the auto-shop and get some of the urgent work done. There I find Marvel who seems to have the same mind as me.

"I hate fuckin' hospitals," he observes, as if I'm going to criticise him for not dropping everything to support the prez.

"Wiz has got plenty of brothers with him," I respond. "He probably won't even notice we're not there."

Marvel can be a dick at times, but he's good at his work. Before long we're working in companionable silence and actually manage to get plenty done.

Mid-afternoon, Nathan, bleary eyed after only a few hours sleep, walks in holding a package.

"I just took up a shift on the gate and there was a delivery."

I reach out my hand to take what's probably an ordered part and start ripping it open without checking the addressee. Instead of something mechanical, a pair of riding gloves fall out. A branded make with armour on the back, the fingertips and palms being of the softest top notch leather. They're large, perfect for hands the size of mine.

"Shit," I say with feeling. "Didn't even check who these were for." I pick up the packaging which I'd let fall to the ground.

The address begins, *Throttle. Satan's Devils Compound.*

"Fuck it!" I shout as once again I go through the routine of checking the envelope, shaking it out and finding no receipt or note inside.

"What the fuck, Brother?" Marvel lays down his tools and asks.

"Another anonymous fuckin' gift." I now notice the writing on the outside looks just the same as that which was written on the box containing my boots.

Marvel, in typical Marvel fashion, doubles up. "Ooh. Throttle's got a secret admirer."

"Shut the fuck up," I growl, tossing the gloves down.

Marvel, of course, picks them up. Not only that, he tries them on, flexing his hands. "These are good shit. If you don't want them, I'll take them off your hands. Hands!" he repeats, bellowing with laughter again. "See what I did there, Brother?"

"Shut it! And give them here."

When he takes them off with a roll of his eyes, I snatch them from him. My mood completely ruined, I leave the auto-shop.

Boots first, now gloves. Someone's sending me a message and one I don't understand. I'm as much at a loss as to who sent them than I was for the first gift I received. That I'm the recipient of someone's generosity fills me with no pleasure.

These have been sent to get a reaction from me. I'm not sure what they expect. Undying gratitude, payment for a service I've not as yet rendered? Or a woman who wants to bribe her way into my bed?

I storm up to the clubhouse, needing a drink.

Hawk's by the bar flicking through some paperwork.

"Throttle?" He can tell something's wrong by the expression on my face.

I pass the gloves over to him. "Same fuckin' thing again. My name on the envelope, no return address."

Hawk whistles through his teeth. "Nice gear." Like Marvel he slips one on his hand, stretching his fingers out then pulling them in. Unlike Marvel, he then slips them off, handing the pair back to me. "No ideas who from?"

"Nah. But like the boots, they're my fuckin' size."

Butcher grabs a beer and hands it to me, but like a good prospect, he stays quiet.

"Wanna talk it through?"

"Nah, Hawk. I can't get my head around it." I return the gloves to the packaging they came in and leave them on the bar. "It's driving me fuckin' crazy not knowing. Anyway, why haven't you gone to support Prez?"

His eyes examine me, then he nods, allowing the change of subject. "It will probably be hours before there's something to celebrate." He echoes my earlier thoughts, and having been there and done that recently, he's speaking with authority. "Wiz has enough brothers around him."

My phone buzzes in my pocket, taking it out I see it's Rascal. I answer immediately.

"Talk to me." As far as I know Rascal is having a boring day waiting for Gwen to leave work.

I grow still as I listen to his update. Not wanting Gwen to worry, I'd instructed the prospects to be discreet. He'd followed her this morning without her clocking him, but now he's fucked up and she knows he's tailing her. Sounds to me like he needs a lesson in surveillance. On the other hand, his mistake means I've been alerted to what went down during her lunch with Lisa.

It didn't surprise me the girls had met up, they'd obviously reconnected when she was on the compound last week. I'd been pleased with that report, suspecting Gwen works too hard to make meaningful friends, and establishing a relationship with Lisa would be good for her.

What I wasn't so happy about was Gwen being covered in what the prospect thought was coke. She'd been drenched in the shit. It could have been accidental, but with everything else going on, I had my doubts.

As soon as Rascal's off the line, I call Lisa.

"What the fuck went on at lunch?"

"Hey, bro. Nice to speak to you too."

"Cut the crap, Sis. How did Gwen get someone's drink all over her?"

"How the hell do you know anything about that?" Lisa pauses, then blasts me again. "Oh, Gwen must have called you."

"No she fuckin' didn't. But," I grin slightly, it never hurts to remind her, "Satan's Devils have eyes everywhere. Now tell me, what the fuck happened?"

"Calm your tits, bro. Gwen was seated with her back to the room, a woman walked past—she said she stumbled, and her full drink went all over Gwen."

"Who was she?"

"No idea." Lisa sounds annoyed. "Gwen thought she recognised her from somewhere, but couldn't place who she was or where she'd seen her."

"What did she look like?"

Lisa is quiet for a second or two. "A bit older than us, maybe. Short, with dark hair pulled back in a ponytail. No makeup, but I can't really remember much, it happened so fast. She wasn't anyone I've seen before."

"Was it deliberate or accidental?"

"It happened fast, I didn't see her trip. I'd have said accidental, except for her attitude. Her apology seemed a bit fake, but that could just have been my interpretation. But if Gwen didn't know her, I can't see why she would do it on purpose. Now is that all, *Brother*, as I've got things to do?"

There's probably nothing more she can tell me. "Yeah. See ya later. Love you, Sis."

"Love you, too."

I end the call feeling frustrated. That Gwen had semi-recognised the culprit sends warning bells through me. A perfect stranger could have been discounted.

Hawk's looking at me with his sharp eyes. "Trouble?"

Fuck knows. "Could be something, could be nothing at all."

"Tell me." Hawk might have stepped away from the VP title, but the snap in his tone demanding an answer shows he can still act the role.

So I explain what I'd learned from the two phone calls, and what went down the previous night. I breathe a sigh of relief when Hawk confirms his gut feel mimics mine, and with everything else going on, that Gwen thought the woman was familiar should be followed up.

"I'll go to the Wheel Inn tonight, then follow her home and see if I can jog her memory." I pinch the bridge of my nose and try to suppress the feeling of pleasure at having an excuse to be alone with her again. The grin that threatens to come to my face is hard to suppress.

Hawk glances at me sharply. "Nah, I'll go."

My brow furrows. "You?" *Cockblocker.*

"Think about it for a moment. It's too much of a coincidence, Throt. You're followed, and someone was waiting for you outside Gwen's house. Could be Gwen's got an ex in the wings who's got a proprietary interest in her. Or it's a woman who thinks Gwen if after her man."

"There's no ex according to Gwen, and she's not currently dating or intending to." *Or, so I hope.*

Hawk shrugs that off. "At one extreme it could be someone she's never met. You know what fucks some people are. Maybe she smiled at someone in the street, some asshole who could have decided she's meant to be his, and is jealous as fuck of anyone else."

My eyes widen incredulously. "A mythical person who loves her enough to beat her up?"

"Maybe he wanted to unsettle her and have her turn to him for support." He presses his fingers to the brow of his nose. "Someone invaded her house, nothing was taken. But what if he rooted around in her stuff? Has she checked all her panties are there?" *What the hell?*

"He pissed in her fuckin' bed."

Hawk shrugs. "Way to mark it, perhaps."

My jaw clenches and my fingers curl into my palms, but Hawk's right. We could be dealing with a sick fuck. "If he wanted to swoop in and make her turn to him for comfort after she was attacked, his plan was fucked as you were the one there for her." Hawk's mouth turns up at the corners. "See? I'm a fuckin' genius. That's the reason why you're in his sights."

He might have until recently been my VP, but that doesn't mean I can't take him down a peg or two when he thinks he's got it all summed up.

"Yeah? So how do you tie in a woman spilling her drink over Gwen?"

Undeterred, he replies, "Even assholes have friends. Fuck

could have a sister or mad ex he could enlist to help. Or, as the girls obviously thought, it was just an accident." His eyes harden, and it's the VP in him who speaks. "Whatever, it needs to be investigated. I don't want you near her, Brother. If I'm on the right lines, it's you, more than her, who's in danger. And hell, yes, I know you can look after yourself, but you getting run off the road won't give us answers."

He's fucking right and I hate it. Tension rises as I realise I don't have an excuse to see Gwen again. Perversely it makes me want to challenge him, to remind him he's in no position to give me orders. But I hold on to my temper, and instead, I'm sneaky.

"You can't go, Hawk. You'll want to go support Wizard."

My brother isn't stupid. He cocks an eyebrow at me as he shakes his head. "Wiz would want me to handle shit while he's gone, and you know," he points his finger at my chest, "exactly what he'd say. He'd think the same as me and tell you to keep out of the way." Then his harsh expression softens. "Fuck, man, I know how you feel. Hurts like hell when a woman you've got feelings for is threatened, but you know you can trust me. This, I'm convinced, is the best way of keeping her safe. I can't help thinking if you're the one drawing the heat, you showing up might bring more down on her."

His final sentence is the one that convinces me. Much as I hate it, much as I want to be the one to protect her, if me staying close to her brings her into the orbit of whoever's after me, my only recourse is to stay well away.

"Hawk," I start hesitantly. "Where do these fuckin' gifts fit in?"

He shakes his head. "That I can't fuckin' answer. Coincidence, I expect." He chuckles. "You've got a secret admirer, bad fuckin' timing when you've got the hots for another."

"I ain't got the fuckin' hots for Gwen."

"Yeah, you just keep telling yourself that, Brother."

CHAPTER SEVENTEEN

Throttle…

Isn't there a saying that absence makes the heart grow fonder? Perhaps it's just me being perverse that having been told there's something I can't have, in my head it blows up into the one thing I really want.

Whatever, staying away from Gwen is fucking hard, particularly now Hawk's got me believing her attack wasn't a one-off, and she could be in danger. My gut screams I should be there to protect her. There are rational reasons why I can't, but that doesn't stop me feeling like a child whose favourite toy has been taken away.

She's on my mind more than any other woman. I wake up, it's her I'm thinking about. I go to bed and begin replaying conversations we've had. Try as I might to forget all about her, she sneaks into my head at the most inappropriate times.

Why does she invade my thoughts so much? Why, when I close my eyes, is it her that I see? Why, when a sweet butt approaches me, my dick doesn't so much as twitch, yet one thought of her gets me at full mast straight away?

It would be driving me crazy were it not that a presumably

irrational part of me enjoys perpetually thinking about her and her luscious ass.

As promised, Hawk had left earlier to go speak to Gwen. Still jealous, while I get his reasoning, I can't settle as I wait for him to return. The prospect's keeping my beer bottle refreshed, but I drink slowly wanting to keep a clear head.

Clover approaches, but I wave her away before she gets close to me, and give her a shake of my head.

"Not feeling it tonight?" Pussy, leaning heavily on a stick, struggles to get onto the bar stool next to me. Gentleman like, I help her up.

"Leg hurting?"

Her face contorts. "You could say that. Fuckin' stupid, slipping as I did."

She slipped because she twisted her knee which apparently was dodgy anyway. Now she's waiting on a replacement joint.

"You'll be right as rain when you've had the op." An operation the club are paying for, a thank you for all the years she's put in at the club.

"I hate being weak," she says, her brow creasing. "Makes me realise I'm getting old."

"Nah, you'll never be an old lady," I note, purely in reference to her age, but she purposefully misunderstands me.

"An ol' lady is something I'll never be, honey." She winks at me. "Decided that years back. One cock was never enough for me."

A woman who sees things just like I do. I grin sideways at her, then a comment that could certainly be taken the wrong way slips out of my mouth. "Don't see you getting much cock lately."

"Choice, hon. Not circumstance."

"Choice?" I don't think I could ever give sex up.

She sighs and nods. "See? I've been through the menopause, and well, what happens to some ladies happened to me. I'm a dried up hulk, probably had more than my fair share of cocks in the day, and now nature is punishing me."

My eyebrow rises. Of course, the mention of the dreaded M word made me want to run, but a reckless part of me wants to know more.

"My vaginal walls have thinned and sex is painful."

"They do that?" My eyes widen. "Isn't there something you can do?" In my mind I have a horrific thought, of her internal parts splitting open while getting fucked.

She places a hand on my arm. "Yeah, they do that. And yes, there's cream I can use. But to be honest," she taps her head, "the inclination isn't there. As I said, I've probably had enough cocks to last a lifetime. Now it's hard to remember what the fuss was all about."

Would I ever get tired of pussy? The thought's too scary to think about.

"I'll tell you. I'm thinking of moving on."

The club without Pussy? Unthinkable. "What the fuck? Where would you go?"

Shrugging, she tells me. "My sister's offered me a place to stay. She's moved to Miami."

"Never knew you had family."

She chuckles. "We fell out many moons ago. But it seems old ladies mellow. We're thinking of spending some time together before we grow too old to enjoy ourselves." She raises her eyes and catches mine. "Nothing's decided yet, so keep it to yourself." When I nod, she continues, "So what's up with you, kid? You look like you've got the weight of the world on your shoulders. And, I watched you tell Clover to get lost."

"Just not feeling it tonight," I respond. She might have confided in me, but I won't be sharing what's on my mind.

Content with a sharp-eyed look, she taps the bar top, and soon has a drink in her hands. "How's Lisa doing?"

To my surprise, rather than my normal method of passing time deep in the cunt of a sweet butt, I enjoy a conversation with a club girl instead. We're soon chuckling as we rehash old memories, and she fills me in on shit that happened way back in time.

When Hawk appears, I don't attack him as I'd previously expected, but allow him to get a drink before commencing my inquisition. Pussy, seeing we've got business to discuss, exits as gracefully as an older woman leaning on a stick can.

"Well?" There is an end to my patience.

Hawk sighs. "I introduced myself at the bar and followed her home as we agreed, and invited myself in for a chat. It was hard knowing how to approach it. I didn't want to worry her. I didn't mention someone's lurking around her house. I kept it casual, Brother, and couldn't get much. But she's convinced there's no ex who might have it in for her."

That's what I'd already told him, I think I could have got more and dug deeper. I wouldn't have been content with a simple no.

"She did push me about why we still had prospects on her. But I said it was for our peace of mind as much, if not more, as hers."

Perhaps he's right. She might not even know her stalker. But Hawk has got nothing more to go on tonight.

Despite him telling me it's safer to stay away from her, as I wind my way up to my suite that night, I'm determined that I'll speak to her when I can. I'm certain she knows more than she thinks she does.

As it turns out, I was right not to rush straight to the hospital. Wizard and Amy's baby was born thirty-six hours after they'd left the compound. Despite the length of time, it all went smoothly, and Prez and his old lady have ended up with their expected boy. That outcome brings grins to the faces of those like me who possess a wicked sense of humour, while a look of horror appears on Hawk's. I visited shortly after the birth, but had declined the offer to hold the kid, unable to see why anyone who wasn't blood related would want to cradle such a disinteresting bundle in their arms.

On Friday morning when they appear on the compound, I'm there waiting like everyone else. I give my congratulations and a gift of a store card—well, I've no idea what a newborn needs. When Wiz appeared in the clubhouse, I bought him a beer to wet the baby's head in the time honoured way.

I stay on the sidelines when an exhausted looking Amy appears, intrigued by the expression on Wizard's face. Such adoration, such fulfilment and more than a tinge of pride, made me believe introducing his son Calvin Andrew was the pinnacle of his achievements.

"You keep your son away from my daughter." Hawk's voice suddenly rings out, followed by an oomph as Olivia's fist hits his stomach. "What?" He turns indignantly to his wife. "You know what's probably going to happen."

Olivia's eyes go wide. "I think you should consider very carefully what you're saying."

As smirks form on faces and sniggers go around, it takes the normally intelligent Hawk longer than it should to realise. It's clear to see when he does, his expression completely changes, and he becomes contrite. "Sweetheart, we were made for each other."

His wife looks him straight on. "Uh-uh." she raises a finger and waggles it at him. "You've just inferred we were forced together and that you had no choice." One eyebrow rises in challenge.

"Um, er…" Flustered, Hawk tried to find the right words. My lips curve as I watch him struggle. He looks like a worm caught on a hook. "Of course not, Liv, sweetheart, we were always meant to be together."

Now Olivia places her hands on her hips and cocks her head to one side.

"Fuck," Hawk breathes out, and throws up his hands. "What will be will fuckin' be." But it doesn't stop him tossing a warning glare at Wizard.

Olivia reaches up a hand, curls it around his neck and pulls his head toward her so she's able to whisper into his ear.

Various expressions cross his face until he finally settles on a grin. Noticing all eyes on him, he announces, "Seems like Liv's got a plan, and," he shakes his head in disbelief, "apparently breastfeeding isn't a reliable contraceptive. We're going to start working on a little brother to keep all the boys away from her."

TMI, maybe, but I'm not the only one to raise my glass toward him, nor the only one who finds their solution amusing. But fuck, if they're successful, that means he'll have two kids in diapers. The horror that sweeps into me at just the thought reconfirms having a baby will never be for me.

Rock pulls out his wallet and waves a note. "Fifty says Hawk's swimmers make another girl." Within seconds he's got brothers surrounding him, Wizard and Amy's baby forgotten for now.

Hawk swings around and raises his middle finger.

Jeez. All this excitement and he's not even yet impregnated her.

"Way to steal my fuckin' thunder, Brother." Wizard, son cradled in one of his muscular arms, ambles across and puts his free limb around Hawk's shoulders, who, it must be said, looks slightly stunned as if the implications of his rash announcement are just hitting home.

Sophie's rushed over and is hugging her daughter, and Sam wrestles Hawk out of Prez's clutches. Drummer looks on, another proud grandparent.

The scene makes me feel out of place. So much so, I mumble about having work to do, and slide away before anyone can object to me getting gone.

I'd far rather tinker with bikes than with babies, so I go to the shop and step to the bike I was working on. I stare down at it. It's being a bitch, the owner hadn't done much maintenance or taken care of it like he should. Each nut and bolt is a pig to turn, but there's something satisfying about breathing new life into an old machine. That doesn't mean I don't swear at it though.

I'm just about to start replacing the oil filter when my phone rings. Grabbing the rag and rubbing dirt off my hands, I take it out of my pocket and answer it, noticing it's from an unknown number.

"You've got Throttle." I wait. All I hear is silence.

"Who is this?" I ask. But no one responds. Instead I hear what could be breathing.

There's someone there.

Well fuck, if it's a wrong number why not just say it? Having a job on my hands I've got no time for games. I end the call.

Maybe it was a faulty signal. Maybe I could hear them, but them not hear me. Sighing, I dial the last number, but my phone doesn't connect. Putting it down to a bad line, I replace the phone in my pocket.

Over the rest of the day I get called six times, long before the last one I'm getting fed up. When I pack up my shit ready to go get changed out of my working clothes for Friday night church, I'm determined to do something about it.

After showering and changing into a fresh shirt and jeans and settling my cut back over my shoulders, I stride down to the clubhouse too early for church, but hopefully in time to catch Mouse in his office.

He looks up as I enter. "Throttle. What can I do for you, Brother?"

I place my phone on his desk. "I think some asshole's got hold of my number. He's playing games. Calling me without saying anything, and I can't get my phone to connect when I call back. Someone's fuckin' there, I know it. I can hear breathing."

Mouse stares at the phone for a second before opening a drawer of his desk. He takes out a box and shows it to me, then opens it up and fiddles with the device inside for a moment. "I'm setting this one up so it mirrors your current one, that way you'll have all the shit that you need. But you'll have a new number, at least temporarily. Leave that one with me. I'll hook it up and monitor any calls."

It's what I'd hoped for. "I might get some bona fide calls…"

"I'll forward them on."

I raise my chin. "Thanks, Mouse. With all the other shit going on, these phantom calls ring warning bells, you know?"

"Mention it in church," he suggests. "Speaking of which, time to get going."

When he stands, I do as well, then lead the way out of his office, taking the few short steps that leads us through to our meeting room. I come to a full stop at the sight that greets me, Drummer sitting at the head of the table.

"Well that takes me back," I observe as I move to sit by the now vacant VP's chair.

"Just like old times," Roadkill comments.

Wraith wanders in, pauses, then smirks. "Wiz can't handle a baby and being the prez? We never got away with that shit."

"Settle down, fuckers," Drum says sternly. "I'm only standing in today to give *Prez*," he pauses to show he has only taken over the seat not the table, "the chance to settle Calvin in."

"So Satan's Devils offer paternity leave? That's new." Joker chuckles. He nods to the empty chair beside Drummer. "Wraith going to resume the VP seat, too?"

"Fuck no," Wraith states firmly, taking his seat at the opposite end of the table. "I find this chair far more to my liking. It means I can give Drummer shit."

At his ex-VP's smirk, Drummer growls in his throat, but his steel-grey eyes have warmth in them as they go to the man seated by Wraith's side. "Hawk, get your ass up here."

"What?" The man in question, stares at his father.

"Oh, come on," Drummer states. "All I'm asking is you're my backup for one meeting."

I grin as Hawk gets to his feet and comes to take what I believe is his rightful place beside me. When he sits, I slap my hand against his cut. "Good to have you back, VP."

"Fuck off," he replies, good-naturedly.

Drummer bangs the gavel firmly. "Now, let's get started. Dollar?"

It's the normal business, and Drummer slips back into the role as though he'd never been gone. Despite the birth of a baby that's got our rightful prez distracted, the businesses are all ticking along nicely. There's not much to discuss as one by one the updates are given and the bottom line is the club remains in the black.

When it's onto other business, Hawk kicks it off.

He glances at me, then looks around the table. "You're all aware that there's some kind of threat toward Throttle or his lady."

"Ain't my lady," I growl.

"You sure of that?" Marvel yells out, chuckling.

Peg, I see, is grinning widely. I raise my middle finger to my old man.

"Continue, Hawk," Drummer rasps, his death stare quietening the table.

The temporary VP lifts his chin. "The prospects have been tailing Gwen all week, and so far no one has tried to follow her. Likewise the security systems have shown no one has attempted to break into her house."

I have to bite back a question about how she is, whether her injuries have healed, and what's her state of mind. While I'm having my internal fight, Lady raises his hand.

"What about you, Throttle? You had any more issues?"

"Nah. I've ridden out a few times, normally with Joker or Marvel." I nod my thanks to the men in question. "But there's been no attempts to run me off the road or follow me."

Joker takes over. "A couple of times I took the SUV and hung back letting Throttle look like he was on his own. No one took any interest in him."

"Could we say the threat, or whatever it was, has passed on?"

Mouse looks over at me. I take the hint. "Probably nothing,

but I've been getting nuisance calls to my phone. When I answer, someone's there, but they don't speak."

"I'm hanging onto Throttle's phone for a while to check it out."

"You able to trace it?" Drummer asks.

"Of course, unless it's a burner and not registered to anyone."

"So someone could still be fuckin' around," Hawk states. He studies me for a moment. "Apart from Gwen getting hurt, nothing else is serious, just things that are fuckin' annoying, almost to keep you on edge."

"Tell me about it," I respond, glumly. "I just wish whoever it is would fuckin' give up."

Marvel snorts. "He just wants to stop getting gifts. Me? I wouldn't turn that shit down."

"Gifts?" Like lasers, Drummer's eyes pin me down. "Plural?"

In the fuss over Prez's baby, those gloves had gone to the back of my mind. "Yeah, got a pair of decent riding gloves sent to me. Same handwriting as the boots, but no return address and no card."

"Told you he's got a secret admirer," Marvel crows again.

But no one else is laughing.

"There's just too many things which don't add up," I tell them, feeling the weight of the unknown on my shoulders. "Being followed, calls which don't achieve anything, and gifts I don't want out of the blue. I'll tell you this, Hawk's right, it's got me on edge, Brothers."

"Who'd want to hurt you, Throttle?" Joker asks.

I shrug. "Can't think of anyone."

Blade spins his knife twin front of him. "Only ones who the club's been up against lately are the Drays. The ones who stole Nathan's bike."

"That was weeks back," I counter. "If they were going to, they'd have made a move before now."

Blade shrugs. "Cedar's hand would have taken a while to

heal. And they might have been plotting and planning in the meanwhile."

Pursing my lips, I dismiss the idea. "A bullet to the head would seem more their style. Or, if they've been doing the following, they could have taken me out when they stopped behind me at some lights."

Drummer's regarding me carefully. "I don't think we should dismiss it so lightly. It's a good idea to look into the Dray twins further. Though I wonder why they'd go after Throttle, if they want revenge they'd take it on the club."

"It could be they're waiting and gathering information. Maybe they're just starting with Throttle as he took the lead in their torture. They could be getting info about his habits and the routes he's taken." Peg glances around. "Maybe time to start taking extra care, Brothers. This may not be Throttle's problem, it may be ours."

Hound gives a chin lift to Peg, then his eyes narrow. "I do think it's time I paid them a visit, it wouldn't hurt to check them out. Mouse, can you check what vehicles are registered to them?"

Mouse nods. "I'll get the drone up to see if anything they have in the scrap yard could be a match for the Ford Explorer that followed Throttle. Even if there's not, it doesn't mean they don't have access to one."

I sit back, folding my arms. "If it's the Drays, the gifts and the phone calls must be unrelated. But seeing as they're the only people we've pissed off recently, I'll go with Hound. I want an end to this Drum. If it's revenge they're seeking, I'd rather they came straight at me. This feels like I'm being played like a cat with a mouse."

"Not you." Hawk's sharp eyes are on me. "I agree with you, Brother. We need to bring this to a head. Someone else can go with Hound, but I propose a different plan for you instead."

I glare at him. This is the second time recently he's stopped me taking the action I want to. "Got a good reason for that, *VP*."

I'm annoyed so I snarl the title he's got back temporarily. It seems to be going to his head.

"I certainly have," he rasps back, his eyes going icy just like his father's. "Things happen when you and Gwen are together. When you're apart, whoever it is backs off—except for the gifts and the phone calls, but I'm discounting those as distractions. I think we need to draw them out."

My eyes narrow. "Draw them out? How?"

"We push the two of you together. You go to the Wheel Inn, be there while she works. Take her home and stay with her. We'll keep a close watch and see whether anyone takes the bait."

Drummer's eyes glow with pride for his son. My own anger has gone, and I'm interested now. Hawk's made a fucking good point. Sitting back in the VP seat seems to have given him new confidence, he's showing a spark of the old Hawk who'd got his position because of his ideas.

And, of course, I'm unlikely to raise an objection. His suggestion means I can go see in the flesh the person who's taking up residence in my mind. Seeing her again might be a cure, and I'll be able to fuck the club girls again. Without giving away I'm leaping at his plan, I give an off-handed shrug. "I'm game."

CHAPTER EIGHTEEN

*G*wen...

Friday night is always busy at the Wheel Inn, with citizens wanting to celebrate the end of the working week. It's also a night when the Satan's Devils aren't likely to be around except for the prospects. Tash has explained that's because they go to church, a pronouncement which had me confused at first not having expected them to be religious. Then she'd elaborated that was what they called their meetings. And though that will end relatively early, they'll party afterwards. An event, Tash explains, that particularly appeals to the single brothers. I'd asked why, then wished I'd kept my mouth shut. Hearing about the hangarounds who went to the compound with hopes of ending the night in bed with a biker was not the best news I'd heard.

Damn it. The thought of Noah taking his pick of any number of pretty city girls free with their sexual ways hurts. He won't be lonely tonight. Lisa had warned me, hadn't she? After that conversation during that fateful lunch, I hold no expectations of anything other than him bedding a woman who gives him as much as a second glance. It's not a case of him resisting temptation, he'd actively be on the prowl for a likely victim to catch his eye.

Why should the truth make me feel as though I've lost something, when I never had it in the first place?

The problem is, all week I've been unable to get him out of my mind which is crazy as I certainly haven't been on his. Sure, he's organised the prospects to make sure I'm not followed from home to work and back again. But he's not taken personal responsibility or even called to make sure I'm okay.

I've come to the conclusion he's only making sure I'm protected as I'm employed by his MC, and that he's got no special feelings for me. He's probably placed me back in the box labelled *Lisa's friend. Do not touch.* I was stupid to think he actually cared.

I should get the handsome bearded biker out of my mind. Easier to say than to do until I focus on what he's probably doing tonight. The thought of him fucking another woman should make me see sense.

I never had a chance with him, anyway. It's not his fault my teenage crush reared its head. It's not his fault I've been dreaming of being in his arms.

Seeing Tash watching me carefully, I do my best to shrug, indicating her words haven't affected me in the slightest, then pick up the tablet I use to take orders, and prepare to start work.

Both Nathan and Butcher are here tonight. Nathan having followed me from my home, and as he sits watching me, is obviously my security for the night. Not that I need it, but it's not worth wasting my breath telling him.

The place is crowded and soon I'm rushed off my feet. As the evening wears on, I see Tash smiling as full tables are good for business, but I'm tired as hell, my feet ache, and I'm fed up with trying to evade a table of handsy men who think they're entitled to touch my ass. Honestly, one more time and I'll dump a tray load of drinks into the offenders laps.

Usually it's a problem I can deal with, but tonight I'm just not feeling my feisty self. I try to avoid the thought it's because another woman is probably already feeling up what I wish was my man.

"Fucking dicks," I mumble under my breath when I return to the bar, but I wasn't quiet enough.

Nathan nods, pushes off his stool and stomps his way across the room. Even though I'm not the one in the wrong, I feel my cheeks burn and can't watch as he goes to confront the men at the table I just left.

"They're leaving," he announces on his return, and holds out his hand. He's got fifty dollars in it. "They left a tip."

"I love you!" I squeal.

"What the fuck's going on? Get out of here, Prospect."

Noah's angry voice has me spinning around. As I turn delighted, I see that his face is set and dark. "You got a thing going with him?" He jerks his head toward the hastily retreating prospect.

"What the hell?" I spit back, my welcome smile fading. "Of course I don't. He was doing his job. He stopped a table of ass feelers and even got me a tip." I wave the notes in his face as proof. "Men!" I finish with lamely, then nod at Tash and, taking my tray of drinks off to deliver, stomp away.

For the next half hour I'm rushed off my feet, delivering food, clearing tables, seating customers and taking orders. The other waiters and waitresses look as frazzled as me on this busy Friday night as we all work our hardest. I don't have time to process that despite my expectations, Noah has turned up. I only have time to wonder quickly what time their party starts, and whether his opportunities will still be around when he returns to the compound later.

I'm going back and forth to the bar to get drinks, but barely have time to notice Noah's still there, and no moments to spare to chat.

"Take a break," Noah growls into my ear the next time I go up to the bar.

I'm just about the blast him and say I'm far too busy for that, when Tash comes in on his side.

"Fifteen minutes, hon. Everyone's getting a moment to take the load off."

Noah jumps on the chance, taking the tray out of my hands and leaving it on the bar. Then he grabs hold of my fingers and leads me out back. He doesn't stop at the employee's breakroom, and unless I wrench my hand out of his huge paw, I have no option other than to follow him through the back door and outside. And why should I do that? Having my hand encased in his feels nice. For a few seconds I allow myself to enjoy the illicit pleasure.

But once outside in the fresh air, I go to pull away and immediately his fingers open freeing mine.

"Why are you even here?" I address my comment to the night in front of me, rather than the man by my side. "Isn't Friday your party night? Or that's what Tash told me."

He doesn't respond immediately, when he does, he chuckles first. "Your tone tells me she also explained what happens at our parties." He moves in front of me, two of his fingers resting under my chin, and raising my head, forcing me to look at him. "We have plenty of party nights, darlin'. And right now, here's where I want to be."

"You haven't contacted me." My statement sounds more accusing than I meant it.

He raises his chin in acknowledgement. "I was keeping you safe. Hawk and the prospects have kept an eye on you, haven't they?"

But not you. All I can do is nod to agree.

"Gwen, I stayed away because people have been following me. If someone's out for my blood, I didn't want you involved."

An acceptable excuse? Maybe. "So have they stopped now, is that why you're here?"

In the light of the streetlight I see him grimace. "Gwen, I'll be honest. There have been no more incidents for a few days. We're stumped babe, as to what it's all about. You haven't been followed and neither have I." He pauses. "Though there have been other strange things."

"What things?" I pick up on that fast.

His face twists as he grimaces. "Those boots were followed up by a nice pair of gloves." I raise my eyebrows in question. "And I've started to get heavy breathing phone calls."

"Heavy breathing?" I snort an unladylike laugh. "You get gifts and I end up in hospital?"

"Yeah, well." A muscle ticks in his jaw at my reminder. "I'm not convinced they're related. Gwen, it's what happened to you that's serious."

"But you think it's stopped?" *That's what he's come to tell me.* I'm pleased, of course I am. While I hadn't complained about the prospects following my every move, I've felt trapped, as if I can't just leave the house to get an item from the store, as they come with me, and I always feel I'm putting them out. It will be a relief if I have the freedom to do what I want without worrying there's danger coming my way. On the other hand, Noah will have no reason to have anything more to do with me.

"Perhaps." His answer is not what I expected, the one word neither convincing nor final. As I stare up into his handsome face, he gives a little shake of his head. "There's a suggestion that it's not you or me, or at least not singularly. But that there's someone who objects to us being together. Maybe an ex of yours."

I recall going through this not only with him, but with his friend, Hawk. "More likely of yours," I refute. "There's no one in my background who'd be jealous of whoever I'm with."

"You can't say that, Gwen." His eyes tighten slowly. "Sometimes people have no discernible motive for what they do. It could be someone you don't even know who decided that you were his. Or," his fingers come to my mouth to stop my protest, "the same could apply to me."

I'm confused. "Are you telling me it's over, or are you saying that we've still got something to worry about?"

"Fuck Gwen, I don't know. I can't tell you whether it is or not. But rather than sit back and wait for someone to make another move, if it's you and I together that they've got a problem with, then let's act like we're a couple and draw them out."

My eyes widen. *Pretend to be a couple?* Of course it's only a pretence he wants. I turn away, not wanting him to see my stupid disappointment, and force myself to think as an adult, not like the child I once was.

The reason I learned self-defence was to prevent me becoming a victim. My first impulse is never to keep my head down, but to confront things head on. While I still believe my attack was a junkie, and anyone following Throttle would be after him, not me, my preference would be to face whoever's causing him problems face on. On that basis, I can buy into his solution.

My sensible thoughts don't prevent the devil on my shoulder whispering, *Pretending might lead to it being real.* Mentally I brush him off and tell him to get lost, and say over-brightly, "So, how are we going to go about it?"

There's a flare in his eyes as he moves his hand so it rests on the back of my head. "First, I'm going to kiss you, then I'm going to come home with you tonight. If there's a guy who thinks he's got a claim on you, that should make him sweat."

Kiss me?

But before I can object, he makes good on his word. His hand exerts pressure, making me rise on tiptoe as he lowers his head. Without giving me time to prepare, his soft lips crush down on mine.

What does a girl do when the man of her dreams starts to kiss her in a way she's never before been kissed, with a dominance that immediately makes my panties go wet? She opens for him, that's what she does.

Somewhere in my brain I'm screaming, *this is fake, he's doing it for a purpose.* But another part replies, *kiss him back with all you've got, make him realise what he's been missing.*

My hands clasp at him, holding him tight. He's controlling the kiss, his tongue invading and retreating, enticing mine to follow his into his mouth, then both knotting and entwining. I try to give as much as I'm receiving, holding nothing back.

His beard is soft, which I wasn't expecting. His lips, smooth, his taste, intoxicating. All I breathe in is the scent of the man with a heavy tinge of leather and whatever soap he's been using. All I can hear is our combined heavy breathing.

I've dreamed of our lips meeting for years, but nothing in my imagination could match the reality I'm now experiencing. This isn't an untried boy, this is a man, far beyond my expectations, and like nothing I've known before.

A clearing of a throat makes me jump, but his arms tighten momentarily, ending the kiss on his terms and not those of anyone else. Luckily he keeps his hands on me else I might have stumbled were he to suddenly let me loose.

My heart is pounding, pumping blood to my extremities so fast, I feel slightly dizzy. But when the cough comes again, I gather what strength hasn't been zapped from me, and turn my head to see Kyla, one of the other waitresses, grinning widely.

"So sorry to interrupt, but Tash sent me out to find you," she explains.

"Shit. Sorry." I start to pull away from Noah, when he growls, hauls me back, plants a kiss to my lips, then, in his time, lets me go.

"Don't apologise to me." Kyla giggles. "I wouldn't have said no, either."

With my cheeks blazing I go back through the door, conscious that Noah's following close behind, his hand resting on the small of my back. When we reach the end of the corridor, he moves his hand to my shoulder, then stops and turns me.

His eyes examine my face, then he beams with satisfaction, his finger tracing what feels like my very swollen lips. "Yeah," he murmurs softly. "That should be convincing."

Convincing? Forcing my features to remain impassive, inside I'm broken as I realise what meant everything to me had clearly meant nothing to him.

Unable to speak I swing on my heels and dive straight into the thick of it, hoping keeping busy will stop my mind dwelling on how amazing his kiss had been, desiring instead to erase it from my memory.

It's not easy. Each time I return to the bar, he's sitting on a stool as though waiting for me. Each time I get a touch on my arm, on my shoulder, or even on my fucking ass, or his hand pushes strands which have escaped from my bun away from my face.

Inwardly I seethe, knowing it's all an act he's putting on. *Doesn't he know he's slowly killing me?*

I try to put to the back of my mind that he said he was coming home with me. *How will I cope? Did that kiss betray how much I want to jump his bones, while he was just acting? I could deny him entry to my house, I suppose.*

As closing time draws closer, I become more agitated. In the moment when we'd shared that kiss, I'd thought something had clicked between us at last, but it was only him acting. What a stupid woman I am. Lisa had tried to warn me, yet all he'd needed to do was crook his little finger, and all my inhibitions had fled.

Had he read that my response was genuine? If he had, would he take advantage? And, if he pressed his case, would I weaken and end up letting him into my bed?

Although I suspect he could fulfil my every fantasy, I know him leaving and walking away without a backward glance would devastate me.

My problem is, I don't know how strong I am, and whether I could turn him down if he offered.

Stupid, stupid woman. Deep down inside, I'm still hoping one taste of me would reform him.

Berating myself, knowing where he's concerned I can be weak, I decide he won't be setting foot in my house.

CHAPTER NINETEEN

*T*hrottle…

As soon as my brothers gave me the go ahead to go to see Gwen it felt like I'd been let off the leash. My pent-up thoughts and emotions which had taken root in my head for the past few days had me tearing to the Wheel Inn as soon as I could reasonably escape.

Had I ever been so eager to see a woman before? Not in my memory, unless you count the arranged liaison with the cheerleader who'd taken my virginity.

As soon as I walked into the restaurant, my eyes were drawn to her as though she was a magnet attracting me. I'd hurried my steps to get close to her, only to hear her telling the fucking prospect she loved him. *What the fuck?*

While the sane part of me knew the words were light-hearted and joking, I'd seen red. Nathan's lucky he didn't get my fist flying at him, but some sense of self-preservation had saved me. Neither Gwen nor Tash would have appreciated the violence in front of them, and my club would have heavily censored me. Satan's Devils can't get a rep for causing a fight in the successful business we have operating.

But my over-the-top reaction had shown me one thing. Whatever this strange attraction is, and wherever it will take me, Gwen's not just my sister's friend, she means something to me. Something that has my gut screaming no other man should get close. *She's mine.*

Could I be faithful? Could her pussy keep me going back for more? Could I step up and be the man she needs me to be? Fuck knows, but for her, I know I want to try. It's not for forever, just for as long as I can to bring this weird possessive feeling I have around her under control.

As I sit at the bar nursing my drinks, I keep a close eye on her. I hate the bastards she is serving, not missing the way she has to evade groping hands from the tables pushed so closely together. Rationally I know we pack so many customers in as it's all money in the club coffers, but personally I'd have placed them ten foot apart so Gwen could avoid the perverts. I should be the one touching her ass, not anyone else.

"She needs a break." *What?* I turn back to the bar which Tash is working behind. "Gwen. She's the hardest working waitress I've got, but she can't do it all. Can you get her to catch her breath?"

I'm certainly the man for the job. Which is how, five minutes later, I've got her outside. That's when instinct takes over. While rationalising it to myself, if there are eyes on us, seeing us together would send any stalker of mine or hers right over the top, I hadn't been able to stop myself reaching for her.

Fuck. As soon as I had my lips on hers I wasn't thinking anymore. I just knew I had to mark her, knew that stalker or not, any other man tonight would see her swollen lips and know she was mine. Her taste, her perfume, was like no other. I was barely able to make myself stop, even when we were interrupted.

Once I'd let her go my arms had felt empty, as though I needed her back and was less of myself without her warmth beside me. I'm stunned by how much I'd enjoyed just the meeting of our lips. She'd fitted against me as though it were me she was made for. The best thing? She'd kissed me back and had obviously poured her heart into it.

Then I went and I fucked up.

My reaction to her had caught me off balance, and I'd run scared, reverting to the character who poured cold water on women's expectations, making sure she understood there'd be no deep meaning to our interaction outside the back door. *It was an act* I'd led her to believe. *Nothing to it.*

She tried to hide her reaction, but I could see she was hurt. For the rest of her shift she tries to ignore me, while I revert to sneaking touches whenever she walks past. Sure, I was stating ownership to anyone watching, but I'm finding it hard to convince myself there isn't much more to it.

I can't take my eyes off of her. When she's taking payment for one of the last tables to leave, she lowers her head, leaning in obviously to hear the punchline of a joke the bill payer is telling. When he places his hand on her arm, I nearly fly off my stool, it's only Tash's sharply barked, *no.* that prevents me.

"Honestly Throttle. Why don't you piss on her?" Tash rolls her eyes.

Frowning, I knock that back. "It's not like that."

"Kid, who you trying to convince, you or her? 'Cause you're doing a shit-poor job on me."

I'm the fucking club enforcer, but Tash, along with the other old ladies, still call us kids having dealt on more than one occasion with our dirty diapers, so I don't call her out on it. Neither does she wait for an answer, she just tosses her hair and walks off to serve another customer.

At the end of her shift, Gwen comes hesitantly across. She's biting her lip like she's got something on her mind.

"Er, I think I'll just go home alone, Noah."

"Ain't happening." I shut that shit right down.

She glances around. "Are any of the prospects here?"

"Nope." I sent Nathan home as soon as I could, and Butcher's outside to check all the rest of the staff get safely to their rides.

"Noah—"

"Got your shit?" I shut her down. Sure, it's delaying the conversation she wants to have, but if it can wait until I've got her home, she'll have nowhere to run when I make clear what I want from her.

Do I know what I want myself? I have to admit, I don't.

"You're not following me home."

I shrug. "It's a free country."

She places her hands on her hips. "Then I'm not letting you in."

She can try to keep me out, but I got her security system installed, and I may have pocketed a spare key for her lock. I counter with a sharp nod which could mean anything.

Huffing, she stomps her way to the staff room where she swaps her apron for a jacket and picks up her purse. Without looking at me she walks off. I don't mind, trailing in her wake gives me a good look at her perfect ass. As soon as we approach the exit I call her back, pushing her behind me so I can step outside first, then, only after having made sure there's no one hanging around, I let her lead the way to her car.

Reaching it, she gets in and immediately starts the engine, then hesitates. I realise she's not as blasé as she seems when she obediently waits until I've brought my bike up behind her. As we drive through the now quiet streets of Tucson, I scan all around me and in my rear view checking for any vehicle that may seem interested in us. We proceed unimpeded and eventually draw up outside her house. I park my bike behind her car.

By the time I've taken my safety glasses and gloves off and tucked them into my cut, she's standing by the door. Her arms are folded.

"Get inside," I direct, as I approach. Taking a quick glance to each side and behind me, I add, "No point courting danger by standing out here."

"Whatever you've got to say, just say it." She doesn't move, and her posture is straight and stiff, as if she's mentally preparing herself.

I hold out my hands in supplication. "Babe—"

"Don't you babe me."

I don't like being exposed, it makes the hairs rise on the back of my neck. Spying the house key held in her hand, I thrust out mine, take the key, then reaching around her open the door to her house.

The alarm starts to beep. She challenges me with one eyebrow raised. With a sigh I input the code to switch it off.

"What the hell, Noah?" I can tell she doesn't like me knowing her code.

"Gwen," I start sternly. "Everything's been done for your protection." I prod her gently to move her out of the way so I can close the door. Then I deadbolt it and reset the alarm. "Let's sit and talk."

She huffs loudly, kicks off her shoes and takes a moment to rub her obviously aching bare feet, then strides to the kitchen. She returns carrying a single glass of water.

"Don't bother sitting, you won't be staying long." She takes out her phone, dials a number. It's on speaker I can tell as I can hear the ringing tone.

Within moments there's an answer.

"Yeah?"

"Er, Wizard. I'm sorry to bother you so late—"

"It's not Wizard. Who's this?"

"Oh, I'm sorry. I thought this was his number." Her brow frowns as she stares at the phone.

"You got Drummer. I'm acting prez while Wizard's settling in his new baby. Now, who are you and why are you disturbing my fuckin' sleep?"

I grin slightly. Trust Drummer to not make it easy on her.

He'll know exactly who's calling and has properly already assessed it's not an emergency.

"Er, it's Gwen. The waitress from the Wheel Inn. I, er, Noah's here in my house—"

"Well of course he fuckin' is. It was what was decided. If you don't know why, then you haven't given him a chance to explain as yet. I suggest you're better off talking to him and not to me."

The phone cuts off leaving Gwen just staring at it. Drummer treats words as if they're a precious commodity. Why waste them just to be polite?

I take pity on her and wipe the smirk off my face. "Wizard's son was born two days ago. He and Amy are tired as fuck, so we've given him a few days off."

She raises both eyebrows. "The Devils have paternity leave?"

"Don't give it a fuckin' name. We're family, we just step up and do what's needed."

She shakes her head. "I've never had family like that."

I rise, going over to her, and fuck if I don't say, "You've got us now. We're on your side, never forget that."

Her brow creases and she shakes her head. "Why?"

I could dress this up, give her all kinds of explanations, could find the words to satisfy her, but instead I decide to cut the crap and tell her what I want before I can second-guess myself.

"Because you're mine," I growl, getting up close and crowding her. "You're fuckin' mine, Gwen. I've tried to fight it, but I can't anymore. Being apart from you this week fuckin' killed me. I want you. I want you in my bed."

She pales and steps back. "I can't be a conquest, Noah. I can't be your Friday night pick up. I don't work like that. Lisa said—"

"Fuck Lisa." My hands go up to the sides of my head, fingers curling into my hair. "Sure, I haven't yet found any other woman that I want to keep close. You're fuckin' dangerous to me, Gwen. You're like my kryptonite, making me want things I never went looking for."

"You want me for sex."

"Of course." I grin, but before she can slap me, and yeah, I can see her hand twitching to do just that, I add, "But I want you on my bike, riding behind me, and babe, believe me, ain't had no one riding there before. Which means I want all of you, babe, and I want to give all of me to you. If you'll have me that is."

I didn't think her eyes could go wider, but they have. Still she's cautious. "For how long, Noah. One night, two? How long before you get sick of me?"

I answer honestly, "Fuck knows. But with you, I want to try."

She's still not convinced. "That kiss was fake. You told me that."

I sigh, knowing that would come back to bite me. "I implied that, yes. You wanna know why? Because it scared the shit out of me. I've never felt a connection like that."

A myriad of expressions chase across her face. A little hope, some sorrow, some doubt. I want to wipe all the negatives away, I want to see her features rearranged to reflect only pleasure. "Maybe it was a fluke," I say, nonchalantly. "How about we find out?"

She hesitates just a little too long. It's enough time for me to close the gap she'd left between us. Taking charge, I fist her hair that's come loose from her bun and pull her into me.

I'm a dominant man. I like to think I give, but first I take. My tongue demands entry, she gives it to me. My free hand reaches down and cups her ass, pulling her into me. Her little gasp shows she can feel my erection digging into her stomach. Moving my hips in the same rhythm as my tongue, I let my body do all the convincing.

Fuck, this woman gets to me. Her taste, her smell—even if it's tinged by the odours of food that she's been surrounded with all night. The feel of her softness, her full breasts crushed against my chest, and those little moans of encouragement escaping her mouth? Well, they've got the power to undo me.

Her eyes are closed, her cheeks are flushed. She looks like a flower just right to be plucked. As I lead, she's content to follow, it makes me wonder about the men she's been with before, and whether they could provide what she wanted. Under my touch I want her to blossom, I want her to feel things no man has come close to.

I want to teach her how a biker fucks.

I want to teach her how a biker makes love.

CHAPTER TWENTY

*G*wen…

I'm not a virgin but tonight I might as well be. I've never been with a man like Noah. Men have kissed me politely, our tongues shared a dance, with no particular partner dominating, or the man politely letting me control the pace.

Noah doesn't ask, he takes, and heaven help me, but I love it. I don't have to think where to put my hands, or whether to push in close. He's got me exactly where he wants me. If I thought the kiss outside the Wheel Inn had been hot, this one is off the scales. I can almost feel my panties melting.

Don't stop, don't stop.

He's using his tongue as though if was fucking me, his hips circling following the movements of his mouth. But although he's forceful, he's gentle even though that might not make sense. There's emotion behind his kiss, laying lie to the rumours I'd heard about him. I'd have had to be made of stone not to respond, and believe me, I'm a woman who's all flesh and blood.

We need to talk.

Hell, that's what the sensible side of me is saying, but I've dreamed about this and all rational thought has fled. I'm putty in his hands, and wherever he wants to take this, I'm a willing participant. My lips feel swollen, my cheeks burn, my whole body is overheated. As for that place between my legs I feel wet and so damn needy. Never have I felt this turned on, nor had the desire to dry hump the man who's kissing me.

When he pulls back putting only a fraction of an inch between us, it's purely to growl, "One chance to say no." Simultaneously, he sweeps me up in his arms as though he'd said the words, but is taking my choice away.

I'd never have described myself as dainty, yet Noah lifts me with ease. I feel protected and safe in his hold, yet at the same time, know I've never been in such a dangerous position before.

He's going to break my heart.

Shut up! I scream at my sensible self. Whatever happens, it's going to be worth it.

Giving me only a second to voice the objection which never comes, he carries me through to my bedroom. Once there, he lets me slip down onto the floor, while still holding onto me tightly. When he starts kissing me again, I melt. My legs feel so shaky I grab onto him just to keep myself upright.

With our lips melded together, he pushes me back slightly, placing both hands on my breasts. He groans, I moan, and when he grumbles about the layers of clothes between us, I can only agree.

Tearing his lips away from mine, he gasps, "I want you naked."

I want him that way too. I want to see everything Noah has to offer me. My chance, my resolve to escape the inevitable has fled long ago.

"Help me?" I ask, weakly, my limbs seeming to have no strength of their own.

Avoiding all thought of how he got his expertise, I let him take charge as he quickly strips me of my clothes. My t-shirt is over my head and discarded in just a blink of an eye, his nimble fingers unerringly find the clasp of my bra and it joins my shirt on the floor almost before I can register it.

His sharp indrawn breath of appreciation makes me feel like a runway model. But he's intent of removing me of all my coverings, as without pause he sinks to his knees, undoes the button and then the zipper, and soon my pants, along with my panties have gone. There's no room for embarrassment, just desire, when he leans forward and places a kiss to my mound.

"Love that you're bare."

"You. Now." I can't even form sentences. My clit throbs with the need for him to touch me, but my eyes want to feast on him.

Again he easily lifts me, lying me reverently on the bed. Then he steps back and takes off his cut, placing it over a chair. The way he rips off the rest of his clothes has none of the respect shown for his leather vest. Within seconds his whole body is bared to me.

I swallow, then swallow again. I've never seen a more magnificent male specimen outside of the covers of the books that I read, and the posts I often view on social media. Is this really me? Am I awake, or am I dreaming? I feel like a fantasy has come to life. My mouth dries as I imagine what this man could do to me. I'm turned on more than I've ever been and he hasn't had his hands on me yet.

Something glints in the light. *Something fucking glints.*

My hand covers my mouth, and I point. "Er...?" I've heard about piercings of course, but I've never seen one in the flesh. Noah hasn't just got one, his whole dick is covered.

He looks down at himself, then at me with a smirk. "Jacob's Ladder," he explains. "Consider it ribbed for her pleasure."

"Oh my God, I need to try it." *Did I say that aloud?*

It seems like I did, as he moves immediately.

When his body comes down and covers mine, I don't have to think about what he's expecting, he shows me exactly what he wants, taking both of my hands in one of his and pinning them above my head. His legs gently kick my thighs apart making a cradle for himself between them.

His lips again meet mine, but only briefly, before he moves

his head down and starts to pay attention to my already aching breasts.

Oh. I breathe in sharply. No one has ever tightened their teeth around my nipple before, the savage pinch hurts briefly, but when a zing shoots straight down to my clit, I don't voice any objection. Then he soothes the ache with his tongue, making me writhe against him.

He plumps up my other breast with his free hand, murmuring appreciatively, "You're so fuckin' beautiful, Gwen. These tits were made for me."

This time I'm expecting the nip, and the effects don't disappoint me.

He suckles my nipples, then moves his mouth around my orbs, every now and again sucking hard, and no doubt marking me. Another first, and one which doesn't raise any objection. No one will see them but me, and hell, it will be something to remind me that I really wasn't dreaming.

Once he's done with my breasts he lifts his chest, and his piercing eyes stare down at me as if checking in. All I can do is wriggle to encourage him. I don't have words to explain how I'm feeling, or how much I want him to continue. Already he's blown my expectations out of the water and I'm excited to discover what more he's got in his repertoire.

A second later he's kissing his way down my torso, occasionally pausing to mark me again. When his mouth glides over my rounded stomach I suck in a breath. Noah's lean, and muscular, and I'm carrying more pounds than I should be.

A growl comes again, with the comment, "Fuckin' perfect. Relax, Gwen, don't tense for me. Well, not yet."

His beard deliberately rubs over my bare mound, it tickles. Despite myself a giggle bursts from me. I hear a chuckle, then he does it again.

Then he continues his exploration, pausing to suck my clit into his mouth. The sensation makes me try to get my hands free, but he's holding them too tightly. It's almost a sense of security, knowing I've no choice but to lie here and take what he's offering me, without having to worry about how to reciprocate.

He circles my pulsing nub with his tongue, then nips it gently. My arousal starts to grow, but before I can get close, he's moving again, this time probing my slit with his tongue.

"You taste fuckin' amazing. I could feast here all day."

I feel a fleeting embarrassment that I haven't showered since this morning, but any discomfiture soon slips away as I realise it doesn't bother him as he licks up my cream as though he could never get enough.

His tongue is replaced by a finger invading me, then he adds another. Now he's back to sucking my clit, while pumping his fingers inside me.

Oh God what's he doing? He's touching a spot that has my muscles contracting without me giving any instruction.

I'm out of control, I can't even think. My body belongs entirely to him. I can't take part, I can only react. My muscles tense, my stomach quivers, my mouth opens and I start to plead.

"Yes, there, yes. God, yes. Oh God..."

I'm ascending to a peak that I don't think I'll survive going over. Never has my body been under such stress before. My heart surely stops beating as I draw in one last breath and hold it, before everything releases and a tsunami of sensation floods over me, making me see stars for a moment. I scream with the intensity, arch of the bed, almost getting my hands free. But I'm locked in place, having no option other than experience what he's giving me.

He brings me down, but I get no relief, as he starts his manipulations again.

"Please, no. Please." I'm unsure whether I'm begging him to stop or to continue.

My second orgasm hits me fast with almost the same intensity. My lungs heave, my eyes water, my brain is mush.

Seconds pass before I realise he's released my hands.

When I force open my eyes I see him sitting back on his

haunches and smoothing a condom over his impressive cock, his brow creased in concentration. As though he feels my gaze on him, he looks up and meets my stare.

"Ready for me?"

I can't reply, but in my head I'm answering, if I'm not now, I'll never be. *How are those piercings going to feel?*

My arms feel like lead but I raise them, reaching up in supplication for him to come to me. Placing one hand by my shoulder he braces himself, using his other to line his dick up. Then, he starts pushing in.

He's prepared me, but it's been a while, and he's big. I suck in air, worry for a second whether we'll fit, but he takes his time, muttering reassurances to me. Just when the burn and stretch starts to become too much, he stops, and I feel the hair of his balls against my smooth pussy lips.

I get a moment to acclimate, and then he starts pulling out and pushing back in with rhythmic movements.

This is nice. Mmm. I feel an odd sensation which must be the piercings. It's pleasant…

Then he picks up the pace. *Oh my God.* He's hammering in, so hard my headboard's crashing against the wall adding a percussion accompaniment to each of his thrusts. Each time he hits that spot inside me and my arousal begins to ramp up, attaining the peaks it reached previously and then exceeding them.

I can't breathe. I'm going to die. There's no way I can survive. I clutch at him as my vaginal muscles clamp down on his dick. My body bucks of its own volition and once again, I scream.

"Fuck, Gwen. Fuck, that's it. Milk my fuckin' cock."

My nails dig into his skin as I try to survive the most intense experience of my life.

Teetering on the peak, I suddenly go over. As I start to come down, I feel him slowing his pace, now his thrusts are firm, controlled and less manic, until suddenly they become short and irregular.

"Fuck, Gwen. Fuck!"

He stills, holds himself as he fills me completely. His eyes are squeezed shut, deep lines appear on his sweat covered brow, and tension presses his lips together.

With a shuddering gasp and an indrawn breath, he finally begins to relax. One eye opens first, and then the other. Tension leaves his muscles and a beautiful smile covers his face as he leans down and moves his lips over mine.

"Fuck," he exclaims softly. Holding the condom with one hand, he twists and flops down on his back, pulling me along and holding me to him. "I have no words, Gwen. You'll have to give me a moment."

I'd give him anything he wants—the moon should he ask for it. Anything that means we'll repeat this again.

He's not going to get up and leave, is he? After this, he's spoiled me for all other men.

Maybe good sex affects the brain but I bite my tongue to stop words escaping. I've liked him for a very long time, lusted after him almost since I first met him when I was fourteen. Apart from what Lisa spilled about his sexual exploits, I know he's a good man. My heart's screaming that I love him, but surely that's just a hormonal reaction to what we've just done?

Don't make a fool of yourself, Gwen. He made you no promises.

What have I done? If he walks out of my life, he'll take my heart with him.

CHAPTER TWENTY-ONE

*T*hrottle...

Brothers, shit, even my father has tried to explain to me what it was like finding their one. How she blindsided them, leaving them with no choice in the matter. I never believed them. I thought I'd been vaccinated or was naturally immune. Gwen's proved me a liar.

I'm not even going to try fooling myself any longer.

Fucking Gwen had been an earth-shattering experience, smashing out of the ball park any previous liaison I've had. I'm not blind to the reason.

I'd wanted to make it good for her, but that's not unusual. I might take sex where and whenever I can, but I'm not a bastard. Unless it's a sweet butt, if the woman doesn't come at least once, then I count myself a failure. I'm a confident asshole, I pride myself on my skills, and while not every woman comes when I'm inside her, she's not left wanting or unsatisfied.

Tonight, though I might not have shown it, my confidence evaded me as I piled on extra pressure. I needed Gwen not just to enjoy it, she had to end up wanting no other. Because, fuck, I knew the moment I'd started kissing her that I never wanted to leave her. Fucking, had only cemented it.

The difference had hit me all at once. I've liked Gwen forever, even when I didn't really notice her and dismissed her as a friend of my sister. Over the past couple of weeks I'd come to admire more about her. Her figure, her shape, well, sure that attracted me, but should she gain weight or lose it, I'm certain it wouldn't matter. As she ages and wrinkles appear, they wouldn't turn me off. It's those thoughts that hit like a smack around the head and I know I can't lose her.

Why was sex with Gwen so spectacular? I'd wanted to please her, and going by her exclamations and the look of wonder on her face, I'd achieved what I'd set out to do. But it went further than simply getting her off so I was free to take my pleasure, I'd wanted to bind her to me. Because an extra ingredient had been added in tonight, something that I'd always been missing. *Emotion.*

Every sigh, every reaction had been like a balm to my soul. It was as if I was not only taking my pleasure, but experiencing hers. The connection between us had been something I'd never felt. Prior sex had been a physical release, our joining was on an almost spiritual plane, the meeting of two people and a sense of becoming one.

Fanciful thinking for a biker? Perhaps, but it's the only way I can explain it.

I'd never worried about my previous conquests. Once I'd had them, they were free to move on. Hell, even before then. If I'd set my sights on a woman and another man swooped in, I'd have wished him good luck and stepped back. One pussy was so much like another and there were plenty to go around. Last night, my possessiveness over Gwen had surprised me, I could have decked Nathan when Gwen jokingly expressed her love to him. As for the bastards feeling her up, they were lucky to escape with their hands. I've never felt this way about a woman before, the only comparison is how I feel about my bike.

After we fucked, I'd dozed, then noticed Gwen was out like a light. I'd got up to deal with the condom, then returned to her side, pulling her into me.

Now the sun's rising. As I lie awake, waiting for her to open her eyes I have to admit this is comfortable. I thought having a person sleeping beside me would be distracting, but instead I slept well, her gentle breathing beside me being soothing instead of annoying. I had no inclination to leave and return to my lonely room.

Yes, this was what my brothers had been trying to tell me.

But how to get Gwen into my life and keep her? Would it even be fair? She's got a good career ahead of her, and I, well, I'm a biker, good with my hands but not much else. Do I even deserve her?

Then I think of my mother, a fire chief in Tucson now. She never looks down on Peg for being a biker.

Would Gwen take to the club? As a citizen, we've always kept her away from the compound, except when I took her there two weeks back. What does she know of bikers and our lifestyle? Would she want to become a part of it? I hate the idea I could drag her down and sully her worldly innocence. Although the club's going through a settled spell now, the authorities don't like us, and we can easily make enemies.

My thoughts lead me nowhere except to acknowledge the fact that I'm a bastard. I want her and I'm going to have her. That's all that matters.

She stirs, stretches like a cat, and then begins to wake up. Her movements are fluid until her leg touches mine, then she starts and half sits up.

"You're still here?"

Pressing myself up on my elbows I rise to meet her. "Good morning, beautiful."

Her hand touches her hair, tousled from our lovemaking, and grimaces, but then she grins. "Good morning, yourself, handsome."

I'm a man, I'm lying beside a naked woman, and my

morning wood is at full mast. What else can I do but grab a condom, roll her onto her back, kiss the fuck out of her, then proceed to make love to her? Me, Throttle. Making love. The thought makes me want to laugh at myself and I would, but this is no joke. How I'm feeling about her is fucking serious.

After we've proved last night was no fluke, and if anything this morning is even better, our stomachs rumble in unison.

Chuckling, I ask, "Want some breakfast?"

She looks contrite. "We'll have to go out. I've only got cereal and…" She waves at my body.

Chuckling again, I nod. "Which won't keep a body like mine in top condition. Not with the workouts it's getting. Christ, woman, to keep up with you I need some meat in me." I wink at her. When she starts to move, then winces, I decide she needs pampering. "Tell you what, you stay here, have a bath or something and I'll pop out pick some shit up then I'll cook you breakfast."

Her eyes widen in disbelief. "You cook?"

"You've met my mom, yeah? You think she'd put up with that chauvinistic crap? I was taught to fend for myself alongside Lisa." I smile as I remember. "I'm actually better than my sister. Mind you, most chefs are male, so I just suppose it's something else we're best at."

"Noah!" she squawks indignantly, but then has to stifle her laugh.

Leaning over I kiss her. "Right, I'll just run through your shower then I'll be off. Take your time."

I make short work of using the facilities, leaving with my hair dripping wet, knowing the wind will dry it off quickly enough. The store isn't busy so I easily get what I want. All the time there's a wide grin on my face which I can't seem to get rid of.

I suppose I'm gone about three quarters of an hour. When I return and use my key to get in, I hear a hairdryer going in the bedroom. I place the bags on the counter, and sort out the stuff that I'm going to cook, putting the rest in the refrigerator.

Does she even eat meat? There's so much I don't know about her. *Is she allergic to eggs?* I better go ask her.

Her bedroom door opens as I approach. She rounds the corner looking delightful in tight jeans and a clingy top. She's got her hand over her mouth, eyes squeezed shut as she yawns widely.

I stand, still grinning, waiting for the yawn to stop.

Then, hell breaks loose.

One minute I'm standing gazing at my girl, the next moment my nose is hurting like a bitch, my arm twisted and I'm on the floor, staring at a leg that's pulled back and aimed straight at my balls.

"Stop!" I shout. "Unless you never want to have my children." If my voice is high pitched, there's a good reason for that —sheer fucking fear of the damage she could do.

She pulls her kick, but stumbles before righting herself. When she looks down, her eyes come into focus. "Noah, I'm so sorry. I'm still half asleep and I thought you'd have to knock to get in. Oh God, I can't apologise enough. Did I hurt you?"

My arm, that she'd twisted, does throb, but my overriding feeling is that I'm as proud as fuck.

"I got a key," I tell her dismissively. What's more important is, "Where the hell did you learn to fight like that?"

"Noah, don't be angry—"

"I'm not angry. I'm fuckin' impressed." *She'll make a great old lady.* Then my pride fades. "Is there a reason you learned to defend yourself?" She was fostered, and I know things aren't all unicorns and rainbows in many foster homes. *If someone abused her, I'll go after them myself.*

She still looks worried, so to convince her I bare her no ill will, I stand, open my arms and she comes into them.

"I was on my own after I parted with my foster parents, and I knew I had to look after myself. I took self-defence classes."

Sensible. "Can you shoot?"

"Uh-huh."

Christ this woman. "Got a gun?"

"Yes. I don't take it out, but it's here in the house."

I can't help it. I kiss her. "Fuck, woman. Just when I thought you couldn't surprise me more, you go and show me those moves."

Her teeth worry her lip. "Are you sure you're not hurt?"

"If I say yes, will you kiss it better? Because, babe, my balls… they were scared to death, and they need some attention." I waggle my eyebrows.

For that I get a fist to my arm, but only gently.

She pulls away from me. "Talking about your balls, what did you mean when you told me to stop if I wanted *your* children?"

Trust her to pick up on that. The words had been driven from me by panic, with no real meaning. But there must have been some instinct driving them, because now what I'm going to say next is a fact.

I shrug. "If you ever want kids, I'll be the father."

I've stunned her. "You want kids?"

Never did. Now? I'm not sure. "If I find I do, you're the only one I'd want them with."

"Noah!" The sharpness in her voice makes me narrow my eyes. "Lisa told me some stuff…." She frowns, then tries again. "I didn't even expect you'd still be here this morning, now you're talking about having kids?"

I'm going to kill my sister. "Would it make you feel better to know I didn't expect those words to come out of my mouth?" Her face falls and makes me feel an ass. "Fuck, babe, I'm going about this all wrong." Drawing my hands down my cheeks, I tug at my beard. "I might not have thought I'd be saying them, but it doesn't make them wrong. You," I point to her, "me," I point to myself, "well, lets just say it wasn't what I expected."

"The sex was that good, huh?" Her expression is unreadable.

"Not just sex," I say fast. "The whole damn package." Frowning, I try to sort through my thoughts. "Lisa's already told you who I am, what I do. From the time we met at the Wheel Inn, there was something about you, and it was more than a connection we had in the past. For the last couple of weeks I've been thinking about you. Yeah, I didn't contact you, because I didn't know what the fuck to do. I care about you, Gwen." My eyes narrow. "Not giving you a lifetime commitment right now, but I want to keep seeing you. I want us to start dating."

"I care about you, too, Noah." Her voice is soft, like a caress. Then she glances down at her hands. "Dating I can do, but I can't share you."

"Fuck, woman. I wouldn't ask you to do that." Reaching out my hand I raise her chin so she can see my sincerity. "The promise I'll make right now is, however long we're together, you're the only one who's going to be in my bed."

"I'm that good, eh?" She's half-grinning, half not, seeming uncertain whether to take me seriously.

Smirking, I reply, "Yeah, you're that good."

"So we're exclusive?"

"Better fuckin' be. Hell, Gwen, I think you've cast some sort of spell over me. I've been fighting it, but I can't run anymore. Let's give us a try."

"Do you mean it?"

I've never meant anything more. "I mean it."

Suddenly she leaps at me. I catch her, her legs go around my waist and her lips find mind. This time I let her kiss me. When she draws back, she stares into my eyes as if trying to read what's written on my soul, then she says, softly, "I like you, Noah, very much. I think part of me always has."

I feel ten feet tall at her declaration, and obviously my first thought is to take her back to bed. But when her stomach rumbles loudly again, I realise I should probably get her fed, and put my baser desires on the back burner for later.

Easing her back onto the floor, I ask, "What do you eat, Gwen? I got bacon, eggs, waffles and sausage links, or fruit if you prefer?

"Did you buy out the whole store?"

"Not quite." I chuckle. "But as much as I could carry on the bike."

"I want all of it!"

Now that's my kind of girl.

I make her sit on a stool while I find my way around her kitchen. After a while she gets twitchy with nothing to do, so gets up to make a pot of coffee. I relax once I find the pans I need and settle into my task.

"Tell me more about you," I instruct, as I place bacon in the pan. "What was it like being in foster care?"

With a grimace, she proceeds to tell me the whole story, and my gut twists for the neglected girl she'd been. Sure, she'd been fed and given what she needed, or everything except love. Now she's mine, she'll never want for affection again, that's the vow that I silently make her.

It becomes clear why she learned self-defence, she's never had anyone to depend on other than herself. That changes from now.

No wonder she was so diligent with her schoolwork, and how she'd come over as such a respectable teenager, never wanting to step a foot over the line. It was because she'd lose her home if she'd been caught misbehaving. All the reasons we kept her away from the compound then mean nothing now.

I start to regret that we never invited her. As Lisa's friend, she would have been drawn into our extended family, and given the love that she'd obviously been missing out on. Yet I was the one who'd encouraged Lisa to keep her at arm's length, such an upright citizen wouldn't have jelled with our way of life.

I find myself secretly grinning, knowing if I introduce her as my old lady she'll gain more friends and relatives than she ever could have dreamed about. Life's soon going to be looking up for Gwen, and I can't wait to see how she takes to it.

Sure, I'm going to get my leg pulled when I turn up with a woman in tow, but the blowback won't land on her. I'm prepared to take whatever's thrown at me, as I understand it now, how the world changes when you find the person you want to ride through life with.

She can't hide her expression of surprise as I place a perfectly cooked plate of food in front of her, and those moans of appreciation make me want to take her straight back to bed. But after the athletics last night and from the stiff way she's moving this morning, she's going to be far too sore, so hold back. I also find the thought that the next time I have her naked under me, it will be in my own bed. A sacred place where no woman has ever slept before.

Discreetly I adjust my cock as I envisage the sight of her luscious hair spread out over my pillow. This time she won't be injured or hurt, she'll be mine to play with.

"So, tell me, Noah. What's all that with the," her eyes crease, then she clicks her fingers, "Jacob's Ladder on your dick?"

I smooth a hand down my cheek. "You going to let me keep that a secret?"

"Nope." She grins cheekily.

I shake my head. "I was a fuckin' prospect, eighteen years of age. Heard some of the guys talking about piercings. Apparently women are quite appreciative." I wink, she flushes. "Blade, well he had a lot to do with setting up our tattoo parlour, which, if you haven't guessed, does piercings. The fucker encouraged me." I wince as I remember. "I'd looked into it, thought a Prince Albert sounded like it would do the job."

"That's just one piercing, isn't it?"

"Uh-huh."

She leans forward, her eyes twinkling. "But you went further. Was alcohol involved?"

"Whisky and a fuck lot of it," I admit with a shudder. "If I was going to let a guy get his hands on my dick, I wasn't going to go in there sober."

"I thought there was a law against that?"

I stare at her. "We're bikers. We own the joint."

"Ah. So what changed your mind? Why did you go for the full ensemble?"

"Because the piercer taunted me into it." And bastard, he fucking had. I didn't even know Blade had put him up to it until after.

Her brow creases. "It must have been painful."

She doesn't know the half of it. I'd gone into it like a stupid kid. Hadn't considered I'd have to lay off fucking while it healed. My naïve eighteen-year-old self had expected to show off what I could do with it, if not that night, then a day or so later. I'd found out how wrong I was.

"Yeah," I say, succinctly. "But what happened after was worse."

"It got infected?"

"Nah." Annoyed as I'd been at the time, I can smile now as I remember. "Blade couldn't keep his fuckin' mouth shut."

"He told everyone? But you said they'd already talked about piercings."

"Yup. That wasn't the problem." I pause, before giving her the punchline. "Blade knew full well another member had a Jacob's Ladder."

"So?" She looks confused.

I take a breath. "My own fuckin' father."

She snorts. "Peg-Peg," she snorts again, "Peg has a..." she points to my lap, "what you got?"

"Yeah, like father like son."

She's still chuckling, it takes her a moment to get enough control to state, "I'm surprised Blade is still alive."

"He wouldn't be, but I was a prospect. And as it turned out, Satan's Devils frown on prospects killing members." Then I'm laughing as well. It had been embarrassing as hell, and the members had got a lot of mileage from yanking my chain. Peg hadn't been particularly happy either to start with, but in the end he'd found it amusing as shit. But in time, the novelty had worn off.

"I don't regret it," I explain, "Not now. But I did at the time. What eighteen-year-old wants to feel like they've copied their old man?"

She's belly laughing now, wiping tears from her eyes. My lips twitch. How Blade tricked me isn't a story I often find myself telling, most times if a woman asks, I get her to focus on how my adornments make her feel, rather than explaining how I came by them. But seeing her cracking up? That's worth every second of my embarrassment.

Enough of talking about my dick for now, else I'll be taking her back to bed and giving her another demonstration.

As if she knows where further conversation might be leading, she changes the subject. "Are you going back to the club now?"

For once in my life, there's something I'd prefer to be doing. I counter with, "You got plans for today?"

She grins. "Not so much now since you went to the store for me. Other than tidy the house and get a start on the laundry, I've nothing planned."

"Okay. So how about I clear away the breakfast shit while you do what you have to. Then, why don't you come for a ride on my bike, and after that we'll visit the compound."

Her eyes widen, and she squeals. "On your bike?" Then crease lines appear. "If we go to the compound, what exactly will I be going as?"

Replacing my fork on the plate, I grow serious. "I'm not messing about, Gwen. You're coming back as my girlfriend. I want everyone to know we're together now." I'll be given hell, but hey, they read the signs before I did. I doubt any will be surprised.

She's stunned for a moment, then she smiles. The expression lights her face and makes her even more beautiful if that's possible. Next, she laughs and shakes her head. "Lisa won't believe it."

"Fuck Lisa," I growl. "Fuck anyone who dares to comment.

You're mine now." I pause and add with a hint of nervousness which isn't like me at all, "Aren't you?"

"For as long as you want me to be."

"For as long as either of us want to," I state firmly.

She reaches forward and places her hand upon mine. "Why don't we take it a day at a time? I might find you snore or something. And you might not like my habits."

I can't believe there's anything she could do which I wouldn't like. *Fuck, I've got it bad.* But if she needs to go slow, I'm happy with that. "Day by day, however you want it."

To my astonishment she giggles. "Then I better make a phone call now. I had a date tonight."

A fucking date? I see red. *She was planning on going out with someone else?* "Who with?" My tone is terse. Another fucking man? That shit ain't happening.

"Oh, a colleague at work asked me out."

Warning bells in my head start ringing and make me tamp my jealousy down. "Gwen." I grow serious. "I need to know who it is. If someone's interested enough in you to ask you out, it's possible he's your stalker."

Again her eyes show astonishment. "Everest would never hurt me. He'd be pretty stupid to attack me as a way of showing his interest."

"Or have you attacked." I decide to explain the ways of the world to her. "You getting hurt and scared might mean you need someone to turn to. This Everest," *fuck, what a name*, "could have been setting you up so he could sweep in and comfort you when you're at your lowest. Tell me his full name, if nothing else, it's worth looking into."

"You won't confront him?" Her brow creases in concern, "He's a lawyer, it could cause problems for me at work."

Seeing she's genuinely worried, I reassure her, "Nah, I won't do that, babe. I'd do nothing to jeopardise your career. I'll just get Mouse to run a background check on him."

She grimaces, then states, "His name is Everest Fontaine. I'll go ring him now."

"You like him?" I challenge, cautiously, wondering if I've got competition, and thanking fuck I came back with her last night. If I hadn't, I might have lost her completely. *Nah, I'd have removed fuckin' Everest from the planet.*

"It isn't like that," she replies, biting her lip. "I don't really know him. When he invited me out, I agreed only to take my mind off the man I really wanted, and the one who I thought I couldn't have."

As her eyes meet mine, there's no doubt she means me. I thank my lucky stars I didn't wait longer to step up to the mark. I don't know anything about this Everest fucker, but I do know any man having a chance with Gwen would be stupid not to take it. If he'd played his cards right, he could have shown her a lawyer was a better bet than a biker. *I could have lost her.*

The idea makes me shudder.

CHAPTER TWENTY-TWO

---

*G*wen...

While Noah starts clearing up the breakfast things, on automatic pilot I start sorting out the clothes I need to wash. My mind is racing. I seem to have fallen into a dream world, and more than once, pinch myself.

I make the phone call to Everest, letting him down gently. When he tries to rearrange our date, I tell him an approximation of the truth, that an old boyfriend has re-emerged and that he wants to make a go of things. I listen carefully to his reaction, but he sighs. When he admits he's disappointed, but wishes me every happiness and assures me things will not be awkward at work, I very much doubt he could be the one who attacked me and violated my house. But without an alternative, I have to accept Noah's right, and nothing and no one can be discounted.

I don't have a second thought about turning a date with a professional man down in preference to spending time with Noah. Deep down I know I'm doing the right thing. I've been attracted to Noah for years. Having been offered the moon, there's no way I'm going to be giving up the chance to see where a relationship with him leads, even if there's a small part of me that's concerned he'll soon get bored.

I'm so excited about going to the compound, not as a victim who's been attacked and needs care and sympathy, but on the arm of the man I'm fast coming to, let's be honest, like a hell of a lot and maybe even love.

What will Lisa say? I'm sure she'll be happy when she gets over the shock. I've no worries about seeing his mom, Darcy's already been lovely to me. I hadn't had much to do with his dad over the couple of days that I stayed, but that was because I'd been laid up hurting and resting. Now I'm to meet his MC brothers. It's scary to think about being thrust into his extended family. I'm not particularly extrovert, and I worry they won't like me.

How do I act? I've never been in that situation before. When I'd once been fostered into a family which already had children, I'd learned to be seen and not heard. I'd had more than my fair share of bullying on the principle I hadn't belonged, on the compound I'll be an outsider again.

Noah will be with me. He won't let anyone hurt me.

One thing that doesn't worry me is the principle of going onto a biker compound. I've met a few of the bikers during my shifts at the Wheel Inn, and so far, have been exposed to nothing that concerns me. I also have a lot of respect for Tash and read her as a woman who wouldn't put up with stuff she didn't feel comfortable with. It's just they're a family, and I've no experience to draw on of being a part of one.

When I finish up my chores, I decide to look forward positively and enjoy this day with Noah. *Just be me.* Noah likes me, and that's all that matters.

"You look deep in thought?"

His voice startles me. I don't tell him what I've been thinking about, substituting, "I'm wondering what to wear on your bike."

Giving me a thorough assessing look, he finally nods. "What you've got on is fine. Maybe grab a light jacket, it's cooler on the bike, and it's late autumn now."

"Do I need a helmet or something?"

"I got you covered. Hey, I thought about riding up Mount Lemmon. Just to give you a feel for riding the bike."

"Sounds good," I reply, brightly, though those twists and turns and the drop offs feel like it will be a baptism of fire rather than a gentle introduction. With anyone else I'd be terrified, but I know Noah would never put me in danger. I just hope I don't unbalance his motorcycle.

"We'll go as soon as you're ready. Take a ride, stop off for some lunch, then go to the—" His phone rings, interrupting him.

The day sounds wonderful, I think dreamily. Better than the Saturdays I spend alone. But my ears prick up as I overhear his side of the conversation.

"Mom?... What, now?... What's the matter?... Dad okay? Lisa?... Give me a fuckin' hint, woman... What, when I get there?" He sighs. "Can't it wait? Okay, keep calm. I'm leaving now."

He hangs up with a heavy sigh, I raise a quizzical eyebrow.

"Mom wants me back at the compound now."

"Is anything wrong?" I'm worried on his behalf. I only heard one side of the conversation but picked up it was something serious.

His brows go down and meet in a V. "There's something up, but she wouldn't tell me what. The family is fine, she told me. And it's not club related as one of my brothers would have called. I'm fuckin' sorry, Gwen, I'll have to put our ride on hold for now."

"You get going." Making a shooing motion I lie and tell him I don't mind, while inside I'm screaming. The obvious disadvantages of having family is being beholden to them.

He steps forward. "I'm not fuckin' going without you, Gwen. I told you I'm taking you to the compound, that's just risen up the agenda is all. We'll do our ride later. I want to spend the day with you, and nothing's going to prevent that."

My heart leaps, but I'm not sure. "If there's a problem..." *I could be in the way,* I add to myself.

"I want you beside me." His eyebrow rises in challenge. "Or are you thinking about calling fuckin' Everest back?"

I snort, silently thrilled at his obvious jealously. "Unlikely. I just didn't want to intrude."

His hand comes out to cup my cheek. "I thought we had agreed to give this a damn good try. We're together now, Gwen. Through the good and the bad. I know we said we'd be dating, but I'm in it for the long haul."

Well, hell. I like the sound of it.

Taking a deep breath, more than a little worried about what family argument I'll be stepping into, I take that leap. "I'm ready." Mentally I try to prepare myself. If Noah needs my support, he'll be getting it.

Grabbing the jacket he suggested, I lead the way through the house, mocking him inwardly when he pushes me back and insists on setting the alarm himself. I exit the front door first, halting so fast, he has to put his hands on my arms to stop himself knocking me flat on my face.

"What the—?"

"Stay here," he commands, stepping forward. His head turns left and right as he clearly searches for anyone hanging around. Only when the coast is clear does he step closer to my car, the vehicle that's now resting on four wheel rims, slashes clearly visible in each of the tyres.

My first thought is the cost of replacing them, and anger rushes through me. I don't work all hours to buy unneeded tyres. Then I feel fear. Someone came to my house armed with a knife.

I stand, staring, then notice Noah carefully inspecting his bike. "Have they damaged it?" At least his tyres look fine to me.

"I don't know. It's strange your car was disabled, but my bike untouched. I'm checking it out in case they cut the brake hose or something."

Suddenly I'm very glad he's taking the time to do that. I leave him be while I wonder what I'm going to do now. Call out rescue to tow my car? Buy tyres first, then get them to fit them? I'm at a loss, never before having to replace four at once. My mind is all over the place and rambling as I try to find an option that will cost the least money.

After a couple of minutes, Noah comes back. "Bike looks okay." He glances down and wipes a tear from my eye, a tear I didn't know had escaped. "Gwen, babe, don't worry. I'll get your car sorted out." He turns and glares at the offending vehicle for a moment, then turns back. "Seems your stalker has struck again."

"I'd rather have your stalker than mine," I respond, glumly. "You get presents, I get hurt and my car vandalised."

"And I get random phone calls," he corrects, then grimaces. "But you're right, you're getting the worst of it. But, this could be good news."

"What?" I gaze at him, perplexed. *How the hell could it be good*?

He nods toward the house. "You've got security cameras now. Have you forgotten? We might be able to identify the motherfucker at last."

I suppose that is a positive. I'd love to discover who the asshole is who's fucking with my life and put a stop to it.

"Come on, I've got to get back."

Suddenly I know I'll have to let him go alone. "I have to stay here. I have to sort this mess out. I'll need my car on Monday."

His face darkens. "Leave you here when that bastard could still be around? No fuckin' way." He shakes his head. "I don't like that he disabled your car. Maybe that's exactly what he wants." Tugging thoughtfully at his beard he adds, "Bikers don't take women on their bikes, not unless they're serious about them. If he knows that, then he could assume I'll go, leaving you here on your own. So you're coming with, no question. As for your car, already told you. Leave that to me."

That makes a chilling kind of sense. I shiver, and wrap my arms around myself, as something occurs to me. "Could he be behind your mom summoning you back? Making it so you had to leave?"

He nods. "I was wondering about that. Come on, the sooner we go, the sooner we'll find out what's got her panties in a twist. And get Mouse reviewing the tapes. Think of this, it sucks about your car, but that can be fixed. Today, he might have slipped up and brought us one step further to identifying him."

I'd rather be with Noah. *Someone came to my house and vandalised my car.* Once again, whoever it is has made me a victim. I hate that. And, maybe, I could do with some time in a different place to regroup my feelings.

Noah takes time telling me all the stuff I need to know about being a passenger on his bike. There seems so much to remember and I get worried I won't be able to lean when he does, preferring to keep myself upright and not risk overbalancing the bike. I'm biting my lip as I sit behind him, already holding fast to his waist.

My hands tighten as he moves off, and I'm just about terrified as he accelerates up the street. But when we hit the first corner I find the bike's momentum makes it easy for me to follow his lead, almost without thinking, shifting my body slightly to lean the same way he does. When we get to the edge of the city, I realise I'm enjoying myself.

My death grip relaxes slightly, not too much, but instead of being tense with fear, I start to relish the freedom that being on a bike gives, and start understanding why he prefers this mode of transport to being in a car.

My focus on the ride helps puts slashed tyres to the back of my mind, rather than it consuming all my thinking.

In the end, the journey's far too short, firstly, because I'm starting to love it and secondly, because as we draw nearer to the compound, I feel Noah tensing. I've no idea what I might be walking into, or what usually fuels his family tensions. I'm not looking forward to intruding on a family row.

Noah zooms through the gates which open automatically for

his bike, then slows as he navigates the track up to the club-house. Once there, he stops, and taps at my leg. Remembering his instruction, I put my hand on his shoulder and get off. Then he expertly backs the bike into what is probably his normal parking spot.

Once he gets off, he puts his arm around me. "We'll stop here for a moment, then go up to the house."

Fine by me, the longer we can put any confrontation off, the better. As we approach the door, Noah doesn't remove his hand, and when we step inside, he tugs at my waist, making me curl against him. *He's making a statement.* I can only hope it's going to be well received.

I'm not stupid, due to his reputation I expected people to be shocked, and knowing how men can be, jokes about how he's been caught at last. But what I didn't expect was for the crowded room to go completely silent, well, except for the crying of a baby that is.

Noah stiffens slightly, but unperturbed, calls out, "Blade? Do me a favour, will you? Some asshole sliced the tyres on Gwen's car. Can you get a couple of prospects to go to her house and replace them?"

That my problem was the first thing on his mind stuns me and also perturbs me. At any other time I'd have objected and offered to pay, but the atmosphere is disconcerting. I notice one or two men looking at me with what can only be described as pity. *Do they think Noah's such a bad bet?* I start to wonder what I've stepped into.

"Prez." Noah nods respectfully as Wizard approaches. "Could you or Mouse look at the security footage from Gwen's house and see if we've got enough to make an identification?"

Wizard looks distracted, and he's another who casts me a compassionate look. "Sure, Throttle. Leave it with us. Look, you better get yourself up to Peg's house."

Glancing up at Noah I see unease on his face. "Is it bad, Prez?"

Wizard doesn't seem to know what to say, and his next words are unexpected. "Leave Gwen with us. We'll look after her."

I don't want to be left with people I barely know, though if this is private between Noah and his parents, I'll make the best of it. But in response Noah's arm tightens around me.

"Gwen and I are together. You better get used to that now. Where I go, she does."

"Throttle—" Blade calls out.

But Noah ignores him. "Come on, Gwen. Let's go face the music." He tosses a glare at the men in the room and leads me out.

Disturbed by the reception I'd just received, I stay quiet as we walk up the compound, holding back the automatic reflex to ask what he thinks is up when he clearly has no idea. When we reach the top, he turns toward his family's house, takes a tight hold on my hand and breathes in deeply. I do likewise, having a feeling I really shouldn't be here.

It's a family matter. What do I know about them?

After his fortifying breath, he strides up the path and opens the door.

His grip on my hand means I'm forced to be at his side when we enter the living room. Immediately I'm faced with two people I expect, and one individual that I certainly don't. My eyes narrow as I take a second glance, then recognise the woman who spilt the drink over me when I was having lunch with Lisa. She had dark hair then, but now back to her original blonde, it clicks where I've seen her before. *The Wheel Inn.*

Why the hell is she here?

Darcy and Peg stand together, presenting a united front when we appear. I anticipate a welcoming smile from Noah's mom at least, maybe a friendly, 'how are you feeling now', but instead I'm greeted with a frown, making me swallow my own prepared greeting down.

A growl, not unlike the sound I've heard Noah make, comes

from the mouth of his dad, and fury fills his eyes. Lisa, my friend, is nowhere to be seen.

"What the fuck are *you* doing here?" Noah snarls. Ignoring his mom and dad, he approaches the extra individual.

The woman stands her ground, throws me a smirk, then her expression changes to one of innocence and hurt. "Throttle, I've been trying to find you." Her voice is breathy, almost like a child's.

"I can't think of one good fuckin' reason why," Noah counters with a look of disgust. "And why the fuck are you here with my parents?"

"I'm fuckin' disappointed in you, Throttle," Peg states, glaring down at our joined hands. His look is so fierce it makes me want to yank mine back, but Noah just squeezes tighter.

Noah's face creases and he looks confused. "What the fuck you talking about, Dad? What do you think I've done?" He sneers at the woman. "Whatever she says, she's no business being here." Through our joined fingers I feel him vibrating with anger.

"Oh, Noah." Darcy seems close to tears. "Hattie's been searching for you. She needs to speak to you. She's…" Her voice trails off as if she can't give words to whatever the person, who I know now is called Hattie, is after.

Noah's rage increases. "Will someone tell me what the fuck's going on?" He drops my hand and stalks toward Hattie. "You, for a fuckin' start."

Hattie widens her eyes and stares at him. She bats her eyelids, places a hand on her stomach, and without giving us time to prepare ourselves, she utters those fateful words. "I'm pregnant, and before you ask, it's yours."

Bile rises in my throat and I cover my hand with my mouth, then I turn and stagger to the door, wrench it open and run into the open air. I bend, with my hands on my knees, trying to get air into my lungs. This morning I woke with Noah giving me the world, hope like I'd never had before. Two words and every-thing's been snatched away out of my grasp.

"Gwen!"

When Noah shouts after me, I straighten and start to run, but my legs are no match for his, he easily catches up.

He wrenches me around to face him. Sounding out of breath, he snarls, "She's lying, Gwen. She fuckin' has to be."

"You fucked her?" Only a negative answer would give me hope.

He doesn't try to lie to me. "Yeah, but I used a fuckin' condom. I never forget. Ever."

Surely, he must know they're not one hundred percent reli-able? *He used them with me. Could I be at risk?* "I can't, Noah," I cry out. "I can't right now." If Hattie is telling the truth, he's got obligations made with her, before any promises he made to me. I gesture back toward the house. "You've clearly got things to talk about. I'm going home."

"She's right, Throttle." Another man appears as though he's been waiting for us to appear. He's older, more Peg's age I notice. "I'll get Gwen home. You've got shit to sort out."

"You know, Wraith?" Noah asks, his eyes creased.

"Yeah, I heard," Wraith replies.

Noah looks at me, he raises his hand to caress my face, but I step back. I feel like I've been physically struck. I'm shocked, hurt, sad and angry all at the same time. He sends me a pleading look, I turn away.

"Wraith, I..." Noah's words trail off. He swears under his breath, kicks a stone, then turns me to face him again. "Gwen, Wraith will take you home and make sure you're safe. I... I've got to sort this shit out. I'll come see you later."

It's on the tip of my tongue to tell him not to bother, but I want more than anything to hear that this is a lie. That that woman in the house behind isn't carrying his child. I don't agree, nor suggest I won't see him. Truthfully, I don't know what my uttermost emotion is right now.

Noah hesitates, his hand hovers in the air, then lowering it without touching me, without his gorgeous lips lowering to my mouth, he swings on his heels and strides off.

"Gwen? I'm Wraith." The other man stares at me for a moment as though assessing how I'm taking what's just occurred, then confides, "I've got four daughters. I know that doesn't negate that I'm a man and don't understand anything, but I do know I'd want someone watching out for them if they were hurting. You can trust me."

I'd trust anyone who can get me out of here, and especially if they can do so without me having to face anyone else. *They knew. Down at the clubhouse. Those looks start to make sense.* "You'll take me home?"

"I'll take you wherever you fuckin' want to go. Your house, a friend's? Just give me directions."

There's nowhere and no one else. I just want off the compound and back to where I can lick my wounds in private.

"Okay," I sob, only now aware that I'm crying, and that traitorous tears are running down my cheeks.

"Come on, then."

Without turning to look back at Noah's house, I match my step to that of Wraith's and try to harden my heart. If a baby's coming along, Noah's got other priorities and a woman to take care of, and that woman isn't me.

CHAPTER TWENTY-THREE

hrottle…

I hesitate before pushing open the front door, turning to watch Gwen walk away from me. I can't blame her. We're too fuckin' new to have built a bond strong enough to overcome obstacles put in our way. Who the fuck am I kidding? Even if we'd been together awhile, being faced with a woman who claims to be the mother of my baby must have been one hell of a shock. As it had been to me.

Focused up to now on how Gwen was reacting, I hadn't stopped to think about myself. I'd driven here with such high expectations. My parents should have been delighted I've found a woman I wanted to make a go with, instead, as it turns out, it was the worst possible timing to bring her home. *Fuckin' Hattie.*

She's lying. She has to be.

At least Wraith is with Gwen, I trust him completely. He's a dad to four girls, and will know what she needs. He'll also know to make sure she's safe to be left alone.

Will she ever forgive me? It's one thing to know I've fucked around, another to have it thrown right into her face. There's no baby, I'm certain of that. I've always been so fucking careful.

Hattie must be lying to get her claws into me. Well her ploy won't work, more than that, she'll learn not to fuck with me.

Why has it all gone to shit? Gwen's already worried I wouldn't be faithful, but to be confronted by one of my conquests must have brought her fears too close to home.

I hate myself, I hate my parents for not saying something to warn me—if they had, Gwen wouldn't have been with me. Most of all I hate Hattie. If there's a kid… No, I don't even want to think about it. Sharing parenting with a bitch like Hattie? I can't even consider it. *I was careful. There's no fucking way.*

Maybe she'll get rid of it when she sees she can't blackmail me. If it even exists that is.

When Gwen disappears out of sight, without a backward glance I notice, I take a deep breath and return to the house. This time, when I step over the threshold, my parents aren't waiting for me. In the living room there's just one person, Hattie.

She stares at me haughtily. "There's no more you and her," she states adamantly.

I see red. Moving fast, I approach her, taking hold of her arms and holding her firmly. "You don't get to say what I can and can't do, you can't dictate to me. You hearing me?"

"Throttle—"

"Get this into your fuckin' head, Hattie. Whether or not you're having my baby, I want nothing to do with you."

Her lower lip trembles. "But—"

"I don't believe you, Hattie. You'll try anything to get back with me. You come to my mom of all people with a fuckin' fairy tale—"

"I *am* pregnant," she cries out.

"Then you'll take a damn test in front of me to prove it. Better still, we'll go to a doctor together."

A sly look comes over her face. "I'll do that. I'll do anything you want, Throt…" Breaking off, she smiles sweetly, and corrects, "Noah."

It sounds so wrong coming out of her mouth. "You don't get to call me that. Only family uses it."

The sweet act disappears. "It was what *she* called you," she sneers.

"She's special to me. You're not," I throw back. "And if you are pregnant, I want proof of paternity." Surely my swimmers have more self-respect than to fertilise anything via her cunt.

She grins, it looks sneaky. "Sure we can. But I don't want to harm the baby. After it's born, we'll do the test. But Throttle, you are the father. I know you are."

She can only just be pregnant. I do not want to wait for eight months. I'll have to find out where I stand. Of course, I wouldn't risk harming a kid, but that feels too fucking long to wait to me.

She'd agreed fast to go to the doctor. The realisation chills me. If she wasn't pregnant, she'd have come up with an excuse for that too. For the first time, I wonder if she's telling the truth. I turn away, forcing myself to think of the outcome if she is, and what would be expected of me.

My tone is still harsh when I turn back. "*If* you are pregnant, *if* the baby's mine, I'll give you money." Hell, I might even step up as a dad though I've no current desire to do so. Looking at Hattie, I might need to consider stepping in and demanding full parenting rights. How could I leave a child of my blood with someone like her? She was alright to fuck, but as a mother? Suddenly I regret the choices I'd made in the past. What attracted my dick certainly wasn't what I wanted in a partner. "Yeah, I'll give you enough to support the kid, but there will never be anything between us. I'm with Gwen now."

"Don't say that, Throttle," she cries out, putting a hand on my cut, but I brush it off. Undeterred, she touches my arm instead. "We're going to be parents. If we give it a chance, we could be good together."

I step away, brushing the leather as though to get any trace of her off. "Get this into your head, Hattie. One fuck, that's all we had. And that wasn't enough to tempt me back. There's no you and me. If that's what you're after, you can forget that."

"I'll get rid of the kid." She says it as a threat, much in the way a player would throw down a winning card.

"Please do," I toss back. "I want none of it." I suppress the thought it's not just any kid she's talking about, but something made of my flesh and blood. Or, at least, my semen. Shouldn't it have a chance of life? But whatever my feelings, it's her body. It's her who's got to carry it for nine months. "If you want to handle it, I'll give you money." Whether it's mine or not, I can do that. It would be worth it to get her off my back.

"You want me to kill it?" she screeches.

"For fuck's sake, I didn't say that." Turning my back I start to pace. "You throw this on me and expect me to deal with it?" Especially after the night and morning I've just spent with Gwen. When I thought I'd got my future sorted, she turns up and fucks it up. "I need time to think, Hattie."

Again her lip trembles. "This is as much as shock to me as it is to you. Do you think I wanted this?"

I don't know what to think. All I know if I stay close to her that I'm in danger of really losing my temper. All I can focus on is the devastation in Gwen's eyes and the possible loss of a chance of a relationship with her.

She gentles her voice. "We can make this work, Throttle. We can both step up and be a family."

"For fuck's sake!" I roar. "That's never going to happen, Hattie. I can barely stand to look at you, let alone play happy families."

"My cunt was good enough for you," she shouts back.

"That's all it was, which I made clear."

She's breathing heavily and her face has gone red. *Is that bad for the baby?* My thoughts pull me up. Making an effort, I gentle my tone. "Give me some time to think about this, Hattie."

"We should talk everything through together."

My fists clench. "That's not going to happen. You spring this on me with no warning. You tell my fuckin' parents before you speak to me. You have me brought back like a naughty child... How the hell did you think I was going to react? Give. Me. Time, Hattie. I can't deal otherwise."

If it was Gwen telling me she was pregnant I wouldn't be behaving this way, but this woman in front of me? I hate her for putting me in this predicament. It's not like I don't know I'm equally responsible, I am. I'm also determined, if I have to, I'll step up to the plate. But it doesn't mean I automatically have to like the mother of my baby. Fact is, I don't. I hate the situation, and I hate her. There's something that warns me she's not being straight with me. I won't believe her until I see evidence of the pregnancy.

I think I'm getting through to her. She walks to the table where there's a purse lying on it, as she picks it up I deduce it's hers. She takes out her phone. "Give me your details, Throttle. Your full name, cell—I take it," she glances around with disdain, "that the compound is your address."

"Why the fuck do you want that?" I don't want to give her anything. My child, yeah, that can have everything, but her? No. If she'd had one shred of decency, she'd have come to me without involving anyone else. Now it's clear why the clubhouse went quiet when I walked in, and why they'd suggested me leaving Gwen there. I should have listened to them. They already knew what we'd be walking into.

"For a start to let you know when I make a doctor's appointment. And, so I can start suing for support." She grins nastily. "I understand your little *girlfriend* works in family law. Maybe I should go to her firm?"

If she wasn't a woman, if she wasn't possibly pregnant, she'd be flat on the floor right now. But all I can do is snarl, "Don't you fuckin' dare. You don't want to cross me, Hattie." My expression, my rage, makes her take a step back. "You're going to stay well away from her."

"Will you?" she bravely throws back. "Can I trust you to leave her alone?"

"Why the fuck should I?"

"Because you owe it to me. And your child."

I see red. I launch forward, she takes a step back. Luckily I stop, knowing I'd hate myself if I hurt her, but she's pushing all my buttons. "Get out of here, Hattie. I don't trust myself right now. And I don't trust you. I don't believe a word that you say. Get out. Contact me when you've made that fuckin' appointment and I'll be there. If you're not fuckin' pregnant you better keep running. If I catch up with you, I won't promise I'll be able to control myself. You've cost me *everything* by coming here." By the time I finish, my fists are clenched, my jaw is tight and if there was steam coming out of the top of my head, I wouldn't be the least surprised.

She opens her mouth, but sensibly shuts it again. Hoisting her purse onto her shoulder she holds herself straight. With one last considering look toward me, she turns and steps away.

Just as she reaches the door, I throw out, "It's Noah Rinter." I take a business card out of my wallet. "And my contact details are on here." Not wanting to go near her, I toss it in her direction.

She bends, picks it up, then smirks as she slips it into her purse. "You'll be hearing from me."

When the door closes behind her, I sink to the floor and place my head in my hands. It's as though she's taken my rage with her, all I feel now is regret. *Christ. What a fucking mess.*

It shouldn't surprise me that I'm not long alone. A door opening and the sound of boots on the wooden floor is followed by a deep voice.

"I never thought I'd be so fuckin' disappointed in you, Son."

I swipe my hands over my face, surprised to find my eyes wet as they move over my eyes. I look up at him blearily. "You told me to find my one, so I have. I brought her to meet you. Only to find—"

"One of your fuckin' mistakes caught up with you. *This* is what you get for fuckin' around."

But hundreds of other men get away with it, including most of the single men on this compound. Just because Peg was more discerning, I've done nothing to feel guilty about. I didn't knowingly do anything wrong, *Except sink my dick in one of the worst places.* For that, I've received a life sentence.

"That's not fair." I get to my feet. "I told that bitch exactly how things were going to go down. I took fuckin' precautions. I always use a condom, Dad."

"Condoms don't work all the time," a more reasonable voice breaks in. Well, to be accurate, a touch more equitable, but it didn't need to be much to be less censoring than that of my dad's.

"Mom." I wince at the condemnation in her eyes. "It was *one* night. *She* came on to me. Sure, I didn't say no. But I never went back. One fuckin' night. Since then she's been trying to get me to go back again. For all I know, this is a ploy and she's going to magically 'miscarry'." I indicate I'm stressing the last word with inverted commas.

Darcy gasps and flicks her eyes towards Peg, but he carries on regardless.

"You should know the risks, Noah. If you're not prepared to step up and face the consequences, you should never have got your dick wet." Peg pauses for that to sink in, then considers my words. "You think it's a trap?"

I glare at him. "I don't trust her. So yeah, I think she's trying to get her hooks into me."

Peg stomps across the room and collapses into his favourite chair, making it groan under his weight. His eyes stare at me accusingly. "If you didn't think she could be trusted, why the fuck did you go there? As to her lying, I think you're kidding yourself. The chances are that she's pregnant and that you're the father. Son, not wanting it to be true doesn't make it false. What I want to know, is what the fuck are you going to do?"

I'm a grown man. I don't need to cower in front of my dad. Inserting as much strength as I can into my voice, I tell him what I'd just told her. "If she is, I'll do what I have to. I'll support her financially if she wants to go ahead and give birth, during the pregnancy and until the kid's eighteen. I know my responsibilities, Dad. But I won't be with her. She and I? It would be a fuckin' disaster in the making. I'm not even sure she's cut out to be a mother."

"She could change," Mom puts in. "People do when they have to. But what will you do if she proves she's not?"

Why are they asking me all this now? I don't have a clue. I grab at the first thing that comes into my mind, with no idea how I would make it work. "Step up and take in my kid I suppose. *If* it's mine."

"You made your bed, you should lie in it." Peg won't give up. "You owe it to her to try. It's not only her fault she's pregnant. If you'd kept your dick in your pants, none of this would have happened."

"I'm not a fuckin' monk," I snarl.

"Some of us didn't need to fuck around." Dad keeps up. "Before your mom, if I went with a woman it was someone I was hoping could be a possible mate for life."

"Well that's great for you!" I'm furious. "Most of the club members used to fuck around, the single men still do. We have sweet butts for that very purpose."

"Calm down, Noah," Mom says, sharply. "We only want what's best for you."

"It doesn't fuckin' sound like it."

"That baby the girl's carrying is our grandchild. Don't we get any say in this too?"

"Butt out of my life, *Dad*." I throw up my hands and scowl. "I'm off, there's no speaking to you."

"Noah." Mom comes running and puts her arm arms around me. "It was a shock to us too. You'd convinced us you were never settling down, now on the same day you bring a girlfriend to meet us, a pregnant woman turns up."

I let out a deep sigh. "I suspect she's an ex-girlfriend now."

"Your first priority is to the mother of your child." Mom pauses, and adds, "Before you speak to Gwen, you've got to work out what you're going to do."

There's only one answer to give. "I don't want Hattie, I want Gwen, Mom."

"You think Gwen can get over your manwhore ways?" Peg puts in, unhelpfully in my view as that's exactly what I'm worried about.

Ignoring him, I concentrate on my mom. "I just need to clear my head. Right now, I need to go speak to Gwen." To see if there's any way I can mend the damage that's been done.

Mom shakes her head. "Noah, this is your problem, and it's on you. It's been a shock to everyone. If you've doubts, maybe you should wait until you have proof Hattie's pregnant. Having a kid is a hell of a responsibility. You might decide staying with Hattie is the right thing to do. I'm sure Gwen will give you some space. You and her, you're very new."

"I don't see you've got a choice," Peg states. "I brought you up to take responsibility for your actions. You get a girl in a mess, it's down to you."

I've got to go before I say something I really regret. Nothing he says would make me start any relationship with Hattie. I can't believe it's the right thing to do.

Hell, maybe I was right to steer clear of relationships. If only I could have stayed away from fucking too.

CHAPTER TWENTY-FOUR

---

*G*wen…

This morning I left my house full of excitement and happiness. Now I'm returning devastated believing I've lost something precious.

Passed around from one foster parent to another, I should have known better than to get my hopes up. Each time, or at least early on, I'd been optimistic that someone would recognise my difficult behaviour as being a cry for help. That this home would be the one where I'd be treated as and made to feel part of the family. Eventually the Pollyanna inside me had given up. The universe wasn't inclined to be kind to me.

I thought I could ignore Noah's sexual exploits before we'd gotten together, had convinced myself what was important was what happened from hereon. I never imagined his recent past could have such shattering ramifications on our fledgling relationship.

One of his conquests is expecting a baby. He's going to have a child, and with another woman. *With Hattie for fuck's sake.* The very same woman I have good reasons to think is a bitch.

Will he want to make a go of it for the baby's sake? Will he feel compelled to stick by her side?

I'm hurting, and more than that, angry. Internally I'm ranting and raging, even though I know it's not entirely fair. Noah hadn't known what he was taking me into. There's no doubt it had been as much of a shock for him as it had been for me, but I still blame him for pulling me into this predicament.

When Wraith pulls up outside my home which suddenly feels empty, I exit the car and walk to the front door. With trembling hands I try to get the key into the lock, but the biker takes it from me and opens the door himself. It's only on the fringe of my consciousness that I register, just like Noah, he seems to know the code to turn off the alarm. It should bother me, but it doesn't. measured against everything else, it's insignificant.

I expect him to leave having done his duty, but he doesn't.

"Sit down, Gwen. You want me to fix you a drink or something?"

I sit only because my legs threaten not to support me, and as for the rest of his statement, the only thing I want is Noah. So deep in my misery I can't even summon indignation as Wraith makes himself at home, settling on the seat opposite me.

I wish he would go. I want to dissolve into a heap of misery and let the tears flow, him being here prevents me.

"Gwen, can I tell you a little about me?"

I say neither yes nor no, nor give any indication. I'm not even vaguely interested in a man I don't know and who's probably three decades older.

He takes my silence for acquiescence, leans forward clasping his hands together between his thighs and begins to speak. "I was like Throttle many moons ago. I fucked every woman who'd consent to be with me without any promise of a relationship. I never believed I'd find the one woman who could tame me." He chuckles at himself. "I didn't want to be tied down and certainly didn't think I was missing anything."

Glancing up he checks to see if I'm listening, then continues anyway, "Back in those days there were only a few men in the club with old ladies. I'd look at Heart, saddled with a wife and child and rather than feeling envious, I pitied him. How could he be content to never again know a pussy that didn't belong to his wife?" He shakes his head slowly. "Boy, it's hard now to believe I ever thought that way."

I stay quiet, just wishing he'd give up and go.

Undeterred by my lack of reaction, he carries on, "All that changed when a cute, at the time, wheelchair bound English-woman came into my life." Once more his low chuckle rumbles. "Sophie was a fish out of water when she arrived on the compound, completely overwhelmed by the biker lifestyle. She and I should never have been a match, but as soon as I saw her, I wanted her. It took me more than a moment to convince her, but in the end, thank fuck, I did. I'd found my one, and from that moment on, wanted no one else."

He's described himself as a manwhore, just like Noah. Is he suggesting redemption is possible? My interest caught, brazenly I ask, "And did you stay with her? Were you faithful?"

"Fuck yes. Once Sophie was mine. I never looked at another." He looks up and meets my eye. "Men like us, Gwen, well, we live fast and on the edge, just riding a motorcycle carries an element of danger. Free and easy sex is part and parcel of our lifestyle, hell, we even have women who live on the compound free in exchange to cater to the sexual needs of brothers who want to use them." That statement does not make me feel better, but he's not finished. "We don't do things by halves, and it seems, when we find the other part of our soul, we're one hundred percent all-in. I have never stepped out on Sophie, and never will. I've never entertained the idea, from the time we got together, she's been all that I want."

I snap, "Fine. It worked for you. But you hadn't gotten anyone pregnant."

He scoffs. "As luck would have it, I didn't. But I could have. Throttle would have used a condom, he wouldn't forget. It's not only pregnancy, there are other risks when you fuck anything that takes your fancy. I've no doubt he took the precautions he could, but unfortunately he lost the lottery. He's been caught in the small two-per-cent. It could have happened to me, or to any of us."

Warring between misery and anger, I can't let the latter comment go. Which makes me retort, "Noah didn't hide that he'd been fuckin' around, hell, his own sister told me. But it's different accepting that on an intellectual level and having it thrown in your face. Are you asking me to forgive him, because I don't think I can. I feel like I've been slapped."

Wraith sighs. "You're going to punish him for something he had no control over?"

My cheeks grow red. "This isn't like accidentally breaking a precious ornament. This is a *baby*, Wraith. If he's half the man I thought he was. he'll step up and take responsibility. This mistake will have implications for the rest of his, and its, life."

"You don't think you could share him, even with his child?"

"No." It's an honest response. I bite my lip as I try to put my thoughts into words. "Were he a single dad already with a baby, I'd think long and hard about taking on a kid, but if I loved him, I'd love his child. But the thought of him having dealings with another woman, being there for the pregnancy and being tied to her for at least eighteen years? That's what I can't handle. Especially as it's *her*."

"You know Hattie?" he asks, sharply.

"I wouldn't say I know her, but I've seen her. What I do know from what I've seen, she won't settle for part of Noah, she wants all of him. She's a bitch."

His eyes narrow. "What exactly do you know of her?"

I shrug. "Seeing her brought it into focus. She's been at the Wheel Inn a couple of times. She complained I was working when my face looked awful after being beaten up. Then, last week she tipped a drink over me when I was having lunch. I thought at the time it was an accident, now…?"

"Throttle said you didn't know who it was."

"At the time I was more concerned with being drenched with

icy cold cola that stained my clothes. I thought I knew her, but couldn't place her out of context, and she must have been wearing a wig. She'd had dark hair, not blonde." I cast my mind back. "She said the right words, but didn't seem particularly contrite. So," I finish, "that's how I know she's a bitch. I also would have to be blind not to know she hates me. Co-parenting would be a disaster. You think she'd ever trust me with her child? She'd make Noah's life difficult, and that would put a strain on our relationship." The truth of my own words hits me. "Noah and I wouldn't work out, there'd be too much coming between us."

Wraith grimaces. "So you don't have feelings for him. I'm sorry, I thought you did."

Immediately I deny his assumption. "I do, well, I was falling hard for him. But it's best to stop this now." Unsummoned, a sob escapes me.

"If you're his one, giving up on him will destroy him." Wraith's voice drips with concern. "If Sophie had turned me down, I'd never have gone looking again. She's the only woman I ever wanted, and I'm certain I'd never have found anyone else. If you are that for Noah, you're condemning him to a long, lonely existence."

"What if I don't believe there's only one person for us in this world?" I spit out. "And if that's true, what about me? What if I can't move on?"

"So stay, fight for him. Stand up for your man and be beside him." He makes it seem so simple.

"But what if he wants to be with her?" I wail. Given the choice, wouldn't he want to be with the mother of his child?

"He doesn't and he won't." Wraith scoffs. "Believe me. Throttle has never walked hand in hand into the clubhouse with another woman. Fuck, he's never brought anyone else onto the compound. It shocked the hell out of all of us when he came in with you. He never brought *her*, and I doubt he'd ever intended to."

But he's missing something. "He's a good man, Wraith. What if he thinks of the best for his child and makes a go of it with her?"

"I doubt he'd do that. He's got a good head on his shoulders. He'll know, unless there's a foundation for a relationship to build on, then it would be doomed from the start."

I wipe a tear away and then need to do it again. As more start falling freely, I take a tissue from the box that luckily is close by me. "Who's to say there isn't some feeling between them that could be built on? Hattie seems to think there is."

I'm tired, exhausted. All I want to do is fall back on my original plan to curl up and cry. I appreciate what Wraith is doing, but I need to work things out in my head. Sure, the older man is putting himself in Noah's shoes, but who's to say the two men are the same?

"I want to be alone."

Wraith gazes at me intently, then he sighs. "The prospects sorted out your car while all this was going down. I'll go, Gwen, but a prospect will remain outside looking out for you." As I go to protest, he reminds me, "Someone came to your house today and slit your tyres. We still don't know who or why, and until we catch the bastard responsible, then the club will have eyes on you."

I want to tell them I don't want any reminder of Noah and am even thinking of quitting my job at the Wheel Inn. But he's right, today or last night, someone damaged my car. I could insist I can look after myself, I know self-defence. But he'd only remind me, last time I was caught unawares and had gotten hurt despite that.

I'd felt safe with Noah, but now, once again, I'm on my own. I'd be a fool to turn their help down.

Wraith gets up, comes over and rests his hand briefly on my shoulder, then goes toward the door, turning with just one last instruction, "Set the alarm after I go."

His words don't register, just the fact that now, at last, he's gone. I wait only until the door closes behind him before sinking to the floor and letting out an agonised wail.

I've been on my own since I was six years old and thought I'd learned to live with it. For a brief moment, hope of a bright future was dangled in front of me. Now it's been ripped away, and I can't summon my accustomed resilience.

I cry until I've no more tears left to weep, then I lie hiccupping. My eyes feel sore and my throat raw.

It's too much for one woman to cope with. First the man I was starting to love has been stolen away, and secondly there's someone stalking me for some unknown reason. Visions come into my head to taunt me, *Noah might be comforting Hattie right now. Making plans which don't include me.*

Why me? I rage at the universe, *why me?*

Hours pass before I get the energy to move, and then it's only to take myself to my bedroom where my sheets smell of Noah. Apparently I'm not completely drained as my tears start again.

I can't sleep here, not with his scent to remind me. I strip the bed, and force myself to put fresh sheets on. Then regret that I'm removing all signs of Noah from my house, while trying to convince myself it's for the best. He was mine only fleetingly, I have to get used to the idea.

He might come back. He said he'd come around. But it's been hours and there's no sign of him.

Hattie wants him, and she's carrying his baby. If he comes back, I should force him to be with her. I know what it was like to be brought up without parents, and I wouldn't wish that on any child. The one innocent in all this is the baby they made, and its happiness takes precedence.

It's still early evening but I've worn myself out. I'm not hungry, so I crawl into bed and will oblivion to take me away. It doesn't, of course. My mind keeps whirling, thoughts of 'what might have been' intent on circling around.

Giving up on sleep that won't come, I pull my tablet toward me.

CHAPTER TWENTY-FIVE

Throttle…

Leaving my parents, I go to my suite and take out the bottle of whisky I keep there. I pour a shot and down it, then a second goes the same way. If ever I needed a drink, this time is it.

Fuck. Fuck. Fuck.

How in the space of only a few hours could I go from feeling the happiest man in the world who finally has his shit sorted, to having my future come crashing down around me?

It takes two to make a baby, I know that. I'd put my faith in condoms, and I'd been wrong. Hattie hadn't pressured me to go bare or use one that she'd provided, I'd used my own for fuck's sake, no blame can attach to her.

But if an accident was waiting to be made, why the fuck did it have to happen with Hattie? I don't even like her. She'd been available, and I'd taken her up on her offer. I hadn't gone with her for her wit or her conversation, in fact we hadn't exchanged more than a few words.

She's a victim too.

She is, but she didn't seem particularly unhappy. She seemed to assume I'd step up and immediately start playing happy families. But I couldn't live a lie just to please her.

I've disappointed my mom and my dad, hell, even myself. As for Gwen... I groan, throw myself on my bed and put my arm over my eyes. *Where the fuck do I go from here?*

On one hand it sounds easy. Go to Gwen, talk to her, like I'd promised. Tell her that nothing has changed.

But it has, and significantly. Before Gwen I never wanted kids of my own, it's been less than twenty-four hours since I ever envisaged having a child, and only then if it was with her. Now, if Hattie's telling the truth, I'm going to be a dad long before I'm ready, and with the last woman on earth with whom I'd want to father a kid.

It's not hard to see Hattie wants me to herself. I don't think I've yet convinced her that's never going to happen. The signs I've already seen warn me she'll be vindictive, and that will include toward any other women in my life.

How could I drag Gwen into this and not turn my back on my child?

I make good money, but supporting a kid will take a hefty chunk of what should have been ours. Time when we should be building our relationship will be stolen because of the hours, days, weeks, months and years we'd have to dedicate to a child. Would Gwen resent that? Or what if, as I suspect, Gwen opened her heart to a baby, would Hattie try to penalise us by restricting access?

Hattie already wants Gwen out of my life. More than that, she wants to punish her. Why else would she have taunted me by threatening to take a paternity case to the company Gwen works for? Only a true bitch would think of throwing that in the face of another woman. Which makes me wonder, how the fuck does she know where Gwen works?

I still, then realise I'm looking for conspiracies where there probably aren't any. Hattie's been to the Wheel Inn, and may have overheard Gwen and Tash chatting. What Gwen does is hardly a state secret.

But it still remains she'll do what she can to drive a wedge between Gwen and me. Nothing about Hattie makes me think she'd play fair.

While I don't see myself as good father material, I could never allow a child to suffer. If Hattie proved an unfit mother, then I'd seek custody for my son or daughter and do my fucking best to step up to the role. Which would mean, if Gwen and I were together, she'd end up mothering another woman's child. How the hell could I ask her to do that?

From whichever direction I try to come at it, I realise there's no easy way out of the trouble that's coming my way, and no way on earth I can stop it.

Hattie might not be pregnant.

I can hang onto that. Maybe if it's a false alarm or an outright lie, then things can go back to normal. But my manwhore ways have now been thrown in the face of a woman with whom I was already skating on thin ice, and who has doubts about my ability to be faithful. Could we ever get over that?

Maybe if our relationship wasn't so new, I'd have more of a basis on which to work. Our tentative declarations—*fuck, was it only a few hours ago?*—when we both professed to being on the brink of, on my part at least, falling in love are too new to provide strength in our relationship.

I can't expect her to stay in the mess that's become of my life.

I eye the whisky, but know getting drunk is no answer. I lie on my bed thinking of Hawk and Wizard and the pleasure they'd taken in their women giving birth to their kids, while I'll be dreading the occasion. I wonder how I'll ever be able to look at the child without thinking of it as a costly mistake, while knowing that I must. It's not the kid's fault, it didn't ask to be conceived.

I ask myself whether I've got the strength to stand by the woman I impregnated, not as a partner, but accepting my equal responsibility. Hattie hadn't asked for it either. I begin to regret being so hard on her.

Maybe she was panicked herself, maybe that's why she hadn't waited to tell me in private. I try to put myself in her shoes, alone, scared, and without a man to support her.

I know nothing about her, or whether she's got family to have her back though, my eyes crease as I remember, she does have a brother living in her house. But perhaps he wouldn't be supportive. Maybe calling her a bitch is doing her an injustice. Perhaps I should give her a chance. Not to come into my life, but to just be more understanding. After all, it's her that will have to suffer for nine months.

Christ, what a fucking mess.

A sharp knock comes at my door. I want to be alone, but automatically, I call out, "Yeah, come in."

It's my father.

I sigh deeply. "What?"

"You drinking?" He pointedly lets his eyes rest on the bottle of whisky.

"No." I don't care if he doesn't believe me.

He goes to my desk and pulls out the chair. "I agree with your mom. I think you should cool it with Gwen. You've got too much on your plate to start something with her."

I don't entirely disagree, but it's the last thing I wanted him to say. "I need to talk to her. I need to explain."

"Explain what? You can't keep your dick in your pants and now you've got to live with the consequences?"

Ouch. That hits far too close to home.

Peg eases the leg with his prosthesis over the other. He grimaces slightly as he takes the pressure off his stump.

My eyes narrow. "You due for a new prosthetic?" He needs one refitted every few years, I've lived with him long enough to know.

Dad's accepting of and not apologetic about his disability. "Yeah," he replies, distractedly. "But let's talk about you. Those consequences I've mentioned, well, you've got to consider they might not be what you expect."

"You think I should make a go of it with Hattie?" My eyebrows raise and my lips purse in disgust.

"Honestly?" He rubs his beard and thinks for a moment. "If you take risks and get a woman pregnant, then yes, I'd expect a son of mine to step up, for the kid's sake if nothing else." Now he tugs at his beard, the gesture I seem to have inherited. "She reminds me of someone I never talk about. A period in my life I prefer to forget. A time when I was faced with the same situation as you."

While I can't see how his history could interest me, I gesture for him to carry on.

"When I was a serving Marine, while I wasn't so free with my affections as you are, I did sometimes hook up when I was on leave." His eyes glaze slightly. "Some of the sights I saw, well, it made me hungry for that physical connection. I dated a woman for a couple of weeks, and before I returned to the sand pit, she told me she was pregnant. I married her." I remember now hearing he'd been married long before he met Darcy, but it wasn't something he'd spoken about. I watch as his face darkens. "With the distance between us, I could barely remember her face, and I kind of blew up her character. Those lonely nights away were mitigated by the thought I had a woman waiting for me. I set up a joint bank account and made sure she didn't go wanting. I knew I'd settled because of the circumstances, but was determined to make the best of it."

"You're suggesting I do that?" I swallow, then open my mouth to tell him I just couldn't.

"Shut the fuck up. Only telling you this once." He glares at me. I shut my mouth. "My tour lasted six months. When I got back stateside, she told me she'd miscarried. I did wonder why she left the news until I came back, flummoxed by her flat stomach. But I accepted the excuse that she hadn't wanted to distress me while I was fighting for my country. She was my wife, despite the rocky start to our relationship, I was determined to make her happy. I thought I had, until the next tour came, and I lost my leg. She used that as an excuse to say it would never work between us. While I was in the hospital she cleaned out the bank account." His cheeks go red with anger. "She was never fuckin' pregnant. She'd been fuckin' around all the months we'd been married. Just wanted a Marine/biker on her arm when it suited her, and the lifestyle my money brought her."

"Dad…" My jaw drops. That wasn't what I expected.

"I know I want you to settle down. I always wanted a family of my own, so I can't understand the way you treat women. My first impulse was to think you should lie on the bed that you made and give it a go with the woman you got pregnant, in the same way I'd had to step up." Again he tugs at his beard. "After you walked out earlier, your mom reminded me of things that happened nearly forty years back. I wouldn't want you to get in the same trap."

"That's what worries me. I think she could be lying, Dad."

"And I think you should do nothing until you find out," he confirms. "But Gwen's a complication you don't need, and it's not fair on her. You've got to sort yourself out. Gwen and you are so new. Hell, I didn't even know you were dating."

We weren't. But I'm not going to tell him that.

I'm about to tell him I won't repeat his mistake, I'll find out whether Hattie's really pregnant, if not, she won't see me for dust. Then I was going to instruct him to keep out of mine and Gwen's business, but just as I'm formulating my reply, another knock comes at the door.

Hell, it's like a turnstile in here. "Come in." *Join the party,* I add under my breath.

It's Wraith.

"Peg," he greets his brother politely, then looks to me. "Sorry for interrupting."

Dad starts to get up. "I've had my say."

"No, I think you should hear this." Wraith waves his hand

for Dad to sit back down. Then his eyes come back to me again. "As you know, I took Gwen home."

"How is she?" I hate that I've hurt her.

"Devastated. Shocked. Upset." Wraith doesn't spare me. "Alone."

Alone. *Shit.* I sit up. "She's in danger. I know it."

"Do you think I don't know that? There's a prospect outside her house." Wraith scoffs.

I might have unwittingly fucked up, but Gwen still needs our protection. I raise my chin in thanks.

"She told me something that resonated." When I gesture for him to continue, he does. "That incident where the drink was spilt on her? She's now identified the woman that did it. It was your baby momma. It was Hattie. It didn't register with her immediately as Hattie was wearing a wig."

What the fuck?

I feel like someone's handed me a piece of a puzzle but I don't know where it fits in. "She knows where Gwen works." I raise my eyes to Wraith. "And now I think about it, I've caught a couple of dirty looks Hattie threw at Gwen when she was talking to me at the Wheel Inn."

"She wants you," Peg states. "Could she be behind what's happening to Gwen?"

I frown. "You think she attacked her and slashed her tyres?"

Wraith shakes his head. "A woman scorned and all that? Seems unlikely. But I do think we need to look into her, even if only to rule her out. You fucked her, then walked away, and brother, I'd be a hypocrite to criticise you for that. But is it a stretch of imagination to wonder, if she believed she should have another chance with you, whether that would lead to her wanting to chase any competition away?"

"One thing's fuckin' clear, Son," Peg growls. "You got to find out if she's really pregnant as soon as you fuckin' can. Because if she's been fuckin' with your woman, what better way to chase her off, than to make up a non-existent baby?"

CHAPTER TWENTY-SIX

*T*hrottle…

When Peg and Wraith leave me alone, I sit a little longer trying to bring things into perspective. If Hattie's Gwen's stalker, pregnant or not, she's going to feel my wrath. I might not be able to hurt her as she's carrying my child, but I'll think of some way to punish her.

All this time I've been thinking the attacks on Gwen were rooted in something in her past, now it seems her troubles could have been down to me all the time. The trouble is, I just can't see how Hattie could have got the better of her in the parking lot, let alone hurt her. Gwen's no slouch at self-defence as she'd proved to me earlier.

Dad had advised me to step away, but my gut tells me I should go see Gwen. How can I leave the woman I love crying alone? She might not want to see me, but I need to take that risk. If nothing else so we can talk through things together. That's what partners do, isn't it?

I've been making assumptions of her, maybe she'll be doing that in reverse. It's possible she thinks I'll go to Hattie and be with her.

Or perhaps, she'll turn to that fucker Everest. That can't happen. It's my place to comfort her.

My mind's made up. I take a quick shower and change into a fresh shirt, then stride down to the clubhouse hoping no fucker will try and stop me. But, of course, my advance to my bike is brought to a halt when someone steps in my way.

"Hawk," I growl warningly.

"You going to Gwen?"

"None of your fuckin' business."

He holds up his hands. "Hey, I wasn't going to stop you, Brother. I think you should." His words pull me up, especially as he continues, "Look I know we all want the perfect relationship with no bumps in the road, but what ride's ever like that? Certainly not mine. I wanted to give Liv the world, and what did I do? I had a fuckin' breakdown instead. Women are much stronger than we give them credit for. Cutting her out and making decisions by yourself is the surest way of losing her in my view. Things between you and Gwen might not work out, this might be too big a hurdle to get over, but you won't know unless you involve her. If you love her man, you go to her now."

He's only telling me what I want to hear, but if any man knows how to fuck a relationship up, it's him, albeit he didn't do it on purpose. For a while Olivia had had to bear all the burdens herself.

I'd have done anything to stop the events of today playing out as they have and to avoid a test so early in our relationship. But if Gwen is going to be my partner, at some point we'll face adversity. This is a chance to see if we can really be stronger together.

He raises his fist, I bump mine against it.

Now I've heard the opinion that matches my own, I don't hang about any longer. Within moments I'm heading out of the compound. With each mile ridden my heart feels lighter, while simultaneously my stomach churns. *Will Gwen listen? Or will she*

decide to call it a day, thinking a relationship with me is too much trou-
ble? In the circumstances, I couldn't blame her.

I raise my chin to Butcher who's waiting in an SUV outside her house, then, having second thoughts about dismissing him, approach the driver's side window.

"You mind hanging around for a while?" If she kicks me out, I don't want to leave her unprotected.

Butcher, who I already know has a mature frame of mind, cottons on immediately. His reaction though, shows even the fucking prospects know what's happening in my life. "Good luck, Throttle." He settles back in his seat, kicking out his legs to get comfortable.

After another chin lift in thanks, with a fortifying breath, I approach the front door, raising my fist to knock on it. But noticing the lights are all off, I take it she's having an early night.

If she's asleep, I won't wake her up just to disturb her. So, possibly for the last time, I take out my key, enter, and prepare to disable the alarm before realising it hasn't been set. I take is as a sign of her state of mind, she's too upset to worry about her safety. Lips pursing, I set it, then pause, listening. When a small sob comes from the direction of her bedroom, I can't hold back any longer.

Moving through her house quietly, not bothering to put on any lights, I enter the room where she's lying. There's a small bedside lamp glowing.

She screams.

"Hey. It's just me."

"Jesus, Noah!" Her hand goes over her heart which I suspect is racing. She takes a moment, then says, "What are you doing here?"

"I thought we needed to talk." *And I needed to see you as much as I need oxygen in my lungs.*

"Have you spoken to Hattie?"

I approach and stand by the bed, uncertain of my welcome should I try to sit on it. "Not for a few hours."

She sits up, allowing me to see she's wearing a t-shirt, and not naked as I'd prefer. Though in the circumstances, I should be grateful. Our conversation will be hard enough as it is, without the complications of a throbbing dick. Her eyes examine me, and I'm gutted to see how raw they look, an all too visible sign of how much I've hurt her.

"Is she telling the truth? And for goodness' sake, sit. I'm getting a crick in my neck."

Planting my ass on the mattress, I take care to keep a respectable distance from her. "Who knows?" I answer her question. "I've told her to make an appointment with her doctor, one to which she should invite me."

She looks down at her hands which writhe together on top of the sheet. "But she could be. You did fuck her."

Her statement's unneeded. I wouldn't be worried if I hadn't, but I keep that to myself. "It was only once, a few weeks back. Before you were attacked." I sigh and pinch the bridge of my nose. "Gwen, I can't hide what I was. Lisa was right in what she told you. I fucked around, a lot. Hattie came onto me. The only attraction I felt was that it was a chance to get my dick wet. I told her that it would be one time only, and she insisted she, herself, wasn't looking for anything else."

"And until me, that was the last time you went with anyone else?"

Shit. She wouldn't find out, but I have to tell her. "I got my dick sucked by a club girl." Raising my eyes to meet hers, I add what I hope is in my favour, "But since then, yeah, nothing."

"Until me."

"Until you."

"Couldn't you find anyone?" she asks, snidely. "Were you that desperate, yesterday?"

"Oh, babe, I could have had a different girl every night." I don't like admitting this, but don't want to keep secrets. "Sable doesn't even count. The club girls on the compound get room and board in return for sexual favours." I shrug. "That was the last time. Since then I haven't even looked. Which, I admit, is unlike me."

"Why not?"

She's folded her arms, looking closed off, and a mixture of upset and angry. I try the truth, and can only hope she'll believe it. "Because, for once, the thought of just sex with a nameless person wasn't appealing. Not when you started to get into my head, and all I could think of was you."

"I'm sorry for upsetting your well-ordered life," she says, with a bite in her voice.

I chuckle without mirth. "Don't be. You know, I thought men who settled for one woman were mad, until I found you."

"Sex with me that good?" She scoffs as though she doesn't believe it.

It's hard to explain, but I try. "Before you, sex was like eating when you're hungry. It's satisfying until you get hungry again. Then, when you do, the same meal isn't what you fancy. With you?" Sharpening my eyes I stare at her intently. "It wasn't just a sexual release. There was an extra ingredient, one I could get nowhere else, and that's an emotional connection. It transcended anything I'd experienced and started an addiction for you that I'm not sure I'll ever stop craving."

Her head falls into her hands, sorrow wins out and she sobs. I know just how she's feeling. If she doesn't take me back, I'll have lost something special. After a moment she makes an effort to gather herself, reaches for a tissue and blows her nose loudly.

Visibly pulling herself together, she tracks back to the main issue. "So, Hattie could be pregnant."

Technically yes, if that condom had been faulty. "I grew up on a compound full of kids, Gwen. Sure, it was great, but many were younger than me, and I got fed up with the stink of diapers and the sound of babies screaming." I note she's looking at me strangely, but I continue with my confession. "Hawk and Wizard have just had their kids, and I admit I thought they were stark raving crazy. I didn't even want anything to do with the babies.

So believe me when I tell you, I never take risks, never rely on a woman telling me she's on the pill, and always use my own condoms. I did so with Hattie, but…" My voice trails off, as my hands make a gesture to suggest shit happens, even though I tried to prevent it. "Yes, she could be pregnant."

"You alluded to having kids with me." She sounds almost accusatory.

"Yeah. Because for the first time in my life, I want everything. I won't say I didn't surprise myself, because I did. A baby with you would be part of you, part of me, part of us. Not an inconvenience, but something to be treasured. Not immediately, but eventually, of course." I grimace slightly. "I was kinda hoping you'd be of the same mind."

"I wanted that too. Though I've doubts on how good a parent I could be."

"You'd be amazing, Gwen. I'm certain of that."

Her shoulders rise and fall as if she's not convinced of it. "Now you could be a dad, but the baby will be Hattie's."

There it is again, that huge stumbling block that's come between us. I decide to put all my cards on the table. "Yeah. Hattie might be pregnant, and the baby might be mine. It's early days, she's only just found out she's expecting, which doesn't mean she'll carry it to term."

"Have you asked her to have an abortion?"

Glancing at her sharply I wonder if that's what Gwen expected me to do. Again, I tell her the truth. "It's the woman who bears the burden during pregnancy. I'd never inflict my views on her, one way or another. If she wants to call a halt to it, I wouldn't criticise her. But neither would I encourage her."

I can't read her expression. Of course, things would be easier between us if there were no baby in the equation. I wonder whether to tell her about Dad's experience, when the pregnancy was faked. But part of me thinks that's too much to wish for, and I shouldn't get her hopes up. One Rinter got lucky, the dice might not fall the same way twice.

She blows her nose again. "So thinking this through. Hattie's pregnant, the baby is yours, it's born healthy… where does that leave us? Are you… are you going to try to make things work with Hattie?"

"Fuck no!" I exclaim. "I'm not saying I won't step up to be a dad, but I won't be anything to Hattie except a sperm donor. It wouldn't be fair on me, or on her. We could never be happy, and I couldn't pretend for the sake of a child, a child who'd undoubtably suffer."

As she breathes out a breath, I assume I've given her the right answer.

"But you won't walk away?"

Even if she wanted me to, I couldn't. "No, I can't. The kid would be a part of me. I'd need to check he or she was looked after and cared for. I might not have much empathy for kids in general, but my own? I'd want the best for it."

For the first time tonight she initiates a contact between us, reaching out and squeezing my hand. "You're a good man, Noah."

I don't know about that. If I was, I wouldn't have gotten into this predicament in the first place.

"Hattie will want me out of your life, Noah. She might make things difficult for you if we stay together. She could restrict custody or poison your child against you. She wants you, Noah. I could see that."

"She might, but she's not getting what she wants," I tell her firmly, then address the implications for her. "I won't deny it would be easy. Instead of us starting our life together cleanly, I come with baggage. Baggage that will be around for at least eighteen years. While I'm selfish as fuck, I want you to go through it with me. I know," my voice breaks, "that it's unfair of me to ask that."

She goes quiet. Her fingers start to twist the sheet, and my heart skips a beat. *Is this where she says she didn't sign up to be a stepparent to a child?* That she's thinking about everything seriously, is obvious.

"I was devastated to hear her announcement," she starts at last. "I knew I should walk away and let you go to her. I knew I shouldn't take on a man who brings so much with him, and what's most important is giving that baby the best start in life."

Here it comes.

"Then I thought of my background. I didn't have the benefit of parents or not that I can clearly remember, and I've seen the worst life can offer a kid. I wouldn't want anyone to go through the horror that I did." Her words make me guilty I'd not known about her background before, back then when I'd have tried to do something about it. I also doubt I know the half of what she's been through. "If you indicated you were going to give it a try with Hattie, I'd walk away. But if you're determined you're not, then I'll do my best to be there for you. Hattie is going to be a problem, I already know that. But it's the child who's important, and I'll do my best to support you, and him or her." She swallows and looks up to meet my eyes. "If that's what you want?"

"Fuck, Gwen. I feel a bastard for even saying it, knowing I'm dragging you into my shit, but that's what I want more than anything." Blinking rapidly I try to suppress tears of my own. "I have feelings for you, Gwen. This hasn't changed anything."

CHAPTER TWENTY-SEVEN

Gwen...

This has changed everything.

Instead of starting a life with just the two of us, now it's likely to have four players in it. I might not know much about Hattie, but I'm normally a good judge of character, and from what I've seen of her, I suspect she'll be trouble. Every instinct I have tells me she's someone not to trust, which is why I still harbour a suspicion about whether she's telling the truth.

Noah makes a move toward me, but I stop him by holding up my hand. If he starts kissing me, I'll lose control and we won't get all the important stuff out in the open first.

"What are the odds Hattie could be lying, and she just wants you to herself?"

He sighs, then sits back. "Of course that's what I've been thinking. Which is why I insisted on going to the doctor to get it confirmed. I guess we'll have an answer if she doesn't set it up."

My lips press together. "What do you know of her? Could she be pregnant by somebody else?"

His mouth twists. "Judging by how she came on to me, I'd say she was used to jumping in and out of beds. She wasn't shy, if you know what I mean?"

"So, you need to get a paternity test." I glance down at my hands, then I admit, "I may have been googling."

"Tell me." He gestures to reinforce my words.

"A simple blood test of the parents can be done at nine weeks. There's a more invasive test that can be done later on during pregnancy, but both seem to have a similar high rate of accuracy, and the first doesn't cause a risk to the baby. Or, you could wait until the baby is born."

"Nine weeks. What would she be now?" he muses.

"If she's only just found out, I'd guess about four weeks. So, another month to wait."

He brightens slightly. "I'm fanatical about condoms, Gwen. I always make sure to apply and dispose of them properly. She could have been careless with someone else and is just blaming me."

"It seems to me you'll have some indication whether that's true, if she doesn't set up the appointment, or if she refuses a paternity test."

One side of his mouth turns up. "I think it's perfectly reasonable of me to promise support *only* after I'm proved to be responsible." He thinks for a moment. "Wraith told me she was the woman who poured her drink over you."

"She was. And, I think, deliberately." It's the reason I believe she wants me out of the way. "She doesn't like me, Noah. She sees me as a threat."

His face darkens. "I've also been thinking about that. All your problems began when we reconnected. I'm wondering if it's her behind them."

It's not that I haven't wondered about that myself. "I don't know, Noah. I was attacked from behind, so it could have been a woman I suppose, and anger would have given her strength. It's possible she was the one who defiled my house. But slashing my tyres?"

Noah rubs at his temples. "We can't rule it out. What worries me is, if it is her and I don't give her what she wants, her behaviour could escalate."

It's not a comforting thought for me either. I shudder. Then, something occurs to me. "What if she's your stalker? Buying you gifts makes more sense than attacking me."

He opens his mouth, then closes it and frowns. "I was going to say she wouldn't know the size of my feet, but she could have checked for the size of my boots when I went into the bathroom. I hadn't thought about that." He winces as he realises he's rubbing my face in it. I shrug. I know he fucked her, and as long as he doesn't share all the details, I can just about deal with that.

"And those calls?" he continues. "Maybe she didn't speak as her voice would have given her away." He looks thoughtful. "But she doesn't drive a black SUV, and it was a good driver who was following me. Not saying women can't drive," he adds fast, with a worried look my way. "But surveillance techniques aren't what I would expect from her."

"Perhaps she's got help? A friend, perhaps?"

"It's worth looking into." Noah pulls out his phone and starts tapping on it. When he's finished, he looks up. "I've asked Mouse to check into her. Family circumstances and everything he can dig up."

"There's one way you could find out." When he raises an eyebrow, I let him in on my thoughts. "You haven't worn the boots yet, have you?" He shakes his head. "So why don't you when you see her next. She's bound to comment on them, or if not, you could draw attention to them yourself. Say you wished you knew who sent them as they're so good."

"It could be her who's my stalker," he says. "But I don't understand why she hasn't yet crowed about the gifts that were sent to me."

"You haven't used them. She might be doubting you liked them and doesn't want you to think she has poor taste."

He raises his chin, as if my suggestion makes sense. "If you're right, then she's been trying to chase you away, and to get her claws into me. Now that hasn't worked, she's gone one fuckin' step further."

My brow furrows. "If she's trying to put pressure on you, then it's far too convenient that she gets pregnant. Either she is, and it's not yours, or she's not and it's all a game."

Noah stands and starts to pace. His hands push back his hair. "If you're right, I'll fuckin' kill her." He stops at the wall, turns, strides across the room again, then turns and walks back. "I never knew how unnerving it was to have a stalker. Even those gifts made me uncomfortable. As for being followed… And you? What she did to you? I could never forgive her."

"Hey, we've got no proof yet."

He changes direction and comes over to the bed. Resting his hands on his covers, he leans over me. "If she's behind every-thing, I'm so fuckin' sorry I brought all this on you." Gently he touches the red line on my cheek. "You got hurt Gwen, and it could be down to one woman who didn't want you near me."

Lifting my hand I place it against his cheek. "It's not on you, Noah. This is on the stalker, whether it's her or not, you've got no responsibility."

He grimaces. "You're wrong, I have. I should have been more discerning about where I stuck my fuckin' dick."

I'm not going to argue with that. But if Hattie set her sights on Noah, she may have made herself hard to resist. Maybe I'm biased, but he is quite a catch. "Even if you hadn't had sex with her, if she's crazy enough, she could have tried to chase me off just because she had thoughts of you and her being together."

He takes a moment to process that. He starts to shake his head, but what he's about to say is lost, drowned out by the sound of gunfire from outside, glass smashing far too close, and the blare of the alarm sounding.

Noah leaps to his feet. "Stay here. Get down on the floor by the bed."

Momentarily paralysed with fear, I don't move. He yanks my

arm and pulls me down to the position he wants. Then, sliding a gun out of his cut, he eases carefully out of the door.

"Noah..."

"Shush."

Oh my God. Visions of Noah shot, lying bleeding, injured or dead on my living room floor fill my head.

Don't let him die, don't let him die, the mantra goes around and around.

I can't cower away like this, not when Noah's in danger. Crawling to the head of the bed I take my gun out of the drawer and load it. Then I take a deep breath and quietly open my bedroom door.

Immediately, I spy Noah at the side of one of the broken windows, cautiously trying to see out.

"Noah?" I speak loudly to be heard over the alarm, needing to alert him of my presence, not wanting him to spin around and shoot.

"Get back to the bedroom," he hisses.

"No." Not wanting to waste words, I don't add that my place is beside him. "What's going on?"

He turns and glances at me, his eyes widening as his gaze falls on the pistol in my hand. When he gives a quick nod of appreciation, his first idea of keeping me locked down seems to disappear.

"I'm going outside to check around. Cover me."

My heart is beating fast, it's one thing to take a gun training course, quite another to be prepared to fire at a live target, I cross the room keeping the wall at my back. When I'm in position, Noah eases his way to the door. Carefully he opens it, looks around, then steps out.

I hardly dare breathe, I'm so scared for him.

Within moments, he's back. Now he inputs the code to switch off the alarm. I watch him carefully as he stares at me.

"Drive-by, I think. Butcher's taken off. Hopefully he's in pursuit of them." His voice falters, and he looks down and grimaces before looking back up. "Gwen, I'm so fuckin' sorry. Your car, it's riddled with holes."

"Your bike?"

"Is a mess." Whatever he was going to say next is lost in the blare of sirens, and he changes it to, "Fuckin' cops."

I live in a residential neighbourhood where drive-by shootings aren't expected. "What do I say to them, Noah?"

His brow creases for a moment, then he shrugs. "They'll have your attack on record, so tell them about your tyres being slashed and now this. There's no point holding back anything. You're the victim in this."

"Why didn't I report my tyres earlier?"

"Because you didn't see anything, and as they haven't found anyone responsible for your attack, you didn't think there was any point."

Blue and red flashing lights illuminate the room as the cops stop outside. I place down my gun, go to the front door, carefully open it and step out with my hands up.

"Stay where you are," a voice shouts at me.

"I'm the home owner," I call back.

"Anyone with you?"

"Yes, my boyfriend."

Noah, minus his cut, steps out alongside, his hands also held in the air.

Cautiously a goddamn SWAT team approach, and soon we have our hands fastened behind our backs. I know it's a precaution, but it annoys me.

"I'm the one who was shot at," I state, adamantly. But they leave us there while they carefully check around the house and then clear the inside.

One officer comes out carrying two clear plastic bags containing mine and Noah's guns.

"That one's registered to me," I state firmly, indicating my Glock.

"The other's mine," Noah states. "Someone shot a fuckin'

AR15 at the house from the sounds I heard and the bullet holes I saw."

"Yeah?" The SWAT team member eyes Noah's bike. "This down to you and your club?"

I wince, his bike has the Satan's Devils MC insignia on it, clearly something with which the cops are familiar.

I try to get my story in fast. "This has nothing to do with Noah. I seem to be the target of a stalker. You've already got it on record I was attacked a couple of weeks back."

Another man, who'd been hanging back at one of the cars, approaches, clearly having heard my statement. "You were attacked at the Wheel Inn which is owned by the Satan's Devils MC." He looks pointedly at Noah. "You got anything to say about this?"

In the light of the streetlamps I see Noah gritting his teeth. "I don't," he states firmly.

"Your gang have enemies?"

"We're not a gang, we're a club. And to answer your question, none that I can think of."

I turn, surveying the damage. Even if our vehicles had been the target, the bullets had smashed through the windows and into the house. If I'd been in the living room, I might have been injured, or killed. Noah too. The thought sends a shiver right through me. My adrenaline rush starts to fade, and I feel like crying again. What the hell have I done to deserve this?

"We'd like you both to come down to the station so we can take statements." It's clear we have no choice.

Feeling like a criminal when I'm shown to the rear seat of a police car and a hand on my head encourages me to get in. There's a grill in front of me making me feel caged. I look around for Noah, but he's being put into a car behind me. I suppose so we can't collaborate on our stories.

How much more do I have to go through today? I start to shiver, and then realise I'm not cold, it's because I'm shaking. I don't think there's any emotion I haven't been through today. Happiness, love, gut wrenching sadness and bone chilling fear.

By the time we arrive at the precinct, I'm a mess as everything catches up with me. When I'm led to an interview room, I'm openly crying. I'm worn out mentally and physically, and it shows. Though I didn't do it on purpose, I think it's that that garners me some sympathy.

A detective walks in and sits opposite. We recap on my original attack, then I bring him up to date with this morning's vandalism to my car. I consider it, but don't bring up Hattie. I still might, but want to discuss it with Noah first. When he's asked me for anyone who might have it in for me, and I'm unable to come up with any names, he ends the interview. When the tapes switched off, he turns to me.

"Not my place to say this, but I think you need to get another part-time job and another boyfriend."

Some of my spirit returns. "You're right. It's not your place."

"Satan's Devils attract trouble."

But I know better. Satan's Devils have been nothing but kind to me.

CHAPTER TWENTY-EIGHT

*T*hrottle...

Satan's Devils have a rule. You don't speak to the cops without a lawyer being present. Cops would love nothing more than to have us at each other's throats, having a witness prevents any accusation of a brother turning rat on the club.

While I'm an innocent bystander in this case, I know they're going to pin the reason for the shooting on my club. I was there, my bike was shot up, and Gwen's attack took place at one of our establishments.

The first signs they're going to put the pressure on me comes when they take my phone and thoroughly pat me down. Knowing my rights, I demand a phone call.

I use it to call Wizard. After I've explained the situation to him, and he's agreed to drag a lawyer out of his bed, I tell him I suspect Gwen will be released first, and ask him to take care of her for me. Then, knowing she'll be in safe hands, I succumb to my fate.

The Satan's Devils deal some unsavoury matters in-house, sufficient that we walk on the side of the line that means we deserve the one-percenter patch. Threaten us and we'll take the law into our own hands. But we don't deal in drugs, women or guns, so normally stay out of the clutches of the police.

From time to time, one of us will get picked up, mainly for being in the wrong place at the wrong time, or sometimes simply for looking at a cop funnily. We're clever enough to cover our tracks, so avoid coming under scrutiny for torture or killing, even if we're guilty.

We keep a firm of lawyers on retainer, but nowadays, not any one individual. So I'm not surprised to find the person who's going to be looking out for me tonight, is someone I don't recognise.

I stand as he enters the room and stretch out my hand. "Sorry for getting you out of bed."

He waves it off, as he might. He'll get a hefty sum for his services. "No worries. I wasn't doing anything. The name's Fontaine by the way." *Do I know that name?* Probably, he could have represented one of my brothers. "Now," he looks down at his tablet, "Noah Rinter, otherwise known as Throttle, what have you got yourself into?"

As he takes a seat, I sink back into mine again. "I'm an innocent bystander." When he cocks an eyebrow, I add, "No, really, I am." Sitting forward I clasp my hands. "My girlfriend's had some things happen recently that makes me believe she's picked up a dangerous stalker. She was attacked and mugged a couple of weeks back. Her tyres were slashed this," glancing at the clock I correct myself, "yesterday morning. Tonight there was a drive-by shooting."

"Your girlfriend's name?"

"Gwendoline Boseman."

His eyes close, his nostrils flare, then he shakes his head and barks a self-deprecating laugh. "Well I'll be damned. No wonder she turned me down. I asked her out."

Lawyer. Gwen cancelling a date. Thoughts flow past behind my eyes. *No wonder his name was familiar.* "You're Everest?" *Christ. How's this going to go?* How can I trust him to represent me?

His eyes narrow. "I am. She been talking about me?"

"Not really." I decide to go easy on him. "We've been moving in fits and starts, there wasn't much between us. But last night we got our act together, and only today entered into a serious relationship."

"So I just missed the boat, eh?"

"Yeah. Thank fuck." I don't sense hostility, so my tone is friendly.

As is his. "You're one lucky man. She's a great woman." He frowns. "But what the hell has she gotten herself into?"

Sitting forward again, I rest the palms of my hands on the tabletop, then continue to tell him everything, answering the questions he snaps at me. I don't say a word about Hattie. I'll be doing that investigation myself, and heaven help her if she's behind this.

By the time I'm summoned for my interrogation, I've come to realise Everest is astute and seems determined to do his job properly. If I hadn't been convinced I'd have asked for someone else to represent me. But he doesn't seem to take umbrage that Gwen preferred a biker to a lawyer. He'd even laughed in stunned outrage when I'd suggested I'd put him on the list of suspects.

As I suspected, the cops do everything they can to pin the blame on me. Not that I shot up Gwen's house, but that I was the intended target. Or if not me personally, my club. I gave them as much as I could, but answered questions about the club and our businesses with a simple 'no comment'.

After a tortuous couple of hours when they could get nothing on me, Everest speaks.

"My client has told you everything he can. There's no reason to believe this was anything but an attack against Gwendoline Boseman. I see you've got no leads for her mugging two weeks ago. The danger is, gentleman, as you must be aware, if you focus on the Satan's Devils who, except for the fact Noah Rinter has a good eye for a pretty girl, have nothing to do with it, you might make a mistake we'll all regret. Which could mean Ms Boseman would suffer for it if the attacker isn't caught and goes after her again."

Once the cops have a Devil in their clutches, they want to hold on to him. I've no priors, so I've no problem with them running my record, they won't find anything. In the end it takes Everest's gentle, but pointed, suggestion that we could all do with getting to our beds, they release me, giving me back my phone, then my gun less eagerly.

Once outside, and after a welcome lungful of fresh air, I shake the lawyer's hand, then scan the parking lot. There's a club SUV waiting for me as I'd expected.

I get in. Nathan wastes no time peeling out of the parking lot as though worried the cops might change their minds and come for me again. As he drives, I take out my phone.

"You a free man?"

I chuckle at Prez's comment opening comment. "Thank fuck. I think they liked my company. Certainly weren't eager to part ways. How's Gwen?"

"Here, on the compound. Couldn't send her back home, Throttle. Not with a shooter on the loose. Butcher and Razza are at hers in case anyone comes back. They'll board the windows up tomorrow."

"Did Butcher get any info on who did it?" I guessed as soon as I'd seen he was no longer in front of Gwen's house that he'd taken off in pursuit of the shooter.

"Nah. He lost them. He's says whoever's driving knew what he was doing."

Which is what I'd thought and rules out Hattie. Unless she's got an accomplice.

"Where's Gwen staying?" I hope Wizard didn't take her to my mom. Though that would have been logical, in the situation it would be fucking awkward.

"I gave her options. She chose your suite, Brother."

I lean my head back, relaxing for the first time in hours. "Fuckin' perfect," I tell him and end the call.

Christ, what a long day it's been. Waking up with Gwen was amazing. When she was riding behind me on my bike, it was as though she'd been born to be there. Then it all went to shit with Hattie's announcement. I'd thought I'd got things sorted with Gwen, then her place, her car and my bike got shot up. And to top it all off, I'd had to sit through an uncomfortable interview with the cops.

I'm a Devil, I've been through shit before, but even this is a lot all at once for me to cope with. As for Gwen? I stare out into the night rushing past us. If this is all down to me, then surely it will send her running for the hills. How could I persuade her this isn't what life with me will always be like?

But what do I know about what life from now on will even look like? I want to be starting out with my old lady, but unless Hattie is lying, I'll have a child in my life. I wish I could go back twenty-four hours and rewrite my story. Actually three weeks, and I could advise myself to have nothing to do with Hattie.

It's a chilling thought that every time I fucked one of the hundreds of women I must have been with, I risked such a scenario, even using a condom as carefully as I had. *Why, oh why did I have to fuck up with someone like Hattie?* I'm hard pushed to say whether it could have been worse. As I didn't research the background of any of my hookups, I can't be certain one way or another. If a lady had been ready and willing, even her name hadn't seemed important.

Nathan drives through the gate and continues driving up to the clubhouse, he pauses to let me out before doing a three-point-turn and heading back to park the SUV behind the auto-shop.

The clubhouse still has lights on, and even given it's the early hours of the morning, there are still members inside. But the only company I feel in need of is the woman who hopefully is lying in my bed.

Within minutes, I'm opening the door to my suite. The light from the hallway filters through allowing me to see a sight that soothes my soul, Gwen, lying asleep. Knowing she must be exhausted, hell, I'm running on fumes myself, I make my way across the familiar room in darkness, unwilling to disturb her. I attend to my bedtime tasks in the bathroom, then strip down to my boxers.

Within moments I'm sliding under the sheet, pausing, then risking pulling her into my arms. I need to touch her, feel her, know that she's really here with me. Fully appreciating what a lucky fucker I am that she's given me a chance, even knowing how Hattie could cause a blight on our future.

Gwen's an amazing woman if she thinks she can cope with me and what I have tagging along. If, as I hope, we stay together, I doubt we yet know the worst that could be thrown at us.

How vindictive is Hattie? Was it really her behind the drive-by shooting earlier?

"Noah?" Gwen's voice murmurs sleepily as she nuzzles in deeper against me.

"Hush, go to sleep." I kiss the top of her head, smiling as I breathe in deep and notice she smells like me. That she must have showered and used my toiletries, appeals to me just as much as it had before. The difference is this time she's got no injuries. Thank fuck. The image of her bleeding from a bullet wound makes me go icily cold.

As she relaxes again, I make an effort to switch my racing mind off. Eventually tiredness takes me under. The next thing I know the sun is blazing in through the gaps in the blinds.

Reaching over to the bedside table, I pick up my phone to check the time. It's ten-thirty in the morning. My movement makes her stir. She stretches and her hand covers her mouth to smother a wide yawn.

I move, hovering my body over hers. Taking my weight on one arm, I brush back her dishevelled hair with my free hand. "You okay?"

"I will be." Her reply is strong and full of determination. Reaching up, she captures my wrist. "Love me, Noah."

She doesn't have to ask me twice. Unworried about morning breath, hell, we both have that, I lower my mouth and capture her lips. After ravishing them thoroughly, I go to move down her body.

"I want you inside me."

I need to prepare her first, but testing with my fingers shows me she's already wet and ready. Pushing myself up, I reach for a condom and quickly cover myself.

She shudders in expectation as I position myself at her entrance, gasping at my invasion, but wriggling as if to impale herself on my dick.

Her arms hold me tight to her. "I need you, Noah."

I know how she feels. After yesterday, I feel the same way myself. I don't fuck her, I make love to her, slowly and languidly. I'll do anything to bind this woman to me, and I try to show my growing love for her in every slide of my cock.

Using every weapon in my armoury, bringing my knowledge of what turns a woman on to the fore, I twist my hips, glide my piercings over her G-spot, and use my fingers to bring her to the edge.

When she tenses and flies over, she takes me with her.

Once her lungs are again filled with air and her heart stops hammering in her chest, she opens her eyes and her hands frame my face. "Hmm, that's how I'd like to wake up every morning."

"That can be arranged," I reply with a wink. I rest my forehead against hers, then as my softening dick leaves her, I ease out and leave the bed to take care of the condom. As I flush it away, I frown at the disappearing latex as though it was a traitor. I've never doubted them before, but now I've been caught out, I'll never trust that method of contraception again.

I wouldn't mind if it was Gwen who got pregnant. Really? I stare at my reflection in the mirror and shrug.

Returning to the bedroom I find she's sitting up in bed, her knees pulled up and her arms around them. "What's going to happen today?"

Perching on the mattress I think for a moment. "I need to catch up with Wizard and Mouse, go over what we know and where we go from here. The prospects are going to secure your house, but for now, Gwen, I don't think you should go back there." I see the pout on her face. "Wherever you are, I'll be with you. If you're determined to go home, I'll go with you. But think about this, it could have been me being there last night that was the catalyst for the attack. You're safer if you stay here with me on the compound."

"But how long for? I've got everything I need in my house."

Forever if I have my way. I'm scared to death of her being out of my sight. Those bullets flying yesterday were so indiscriminate, they could have hit a human target. Which means whoever shot her house up didn't care what damage they did. I shudder.

"Until we know you're safe."

She looks so glum, I feel fear trickle through me. "Don't you want to stay with me? Is it too much, too soon?"

Shaking her head, she explains, "It's not being with you, I want that, Noah. It's your parents and this whole Hattie mess. I know your mom and dad want you to play happy families, and I'll only be getting in the way."

"You leave my parents to me, Gwen. I'll make them understand that there's no Hattie and I, nor will ever be. Pregnant or not, there's no way I'm staying with her." Just the thought fills me with horror. I change the subject. "How did your interview go with the cops?"

"They tried to paint you as the villain." Her lips press together. "Honestly, Noah, they made me so damn angry. They discounted everything but that I'm being targeted as you're a Satan's Devil."

Much as I suspected. I do, however, have sympathy for the view of the cops. Except for the club's involvement. If it turns out Hattie's behind this, she's my enemy and mine alone.

"Hey," I grin suddenly, "you'll never guess who the lawyer the club called in was."

She shrugs. "Who?"

"Everest Fontaine."

"What?" Her hands unwrap themselves from her knees. "You're kidding. Did he know I was there?"

"He did." Interpreting her worrying her lip as concern, I reassure her, "He congratulated me for winning you, didn't seem put out at all. I think we can safely cross him off the stalker list."

"He was never on it as far as I was concerned," she tells me, primly.

At that moment, my phone pings. I reach around her and pick it up. It's a summons from Wizard. Church at noon. In fact, fifteen minutes from now.

"I gotta run," I tell her. "We're going to have a meeting."

She frowns. "You go on. I'll just stay here and wait until you get back."

I hate her thinking she's confined to this room. "Come down with me to the clubhouse."

I might as well have asked her to attend her own execution. "No. I'll wait here."

Realising she'll think she'll be the topic of gossip, I don't push.

Church will have been called because of what went down yesterday and as I'm effectively the guest of honour, I have to be there. Pulling on a fresh t-shirt and jeans and easing into my cut I make myself ready. As I put on my socks and boots, I come up with a plan.

"I'll be back as soon as I can," I tell her, leaning in to steal a kiss.

"I'll shower and dress..." She eyes yesterday's clothes with distaste.

CHAPTER TWENTY-NINE

*T*hrottle…

I hate leaving her like this, but haven't time to spare. I all but run down to the clubhouse, and once through the door, assess the people who are there. My gaze lands first on Mom and Dad who are deep in conversation with Wizard.

Like the sergeant-at-arms he was for many years, Dad's turned at the sound of the opening door. Seeing me, he waves me over to join them.

Damn. Gritting my teeth, I close the gap between us.

Mom speaks first. "I hear Gwen's on the compound."

My jaw tightens. "Her fuckin' house was shot up. Her car is riddled with bullet holes. What was I supposed to do, Mom? Let her go back there?"

"You think Hattie had anything to do with this?"

"Darcy, that's what we're going to be talking about." Peg casts a stern gaze in the direction of his wife.

Mom stares at me. She can read me better than anyone and knows I'm giving off a *don't fuck with me* vibe. Bravely, she reaches out her hand and touches my arm.

"Noah, I was hard on her yesterday. Gwen's innocent in anything you might have done."

"She is," I come back at her quickly. "Her only fault is falling in love with *your* son."

"Love?" Her eyes widen. "It really is serious?"

"On my part as a fuckin' heart attack. There's no way on earth I'm leaving her for a conniving bitch. On hers, well, that's what I hope."

"What she say about the baby, Son?"

Now I round on Peg. "She'll be with me every step of the way. If need be, she's willing to be a stepmom."

"Darcy," Wizard starts deceptively calmly. "I already told you, if it came to it, we'd vote on Gwen as Noah's old lady. Hattie, not so much. Most of us aren't angels, and what happened to him could happen to anyone."

I gather they've been discussing me already. I shouldn't be surprised. But I am, when Mom says next, "Is she in your suite, Noah?" When I nod, she continues, "I'll go talk to her while you're in church."

"I'd rather you don't." I throw away her offer. "She's worried enough as it is."

"Your mom and I have been talking," Dad informs me in his *you're going to listen to me* voice. "We reacted yesterday without thinking. Now we'd like to get to know our son's old lady. Trust your mom, Throttle."

I'm not happy, but there's no stopping my mom when she's got a bee in her bonnet. "I'd be grateful if you make her feel welcome. If she runs—"

Mom chuckles. "If I can make her run, she's not the woman for you, Noah."

"Church," Wizard reminds me, pointedly looking at his watch.

I nod at the prez, then narrow my eyes at Mom. "No bloodshed," I tell her, adding warningly, "Gwen's got a mean right punch."

"Come on." Dad jerks his head toward the meeting room and the brothers who are heading that way.

Reluctantly, worried about what Mom will say to Gwen, but knowing I need to have confidence in my woman's ability to handle her, I follow Peg into church.

Drummer's already seated in the VP's seat as Wizard takes his place at the top of the table. His glare, almost as piercing as his predecessor's, is effective in making sure brothers quickly find their own chairs. When Marvel, the last to arrive is in the motion of sitting down, Prez bangs the gavel.

"This meeting's convened," he begins, "if anyone here is in ignorance, to discuss Throttle and Gwen's stalker issues. Throttle," he addresses me directly. "You must have been thinking about it. Any ideas from your end?"

I clear my throat before speaking. "Seems a fuckin' coincidence Gwen and I have both got stalkers, so my gut feel is that they're one and the same. This shit only kicked off when our paths crossed." I nod toward Hawk. "I deliberately went to the Wheel Inn to see whether me making a move on her would draw them out. Seems that was too successful."

"It certainly fuckin' was," Hawk interjects.

"Anyone from her past?"

I shake my head at Rock. "Nah, or none she can think of. There was a fucker who asked to take her out." I chuckle, then look up to see puzzled faces. "It only turned out he was the fuckin' lawyer sent to get me out last night."

"Fontaine?" Wizard's grinning. "That must have been embarrassing. Was he okay? What's he like? I must admit I thought he was straight when I was introduced to him."

"Too fuckin' straight!" Marvel shouts. "Him having the hots for Throttle's woman proves that."

"And is she?" Joker asks, pointedly ignoring the rest of Marvel's comment. "Your woman?"

I nod. "Let's just say if we can get this crap sorted and behind us I'll be bringing it to the table to vote on her old lady patch."

"Never thought I'd see the fuckin' day," Hound breathes out.

Prez bangs the gavel. "Can we move this along? Throttle, apart from Fontaine, which appears to be a non-starter, there's no one else in her background or someone she's crossed?"

"No," I tell them. "She's pretty damn certain on that."

"We think it's Hattie." This comes from Peg.

"She'd need help," Roadkill observes.

Mouse waggles his hand. When eyes go to him he flicks his long greying hair over his shoulder. "Whoever it is, does have help. Here's what I've got." I sit forward, listening carefully. "I've looked at the security footage from Gwen's house. Both times, when her tyres were slashed and the drive-by shooting last night, a black SUV was within sight. Same make and model as the one that was following Throttle. I couldn't get a clear look at the number plates. At the mall I picked up a driver only, outside Gwen's there were two people involved, the driver and the shooter, but the flashes from the gun obscured any view of a face." He slides a grainy photo across to me. "Here's the clearest shot of the person who slashed the tyres."

It's a figure wearing a hooded t-shirt, no facial features visible. "I don't think that's Hattie. She's not tall or broad enough."

"Whoever it is has an accomplice, or at least, according to Mouse, did have last night. Unless we're going to discount Hattie, and I don't think we should, we're better to assume she has an accomplice."

"Prez, you reckon a woman is capable of this shit?" Heart's brow creases.

"Never underestimate a woman scorned," Wizard states. "She wasn't exactly discreet when she came to the compound. That woman was determined everyone learned she was pregnant, and who the father was."

"Yeah, glad you're not looking to give her a property patch. I didn't take to her," Wraith states firmly.

"Nor did I," comes from Lady, and Joker nods his head as if he agrees.

"She wanted you." Again Wizard ignores the other comments. "She had one thing on her mind, and one only. Getting you to step up to be her man." He drums his fingers on the table. "She had expectations, thought she held a winning hand. Woman like that would be fuckin' upset when things don't go to plan. If she's been keeping tabs on Gwen, then she sees your bike outside hers last night, it could have set her off. It escalated yesterday, Brother. Someone could have died."

I'd rather he not remind me of that. "But it could have been me. Me being dead would have upset those hypothetical plans of hers."

Shooter shakes his head. "You were in bed, the lights were off. It was a warning."

"I could have been getting a fuckin' glass of water," I counter.

"In the dark?" Dollar objects. "Much more likely Gwen would be the one walking around her own house without light. You, being a stranger, wouldn't have known where shit was. If anyone was going to be collateral damage, it would have been your girl."

I really don't like the reminders that Gwen could be injured or dead.

However much the timing points toward Hattie, I don't want to run off half-cocked. "Two people were involved. If we go after Hattie and find ourselves disappearing down a rabbit hole, we might find we're wrong to our cost. That there were two screams the Dray twins to me. Aren't they more likely?"

"Not so fast." Mouse's dark eyes come to my face. "Although I found nothing to prove Hattie's involvement, I didn't find anything to exclude her either. So I looked deeper. She's not been married, and her use of social media doesn't suggest she's been in a steady relationship. What there is is a fuck ton of stuff about her and her brother. He's two years older than her, and they seem inseparable. She's not got a long friends' list, and when she goes out, pictures show it's mostly her brother who's with her."

"He sounds overprotective." Blade butts in. Nothing wrong there, we're all guilty of that. "She ever mention him? Was he there at the Wheel Inn?"

I try to think back, but can't remember her with a guy, overprotective or not. "She lives with him, or at least, he's shit was in her bathroom. There was no one with her at the Wheel Inn. As for conversation, we didn't have any." I scoff. "I didn't go with her for her debating skills."

Heart frowns. "If she knows as little about you as you do about her, why has she zeroed on you as the one? Why be so desperate to have a relationship with you?"

"Well it's not his tiny dick," Marvel shouts out.

Ignoring him, Joker sits forward. "That's simple, isn't it? If she's pregnant with Throttle's baby, wouldn't any woman want a relationship with the father?"

"What do you know about fuckin' women?" Roadkill asks with a wink.

"Thankfully absolutely nothing," Lady breathes out, taking the hand of his man, and grinning.

Rolling my eyes, I explain, "She wanted me before she knew she was pregnant. I'd made sure she knew it was one night only, but she kept trying to get me to go with her again. And those gifts, if they were from her, that started before anyone, even she, could have known there was a baby."

Heart grins. "Then you must have some *fuckin'* skills, Brother, if it only took one night to convince her."

"Or," the voice of reason sounds from the prez's chair, "it didn't matter who, just that she wanted to be a biker's ol' lady."

Thanks for that, Prez. Though I wish Hattie hadn't set her sights on me, it wounds my pride to think she'd have settled for anyone wearing our cut.

"That makes sense," Drummer intones. "She was hanging around the Wheel Inn."

"Yeah, Tash said she'd been coming in for a couple of weeks, ostensibly to arrange the bachelorette party. She had plenty of opportunity to shop for a likely suspect."

"So why did I pull the short straw?" I ask Blade.

Blade grins. "I've been there a lot recently. Dollar was there with Carmen. I asked Tash to think back. She remembers Joker and Lady being in attendance when Hattie appeared, and on another occasion, Shooter." He breaks off and smirks. "Seems she only goes for the young men."

"Hey, who you calling old?" Shooter looks disgusted. "I'm only forty."

"Yeah, and the rest," Wraith teases him. "And you're not unattached."

"True dat." Shooter grins.

"Drifter too," Blade continues. "But he's almost as old as Shooter." He gets a finger from Drifter but ignores it. "Otherwise it was just the prospects who were closer to her age. If she had any sense, she'd want to target a full member."

Drummer stares at me. "Looks like you were the first that met her criteria."

"Shows she's not fussy about looks or dicks."

In a move more likely to be used by my mentor, I take my knife and sink the blade into the tabletop right in the marks already left there by my predecessor. "One more fuckin' word, Marvel, and I'll gut you."

Wizard bangs the gavel, accompanying it with a glare worthy of Drummer. "Mouse, have you got more?"

"I have if I can get a word in," Mouse drawls, his eyebrow rising in challenge as he glances around the table. "It might interest you to know, the brother has a Ford Explorer, the same colour of the one that's been following you and Gwen."

My interest is caught, but I push down the building excitement. *Get this wrong and Gwen might end up dead.* "There must be hundreds of those around. With no identifying features, that doesn't prove anything."

Jekyll flexes his hands, making his knuckles crack loudly.

"But it's a start, isn't it? I, for one, think we ought to be looking very closely at Hattie and her family."

Joker holds up his hand. "I may not have experienced the mechanics, but I do know how things work. Theoretically," he winks at Lady, "you used a condom, Brother. Everyone here believes you. Hell, you can't stand kids, you'd never have risked having a baby. Isn't it a bit of a coincidence that she sets her sights on you and then conveniently falls pregnant?"

From everyone's reaction, he, and I, aren't the only ones thinking it.

"Even if she is pregnant," I tell them, rubbing my beard, "I want a paternity test done. Gwen's looked into it, a simple blood test can be done at nine weeks."

"And she's what, four or five now?"

I nod. "I suppose about that. Unlike Joker, I don't claim to know the mechanics. But he is right in one thing, I never wanted kids." Peg, who's been silent up to now, shoots daggers at me. So I don't stop there, I continue, "Until Gwen, when it's gone from never to maybe." I stare my father down, letting him know how serious I am about the woman who's currently in my suite.

Peg's face goes through a number of transformations, from disappointment, to resignation, then he even offers a half-smile at me, before going back to being serious. "Then Throttle, you need to get Hattie to the doctor to get that pregnancy test done. If it's positive, there'll be a new problem, waiting until the paternity can be established. If Hattie's behind this, as I'm coming to suspect, then Gwen will be in danger."

"Just what I was thinking." Wizard raises his chin toward Peg. "It might be safer if you cut all ties with her until we can rule Hattie out."

"Probably for the best," my traitorous *friend* Hawk says. "Whoever it is, the catalyst is Gwen and Throttle being together."

What? Stay away from Gwen for four weeks? I shake my

head furiously. "No fuckin' way. What if we're wrong? What if someone else is after her?"

"She stays on the compound," Drummer pronounces, his eyes on Wizard allowing him a chance to object. "We cover her whenever she goes to work."

Wizard nods. "We can do that. But if that's the solution, she stops working at the Wheel Inn. The less she leaves the compound, the better."

Blade sinks down in his chair, mumbling, "Fuck, Tash is going to love that. She's her best worker."

The offered solution is just what I want. I can't walk away from her, even temporarily will fuck with my head. Now I've just got to go and convince Gwen she's better off staying with me. If I have my way, indefinitely.

Hawk's staring at me. "This is really serious for you, Throttle? Gwen and you?" he adds, to qualify.

I find myself saying, "I wouldn't be mentioning 'ol' lady' in the same sentence as her if it wasn't. Adversity may have had a hand in bringing us together, but I know she's my one." It's sappy, but one hundred percent true.

"Then why don't we cut to the chase and vote on her then? Seeing as we'll circle back to it sooner or later."

Wizard looks thoughtfully at the man who should be sitting in the VP seat. "It brings her into the club and justifies the manpower to protect her. I'm satisfied with the background check we did before employing her at the Wheel Inn. I vote, aye. Anyone else?"

Before I know it, everyone's raising their hands. Except for me, I sit dumbfounded by the speed with which things are moving. In my mind I see her wearing my property patch, and I'll be fucked if both I and my cock like the sound of it.

"Throttle, this what you want?"

Returning from the image of me fuckin' my lady and her wearing just my patch, I clear my throat and answer the prez. "Yeah." I try again, getting over my own astonishment that I,

Throttle, confirmed bachelor, am sat at this table discussing taking an ol' lady. Something we view more seriously than marriage. "Yeah," I say more forcibly. "That's what I want."

With that, Wizard bangs the gavel, and as long as I can persuade her, Gwen's my ol' lady.

I glance at Peg. He's nodding slowly, and a grin spreads across his features.

CHAPTER THIRTY

*G*wen…

Is there anything worse than wearing yesterday's clothes? Jeans are okay, but my top isn't fresh anymore, and as for the thought of wearing dirty panties, *ew*.

I'd been ready to collapse when I came here last night and had given no thought of what would happen this morning. Hence it's only now I'm viewing my underwear with disgust.

Taking them into the shower with me, I wash them out using Noah's soap, but can't put them on until they're dry.

Going commando isn't something I like, but it's all I can do. I do, however, steal a t-shirt out of one of Noah's drawers. It drowns me, but at least it's fresh and clean.

Once prepared for the day as best I can, I glance around his room. It's functional, but not particularly homely. The only personal things are a couple of photos. Being nosy I pick them up and glance at them. One is a photo of Peg, Darcy, Noah and Lisa. They make a lovely family, and Noah looks so much like his dad. The other is a group photo, of Noah and all the members of his club. I recognise a few of them.

Replacing the photos, I note the rest of the room's contents. There's a television on the wall, and a DVD player under it.

There are a few DVDs on a stand, and a pile of magazines. Hoping to find something to read, I flick through them, only to find they're all about bikes and bike parts. *Typical.*

Opening the patio doors, I find they lead out onto a balcony. Going outside, I lean over the railing, gazing at the glorious view of the Tucson Mountains beyond. It's a lovely autumn day, not hot nor chilly, but balmy. I sit on one of the chairs and turn my head to face the sun.

A sixth sense seems to warn me there's someone walking up the track. Opening my eyes, I glance down, seeing Noah's mom on a trajectory that will take her past this suite. Not in the mood for a confrontation, I duck back into his room. But only a short while later there's a knock on the door.

Knowing it can only be Darcy, I wonder whether to pretend I'm not here, but quickly realise that's not very adult. For some reason, as though it matters, I wish I was about to face Noah's mother wearing panties, I go to let her in, then step back, allowing her to enter the room after me.

She goes to the window and looks out, then turns. "I'm sorry about yesterday."

I shrug dismissively. If I'm going to be with Noah, I have to stand up for my man.

Seeing I'm not going to immediately accept her apology, in truth I don't know exactly what it's offered for, Darcy shakes her head. "May I sit?" When I nod my permission, she takes the desk chair while I sit on the bed. "Yesterday, a woman came to the compound and announced to everyone she was pregnant by my son." She pauses, and glances to see if I'm listening. I am. "She was brought to our house. Peg and I have wanted to see Noah settled for a while. I was flabbergasted by the thought my son had gotten a woman pregnant and hadn't told me or his dad. Until she explained, he didn't yet know."

"He didn't even think there was a chance," I tell her, wanting to put her straight if she thought Noah had been careless. "He used protection."

She grimaces. "I know that now. But then? I thought he'd been reckless, swept away in the heat of the moment, or even maybe, that he wanted a child with her."

"Hattie?" I snort.

Giving me a sharp look she says sternly, "Who am I to question the choices my son makes?"

Well, that's put me in my place.

"Anyway," she picks up the thread again, "Peg was as surprised as myself. He's a good man, Noah's dad, and our immediate thought was Noah should step up and do what's right."

I'm not letting her get away with that. "Peg should know better. Noah told me Peg had been tricked himself."

She has the grace to look sheepish. "Hattie was gushing about how much she loved Noah, and how she thought he'd make a good dad. She led us to believe Noah loved her just as much in return. Peg was taken aback, but put on the spot, he did suggest Noah would do the right thing *if* she was pregnant, and *if* he was the father."

I interrupt, "What I can't understand is how you would push your son into the hands of a woman without asking what he thought first."

"Oh Gwen, it wasn't like that. We wanted him to accept his responsibilities. It was her who was talking about playing happy families. For Peg and I, it was more about staying involved in the life of perhaps the only grandchild we'd have. We never saw Noah settling down, he was adamant that he never would."

A shiver of doubt runs down my spine. He said he wants me in his life, that's a one hundred and eighty turn from what he ever wanted before. Who am I, so new to his life, to say I know him better than his family?

"I actually tried to downplay the chances of Noah doing anything more than supporting the child, but then," Darcy continues, "you walked in with Noah." She turns away from me. "You're a nice girl, Gwen. Always were. You never came onto the compound, but I knew you and Lisa were good friends. She'd often spoken about you, and recently about how you'd reconnected. I just didn't see you as someone for Noah. If I'm honest, I could probably see him better with someone like Hattie."

"You prefer her to me?" My eyes widen in astonishment.

"No, no," she contradicts quickly, her hands fluttering as she tries to make a U-turn. "That's not it at all. You're the epitome of someone I would want Noah to end up with, but the women he went with were different, and how could I do other than assume that's the type he would want."

"He used women," I confirm I know everything about him. "He went with those he knew didn't expect a ring on their finger. Not girls you'd bring home to meet your mother."

"I was shocked when he came in with you, holding hands together. It was obvious he was making a statement."

"His timing was off." I grin slightly, macabrely thinking it could hardly be worse. For me, for Hattie, or for Noah and his parents.

Suddenly she swings back to me. "Are you okay with this, Gwen? Are you serious about taking on Noah and his baby?"

It's my turn to be honest. "Noah's worth me putting in the effort to make it work. It's not ideal, but what is? It's Noah's child at the end of the day, and I'll love it because it's part of him. Though heaven knows what I'll be like as a stepmom, I suppose I'll just have to learn."

She eyes me carefully. "I wish this hadn't happened, Gwen."

So do I. "What's the point in wishing things could be different? There can be bumps in any road when you least expect them." Raising then lowering my shoulders I add, "There will always be things we'll need to deal with."

"Gwen." She steps forward, holding out her arms. "I'll help you. I'll be there for you both. This whole situation blindsided me. You're right, if your relationship's strong enough, you and Noah will cope with anything."

Taking her unspoken invitation I step into her arms, allowing her to hug me. It feels odd, awkward, it's been so long since another woman has shown affection to me, so far back I barely remember it.

The door bangs open.

"Unhand my ol' lady," Noah says loudly, but his tone is gentle, slightly mocking. "And here I thought I was going to have to tear you two apart and mop up blood."

Darcy lets me go and steps up to Noah. "I owe you both an apology."

"Nah, Mom. You and Dad were disappointed in me. I get that."

Mother and son hug, and I wrap my arms around myself. Noah catches my eye, lets his mom go, and steps forward to me, and now it's my frame that he's pulling into his body.

Darcy suddenly stills. "Ol' lady, you said? You're patching her?" She sounds delighted.

"Well, I haven't asked her yet," Noah admits, smiling down at me. "But yeah, it's official. Club's voted on her being mine."

"Do I get a say in this?" I ask, trying my hardest to look at him sternly.

"Not if I have my way." His mouth quirks.

Darcy chuckles. "Good luck telling him no. Oh, I forgot. I brought this." She steps to the door and picks up a bag I hadn't noticed her bring in. "Lisa left some of her stuff here, mostly clothes she doesn't want. You're about the same size as her top wise…" Her voice trails off, making me glad she didn't draw attention to my broader hips. "And I donated some new underwear."

"You're a lifesaver," I tell her, though don't admit I'm currently panty less.

Noah turns, keeping me tucked under one arm. "Mom, much as I love you, will you give us some space?"

Darcy chuckles. "Seems I've outstayed my welcome. Why

don't you both come up to the house later, have some dinner with us?"

Raising an eyebrow and looking at me, I love how Noah silently asks my opinion. What can I do but nod my head?

"We'll be there," he confirms to his mother.

When the door closes behind his mom, I stare down at the bag. "It's lovely of her to bring clothes, but I prefer to go back to my house and get my own."

He moves his finger under my chin and tilts my head to look up at him. "You can't go back, Gwen, not yet. Last night one of us could have been killed. I don't think that was their intention, but it might have been the result. Can't take fuckin' chances, not with you."

I don't appreciate the reminder which sends a chilling shiver down my spine. "If I don't, whoever it is will have won."

"No, you're wrong. They'll have lost. Because you're with me, Gwen. All our stalkers have done is accelerate our timetable and forced us to face our feelings sooner rather than later. You're my ol' lady now, and nothing they can do will part us."

"I haven't agreed to be your old lady."

He chuckles softly. "I'm presuming you'll say yes."

I could hold out, take a stance on my independence, but my heart isn't in it. "When I think about how you could have caught a stray bullet last night, I stop myself playing games. If I lost you, I don't think I'd ever recover. Logically it's far too soon for the intensity of the feelings I have, but my heart doesn't give a damn about logic. I love you, Noah, so, yes. I'll be your old lady." A weight lifts off me as I get my admission off my chest.

He stares at me intently. "I never expected to feel this way, to want a woman more than I want my next breath. But that's what you do to me, Gwen. You're not alone in this, as much as you love me, I love you back." He gives me a moment for that to sink in, for my heart to skip a beat. "You will stay with me? Let me keep you safe?"

I glance around his suite. For a single man it's more than adequate. For two, not so much.

He notices what I'm looking at and turns my head to face him again. "Gwen, if you go home you could be in danger, and so will I, or anyone else you have with you. Here's not a long-term solution, just until we can sort out what's going on. I want us to be together. We can talk about where we'll live, here on the compound, or in town."

"We could move into my house."

"We could, once the danger is past, or start over anew." His brow furrows. "I'd prefer to build a house at the top of the compound. If we have kids, I'd like to think about them growing up with all their cousins."

He doesn't say it, but he's sure to be thinking he might have a child even before we could complete the build of a house. It hits me he's going to be a good dad, he's already thinking about bringing up his son or daughter in the happy environment he had. Even if it is half Hattie.

When I don't immediately jump at his suggestion, he adds, "We've got time to think about it."

"It's a lovely idea." I go on my tiptoes to kiss him. "Everything's just overwhelming right now. But I still need stuff from my house. Can we go and get it?"

"Make a list. The prospects are there now getting your windows fixed and assessing the damage. They'll bring what you need to you."

"You want them going through my underwear?" I widen my eyes.

He frowns. "I'll tell them to bring the drawer."

I chuckle softly, then realise, "What about my car? I need to go to work."

He pulls me in close. "The tow truck brought your car back to the auto-shop, I'll need to check it over to see what needs to be done, whether I can fix it or if we need to get you another. In the meantime, I, or a prospect, or one of the brothers will take you to and from work."

"That's too much bother. I'll rent something."

"It's not too much bother, Gwen. It's what we do. You're one of ours now. Not as an employee, not as a friend of the club, but you're part of the Satan's Devils' family as you're mine."

I've never had a family of my own, never had somewhere I belonged. I stare at him seeing the earnestness on his face, and fuck it, but I'm weeping again.

Noah's giving me so much more than himself, he's giving me a new family and a whole new life.

CHAPTER THIRTY-ONE

Throttle…

Gwen's always needed to find a place in the world, a place where she could feel accepted and where she belongs. I don't need to ask why she's crying, it's written all over her face.

I hate that I kept her away from the compound all those years ago, thinking she wouldn't fit with the rest of the kids here. My conscience is somewhat salved considering her foster parents would never have allowed it.

Resolving to make up for it now, I wipe away her tears and kiss her, first in a comforting way, then, when she responds, it turns into something more. Before we leave the suite, I'd coaxed her into consummating her agreement to be my old lady in the time honoured manner, the one that had us both naked and her screaming. When we'd sufficiently recovered, I'd taken her down to the clubhouse, this time, properly introducing her around.

Something changed while she was being greeted and congratulated by everyone. All the members were slapping my back to congratulate us, and the old ladies and other assorted women were hugging her, while jokingly asking if she knew what she was getting into. Joker and Lady stepped forward enveloping her in their embraces. Those I permitted, but drew the line at Marvel and Hound.

Hawk had brought Liv over, him carrying Layla as though he couldn't bear to put her down.

"You done good, Brother," Hawk says, knocking his shoulder against mine. "She's a good fit."

As I watched her cooing over his baby, I found myself wondering what she'd look like if that was our kid instead, or mine, I think more accurately. *Damn Hattie.*

Once she'd been introduced to everybody, including taking time to speak to Tommy, whose 'bike' I notice she was quick to admire, it was time to drag her off for dinner with my parents and Lisa, who'd come back from town for the evening.

I'd had my doubts about how the evening would go, but the only awkward moment had been when Lisa wanted to drag Gwen off for some private girl time, and I'd wanted Gwen to stay by my side. Gwen was torn by the changed dynamic, but handled it with diplomacy and aplomb. Her solution was to arrange to meet Lisa for lunch the following week, a lunch she'd be escorted to and from.

Peg won her over very quickly, so much so she said she could see where I got my charm from. Mom had snorted, saying that wasn't how she'd describe me. The conversation as well as good food flowed, and when we returned to the suite, I could see Gwen was happy with the way it had gone.

We made love, and then I slept with her in my arms, thinking what a lucky asshole I was. I cherished every moment of her being with me.

But now Butcher's driving her to work. As soon as she'd left, my suite had felt empty. I could have taken her myself, but as I knew I'd have found it hard to leave her, it's better this way. I'd probably have camped outside her office if I had my way.

While she was in the shower I'd phoned Everest Fontaine. He'd assured me the security was good at the law firm where she works, because not everyone got off, and occasionally, though he drily suggested, while I probably wouldn't believe it, sometimes the lawyers got blamed. I'd chuckled, having no problem thinking it true. He also added he'd make sure to watch out for her, family law was on his floor which is how he'd come across her in the first place. Again he seemed genuine, and I thanked him for his concern, and whatever he could do to ease my worry about her.

Not wanting to spend time moping by myself, I go down to the shop early and inspect Gwen's car. Another sign of how much I care for her as I approach it first, even before my precious bike. The windows are gone, the bodywork riddled with bullet holes, and the gas tank needs to be replaced. It's not a new model, so I wonder whether it's worth it.

"What d'ya reckon?"

I turn to see Hawk yawning and rubbing his eyes. "It's a write-off, but she likes it." At that point I'm veering toward doing what I can to restore her car.

Moving closer, he opens the door. "You checked the upholstery yet?"

Shit, no. I've been looking at the engine and exterior. Peering in alongside him, I close my eyes and shake my head. The speedometer has a hole right in the middle of it, and the seat coverings are shredded.

"You could waste money and time on it, Brother. Or get her something else."

"Something bulletproof," I grumble. He's made a good point. Much as I want to please her, this car will never be the same again. "I'll speak to her later and explain."

"I looked at your bike last night. It'll need a new tank, but that's about it."

Is it a clue that her car was shot up worse than my bike? Or just coincidence as it was a smaller target? It is good news about my ride though, I just want to be mobile again.

"Have we a tank in stock?" I wonder aloud.

"Already checked." He smirks. "And yes, we have. Want to wait until it's painted?"

"Nah. I want my wheels. There'll be time to pretty it up later."

When Blade comes in, heading for the office as he can still type on the computer even though his hands aren't up to physical work, Hawk and I are near done putting on the new gas tank.

"Gwen's car?"

I give a sad shake my head in answer to the ex-enforcer, who thinks for a bit. "How about taking it to the Dray's scrapyard? Maybe get a chance to see how the land lies. If it was them, they might give away some clue. Maybe shit themselves when they see what we've brought in."

It's a good idea with one snag. "Great plan, but I need to get Gwen on board first as the car is hers. Maybe that's an outing for tomorrow." I'd prefer to give her the bad news in person and not do it over the phone. While I have no qualms paying for a new one, her desire to be independent is likely to flare. I may have some ideas about how to persuade her, hopeful my cock will find ways to override her objections.

As the day gets going in earnest, Marvel and Drifter turn up and get stuck into their jobs. Once I've finished the work on my bike, I, too, get my head down, working on the shit we get paid for. We've got a good reputation for fixing both cars and bikes, and know how to maintain it. I take on a Mustang someone's brought in for a tune up.

The radio is playing in the background and I'm concentrating hard when my phone rings. Taking it out, I see it's an unknown number. My brow creasing, I answer, slightly surprised when I don't hear heavy breathing.

"Throttle."

"It's me, Hattie." She's obviously using what I believe is a seductive tone. It grates on my nerves. "I rang your number, but

I got through to someone else first?" she asks, her voice raising and posing it as a question.

I don't bother explaining that Mouse is monitoring my calls. "Have you made that appointment?" That's the only conversation I want to have with her. As she's my most likely suspect, she'll know why Mouse is monitoring my incoming calls.

Getting the hint I'm not down for idle chit chat, she's silent for a moment before telling me, "Actually, I have. The clinic had a cancellation this afternoon. Are you free at three?"

My gut rolls. "I can be. Where?" Grabbing a pen and paper, I jot the details down. I'll be giving them to Mouse later to make sure it's a reputable clinic, and not full of sketchy assholes who could be bribed. "I'll meet you in the parking lot at five to."

She can't hide her disappointment when she tells me, "I thought we could meet for a late lunch."

I decide to test her. "Can't. I won't have my bike fixed that early. It will be a push to get it sorted by then."

There's silence, followed by, "Oh, I didn't realise you had a problem with it."

Is she genuine or not? It's hard to tell when I'm unable to watch the expressions on her face.

"Later." I end the call with the one word, then breathe out, seeing Hawk watching me with interest. "Today's the day I find out whether Hattie's lying or not, as long as the clinic's legit."

He grimaces slightly, his discomfiture echoing my feelings inside. If she wasn't pregnant, she'd string me along for a while and not set up an appointment so fast.

I text Mouse the details for him to check, then go back to the Mustang with far less enthusiasm than I had before. I'd been hanging onto the hope that she'd been lying. Of course, it could still be it wasn't my kid, but I'm starting to think that's very unlikely.

Gwen doesn't deserve this. She deserves a man who's fully focused on her, and not one involved with another woman's pregnancy. As I work, I think about Hawk. He'd been to every doctor's appointment Olivia had had, at least until he descended into the depths of his despair. Before his breakdown, he'd been as excited as she was when they first had sight of the fetus in her womb. I remember him showing the sonogram around so proudly.

Would I want to be involved at all? Would I be content to just throw money at Hattie and keep my distance? I don't know if I could. If it's my baby growing inside her, much as I have no feelings for its mom, I'd want to know it was developing as it should and was healthy.

Not for the first time I wish I wasn't in this mess. I know without her telling me that it would stretch Gwen's compassion to breaking point to give up even that little part of me.

Why the fuck did I have to fuck Hattie?

But if I'd been carrying a defective condom, if it hadn't been her, it might have been someone else. If it had been Gwen, I'd have been shocked at first, but I'd be able to cope. It wouldn't have provoked such devastation.

"Damn it!"

At my exclamation Hawk swings around. "Problem?"

"Nah, just overtightened this nut. Need to back it off a bit." I nearly break my fingers as I proceed to do just that. But how could I be blamed when a vision of Gwen's stomach growing round with my baby enters my head?

Mouse calls just before lunchtime with the news the clinic is genuine. He's dug as deep as he can, but was unable to find any suggestion of a nefarious reputation. He's also checked out all the profiles of the staff, and can find no one with a connection to Hattie. Of course, we can't be one hundred percent sure, but Hattie being able to coerce one of them to lie seems unlikely at best.

Which leads me to be convinced that later today, I'll have the confirmation that she is pregnant. Then we'll have to wait until she has that paternity test, but my exit routes seem to be closing, and I believe I'm going to have to step up to the mark.

I just don't know how I'll keep my baby momma happy enough to grow a healthy baby, while keeping hold of Gwen. Neither will be able to have all of me.

My bike looks a rat with a gas tank covered only with grey primer, but at least it will get me from A to B, and that's all I need. In a mood that's halfway between anger at myself and sadness, I leave in good time. Arriving early, I stay on my bike to wait, knowing I'd be no less happy if I was going to my execution instead.

No wonder my parents are disappointed in me. Part of me understands why Mom had so wanted it to work out between me and Hattie. Instead of a straight line heading into the future, I can see a road with so many twists and turns it's impossible to see the journey's end.

When Hattie turns up—not in a black SUV I notice—she's made an effort. She's wearing a pretty sundress with a cardigan around her shoulders, a nod toward the slight chill of the autumn air, more noticeable to us Arizona residents than visitors from out of state. She's wearing less makeup than normal and has a huge fucking smile on her face.

"We better get inside," she informs me, reaching for my hand.

I take a step away, putting myself out of reach. As we walk toward the building, I feel physically sick.

The waiting room is full of women in various stages of pregnancy, or so I assume. Some aren't showing like Hattie, but why else would they be there? Many are accompanied by men who're looking adoringly at the lady by their side, anticipating good news, unlike me. Imagining Gwen beside me, I know I'd feel like them. With Hattie, it's like waiting for a judge to pronounce sentence.

It's only a little past three when we're called in. Hattie's given something to pee into and disappears where she's told. I'd pointedly asked her to leave her handbag with me, having noted there was nowhere to hide anything under her dress. Yeah, I trust her so little, I half-expected her to bring a sample from a pregnant friend.

When she reappears, we wait in silence for the doctor to arrive. Well, I do. She tries to talk to me, prattling on about how exciting this is. How she's sure I'll make a great daddy. I tune her out, pretending my attention is fixed on the posters that cover the walls. I learn more about pregnancy and the development of a baby in those few minutes than I ever wanted to know.

Unless she was Gwen. Then I'd want to know everything.

"Good afternoon. I'm Dr Griggs." The doctor introduces herself breezily as she walks in. She wastes no time, speaking while she's seating yourself. "Congratulations. You're pregnant." She beams at Hattie, and then at me.

Though it's just what I expected, I feel my gut sink, and mentally take a moment to pull myself together. Bowing my head, I try to take deep breaths having just received the worst news ever. How can I begin to deal with it?

Hattie's returning the doctor's smile, but nodding as well. *She knew.* The news was hardly a surprise to her. Again, her hand reaches out to me, and I don't give a fuck how it looks as I shift my chair further away from hers.

"When was your last period?" Dr Griggs asks, pulling a keyboard toward her, and opening up a file on the screen.

"I can't remember," Hattie says.

"Are you irregular?"

"I am."

"Okay. Well, we'll do an ultrasound to check your dates."

"Oh, it's far too early for that," Hattie states, biting her lip. "I can't be more than a few weeks. But I do know the date of conception, three weeks and two days ago."

"Hmm." The doctor pulls down her glasses and peers at her over the top. "We do need to confirm your dates, Ms Sowerby.

"I've told you. It had to be then." Hattie shifts uncomfortably.

"Ms Sowerby." The doctor takes her glasses right off, and

twirls them around with her fingers. "Babies need to be monitored at various stages of their development. To book your appointments correctly, it's best we check and know what we're dealing with."

I'd kind of zoned out, trying to process that nothing was going to swoop in and save me from an eighteen year fate, but the doctor's tone makes me start paying attention. There's something about Hattie and her reaction that makes me suspicious, something that even at this late stage gives me a glimmer of hope. Of course, it could just be wishful thinking. She is pregnant, of that there's no doubt. But if the dates don't match, it might not be mine.

I cock an eyebrow at Hattie who's squirming awkwardly.

She sniffs. "I don't want a scan. This early it will be one of the invasive ones, won't it?"

"There's no danger," the doctor tries to reassure her. "It's better to make sure baby's looking like it should and we'll be able to assess your due date."

"Why do I need a date now?" Hattie sounds stubborn. "Can't we just work that out from the date of conception?"

"Ms Sowerby." The doctor sighs patiently. "I have a strong suspicion you've got that wrong. We detect pregnancy by measuring the levels of hCG in your body. It's the first hormone produced by the embryo. At first it's present in small amounts and increases until it reaches a maximum level between eight and eleven weeks of pregnancy. Your levels are raised considerably, so I'd put you at the higher end of the spectrum. That means you're quite possibly wrong about when conception was, and that's why I'd really like to check."

Wait a minute. What? My heart skips a beat. When it restarts, it's racing.

Turning to look at Hattie, I try to read her face. She's flushing as though she doesn't like being challenged, and her next words show she isn't going to give up.

"Maybe I just have higher levels."

The doctor maintains her composure, but I see signs she's getting frustrated. "Have you had any symptoms? Morning sickness, headache, fatigue?"

"No." Hattie shakes her head emphatically. "It's too soon for those."

Fucking liar. I noticed the way her eyes shifted when she supplied her answer.

My brain's thinking fast. "At nine weeks you can do a paternity test, can't you?" When the doctor nods, I ask probably just a little too eagerly, "If you think she's that far along, can we do one now?"

"I'm not risking our baby," Hattie cries out, her hands protectively covering her stomach. "And I told you, I'm only just pregnant. Your tests must be wrong or something."

The doctor narrows eyes which flick my way before returning to the woman in front of her. I begin to think she's cottoning onto the fact that Hattie might be leading me on. "It's just a simple blood test, and of course we can do that now."

"I don't like needles."

The doctor opens her mouth, but I shake my head, and instead turn to Hattie. "Ultrasound and/or blood test, or I'm walking out of here now."

When she bursts into tears wailing that I'm bullying her, I stand, raise my chin toward the doctor and walk out.

CHAPTER THIRTY-TWO

*G*wen...

Though I'd expected a prospect, it had been Peg waiting for me when I left work today. I'm surprised, and not a little unnerved to see him there.

Peg's a daunting figure of a man, standing as tall as his son, and with an even more impressive beard and neatly trimmed hair which is more grey than dark now. Despite his advancing years, his bearing remains military straight. He's quite intimidating, and I wonder why he's the one come to pick me up.

He's leaning against the club SUV, the same one they all seem to use. He looks different, then it hits me why. It's the first time I've seen him without his cut.

Seeing me exiting the building, he beckons at me from across the parking lot. My heart starts to beat fast, for a moment I wonder whether something's happened to Noah.

"Gwen." His eyes light up as I near him. "Did you have a good day at work?"

If it were something serious, then he wouldn't preface bad news with such a polite enquiry.

"It was good," I tell him. "At least I'm not frightening the clients now. I'm back to meeting and interviewing them. Less boring than paperwork."

"I can see how it would be." He chuckles softly as he opens the door to the car. When I get myself in, he shuts the door for me. *Such a gentleman*, I think.

I'm worried why he's here. *Does Noah know?* Had Peg swapped duties with a prospect? And if so, why? Last night I thought I'd got along with him.

As it turns out, I don't need to ask or wait long for an explanation. "Noah's gone with Hattie to visit the doctor to get a pregnancy test done. I thought you'd like to know."

Swallowing rapidly, I wonder whether he's giving me space to prepare myself. Sure, I knew Noah was going to press Hattie to go to a doctor, but I didn't know it would be as soon as today. I stare out the windshield. There was a large part of me that had hoped Hattie had been lying. That she'd arranged an appointment so fast strongly suggests she was not.

"You okay?"

"I guess," I respond to Peg. "I knew it was coming."

"You know my story?" he asks, then continues as though assuming I don't, "I was told the woman I was seeing was pregnant. I married her. Biggest mistake of my life. It was a lie to get my ring on her finger, or more accurately, to give her access to my bank account. It's the only time I've been grateful for losing my leg as it was that that made her come clean. I've often wished I'd approached it more like my son. Noah's right to make sure Hattie's telling the truth."

But I wish Hattie had been lying, just like Peg's first wife. "Why did you come to get me, Peg?"

He sighs, then is quiet for a moment as he navigates a turn. "When Hattie told us, I feared there'd be a fight getting Noah to have a relationship with her and the baby. Not because of who she was, but because he'd recently told me in no uncertain terms, he was never going to settle down. He was going to continue sowing his wild oats everywhere." He snorts. "I tried to tell him one day he'd meet his one, he told me such a person didn't exist."

We head onto the interstate and he overtakes a car. When he pulls back into his original lane, he carries on. "So, there was Hattie and I knew how it would go, then he walks in with you hand-in-hand. A fuckin' feather would have knocked me down. Yeah, I handled it badly."

I chuckle but it's mirthless. "On one hand you thought you had something that would make Noah settle down, and a potential grandchild being dangled in front of you. On the other Noah's relationship with me that came out of the blue. I can see how you were torn."

Turning my head, I can see him nodding. "I've had words with Noah, and Darcy has spoken to you. It's clear what happened. Despite the odds and his protestations, Noah has found his one. The other half he didn't know he'd been searching for, and even if he did, what he thought he'd never find. Sometimes I think Darcy and I set the bar too high for our son. I still love the fuck out of her, and she, God help her, loves me back."

The tone of his voice alerts me. "What's worrying you, Peg?"

He glances at me quickly before turning back to the road. "I'm worried that knowing another woman's carrying your man's baby will be too much for you. I know my son only too well, he's got a lot of me in him. Now he's found you, he's all-in, with Noah there are no half-measures. Losing you would damage him forever."

"I already know Hattie's pregnant. I'm still here."

"Do you? Or were you hoping that it was a mistake?"

Am I that transparent? Part of me did indeed have such hope. "Today, we'll know for certain." It's then the notion occurs to me. "Are you here, Peg, to persuade me to stay?"

"No, I'd never do that. If you can't cope, it's best to be upfront now. Nor would I tell you to step out of the way to let Noah be with the mother of his baby. I just thought you'd appreciate some time to think and a head's up before Noah gets home."

He stops talking, presumably allowing me said time, which I take gratefully.

Noah was adamant he wouldn't attempt to work things out with Hattie, but would that change once he knows for certain she was pregnant? What should I do if he'd changed his mind? Walk away for his sake and that of his child? Or, tell him that I think he's crazy?

"If he wants to try with Hattie, I'll step back, Peg."

"Fuck no, I'm not asking you to do that. Club voted on you being Noah's property, Gwen. They'd never vote Hattie in."

Much as I hate the word property, I know it's just how they are. Peg's own wife has a property patch, and she's about as independent a woman as you can get with a high-level job as well.

I'm curious. "Why wouldn't you vote Hattie in?"

He snorts. "That afternoon, when I thought Noah should step up as I had done and support the woman he'd gotten pregnant, I hadn't had all the facts. As soon as I did, I knew she wouldn't. For a start, because she blurted out she was pregnant as soon as she turned up on the compound. Old ladies are supposed to be discreet, and she failed at the first hurdle. When I considered that, I soon came to realise she cared fuck all about Noah, and it was about what she could take him for. Don't forget I had a woman who cared more for who I was and what I could give her, rather than me myself."

He stops talking after that. My fists clench and unclench as I think about how Noah must be feeling, now he must know for certain Hattie is pregnant. It's me who breaks the silence. "Noah's going to be gutted, even though he knew it was coming."

He grunts at my observation. "He's going to need you Gwen. You're going to have to help him figure out how this works. There will be more than two of you in this relationship."

"I lost my parents when I was six, Peg. I grew up in foster homes. I've never seen a good example of a family. Even if the foster parents were good, the other kids came from broken homes, and most of their energy went on sorting out their problems. Who's to say what a relationship should look like?" Feeling on a roll, I continue, "Do I like the idea that Hattie will try and come between us, no. Would I give up before we get started because it might be difficult? Again, no. Noah means too much to me."

A grunt then, "Will you come up to the house and wait for Noah with me and Darcy?"

I take it he's as eager to hear the outcome as much as I am. I can't see the harm in it, it's better than waiting for Noah to come home alone.

"Sure, Peg."

He sighs with relief. "I'll text him to tell him to come straight up."

By now we're at the compound. Peg drives through the gates then up the paved track that leads to the houses. He parks, tells me to wait, then comes and opens my door for me.

Darcy hugs me as soon as I enter.

"You not at work?" I ask Darcy.

"I took the afternoon off as soon as I heard where Noah was going." She gives me a weak smile. "I've got enough leave, and I didn't want to hear the news over the phone."

"It's only going to be confirmation of what we already know," I tell her, sadly.

There's not much to say that hasn't already been said. Darcy tries to keep a conversation going, asking me about work, and talking about some of the fires she's been to, but no one's really interested as we wait for the hammer to drop.

When the front door bursts open, and Noah walks in, all three of us stand.

This is it. My gut rolls, not wanting to hear the words from his lips. I'd cover my ears if I could. *I don't want to hear.*

Noah comes to a halt, his fists bunched at his sides, his eyes going between us. After a moment he takes a deep breath.

"Hattie's pregnant." Though I thought I was prepared, I feel like wailing out loud. Darcy's hand reaches out to touch mine. Noah's eyes flick down to our joined hands, then his mouth quirks. Watching him closely, I wonder at his expression. After waiting a beat, he delivers the punchline. "And I'm fuckin' certain it's not mine."

What?

"Noah?" Wrenching my hand out of his mom's, shakily I stand and run toward him. "What happened? Are you sure?"

"Yeah, Son. What the hell went on? Did she change her story?" Peg growls.

"Noah, tell us," Darcy demands.

Noah's face is almost unreadable. As he's not wearing quite the expression of relief he should be, I reckon there's more to it.

"From her hormone levels the doc reckons she's further along than she says she is, which would put me out of the picture. She denied it, of course, but refused to have a sonogram. The doc reckons she could already be nine weeks or more, so I asked her to have a blood test to prove I'm the father. She refused that as well."

"Fuckin' bitch liars!" Peg roars. His face grows red, then he walks over to his son, slapping him on the back. "Fuckin' glad you did what I should have done. Got the bitch to prove it."

"It was a different time, a different situation. You were dating, Peg." Darcy runs over to throw her arms around her man. "You can't be blamed for taking her words at face value."

Ignoring his parents, Noah's eyes are focused on mine, a small smile tugs at his lips.

He's mine. Not hers. He never was and never will be. I should be over the moon, but there's something niggling at me.

Wrapping my arms defensively around my torso, I ask the question that's burning at me. "Why you, Noah? Why not put the blame on the real father?" His head tilts to the side. "Lack of evidence isn't proof. Until we get the something concrete, there's a chance that you're still responsible, and the doctor's test could be wrong."

At first hearing the news, I'd been elated. Cautious by nature, I'm worried he could be mistaken.

"Gwen." Noah closes the gap between us. "All the evidence, as you call it, points to Hattie pointing the finger at the wrong man. Sure, there's the question of why, but isn't it better to focus that I'm not going to be a dad?"

Peg's eyes are on me, and I sense approval in them. "She's right, Noah. It's your word against hers, and all you've got is supposition. We need to get that fuckin' paternity test done and know for certain."

Darcy's also watching me and Noah. Her brow furrows. "What exactly did you say when you confronted her?"

Noah stiffens. "I didn't. When she refused the tests, I saw red. It was either walk out or put my fist in her face."

Agreeing all the indications are there that she'd been, to put it kindly, economical with the truth, Noah—and I—need to know for sure. "Perhaps you ought to speak to her?" After nibbling my lip I add, cautiously, "She must have a reason for telling such a huge lie."

"I don't trust myself near her," Noah admits. "Fuck, Gwen. She nearly ruined our relationship. I could have fuckin' lost you. If I see her again, I don't know if I could control myself. I *never* hurt women, but her?" He stares down at his fists.

"She's pregnant, Noah," Darcy reminds him. "And your dad's right. We need proof the baby's not your daughter or son."

"Why's she not naming who's really responsible?" I repeat, unable to get that thought out of my head.

"Maybe she didn't bother to get his name," Noah all but snaps. "Fuck knows. All I know is the kid's not mine."

"Gwen's right," Darcy gently admonishes him. "The doctor could have read the test results wrong, or something malfunctioned. Though I do accept her refusal to find out for sure rings a lot of warning bells. In my line of work, Noah, I know that where there's smoke, there's usually fire. But we need to find out for certain."

"Fuck it, Mom!" Noah turns on her. "Do you fuckin' want that kid to be mine? Would you prefer that?"

Peg growls in response to his son's attack on his wife. Noah's hands form fists and he takes a challenging stance.

Darcy steps between both of her men, one hand on each of their chests. "Calm the fuck down!" She glares from one to the other. "I've dealt with wildfires giving off less heat than you are right now. As for you, Noah, I just want you to face facts. We have suspicions, but can't prove shit right."

Suppressing a smile I realise, despite the two burly bikers who tower over her, it's Darcy who wears the trousers in this house. I decide I'll be getting some tips from her.

Both men step back, turning away from each other. But before either can speak, Noah's phone pings.

For a second I think he's going to ignore it, but then he takes it out.

His cheeks blaze as he reads the message. "Fuckin' hell. That's all I need." He starts typing a response out.

"Trouble?" Peg's attitude has changed completely. He's straightened, and his eyes are sharp.

"Hattie's at the gate. Butcher's asking if he should let her in."

Darcy moves quickly, putting her hand over the phone. "What are you replying?"

"What the fuck do you think? I'm instructing him to tell her to fuckin' get lost."

"Don't do that." Her eyes sharpen.

"What?" Noah's eyes open wide. "That's a step too fuckin' far, *Mother*. I'll kill her if I have to speak to her right now."

"Trust me," she says quickly. "You don't need to see her. You and Peg go the back way down to the clubhouse, but get Butcher to escort Hattie here."

"Why the fuck do you want to see her?" Peg asks, his eyes wide and incredulous.

But his wife simply taps the side of her nose. "Leave it to me. Just trust me."

"What should I do?" I notice she hasn't asked me to leave with Noah.

She smirks. "You stay here and follow my lead."

Noah looks undecided, looking from her to me. "You sure you know what you're doing, Mom?"

"Noah, I run a fire department. I think I can handle one stupid girl."

With obvious reluctance, he deletes his unsent text and types out a new one. Then he nods at Peg, and both men look ready to leave. Before he goes out the door, he pulls me to him, kissing me gently, and telling me quietly, "I know you can handle yourself, Gwen. But take fuckin' care. I don't trust that woman."

Noah and Peg have only been gone a few minutes when a car pulls up outside the house.

As I'm trying to prepare myself mentally to face the woman I hate with every fibre of my body, Darcy sends me a wink and mouths, *go along with it*. Then she starts speaking loudly.

"Gwen, I'm sorry, but you must understand. Noah's focus has to be on his baby. There's really no point in you hanging around. Hattie and Noah need space to start their family."

"Darcy," I cry. Knowing she's acting, I manage to add a note of pleading into my voice. "Please listen to me."

There's a rap on the door. Darcy steps forward to open it. When Hattie enters, she goes as far as to pull her into her arms.

"How are you Hattie? How's my grandkid doing? What did the doctor say? Noah hasn't spoken to me."

Hattie returns her hug, spies me and smirks. Then, to Darcy, asks, "Where's Noah? I thought he was here."

"He will be soon. He and Peg had club business to deal with. I'm getting dinner, you want to help me?"

Over the head of Hattie, I swear Darcy mouths at me, *offer to help.* So I do. "I can help you, Darcy."

Hattie turns and glares at me. "You're not wanted here. You're nothing to Noah. I'm carrying his baby."

Darcy's greeting has clearly given her confidence, making me think Noah's mom has missed her calling as an actor.

Quick as a flash an excuse occurs to me. "I'm waiting for Lisa. You can't stop me from seeing her."

"Who the fuck's Lisa?" Hattie's eyes sharpen, as if thinking she's got more competition.

"My daughter." Darcy, in clear view of Hattie, frowns at me. Then her arm goes around the other woman. "Let's go to the kitchen. Gwen can wait here."

Hattie tosses her hair over her shoulder and gives me another one of her sneering glances. "We don't need you," she informs me cattily. "In fact, no one needs you. I don't know why you're here."

I don't say anything as Darcy leads her into the next room.

What am I supposed to do now? Follow them? *What does Darcy want me to do?* Argue my case in front of Hattie? Cause a scene by accusing her of stealing my man? *But in her eyes, she had him first, so perhaps that makes me the thief?*

For a moment, I do nothing, except listen to the voices easily heard over the clattering of pans. Darcy's making polite enquiries about morning sickness and the like. It's painful hearing Hattie explaining just what Noah's baby is doing to her. Yeah, she's claiming him as the father at every opportunity.

It's going to be a big baby, I mean, just look at the father.

What was Noah like as a baby? His kid's going to be just like him.

Noah's going to make a great dad, isn't he?

I don't want to listen to this, but knowing Darcy's up to something makes me stay. There's a reason Noah's mom wanted me here. She must think I've got broad enough shoulders to deal with this.

"Do you mind chopping the carrots, Hattie?"

"Of course not. I'll help any way I can. I'm part of the family, aren't I?"

"Of course you are," Darcy replies airily. "Here, use this, be careful it's…" There's a loud screech, then "Oh my God! I'm so sorry. I wasn't thinking of what I was doing. I'm so sorry Hattie. Let me see. Oh, it's not much, just a scratch. Here, put some paper towel around it."

"I'm bleeding," comes out of Hattie's mouth as a wail.

"It's not too bad, you just need a Band-Aid, I'll go get one."

Darcy exits the kitchen, heading for me. She winks, shoves something into my hand. "Get this to Noah. Mouse will know where to get the DNA test done. That man can do anything."

Jesus. My eyes widen as I clutch the balled up paper towel in my hand. This woman will be my mother-in-law if things work out between Noah and me. *She's scary.* I love her already.

CHAPTER THIRTY-THREE

*T*hrottle…

I trust my mother to have my best interests at heart, though I can't help wondering whether her idea of what they are coincide with mine right now. I hate that Hattie's on the compound, and more than that, hate that I left Gwen to be faced with her. If I had my way I'd protect Gwen from everything, and that includes any unpleasantness that's in my power to keep from her life. I've abandoned her, and I don't like it.

"Your mom's got a plan." Peg tries to reassure me. "You can trust her. You know why she rose through the ranks in the fire service? Because she was always one step ahead of the fire. She knows what she's doing, Noah."

"I hope you're right," I respond, tugging at my beard. "She could make matters worse."

"Fuckin' trust her, Son," Peg repeats firmly.

When we enter the clubhouse via the door to the kitchen, having taken the back route instead of walking down the track, I'm greeted by inquisitive women and brothers all wanting to know what had happened today. And also, why the prospect was seen driving Hattie up to the top of the compound.

Of course, when I explain, they all agree with my interpretation that Hattie's lying through her back teeth. I end up receiving numerous back slaps for being off the hook. But Wraith eyes me, and then Peg quizzically. You don't have to be a mind reader to see he's wondering, why, in that case, Hattie has gone to our house. As I've no explanation to give, I stay quiet on that topic.

Mom's got a plan. But can I trust her? In her efforts to do what's right, she could make the situation worse, if only painting a larger target on my old lady's back.

Drinking a beer I don't really want, I wish I was a fly on the wall and could know what's going on. Deep down I know, however good my mom is, words won't cut it with Hattie.

The minutes go by slowly. I'm on tenterhooks waiting. A few times I'm about to say *fuck this* and go back to rescue Gwen, but Peg stops me with one of his growls rooting me in place. I'm anxious and worried, then when I'm just about to get up and do what the fuck I want, the clubroom door opens and Gwen rushes in, her eyes searching the room until they land on me, then she heads straight over.

"Give this to Mouse!" She passes a carefully held piece of kitchen towel to me.

"What the fuck?"

She's outright grinning. "Remind me never to cross your mom. That's Hattie's blood, she cut her."

"What did you fuckin' say?" Peg snarls. "Darcy did what?" The extent to which his eyes have widened would be comical in any other situation.

"Oh, it was 'accidental'." She uses air-quotes as she laughs.

I'm standing staring down at what I'm holding, shaking my head dubiously. "Will this work?"

Gwen shrugs. "Darcy seemed to think Mouse could do anything."

"If he can't, I fuckin' will." Wizard's voice sounds from behind me, and he's holding a plastic bag open in his hands. I drop the paper into it, dubious that it's only a tiny amount. "Will need to bleed you too, Brother."

"You got a DNA lab on speed dial?" I ask.

He chuckles. "Not personally, but there's always Utah."

"Fuckin' Utah." Drummer overhears and walks up. "But using their contacts is a good fuckin' idea, Brother."

I hide my grin. Drummer's never been completely comfortable with the Utah chapter, not since he discovered what they really were twenty years back. They're Satan's Devils like we all are, but they work as vigilantes on the side of right. Their contacts are far ranging, and they've solved more than one kidnapping or brought traffickers down due to DNA being left behind.

"Hey, Throttle. I'll do the honours!" Blade's eager voice joins in, and he's got a huge fucking knife in his hands.

"You'll take my fuckin' finger off." I roll my eyes. "I can do it myself. Someone get me something to put it in."

Sophie appears from the kitchen with a small jar. "I just washed it out with boiling water."

Great. Looking around I nearly the whole darn club around me. Manning up, I slide my knife out of my belt, and hold it over my finger.

"Just do it already," Hound shouts.

I can slice up any man I'm questioning, but cut myself?

"What you waiting for?"

But as Marvel speaks up, Gwen moves in front of me, rising on her tiptoes. I lower my head to allow her to give me a supportive kiss, when in one swift move she pulls the knife from my hand and I feel a sharp sting on my finger.

"All done," she tells me in a perfect mom's tone. Then she presents the receptacle and I let blood drip down into the jar.

"Man was too fuckin' chicken to do it himself!" Marvel yells out.

"Nice one, Gwen. We'd have been waiting all fuckin' day." That, I think is from Roadkill.

While I'm the butt of the jokes going on around me, Wizard steps up and takes my donated blood from my hands.

Hawk, like his namesake has been hovering, he swoops in now. "Think it's time to go face Hattie. Mind if I tag along?"

"Just what I was thinking," Dad states, with a grin worthy of one of Blade's nastiest coming over his face.

"I'll stay here."

"Like fuck you will," I say to Gwen. "You won't want to miss the fun." She looks puzzled, but I don't enlighten her. I just take a firm hold of her hand, leaving her no choice.

The four of us take the direct route up to the top of the compound. Entering my childhood home, I inhale an aroma that takes me straight back to my younger days. Mom doesn't cook often, but when she does, she shows some wicked skills. *Pot roast* is on the menu if I'm not mistaken.

Hattie is obviously helping, she's carefully setting out silverware on the table. Her eyes light up as they land on me, and she comes running across. When she reaches me, her welcoming smile fades, and as she holds up a finger wrapped in a Band-Aid, her bottom lip trembles.

"I got cut."

She's clearly looking for sympathy, but she's come to the wrong person. I hold up my finger where my own cut has already dried. "Coincidence, huh? I got cut myself." Raising my eyes, I cast a look over her shoulder. "Thanks, Mom."

Hattie shakes her head as though she can't make sense of anything, but as her gaze finds the woman who's come in with me, she glares, places her hands on her hips as though staking her territory and spits out, "*You* are not welcome here."

"She's more welcome than you," I say abruptly.

Hattie's brow creases, and again her bottom lip trembles. "But your mom… she and I have been cooking dinner together. I don't want her here." She turns and appeals to Mom. "Tell her to go, Darcy. She's coming between me and Noah."

Mom's eyes flare as she steps forward. When she speaks, her tone reminds me of times I did something stupid when I was young. "Hattie, are you really that dumb? Firstly, that you don't realise there's no you and Noah and will never be. And secondly, do you really think I'm as careless as to hand a sharp knife over point first?"

So that's how you did it. Good for you, Mom. I snort.

"I don't understand," Hattie cries, her eyes flicking to the woman behind her, then to Gwen, then me, then back to my mom. "Why did you cut me?" She turns back to me, and stares at my own hand. She pales as she starts to realise. "Noah, how did you get hurt?"

Hawk chuckles behind me and it's like I can read his mind. I decide to put her out of her misery. "Blood, Hattie. Yours and mine. Only takes a little to get a full DNA profile."

She goes white as she stares open-mouthed at me. Then screams, "What have you done?" She launches herself at me, but Peg's there, pulling her away and securing her hands.

"You're this baby's daddy," she screeches.

I shrug nonchalantly. "Guess we'll find that out in a couple of days."

"You are. Believe me. You can't have my blood tested, I forbid it."

I walk up closer. "You forbid it? I'd have thought you wanted proof as well. See, say it proves I'm the father, you'll have me just like you want. You protesting sounds like you got a confession to make. Just admit it. You're pregnant, but it's got nothing to do with me."

"There are more questions we want answered," Hawk says, threateningly. "Like, were you responsible for stalking Throttle and Gwen, and shooting up Gwen's house?"

A flicker of fear comes over her face, she bites her lip, then says, "I know nothing about any shooting."

"Really?" Hawk presses her. "But you're a little liar, aren't you?" Then he turns to me. "Think that's something else you need to get answers for, Throttle. "

Peg leans down and speaks into her ear. "You do know Throttle is the enforcer for the club, don't you Hattie?" She demonstrates she does when her eyes come to my patch. "You know what an enforcer does?" Her eyes are wide as she shakes her head. Peg gleefully enlightens her. "He forces people to tell him the truth, and though he's my son, even I don't like to watch him at work. He's an expert at torturing information out of our enemies."

"You can't… You won't."

My hardened gaze suggests I can. Though the softer side of me protests I'd never hurt a pregnant lady, however obnoxious she might be.

"Why don't you just admit I'm not the father? Might save me the bother and you some pain." Verbally I don't pull my punches.

She struggles against Peg, but he's lost none of his strength over the years. She's crying and screaming. "Let me go, you assholes."

"What do you want to do, Throttle?" Somehow Hawk manages to make himself heard over the noise she's making.

"I want the truth, Brother. If she gives me that, and a promise she'll never again come near me and my old lady, she can go." If she was a man, she wouldn't be walking away, but she's not. And she's pregnant. Evil she might be, but that poor baby's innocent.

"So how about it, Hattie? You admit to Throttle you lied about paternity, and we'll let you go unharmed. If you refuse to tell us the truth, then we'll extend our hospitality for a few days until the proof comes in from the DNA lab. I actually wouldn't advise it, I don't think Throttle's feeling very hospitable right now."

I fold my arms over my chest and fix my stare on her. "Oh I can be hospitable. Got a nice hard chair and handcuffs to tie her to it."

Hawk snorts, but Hattie pales even further.

"Darcy?" she appeals to my mom.

Mom stares back at her. "You wanted a biker's undivided attention, now it appears you have it. None of us like liars."

Why doesn't she just go?

Hattie seems undecided. She looks at Hawk, then Peg, then flicks a glance at Mom. None show the slightest sympathy for her. On my part, I could give zero fucks. She tried to come between me and my old lady, more than that, if she'd had her way, she'd have destroyed my life. Did she really think I'd play happy families and manage to successfully pass me off with a kid that wasn't my own? There's no pit in hell deep enough for her.

Finally Hattie looks at Gwen with an expression that makes me fucking grateful looks can't kill. She spits on the ground. "I had nothing to do with any stalker activities, and I don't even know how to shoot a gun. I'm certain you're the father, Throttle, and I'll make you eat your words."

"If," I start. "If I ever see you near Gwen, near her work, near her house or in the same fuckin' grocery store, pregnant or not, you'll be dead Hattie, and no one will ever find your body. Am I making myself clear?" She's paled, it's a good look on her. "I mean it Hattie. And you can leave the fuckin' gifts out. No stalking me, no coming on to me else you'll face the same outcome. You feel me now?"

"I don't know what you're talking about," she cries out. Her eyes scan around, landing on each of her audience. No one speaks, and no one shows any compassion for her. After a moment, she throws up her hands. "You're all fuckin' crazy. I'll go now."

"Too fuckin' right you'll go," I snarl at her. She hasn't admitted it, but I'm sick to death of looking at her. I've got better things to do with my time. "I never want to see your face again. Don't ever come near me or my old lady, else pregnant or not, a little pain will be the least of your worries."

Hawk catches my eyes, then he, too, nods, as if realising we'll soon have the proof and her admission isn't necessary. "I'll escort her down to her car," he offers. When I raise my chin, he takes hold of her arm and doesn't hang about.

As soon as Hawk and Hattie leave, there's a palpable change in the air, as though we've all breathed out a collective sigh of relief. The silence is broken when Mom speaks.

"Oh well, now that's over. I'll go and finish off dinner. You two are staying, I take it?"

I snort. "Yeah, thanks, Mom. Unless Hattie spat in it or slipped a vial of poison in."

Mom's eyebrows rise and she responds utterly seriously, "I was watching her carefully." Then, she turns to Peg. "You can come help me."

"Yes, ma'am," Peg responds with a sharp salute.

I'm chuckling when they walk off together, then I look down at Gwen. I notice her face is flushed.

"What's up, babe?"

"Er? Oh, I was just thinking."

"Yeah?" That concerns me. We should be concentrating on us and building our new relationship and not letting Hattie's machinations influence us. Fuck knows what damage that bitch has already done. *At the least shoving it in Gwen's face about what a manwhore I am, or rather was.* Just having Gwen close reminds me I'm a redeemed man.

"Yeah," Gwen repeats, biting her lip, and looking up at me through her eyelashes. She seems hesitant to tell me what she's thinking.

Of course, my mind goes to the worst it could be. "Gwen, don't let her come between us. Hattie's in the past, along with how I used to behave. I promise you, you're who I want."

"Huh," she states. "But you offered her preferential treatment."

I swing her around to face me, putting my hands on her biceps to hold her in place. "What the fuck are you talking about? I've never offered her a goddamn thing."

"Er, you have." Her face grows red, and her pupils dilate. I'm running over everything I've said to Hattie in front of her and coming up blank. My mysticism much show on my face, as she lets me out of my misery. "You offered to tie her up with handcuffs and interrogate her."

Fucking hell! Suddenly I compute she's not angry but aroused, and she's suggesting she wants to play games that I can get fully onboard with. *Gwen in my handcuffs and at my mercy?* Fuck yes.

"You got a confession I need to get out of you?" Raising my eyebrows I try to keep the excitement out of my voice.

"Maybe." She's back to biting her lip again.

"Mom!" I yell loudly. "We're skipping dinner."

CHAPTER THIRTY-FOUR

*G*wen...

I have to run to keep up with Noah's long legs as he takes my hand and drags me down the track. Seems like I've woken a beast. Rightly I should go to hell for getting aroused with that oblique reference to bondage, it was not the right time. Me in his handcuffs and at his mercy?

Yes please.

Being tied up is something I've never experienced, all my limited sexual exploits to date have been very much on the side of vanilla, I've read though, extensively, and enough to know the idea excites me.

I have no idea why, at such an inappropriate time, while he was threatening Hattie, my brain envisaged me being the one in his restraints. But once the idea lodged in my brain, I couldn't get rid of it.

His reaction makes me wonder what I've let myself in for, but there's one thing I know, whatever he does, I'll enjoy the hell out of it. Noah would never hurt me, I trust him implicitly, but letting him take complete control? It's not just my mouth watering at the thought of it, my panties are wet as well.

When we reach his suite, he pushes open the door and stands

back to let me inside. Stealing a glance at his face I see his jaw is set, his countenance so stern it sends a shiver down my spine.

With a hand on my shoulder he stops me as soon as we're in this room, and the door is kicked shut behind us. My back to his front, he speaks directly into my ear.

"You've been holding your fantasies back from me. That makes you a naughty girl, Gwen. And bad girls get what's coming to them."

That shiver wracks my body again.

"Get rid of the clothes."

His tone, so dominant, so demanding makes my whole body flush. Overheated I do just what he asks. First, I kick off my sandals, then discard my tee. Risking a glance behind me, it's to see him staring impassively on with his arms folded.

Knowing to expect no assistance from him, I continue. Unzipping my jeans I push them to the floor and step out.

"Now the rest. You're going to hide nothing from me."

Hoping this wasn't exactly the way he'd intended this to play out with Hattie, I unclasp my bra and let the straps slip down my arms, then allow the whole thing to drop onto the floor. With a shuddering indrawn breath, a slight hesitation, I pull down my panties, rewarded with a sharp indrawn breath that he can't quite suppress.

"That ass should be classed as a dangerous weapon," he states, his voice catching. Then he gets back into character and demands, "Get on the bed."

Feeling emboldened, I put a sway into the movement of my hips as I do what he's asked. Knowing how appreciative of that asset he is, I crawl up the mattress, wriggling my fanny, and taking my time.

"Stay like that," he commands.

I do, my knees and elbows pressed into the covers. I hear his steps and out of the corner of my eye I see him stepping up to his bedside table. He fumbles around, then pulls something out.

Seconds later he grabs my hand, and before I know it, I've a zip tie attaching it to the headboard. Then, he does the same to the other. Finally a sharp blade appears in my line of vision as he lays it down on the table.

Intaking a breath sharply, I ask, "What's that for?"

"To quickly get you out of the restraints should I need to." A reassuring hand rests between my shoulder blades. "Your safety comes first, always, Gwen." Then again, there's a swift change of tone. "So, you've been keeping things back from me. You want to start talking?"

"No," I cry out, playing my role. "You'll never break me."

He chuckles an evil sound as I've ever heard.

"Seems like you need some persuasion." He pauses, when I glance back, he's looking around the room carefully, and mumbling to himself, "Fuck, I wish I was better prepared."

He walks to the closet and opens it, rummaging around for a while. When he comes back, he's got something that looks strangely like a tie which I can't imagine him ever wearing, and in his other hand, a belt. Then my legs are yanked back making me flop to my stomach. With strong but careful movements, he takes one ankle and fixes it to a bed post, then does the same with the other, tying it to the opposite one. I'm spreadeagled before him.

I think he has me just where he wants me, but he does not. Now he fixes a blindfold around my eyes, stopping me sneaking quick peeks anymore.

He leans in, his mouth so close to my ear I can feel his warm breath when he tells me. "You're allowed to scream." He then backs away as I shiver, delightfully wondering what he's going to do to me which will elicit such sounds from me.

"You're going to think about what you have to tell me. When I've finished, *little girl* you're going to tell me everything."

"You certain of that?" I taunt him.

"Fuck yes," he breathes. "You won't hold anything back."

To my astonishment my ears are covered with headphones, they're good ones, meaning I can't hear him anymore. I don't know where he is, or what he's doing. I shudder as a tantalising fear washes over me. *I trust him.* Should we have agreed a safe word? *No, it's Noah, he'll stop if I ask him.*

It feels as though my skin has come alive. My body starts twitching in anticipation, muscles contract without any instruction as I've no idea what he's going to do, or where he'll touch first. I don't even know if he's still in the room with me. Although I trust him, panic starts to rise.

But before it can take hold, his palm gently comes to rest between my shoulder blades. The warmth reminds me I can do nothing but feel. As his hand is joined by his other, and he starts to stroke me, I begin to relax. *It's Noah. He won't do anything I don't like.*

He circles his hands around my shoulder blades and then continues the movement down to the small of my back. Digging in a little, it becomes a massage that I'd pay good money for, I moan softly.

But my pleasure is short lived as he gently moves his hands from my armpits, over my ribs then his fingers move to my sides, making me jerk violently. *I'm ticklish.* I open my mouth, but it appears my reaction was enough, as to my relief, he lifts his hands momentarily before placing them on the cheeks of my ass. For a moment he palms the globes gently in a smoothing movement, before his fingers flex then tighten, kneading the parts he'd previously admired.

Then, there's nothing. No part of him is touching me. I inhale and hold it, wondering what he'll do next when suddenly a sharp pain goes through me. *He's spanked me.*

"Oh!" *No. I don't like that.*

But the sting is followed by the warmth of his palm, as he massages the ache away. And I'll be damned if there's not a connection between the discomfort on my ass cheek and my clit which is throbbing mercilessly.

The flat of his hand meets the other side of my ass. This time

I'm more prepared for it and eagerly anticipate the effect. I'm not disappointed.

He spanks me a few times more, and I feel my skin burning, but that's nothing to how my clit is screaming for his attention. As if to check what he's doing to me, I feel his fingers probe, and by the ease with which they move into me, I'm sure I'm so wet I'll be making a mess on his sheets. For which, he's no one to blame but himself.

"Noah, please!" I'm not too proud to beg.

I can't hear or see if I've influenced him, but next it's his mouth that he uses to taunt me. Starting at my right foot, the base of which luckily he avoids as again he'd tickle me, he starts to kiss his way up my calf and along my inner thigh. I buck my ass, and my legs try to close of their own volition, but I'm open to him, unable to prevent him doing anything he likes. The knowledge I'm his toy and under his control does something to me. My muscles start to tense and I'm so aroused I think a breath of air would tip me over.

"Noah," I plead.

But the bastard backs off, and now starting at my left foot, repeats the process.

"Touch me. Please. Touch me."

Touch me. Touch me. I also try telepathy to get him where I want, but again he stops before reaching the place where I need him the most. Futilely I tug my hands against the restraints, wanting more than he's giving me.

I'm cold now as for a second the warmth of his hands leave me, but not for long. *What's he doing now?* He's parting my ass cheeks. *Oh good Lord, he's looking at what no person has ever seen before.*

"Noah? What are you doing?" I try to protest and feel my skin burning in embarrassment.

Whether he answers, I can't hear, but my words don't stop him. I'm powerless to do anything as I feel his finger rimming my asshole. Then, his hand touches my dripping slit, but instead of probing in, he slides his hand up, and starts to press into that most private place.

"Oh!"

It burns, I don't like it. But I've nothing with which to prevent him. He keeps pushing until he breeches me. *I hate it…* Don't I? It's different, odd, invasive, but it's also arousing me. *He shouldn't be there.* Maybe it's the wrongness that's making me so turned on. Now I'm silent, not knowing whether to encourage him to continue or demand he stops.

Keeping one finger where I don't think it should be, he moves his other hand, and finally touches where I want him. My poor abandoned clit given some attention at last.

Yes. Please. There.

The pressure of his finger in my ass as he moves it in and out, seems to make me feel more intensely than ever before.

I'm on a hair trigger. My stomach contracts, my muscles clench, I take advantage that my mouth is already open and suck in air ready to let my muffled scream escape when he stops.

His still clothed body comes over me, illicit intense feelings fill me at the thought I'm naked and totally at his mercy while he is still fully clothed. I feel him vibrating against me. *He's chuckling.* The bastard knows how close I was.

Gentle kisses pepper my shoulder blades, then he places a trail of them down my body. His teeth close on one of the globes of my ass. A sudden sharp bite that does nothing to dampen my arousal, in fact he only increases it more.

I'm desperate, I writhe, trying to get his attention to that spot where I need him the most.

"Noah, I'm fucking begging you."

All the while, one finger remains in my ass. Now I feel more pressure as he tries to add one more. I clench, trying to keep him out, but a rapid slap to each side of my rump makes me forget what I'm fighting, and the second digit takes advantage and gains entry.

What the fuck is he doing? His fingers are moving like they're scissoring inside me. My clit cries out. To try to get relief I press my mound down to the sheet and writhe. *Have I ever been this aroused before?* Fuck no, before now, I didn't know that meaning of the word.

I sigh with relief as he remembers that place which I'd feared he'd forgotten. As he starts to play with my clit once more, I try to hide my reaction fearing again he'll stop. But it's impossible, my body is under his control. I'm like a finely tuned instrument that he's playing like a virtuoso.

I've fingers in my asshole, fingers expertly toying with my clit. When his teeth again close on my flank, it's like an off the scale earthquake rocking my world. I already knew I respond to Noah like no other, but there are literally no words for this. My climax is almost painful in its intensity, I now know why they call this the little death. I'm never going to survive it...

I think I black out, as the next thing I'm aware of is my legs are free and I'm pulled up onto my knees and the headphones are off. As I try to swallow the saliva that's filling my mouth, I realise he must have freed his dick as he pulls me back and there's a probing at my slit.

"Noah. Yes. Noah." I'm incapable of using my voice other than to beg. "Please, Noah, please."

"Told you, you wouldn't hold anything back," Noah stammers out as he grunts and pushes his way into me, sliding in easily as I'm so damn drenched.

"I love you," I scream out, feeling full of him, my sensitive clit already throbbing again.

He chuckles at my declaration. "Want you to strangle my fuckin' dick," he pants out. "Let me feel you, Gwen."

Obediently I clench, making him gasp. *Jeez, he must have made me extra sensitive, the piercings of his are more noticeable tonight.* As he moves, a shiver runs through me, and I start to wonder whether I'm going to survive.

"Gwen, with my handprints on your fuckin' ass... Your

perfect," *thrust*, "delectable," *thrust*, "ass. You'd let me do anything I fuckin' want to you because you're mine."

"I'm… yours." It's the truth. I would.

"Too," *thrust*, "fuckin'," *thrust*, "right."

Then he forgoes words, as he starts to hammer in earnest. The headboard bangs against the wall making me pleased the adjacent suite's on the opposite side of the building. My orgasm builds as his piercings hit the right spot time after time. I'm out of control as my body takes on a mind of its own, bearing down on him, I soar into the heavens once more. He pauses a moment, groaning louder, his face clenched as he fights to hold himself back. He's not finished, however neither, it would seem am I, when a second powerful orgasm, my third of the night, follows almost immediately. It's this last one that makes him reach his limit.

He grunts, groans, and exclaims, "Oh fuck. Fuck, fuck. *Fuck.*" His body stills and I swear I feel a rush of warmth inside me.

But it's Noah. He always uses condoms.

It must be a sign of how wet he made me, as when he pulls out, I feel a wetness leave me. *I really have made a mess of his sheets.*

"Jesus." Noah's body rests lightly on me, his hands planted each side of my body holding his weight. "Fuck, Gwen. You're going to be the death of me." His lips touch that spot between my shoulder blades making me quiver with pleasure. "And if you were wondering, I love you too."

I feel his weight shift, then see flashes of the knife as he cuts through the ties binding my hands. It makes no difference, after coming so hard, even free I'm unable to move.

"You okay?"

"Apart from dead, yes." My reply makes him chuckle.

"Have a nap while I go get cleaned up." He bends so he can place a kiss on the side of my lips, then pushes himself up. It's then I hear him exclaim, "Fuck, Gwen."

The dismay in his voice gets me to push my overworked

muscles into turning myself over. "What?"

He points to his dick, sticky with our combined juices. My mouth opens wide, and I don't need him to say the words.

"I'm so fuckin' sorry. I forgot the condom." Tortured eyes rise to examine my face. "First time in my fuckin' life."

Quickly I do some calculations. "We should be safe. I've only just had my period."

His eyes close briefly, I assume in relief. When they open, he informs me. "Knew it felt fuckin' better than ever. Gwen, you need to go on the pill or something, or we'll be facing the consequences."

I suppose it will be up to me. Always on the woman to take precautions. A little grumpily I ask, "What if I preferred to face the consequences."

I expected him to be horrified, but I'm wrong. Instead his face splits into a wide grin. "Then you'd better get ready, as I'll be fuckin' you bare night and day."

Shocked, I state what that outcome might be. "You'd get me pregnant?"

He places his hand on my belly. "I never wanted kids, I'll be the first to admit it. But over the past few days, I've had to deal with the fact one might already be on the way. To my shock, it wasn't having a child in my life that I regretted, but the circumstances. I was scared at the thought of being responsible for a baby, but not horrified except for the thought of sharing parental duties with Hattie. I've compared my feelings to how I'd feel were it to be you who was pregnant instead—" He breaks off, and his eyes meet mine. "Would you understand if I say there's a tiny part of me that's disappointed? Not about Hattie, but that there's no baby?"

Is it as equally strange that I'm a bit disappointed myself?

But in reply, I huff. "So you want to use me as a substitute baby momma."

As his face goes blank, I sit up fast, placing my hand against his cheek. "I'm teasing you." When he relaxes, I add, "I'd be over the moon to have your baby. I'm just not sure of the timing. We're young, we're just starting out and I want to get through my internship first." But as the sensible words come out, I can't help thinking what it would be like to have a baby with him.

Like he said, Hattie's condition had caused me to do some heart searching. I knew I'd try my best to be a good mom to Noah's baby, even though I'd have resented its birth mother. It's nine parts relief that I feel, though that final tenth regrets I won't be seeing a little Noah anytime soon.

"You're right, of course." Do I detect regret or relief in his voice?

Noah gets up. As he does he shucks off his boxers jeans, grimacing at the mess congealing on them. "Messy business, this getting pregnant," he states with a grin. Then he strips off his t-shirt and lays his naked body on the bed. "If you think it's safe right now, can I come inside you bare again."

"You do know there's still a risk, don't you?"

His mouth quirks as his hands cup my face. "Seems like that boat has already sailed, and some risks are worth taking."

"Like letting you tie me up and torture me?" I narrow my eyes at him.

He chuckles. "You enjoyed giving me all the control."

I'd be a liar to deny it. Shyly, I bite my lip. "Can we try that again sometime?"

Snorting, he confirms he's willing. "I can certainly see us visiting that again." Then his brow furrows. "Unless there's anything you don't want repeated?"

I'd been shocked at first, nervous, but then blown away by sensation. "Nothing," I admit. "It just enhanced everything."

"I'll never do anything that you wouldn't enjoy, babe. I'll never hurt you."

I know that. That's why I trust him. "I love you, my twisted Throttle."

"Twisted?" He shakes his head and quivers with laughter. "Babe, you ain't seen nothing yet."

CHAPTER THIRTY-FIVE

*T*hrottle...

Yesterday Gwen and I spent most of the evening in bed, only emerging to grab some sustenance before heading back there again, falling asleep when we were both exhausted.

This morning I've woken with a smile on my face, and, I have to admit, a slightly sore, overworked dick.

But hell, it was worth it. My abused cock twitches as I brush my teeth, remembering how she'd responded when I went, as she termed it, twisted on her. As I stare into the mirror, it's not my reflection I see, but the red handprints on her delectable ass. *She enjoyed it, thank fuck.* There couldn't be a woman more perfect for me.

Over these past few days Hattie had had me twisted in knots. I'd felt adrift, being swept along by a tide of her making, not having a say in my future myself. Obviously I'll be happier when I hold the actual proof in my hands, but I'm already convinced that's all behind me and at last I'm back in control of my destiny.

I'm almost certain Hattie was our stalker, though she hadn't admitted it. While I can't touch a pregnant woman, she had to have an accomplice. Now him, I could tear apart with my own fucking hands.

But how am I going to find out who he is? We'll have to do some digging.

Will she stop now there's no benefit to be gained? I spit out toothpaste and saliva and carry on thinking. Or am I being stupid trying to pin everything on her. What if she's being truthful and she had nothing to do with it? It could be dangerous to go down just one road and find a dead end when the pavement runs out.

Thinking about dangerous, what a fool I was last night. I'd taken Gwen bare, fuck, I've flooded her with my semen. Hopefully she's right, and there's no chance of her being pregnant. It's far too soon, we've got too much else to worry about, and fun to be had starting our life.

But if she's wrong and foregoing the condom wasn't safe? I wait for the sense of panic, but it doesn't come. It's true I kind of got used to the idea of stepping up and fathering a baby, and if that baby was Gwen's, my life would be fucking perfect. This time it's my own smile I see reflected at me.

Gwen's still sleeping, so I leave her, chuckling at how tired she must be. Now I'm dragging my sleep-deprived self down to the clubhouse for the emergency church Wizard has called.

Entering the clubroom I find the room is full already. Hawk, as usual, has his daughter in his arms. Now he's joined by Wizard cradling his own baby, while Amy and Liv watch on. *That could be me.* For the first time, I feel envious, no longer smirking and thinking them fools. *My baby would be a mix of Gwen and me.*

I've stood there too long, all but drooling with my strange impatience to move nature along, as Hound notices and comes over.

"You upset you're not pregnant?"

I start, his words so close to my thoughts, it takes me a moment to realise what he means. "Never accepted I was." I spin around. "Fuck knows it's a relief. A baby with Hattie would be a fuckin' nightmare."

"Lucky escape, Brother," the sergeant-at-arms says. "Any idea why she named you as the father?"

I shrug. "Probably because I was a better choice than the sucker who knocked her up."

Hound gives an exaggerated shake of his head. "An asshole worse than you? I almost feel sorry for her."

My fist is fast, I catch him in the stomach. He folds, but while he clutches his body, he laughs.

My attention switches back to Wizard, and I watch as he carefully hands his son back to his wife. Then, when Hound's caught his breath, I address him. "Any idea why we've got church?"

Hound grows serious. "Prez wants to get your protection detail straight. To talk about the ongoing need for it."

I've been wondering that myself. When Wizard catches me staring at him, I raise my hand and give him a mock salute. Prez's caution mimics my thoughts of earlier. I'm not risking Gwen getting hurt again so I'll be grateful of other minds on it. I'll appreciate knowing what everyone else thinks.

"Noah!" a deep voice full of pleasure booms. "Tommy cleaned his bike."

Grinning, I turn and acknowledge the 'prospect' wearing his cut and riding his mobility scooter into the clubroom. "Looking good, Brother."

"Hey, Prospect, you can do mine later."

"Sure, boss man," Tommy answers Drummer who's walked in behind him.

Drummer's eyes roll, while Wizard snorts. Tommy will never accept that Drummer's no longer the prez and always defers to him.

I notice Tommy looking around uneasily. Trying to be discreet, he rides his scooter over to Hawk. "Is *she* here?" But as it's said in a stage whisper, I overhear.

Hawk shakes his head. "No, Tommy. The nasty woman has gone."

Intrigued, I raise my eyebrow. Hawk notices. Leaving Tommy cooing over the babies, he crosses the room to me. "We met Tommy yesterday when I was escorting Hattie to her car. Fuckin' bitch called him a halfwit."

I bristle. Just one more crime to lay at her door. No one insults Tommy and gets away with it. If I needed one, it's another reason why Hattie and I would never have worked. The guy's been a fixture in our club ever since I can remember, and no one has a bad word to say for him, or would tolerate one being said about him. Sure, mentally he's still a kid, but he's one of a kind. He's *our* Tommy.

"Church!" Wizard announces.

Hound, me and Prez are the first in. I take my seat, part of me still seething about Hattie's cruelness. I watch the others enter. Truck and Cast are next to arrive, followed by Dollar and Bullet. Joker and Lady turn up together, then comes Marvel. After a moment the FOGs turn up, Drummer first, followed by Peg, Wraith and Blade. That they're together could mean something. *Have they been plotting?* When I catch Hound's eye, I see he's noticed and also reads significance into them turning up together. He rolls his eyes and grins at me. Then Heart, Rock, Mouse and Shooter arrive one after the other, with Jekyll, Roadkill and Drifter being the last to arrive. It's then I notice Drummer hasn't sat down. He's leaning over Blade and chatting at the end of the table.

Prez bangs the gavel and narrows his eyes. "VP, you going to grace us with your presence?"

Drummer points to where Hawk's sitting. "This asshole is in my seat."

"Yeah." Wraith turns and glares at Hawk. "Old-timers only down at this end."

Blade gets out his knife and points it at the brother sitting one over from him. "Show some fuckin' respect to your elders and get out of that seat."

Wizard stills, then wipes his hand over his face. But when he looks up, his eyes have a twinkle in them. "Drummer?" he asks.

Drummer shrugs. "Sitting in for you reminded me why I jacked it in. Time for Hawk to step up again."

"Too fuckin' right," Wraith endorses.

Hawk's expression is unreadable.

Prez stares at Drummer who raises his chin. Then he glances around the table. "Seems like we've got a motion to consider. Hawk coming back to be my right-hand. Hawk, how do you feel about it? Is it time?"

Hawk swallows, then glances down, his lips press together as though he's thinking seriously. "Got a taste last week and it didn't send me running."

Thank fuck.

I decide to hurry it along. "I vote, aye."

"Aye," Heart says from his seat next to me.

One by one we go around the table. No one dissents, so Hawk is back in. I watch him carefully as he vacates the chair which is quickly taken by Drummer. Examining him I see him walking briskly to the top of the table, his back straight, eyes clear, and he's even grinning.

"About fuckin' time," Shooter remarks. His eyes follow Hawk until he sits down.

"Too fuckin' right," Drifter agrees.

Drummer simply eases into his chair with an exaggerated sigh, exchanging a fist bump with Wraith.

Prez bangs the gavel. "Now that's sorted," his harsh tone is softened by a wink toward his VP back in his rightful place, "let's get down to what you're all here for." He directs his stare toward me. "Throttle. Where are we at with your stalker?"

Clearing my throat, I sit forward, my hands clasped on the table. "The baby Hattie's carrying isn't mine." I'd be surprised if this was news to anyone.

"Lucky fuckin' break."

Glaring at Marvel, I carry on, "My stalker tried to butter me up. They sent gifts which is something a woman would do, so on that basis, I'd be content to say it was Hattie."

"You were also followed." Hawk's eyes regard me sharply. "She capable of that?"

I can't remark authoritatively on her driving skills, but I think it doubtful. "She have had to have had help. The shooting needed two people. I want to know more about her brother."

Peg's eyes meet mine. "You told her to back off even though she denied she's the stalker. You think she's going to heed that?"

Shrugging I respond, "What purpose has she got to keep it up? She knows I'm not the father of her kid. But, I am worried."

Wizard frowns. "Unfortunately women aren't the most predictable. She might not have given up yet. You reckon she was also Gwen's stalker?"

"Circumstances fit," I reply, my brow creasing. "Gwen's problems only started once we began talking to each other. It's not a stretch to assume Hattie wanted to get rid of the competition."

"If it is her, you think she'll stop now she knows she's got no chance with you?" Hawk's tone suggests he does not.

"Wish I could say that, VP." It feels right giving him that title. "It might make her even more determined to hurt Gwen."

Prez dips his head up and down. "I was worried about that. My recommendation is we keep watching out for both you and Gwen. And keep a close eye on what Hattie's doing."

"I'd like to know who is responsible for her baby bump," Mouse interjects. "And why she tried so hard to pin that on Throttle."

Joker raises a finger. "Maybe the real dad's the one helping her out. Perhaps he doesn't want to play happy families, so agree to help set up a patsy to take the fall for him."

"Bit of a stretch." Lady regards his man. "But it could make a kind of twisted logic."

Could it be that? What man would want to saddle a stranger with his baby? Or see his kid raised by another man. "Or," I state firmly, telling them the solution that makes most sense to me, "she doesn't know who the fuck it was. It could have been a one-night stand."

"Shame you couldn't hide who you were, Throttle. Next time you want to get your dick wet, leave your fuckin' cut behind."

Drifter gets the full force of my glare. "Won't be another fuckin' time. Not now I've got my ol' lady."

At Marvel's snort, I make a mental note to kill him.

Prez bangs the gavel. "Right, all I've picked up from this is while Throttle is off the hook, and that will be made final when we get back the results from the DNA—what's that Mouse, a couple of days?"

"Yeah, Prez. Utah said three days at most."

"Okay." Wizard continues, "I'm worried we could be going for the obvious, and don't want to overlook other stalker possibilities."

"There are the Drays," I put in. "I can't rule them out. They've got a reason to hate me, and I suspect could shoot a gun. More so than Hattie."

Blade raises his hand. "We took Gwen's car down to the scrapyard."

"You did fuckin' what?" My eyes blaze. "I haven't had a chance to talk to her yet."

"Calm your fuckin' horses," Blade shoots back. "I was going to refuse the offer they made. But it gave me an in to go down there." He stares, when he sees me calm down, then he grins sheepishly. "I, er, might have used a few of my old methods. Scared the shit out of them with my knife play, especially considering how I am now."

Truck snorts loudly. "Yeah, turns out an unpredictable grip on a knife is as scary as a firm one."

"And," Blade winks at the man who's just spoken, "they

nearly pissed themselves at the sight of Truck. Especially when he took out his eye and asked me to take care of it."

Wizard rolls his eyes. "Get to the point. They responsible or not?"

"Nah," the ex-enforcer remarks, sounding disappointed. "I don't think so. Their reaction to the car seemed genuine, as if they'd truly never seen it before."

"You sure?" I ask. It's my life on the line here.

Blade lifts his chin. "As I can be, Brother."

Wizard seems satisfied. "So we're back to Hattie, unless we've got an unsub we know fuck all about."

"I made sure she knew she'd be the first place I'd go looking if anything continued to happen to me," I tell him firmly. "Same goes if she's the one targeting Gwen."

"She believe you?"

"Oh yes," I answer him. "I made sure of that. But whether she'll heed it, I don't know. If she doesn't, it will be Gwen she's after."

"And again, Gwen's stalker could be totally unrelated." Hawk brushes a hand over his face. "We need to keep eyes on Gwen. If the shit dies down, then we can back off. If anything else happens, we'll have to keep trying to smoke this asshole out."

"Okay." Wizard raps his knuckles on the table. "I'm happy with that. Gwen remains under protection."

"She's not going back to her house," I state. "She's staying with me."

"As she should, Brother." Hawk grins at me.

"Oh fuck." Marvel looks disgusted. "I'm going to have to put up with shit like I did last night. You do know your woman's a screamer, don't you, Throt? *Yeah, fuck me, Throttle. Fuck me hard.*"

I can't remember Gwen saying that, for one thing she never uses my road name, but I get the idea. But I've no sympathy for him. Unlike me, Marvel takes sweet butts back to his suite all the time. I show him my finger.

"If you don't like it, why don't you move out?" Shooter queries. "There are a few suites we've recently refurbished."

"Hey," I protest. "Surely me and my old lady should get one of the new ones?" I recall a few cracked tiles in my bathroom and wince, wondering what she made of them.

"What are you going to do long term?" Peg's watching me closely.

"Build a house on the compound, or buy somewhere in town. We haven't gone into the details."

Shooter grins. "How about, to give you time, if Marvel moves out, we can convert his suite into a sitting room and kitchenette for you? Just like what was done to Peg's back in the day."

"We did that 'cause no one wanted to live next to the grumpy fucker," Drummer delights in reminding us. "Long before he got hitched."

Peg's mouth quirks and I chuckle with everyone, but the idea is sound. "That would give us time to consider what we're doing. And a place to live if we end up building a house. If you need us out while you're working, we can stay in Gwen's house once the threat is removed."

"Marvel?" Prez asks.

The man in question shrugs. "If it means I don't need earplugs, and I get better accommodations," his eyes query Shooter then Bullet, "I don't give a fuck."

Bullet's brow is creased. "Reckon we could get a team to start the work next week. Shouldn't take long, Throttle." He winks at Peg. "After all, we're practised at doing it."

"Or we could just chuck Drifter out." Marvel grins widely.

"I've had Peg's old apartment for years," Drifter protests.

"No one's chucking anyone out." Wizard slams his fist on the table.

"Except for me," Marvel grumbles.

"Stop stirring shit!" Prez shouts.

Marvel sits back and folds his arms. His eyes narrow as he

lays them on Shooter. "These refurbs. Got two free adjacent suites?"

I get where he's going immediately. "Fuck, Marvel. Why do you need so much room to yourself?"

"Why did Peg?" he counters.

"Marvel's as much an asshole," Drifter observes.

"Hey." Bullet, normally quiet, leans forward, waving his hand to get everyone to pipe down. "We can make another apartment. Shit, doing two together won't be too hard. If that's okay with you, Prez?"

Wizard shrugs, he looks fed up, and I reckon he's itching to get back to his wife and baby. "Anything to make Marvel shut the fuck up."

Marvel sits back smirking widely and opens his mouth. Blade points his knife toward him before he has the chance to say anything, and he has the sense to keep quiet.

"Right. That all?"

It seems like it is.

As Wizard wraps up the meeting, I wonder whether I can hope this is over, and the precautions we're taking are unnecessary. Hattie knows she's lost. I know the baby she's carrying isn't mine, and she knows Gwen's my old lady now. Unless she's fucking stupid, she must accept, even if Gwen wasn't in the equation, she'd still have no chance.

Surely, this is all over?

CHAPTER THIRTY-SIX

*G*wen…

"Oh, they're just adorable."

Amy, who I'd last seen still pregnant and looking ready to burst, looks up with a soft smile. "They're getting on like a house on fire."

Glancing down into the crib again, I see Layla, who I've seen before, now snuggled up against the new baby Calvin. As they are fast asleep and as yet barely capable of moving independently, I wonder how she can tell.

Even if it's only wishful thinking, I hope she's right. Having been an only child, I've longed for a sibling or even a cousin most of my life. "It will be lovely for them to grow up together."

My comment gets a snort from Layla's mom. "Just don't say that in front of Eli." She chuckles.

"Eli?"

"Hawk. He was born the president's son," Amy answers for her.

Olivia gives her side of the story. "And I was the VP's daughter." She points down into the crib, indicating that so, too, is Layla. "We were put together when we were about the same age."

"You grew up together? Friends to lovers?" If so, what a wonderful story.

Olivia raises and dips her head then laughs. "Now Eli is worried it's going to happen all over again."

"Worried?" Gratefully I accept the seat that Amy's waved me to. "What would he have to worry about?"

Amy grins widely, saying with an exaggerated wink, "Because he's a man, and he knows exactly what teenage boys are after."

A giggle comes from Olivia. "Believe me, we were experts at sneaking around. Our parents still don't know the half of what we got up to."

Catching on, I'm chuckling. "But Layla's what, only a couple of months? It's far too early to tell. They could end up hating each other. Just because you and Hawk were presumably inseparable, doesn't mean these two will be as well."

"Exactly," Amy pronounces as though I'm the voice of reason. "But the thought really winds Hawk up. When he sees this," she points down to the two babies snuggled up, "he'll lose his shit." She and Olivia exchange smirks.

Calvin's just born, Layla not much older. Personally, I reckon it's far too early to start worrying about future wedding bells, or more correctly, what happens before them.

"Where's my grandson?"

I look up on hearing a new voice.

"Marcia." Amy's face beams. "I presume you want to hold him?"

When she nods, Olivia sighs. "And we'd just got it all set up for Eli."

Marcia snorts, then waggles her fingers. "Granny time is far more important."

When Amy lifts her son and passes him over to his grandmother, Layla senses her companion has gone and starts to fret. Olivia lifts her, sniffs her to make sure she's clean, then hands her out.

"Want a cuddle, Gwen?"

Do I? I've never had anything to do with babies. But I don't want to offend her, and when she places her baby girl into my arms, she settles and goes back to sleep. Guess it was just the warmth of another human she wanted. A case of any port will do in a storm.

"So, what's going on with you and Throttle?" A teenager comes over, peers down at the baby in my arms, and then settles down next to me.

"This is Hilda, my youngest," Sophie explains as she walks up. "And Hilly, that's between Gwen and Throttle and no business of ours."

While I don't really mind talking about me and Noah, I don't know if it's my place to introduce myself as his old lady.

I try to change the subject, so I ask Hilda, "I suppose it must be great that you have lots of cousins living on the compound."

Hilda grins. "You could say that. Though some of the boys have gone now. There's Jacob…" I can't help but notice a flare in her eye. "Jacob joined up and is in the Marines, but Isabel is still around. Maya's gone to Vegas, and my sister Zoey has an apartment in town. Rose and Hope are somewhere around. Lisa, as you probably know, has already moved out. Zane has his own place, Mason is away with the Marines, and Maria, Tanya and Yiska live off compound with Mouse and Mariana."

"Jesus," I breathe out. "I had no idea there were so many of you."

"And some she's not mentioned," Amy comments. "I myself often lose count. Let's just say it was a lively place to grow up."

I knew some of them from school, of course. There always seemed to be a crowd. But some of the younger ones such as Mouse's kids, Hilda herself and Alexis, were too young to mix with us.

"Now we're starting on the next generation." Amy nods to Marcia cuddling Calvin. "You and Noah going to add to that?"

Olivia laughs. "Not if Throttle has his way. He runs a mile if you try to put a baby in his arms."

Amy just acknowledges her comment with a smile. "Things change when you find the person you want to spend your life with. What about you, Gwen? You up for repopulating the clubhouse?"

Again Olivia snorts. "If she moves onto the compound, the decision will be taken out of her hands." Turning to me she offers some advice, "Best you avoid drinking the water."

As my brow rises and I'm about to ask what the hell she means by that, there's a clomping of heavy boots which makes me glance over my shoulder. One by one the men appear from their meeting. Noah's one of the last out. He pushes through his brothers, halting when he spies me, and a beautiful smile covers his face.

"Gwen. Glad you made your way down here." He sends a shrewd look toward the women sitting around. "Hope you've all been looking after her?"

"Of course we have." Amy rolls her eyes. "And we've got her babysitting. You know, to get her in practice."

Noah's eyes at last land on the bundle in my arms. His expression doesn't shout his joy at the sight. It's hard to tell what he's thinking. It makes me hope there'll be no outcome for our mistake last night, an error of judgement we made more than once. Quite a few times to be honest, my lack of protestation I put down to the incredible feeling of those piercings of his. Whatever, we shouldn't repeat it. Noah certainly doesn't seem appreciative of me holding a baby in my arms.

"Here." Hawk appears beside him, leans over and takes Layla from me. "You could do with a bit of baby familiarisation." He chuckles as he holds his child out to Noah.

Noah stills, then gingerly takes Layla from his brother. Conversations around me stop completely, but Noah seems unperturbed. Holding her as if she's as fragile as the thinnest of glass, he cradles her carefully in his strong arms.

Best remember to use condoms later, I remind myself, as the sight just about makes my ovaries explode.

Before anyone can comment, a number of phones go off at once. Noah goes to pass the baby to her father, but Hawk steps back, gesturing to Olivia as he too takes out his phone.

The women around me tense, and I pick up on their worry. Something's happened to alert at least the officers of the club.

"Fuck," Noah breathes, his eyes landing on me.

"Noah?" I ask, sitting forward. "What is it?" I notice Hawk's looking at me with sympathy.

"Gwen," Noah starts.

His tone suggests the incoming message is very much something to do with me. "What's happened, Noah? If it's about me, let me know."

"Gwen, I'm so fuckin' sorry." He's scaring me, especially when he comes and kneels at my feet, taking hold of both of my hands. "The prospects said someone has firebombed your house."

"What?" I can't compute. Taking my hands out of him, I pull myself to my feet. "My house is on fire? Noah, I've got to get there. Is anyone hurt? Are the prospects all right?"

As though unwilling to let go of me, Noah takes me into his arms. "Razza's in the hospital with smoke inhalation. They'd already packed up your bags, and he ran back to bring them out."

He shouldn't have done that. Possessions aren't worth a man's life.

"I'm heading out to see Razza now," Hawk explains. "Butcher's dealing with the cops. I think you need to go down there, Throttle."

"They'll need to speak to me," I state, my voice quivering. "Noah, who's doing this to me? I thought it was Hattie, but she knows she's lost now. It can't be her." Despite myself, my tears start falling. It's not so much the loss of my house which was rented in any case, though losing it is devastating enough. It's that someone is still coming after me. I've no idea who it could be.

Noah's reluctant to take me, and while it's true I'd rather not see what's left of my home, I know I have to be there. I feel like the stuffing's been knocked out of me. In the last twenty-four hours I've lost almost everything I own, all I have is what the injured prospect managed to pull out. My car's been shot to pieces, and I've no idea if it's salvageable, and now, no home.

"You've got me." Noah's voice is forceful, as though he can read my mind.

I hadn't noticed Amy had stood when I did. "And you've got us. You've got family now."

I'm shaking, I'm scared. I'd thought it was over, instead, it's escalating. Again Noah understands.

"I'm not going to let anything happen to you, Gwen. Trust me."

I do trust him. Implicitly. But for how long will I need his protection? What if the attacker is patient and waits until I let down my guard? If it's not Hattie, who's got it in for me? I've told the truth, I'm unaware I've ever upset anyone in my life. Could a perfect stranger really want to hurt me this much?

Brushing away my tears, I tell him, "I've got to go and speak to the police now. Maybe this will make them sit up and take notice."

"You do need to go." Wizard's deep voice sounds from beside me. "Throttle, take her down there. I'll call Fontaine. The cops need to get off their asses and do something and not try to pin her troubles on non-existent trouble with the club. I'll make sure the lawyer understands that."

The rest of the day passes in a blur. My house has literally burned to the ground, there's barely anything left saving, and certainly nothing that can be salvaged. By the prospects' truck are two bags which contain the only possessions I now have. That a quick glance shows the new toy dog and teddy bear sitting on the top, requires me swallowing rapidly to prevent fresh useless tears falling.

The landlord turns up, and he's certainly not happy with me, his scowl suggesting he thought I'd left the stove on or something. Before he can voice his accusations, Noah silences him with one of his trademark warning growls, making him back off.

Once I've spoken to the fire investigators—*no, there was nothing flammable stored in the house*—I speak to the cops who seem to view me with suspicion, which intensifies as I see the landlord pointing at me and frantically gesticulating with his hands.

We go to the station and go over the same ground as we have before, the only difference is now there's another thing to discuss on the list. As before, Noah's taken off separately, as the cops try to impress on me these things wouldn't be happening if I kept better company.

However much I tell them it's nothing to do with the club, I can't get through to them. The main problem being, I've no other culprit to offer up.

This time I do mention Hattie, though in my view she's nothing to gain. Burning my house would only be vindictive, and it hurts to think she could stoop so low. But it's the only suggestion I can make to them, that she's a woman scorned, and I'd walked off with the prize. With a rolling of eyes, the cops convey they can't understand why women would fight over a biker. In their eyes, he's a criminal who's never been convicted of anything illegal. He's a member of an outlaw motorcycle club, and apparently, that's enough for them to look no further.

Again they spend less time with me than they do with Noah. Unlike our last visit here, I wait for his interview to conclude. When I see him walking out with Everest, his face is blazing with anger.

Giving him a glance full of concern, I voice my worry to the man who I work with. "Everest, they can't implicate, Noah, can they?"

"Not at all," Everest shoots back.

"But they're not fuckin' looking for anyone else," Noah spits out.

"You sure no one in your past would hurt you?" Everest asks, wiping his brow. "Until we can get some names to distract them, there's only one direction their fingers will be pointing. A mythical enemy of the club."

"But why? That makes no sense."

Everest shrugs. "They think anyone associated with the Satan's Devils deserves what's coming to them." At my raised eyebrow, he continues, "Gwen, I've known the Devils a while now. And in this, I trust what they tell me. Cops are taking the easy way out."

Noah glances at him, then back at me. "I know you don't think it's something to do with you, Gwen, but I think it's time you sat down with Mouse. Go over everyone you've ever been in contact with. Old foster families, boyfriends, fuck, even drivers you might have cut off. Each one will need to be eliminated."

I'm scared. Scared in case they find nothing, and I'll always be looking over my shoulder. Equally scared they do find something suspicious, and Noah gets fed up with me bringing all this hassle to his door. He can't be happy with the cops always taking him in and blaming him.

"Whatever's going on in that head of yours, Gwen, forget it." He looks down at me sternly. "We'll figure this out and sort it, okay? Then, we can get on with our lives. You've got me and the club now, fuck the cops." He waits for a second, for me to react.

"I don't deserve you, Noah."

"I'll leave you too lovebirds." Everest chuckles. "Let me know when the cops question you again, Noah."

"Haven't they finished with you?" I'm worried now.

"I'm a Devil, Gwen," Noah says tiredly. "They'll never be finished with me."

"Oh." I remember belatedly, that I'd passed the time making

a phone call. "Razza's being kept in overnight, but he should be home in the morning. They just want to keep an eye on his chest as they're worried the smoke might have damaged his lungs." I'm crossing my fingers and praying he'll be alright. I don't want that on my conscience.

"You checked?"

Well of course I did. Rascal got hurt on my behalf. But the fact I cared seems to please Noah.

"Fuckin' love you, Gwen."

"You sure I'm not too much trouble to keep around?"

"Babe, you're with a Satan's Devil." He rolls his eyes. "We live for this shit."

CHAPTER THIRTY-SEVEN

*T*hrottle…

Why the fuck did someone have to burn down Gwen's house?

Heading back to the compound I keep glancing over to see her staring ahead without really seeing anything. Since leaving the police station it's all caught up with her. Her hands writhe in her lap, and her teeth keep worrying her lip. I notice her wipe away a tear that's escaped. My gut twists. She deserves none of this. First it was her receiving a beat down, followed by them trashing her house. Then they destroyed her car, and now her home and everything she owns are reduced to ashes. All she's got are a couple of bags of clothes, and the stuffed animals that I'd replaced, seeing how much the loss of the threadbare toys had upset her.

If there were enemies of the club, I'd feel guilty that it was my fault. But try as I might to think of any name I could put on a list, I come up blank. Not now Blade's told me he's pretty certain the twins are out of the picture.

But was Blade right? He's the one who vouched for them, but he also went there with threats yesterday. Were they better actors than we thought and is this their retaliation for his accusations? I think it's time I go pay them a visit myself.

But first I've got to look after my old lady. She's taken knock after knock. I hate that she's gone so quiet.

I hate it even more when she finally speaks as we near the compound.

"Perhaps we should split up, Noah." When I growl, she says fast, "No, listen to me. If there's someone who's set his sights on me for some unknown reason and hates that I've chosen you instead, or even if this is down to Hattie, us splitting up may make her leave me alone." She pauses, then *fuck it,* adds, "We can't even discount it might be another woman who wants you to herself." Though she doesn't add it, I hear the unspoken part of her sentence. *You've fucked around enough.*

"There's no other fuckin' woman, Gwen. I made sure they all knew I was offering nothing."

"That's what you told Hattie," she counters.

"We're not fuckin' breaking up," I say firmly. "I don't run from anyone."

"But you're not the one who's lost everything!" she cries out.

She's right, I'm not. "You want them to win, Gwen?"

"No. But what are they going to do next? I don't want them to kill me." That thought pulls me up. "I might not want to live a life without you in it, but I don't want to die. I could have been shot yesterday, today if I'd been there either alone or with you, one of both of us could have burned to death."

It's now she starts crying in earnest. My brave girl has succumbed as the adrenaline has worn off.

I wait until we're on the compound, and I've parked the car before pulling her to me. "I'm not going to let that happen, Gwen. Someone will always be with you. Me, the prospects, or one of my brothers. Whoever it is is going to fuck up and we'll be right there waiting when they do."

"I'm so scared," she sobs. "Maybe I should go away and leave town. I don't want to put you in danger."

Each time something has come at Gwen, I've been impressed by the way she's bounced back. This time though it's hit her hard and she's starting to worry me. As I walk her up to my suite, she's oblivious of the people I pass or that I exchange chin lifts with a number of brothers.

Once there, I sit on the bed, pulling her down onto my lap. Rocking her gently I try to say soothing things, but I'm not even sure if she hears me. She's drowning in the depths of her misery. Do I think she's weak? Fuck no, she's been hit by blow after blow. A woman, or man for that matter, would be devastated to learn there was someone who could hate them this badly.

I'd rather they directed that hatred toward me. I'm no angel, I've tortured, hell, I've killed for my club. If I've upset someone, I'd deserve it. I remember how at first I thought Gwen was too good for me, too gentle, too peace loving. Is she being hurt because I brought her into my world?

Maybe I should let her go. But I'm a selfish bastard, I dismiss that thought immediately it occurs to me.

There's a knock at my door, I hadn't locked it so I simply call out permission to enter.

"Mom." I raise my chin in greeting.

She eyes Gwen, then comes over, sinking to her knees in front of us and taking Gwen's hands in hers. "Gwen, honey, I'm so damn sorry."

Making an effort to control herself, Gwen sniffs loudly, and blows her nose in a tissue I've placed there. It makes me remember how many tears she's cried since she met me. I vow I'll do whatever it takes to ensure she never has cause to weep again.

"The fire investigators have finished their report. It was arson. A Molotov cocktail with a fast-acting accelerant." Mom gives her professional update.

"So if I'd been there, or me and Noah, we'd have been dead." Gwen's voice has no emotion in it.

"Why the fuck are you telling her this, Mom?"

"So she knows there wasn't a fault with the wiring, or anything else. I'm sure the police have, or will, suggest."

"They did," Gwen agrees. "Or that one of the prospects deliberately set the fire."

"They fuckin' what?"

Mom waves me down, and I swallow my temper. Gwen needs me to be supportive right now.

Another knock comes. When the door opens, Nathan enters, he's carrying a tray piled with food. Behind him comes Butcher who's carrying a cooler.

"Sam sent fried chicken up, thought you both might need some food."

"I got whisky." Butcher flourishes a bottle. "And in here's some wine. Tash said it was Gwen's favourite sort."

I thank them, and they go. Gwen seems bewildered.

"I'll leave you alone," Mom suggests.

After she leaves, Gwen picks at the food, and more eagerly approaches the drink Butcher had left.

It seems she wants me to do little more than hold her. We watch some mindless television for a while, then I put her to bed where all I do is lie with my arms around her.

After a night fraught with nightmares, she wakes anything but refreshed, but I can't persuade her to take time off work. So I drive her there myself, taking the club's SUV instead of my bike, mindful of the enhanced safety features. She leaves me with a half-hearted kiss that betrays she's not really with me. I hate watching her walk into the building and remain standing for a moment staring after the doors have closed behind her.

"Throttle." Turning I greet Fontaine with a chin lift. "How's Gwen?"

"Going through the motions. This has knocked it out of her. I'm worried about her." I admit.

"She's a strong woman," he tells me. "She'll be fine. Want me to check in with her?"

Again I raise my chin. "I'd appreciate that." He's no threat and definitely no stalker. I mock salute him and turn away, feeling slightly easier that she'll have eyes on her inside.

Then I drive off, heading for the scrapyard, unsurprised to pick up a tail before I'm halfway there. This one, though, doesn't bother me.

Having parked, I get out and walk over to the bike. "Peg."

He cracks his knuckles. "Knew you'd come here, Son."

Narrowing my eyes, I respond, "If you're here to tell me Blade's already checked it out, don't bother."

"Whoa." He holds up his hands. "You're only doing what I'd do myself. Seems they," he jerks his head toward the reception, "have reason to fuck your life up. They overstepped the mark if they're targeting that woman of yours. And," he winks, "my future daughter-in-law."

I don't tell him the subject of marriage hasn't yet been approached. But as there's no way I'm letting her go, the details don't matter. I'm happy for him to be at my side. He's a scary fucker, another trait I've inherited. I reckon the ex-sergeant-at arms and the current enforcer should get the truth out of the bike thieves inside. Returning momentarily to the car, I pull out my cut and slip it on. What I'm going to do has no need for me to be incognito.

A sign which has seen better days hangs above the entrance denoting the place as *Dray and Sons*. When I push open the door, an old-fashioned bell sounds.

"Be right out."

There's the sound of clattering and banging from the back office. The sounds draw closer until a man emerges. Immediately he sees me, he turns to run, but Dad's there, stopping his escape.

"I did nothing!" he screams and automatically cradles his right hand.

"You sure about that, Cedar?" Dad says menacingly from behind him.

"What's going... oh." An old man, who must be the father

due to the resemblance to Cedar and Oak, steps out. "You lot again." He eyes his son. "We don't want more trouble. Whatever you think my crazy sons have done, they haven't. They're too fuckin' scared of you."

I'm not taking his word for it. "So you weren't near my girlfriend's house when it burned down yesterday?"

Cedar actually whimpers. "Not us, no. Oak and I were out drinking last night."

"From what time? And where?"

"About five pm. We had food and stayed there past midnight. Oak's got one fuck of a hangover today."

"I had to go and ferry them home," the old man confirms.

Dad catches my eye and nods downward. Well, I'll be fucked. Cedar has pissed himself. Guess his bladder is as weak as his brother's. Dad and I do make a scary pair.

"What can I say?" The old man's face wrinkles with disgust. "They stole a fuckin' Satan's Devils bike. Shows what idiots my sons are. But they do have some sense. Shooting up a car and bike, like your friends who were here yesterday suggested, and now setting fire to a house, even they wouldn't be stupid enough to do that."

Do I believe him? I'm not sure. Signalling to Peg, I step forward. Peg envelopes Cedar in a bear hug, and I grab his uninjured hand and force it down onto the desktop, then take out my knife.

"Don't hurt me," he sobs. "I can barely work now. Please I beg you. I had nothing to do with your girlfriend. I don't even know where she lives."

A shot is fired behind me. I duck down, Peg crouches pulling Cedar with him. The old man? He stays standing.

"What's it going to fuckin' take to persuade you we don't know what you're talking about?" a voice calls from outside. "We learned our fuckin' lesson not to fuck with your bikes. Let my brother go now. We want no war with the Satan's Devils."

"Get in here, Oak. And put that fuckin' gun down," their

father growls, then his eyes come to my face. "Oak's over-wrought, he's doing two men's jobs now. You've done enough."

"He's got a gun," I comment. "And he's not fuckin' afraid to use it."

"And he could walk right behind you and still miss." He rolls his eyes. "Fuckin' waste of space, both of them." He yells out, "Oak, put the fuckin' gun down like I told you, and come inside."

Never one to trust a man who's armed, I go and stand behind the door. Peg moves Cedar in front of him like a shield. That darn bell rings like an alarm, and, as I suspected, Oak hasn't obeyed his dad, but a karate chop has the weapon falling to the ground, and Oak screaming like a child.

It's clear that the Drays aren't skilled and are definitely cowards. What's happened to Gwen might be right up their street. An attack on an unarmed woman from behind, a drive-by shooting, and throwing a Molotov cocktail into a house are actions of men who don't want a confrontation. The question is, even that takes balls which I'm not sure they have.

I pick up Oak's gun in my gloved hand, and motion at Dad. He interprets it and pats Cedar down, then does the same to the old man, relieving him of a pistol.

"Kneel, fucker."

Oak whimpers and complies, and I put the barrel to the back of his head.

"Hey, Peg." My tone is measured, reasonable. "If I shoot Oak, do you think Cedar will fall down dead?"

Peg chuckles evilly. "Interesting experiment. Why don't you try?"

"You're fuckin' crazy!" Old man Dray has paled.

A jerk of my head has Peg coming to stand beside me. With both of us covering three unarmed men, we're in control. I assess which approach might get us answers quickly. From the way the old man had spoken, he's got sway over his sons. I decide to focus on him.

Raising my weapon, I aim at Dray senior. "One fuckin' chance to tell me the truth or the old man goes down."

"Step back," Dad snaps as Oak tries to cover his father. "No one fuckin' move."

"One last chance to admit you've been jerking the Satan's Devils around. Or you'll have to alter your business sign."

"How can we admit something we've not done?" Cedar screams out. "Check out our alibis. We weren't anywhere near your girlfriend's house last night."

Peg growls softly, making me quickly turn to him. Keeping his gun trained and eyes to his front, he tilts his head sideways. "More than one way to skin a cat, Son," he says sotto voce directly into my ear.

I frown, then grin, as I get his meaning. Maybe we can do this without leaving a mess for the prospects to clear up. I change tack immediately.

"Oh, I won't bother checking your alibis out." At my word all hope seems to flee from their eyes. "I'll let the cops do that. And, I'll also offer them a suggestion that they might want to look deeper into your business."

The look on old man Dray's face is priceless. He goes pale, then flushes, then somehow manages to do the impossible and appears to do both at the same time. He moves fast, grabbing Cedar by the throat and slamming him against the wall behind.

"Did you or your brother burn down that fuckin' house? Answer me you piece of shit. You fuckin' answer me now." For good measure, he bangs the twin's head against the woodwork, making me wince in sympathy, but observing, out of interest, how Oak rubs the back of his head.

"We had nothing to do with it, Dad!" Cedar screams out.

Old man Dray studies his son's face for a moment, then lets him go. Cedar drops to the ground whimpering in agony.

His rheumy eyes rise and settle on my face. "I can't stop you doing what you're going to do. My boys wronged the Satan's Devils once, stole a fuckin' bike they had no business taking. I know my sons, know when they're lying. While they're not fuckin' angels, they can't lie for shit, at least not to me. I believe them when they say they have nothing to do with the attack on your lady." All fight and bravado leaves him. "I can't do anymore to convince you."

I glance at Dad who's watching me. In my gut there's a dread that all Gwen's woes are down to me, that it was the Drays and what happened to her was as a result of the revenge I sought for Nathan's bike. But does it make sense? The old man's strong, but his boys are blubbering wrecks.

They could be lying, all of them. But I don't feel I have enough to end them. Instead, I decide to resort to a threat. "Your partners wouldn't be happy to know you stole a bike from an MC, or that you've fucked with a friendly club. If one more hair on the head of my woman gets harmed, the next MC visiting will be the Wretched Soulz, and you'll lose your profitable business, if not your lives."

"You know?"

I nod at the old man. "Money laundering? Yeah, we know. It's why you don't want the cops looking into your business." I owe Mouse a drink for the suggestion.

Peg clears his throat beside me. "I think you better start praying for the continued health of Throttle's ol' lady." He shifts his gaze my way and raises his eyebrows.

I'm still not one hundred percent whether it was them, but the threat I made should stop them doing anything more. My proof might come by nothing further happening to Gwen, which, in itself, is satisfying, though less so than removing them from the face of the earth.

CHAPTER THIRTY-EIGHT

Gwen...

I learned early on to stand up for myself. To take whatever life threw me on the chin. Although it took mental strength and resolve, I've never allowed myself to wallow in self-pity. People take knocks and setbacks, learn from them and move on.

The aftereffects of my original attack had left me feeling vulnerable and scared, but instead of giving in, I was determined never to put myself in that position again. Since then I'd been more aware of my surroundings and more vigilant. I'll never let anyone sneak up on me again.

The vandalism of my house I put down to my own stupidity, of allowing my purse to be stolen, and leaving inside my house keys. Another lesson learned, I should never keep my driving license, or anything containing my address with my keys.

The drive-by shooting isn't quite so easy to put behind me, but the culprit seemed focused on causing damage to my car and Noah's bike rather than killing either of us. The loss of a car is to be regretted, but can easily be replaced. A foster kid learns early not to become attached to possessions, moving on they can only take as much as can be stuffed into a garbage sack.

If I wasn't learning to respect and admire the men and women of the Satan's Devils MC, maybe I'd blame my attachment to them on what had happened to me. But even if they had garnered an enemy that had bizarrely decided attacking me was a way of getting to them, I'd suspect the reason in the Devils' eyes was a just one.

If Noah, himself, had done something to cause this, the only people I blame are those that would choose to wage war on a woman. His response, his devastation on my behalf, had made me more determined, not less, that Noah was the right man for me. All my life I've longed for someone to watch out for and protect me, whose sole focus was me. I won't walk away, just because he made a mistake. It's the bastards that are doing this to me who are to blame, not Noah, and not the Satan's Devils MC.

My house was small, but it was the first home of my own. I struggled with the finances, but it belonged to me. For a foster kid always moving around, getting bricks and mortar gave me permanency. I didn't even realise the significance until it was gone.

That's what's taken the wind out of my sails. The final blow that I'm finding it hard to put behind me.

I could be dead if I'd been staying there.

Had the perpetrator known I was away that night? Or did they not care?

There's no one in my past who wishes me dead. I've dredged the depths of my memories and have come up with nothing that would deserve such a penalty. However I think it, my thoughts always come around that whoever it is wants Noah to suffer, and wants to hurt him by hurting me.

Without knowing club business, the only name I can come up with is Hattie. Though she'd have to be stark-raving mad to think she'd get Noah if I was out of the picture. She'd have no chance, even if she was carrying his baby. Now the truth's coming out, she's got no hold on him at all.

Maybe that's why it's escalated? If she can't have her happy ending, neither can he.

Yeah, I suppose there could be some rationale for Hattie wanting to get rid of me permanently.

The thought is chilling. Unlike anything else, I can't prepare. Though the Satan's Devils are protecting me, I can't get the thought of a well-aimed bullet striking my head when I least expect it. No amount of self-defence training would protect me. And what if they took out a bystander as well, or one of the prospects or brothers who were with me?

The weak person I've been since returning to the compound isn't me, but I can't shake my trepidation off.

This morning I went to work even though Noah told me to take a personal day. Hurrying through the front doors and past security I didn't feel safe until I was inside. But I couldn't relax. Every interview I was asked to conduct or sit in on, I wondered if someone was using a ploy to get at me. *Hattie must have an accomplice.* For a start, she couldn't drive a truck while aiming at gun at my house.

Returning to the compound that night, I still can't relax, even in Noah's arms. He's patient with me, mumbling words about PTSD and that my reactions, my depression, my loss of self are to be expected.

The cops have no leads, but I'm not surprised. I'm tainted by my connection to the MC, and pick up the vibe that if criminals take each other out, that only works in their favour. If I wasn't with Noah, they'd be moving heaven and earth to discover who's targeting me.

I need to do something. I can't live like this. I'm being swept along by the tide, with no control. I hate it.

We're sitting in the clubroom, me snuggled into Noah's side. I'm there, but I'm not. Life is going on around me, but I can't take part in it. *What's the point of getting more friendly with women, if someone's going to end my, or heaven forbid, Noah's life?*

Suddenly I know I can't live like this. Satan's Devils are

protecting me now, but what if my assailant is patient? What if they wait until the club drops their guard?

I suddenly spin in my seat, turning to face Noah. "I can't be a victim anymore."

"Gwen, you're not a victim."

"Don't," I warn him. "Don't say I'm a survivor. I'm alive now, but if those bastards have their way, I won't always be. Even if it's by accident and not design, one day they'll go too far."

"You don't know that. They might have been watching, knew you weren't in the house. Fuck Gwen, they'd have seen the prospects packing up your stuff."

"Or they might have assumed I'd be back. And if I was, I'd be dead. Your mom said it went up quickly."

"I don't believe that. It's a message to me, not a death threat to you."

"Aren't those two things one and the same? I can't do this, Noah. I can't take this feeling of being scared."

He sighs deeply, pain etches his forehead. "You want to leave. Gwen. I can make that happen. We'll go away, go to another chapter. Get new identities if you want."

I shake my head. "That's not what I need. I don't want to be hiding forever."

"You want to leave me? Gwen, we don't know that will be safe."

"For fuck's sake, Noah, I know." My burst of anger is frustration, not at him, but with the situation, but he flinches anyway. "I'm not giving in to them, but I'm suggesting we draw them out. You and me together triggers them. So let's go out together, be seen. But we'll be prepared. You think your brothers would be up to that?"

He looks at me. For a moment his expression is unreadable. Then worry lines crease his brow and he gives a shake of his head. "I'm not putting you in danger, Gwen."

"You're putting me in danger every day, Noah, if only to my

mental health. Even driving with you to work the hairs stand up on the back of my neck and I wait for that bullet to come through the windshield. I can't live like this."

"It won't be for long…"

"You can't know that! What if they're just waiting for us to relax? Or what if things escalate and they go after you?"

He raises his hand and cups the side of my face. "I'm not taking risks with you, Gwen." His finger covers my lips. "Not saying it's something we've not considered. But I'm not using you as bait. There may be some way to get them to come after me."

"So you'll ride around putting yourself in danger just on the off chance? Noah, can't you see, it's me and you together that triggers them. We both need to do this."

"She's right."

The interruption makes me realise my voice has got loud. I swing around to see Hawk handing off his daughter to his wife.

"Prez's office, now."

Noah stands and waves at me to stay put, but Hawk shakes his head. "I think she ought to be in on this, Brother."

It's clear Noah doesn't like it, but giving him no choice, I stand, and stride off in the direction where I think the prez's office is. Hawk follows fast, steering me to the second door along instead of the first.

He knocks, then opens the door when permission is called out for us to enter.

Wizard is my overall boss at the Wheel Inn, but he's been so kind, I sort of overlooked that. However, in his domain he doesn't look like the new father proud to show off his baby. He looks like an MC prez.

Behind his desk is an imposing flag showing the insignia of the Satan's Devils MC. Blown up so large it's more intimidating than the patch they all wear on the back of their cut.

Wizard doesn't stand or offer to shake hands. He pushes aside his monitor and steadies his eyes on us.

"VP, Throttle. Gwen."

Unperturbed by the lack of warm welcome, Hawk plops himself down in one of the seats and takes it upon himself to wave me and Throttle to the other chairs. Throttle points me to the one next to Hawk, while pulling out a spare for himself. To my amusement, he turns it around and straddles it so his front is to its back. He then clasps his hands and rests his chin on them.

"Gwen wants to draw whoever's fucking with Throttle and her out."

At Hawk's pronouncement, Wizard's eyes fall on me. "Dangerous gamble," is all he says.

Throttle goes to speak, but I get in first. "I hate reacting, Wizard. I'm a woman who likes to plan. These things coming at me when I least expect it are screwing with my head. I can't live like this. I want to be in the driving seat and turn the tables on whoever it is."

Wizard raises his eyebrow at Noah.

"I don't like it, Prez, but Gwen's got a point. It's not like it's something we haven't already considered."

"You got a plan?"

I'm not quite sure who Wizard has directed the question to, but Hawk is the one who answers. "Throttle and Gwen being together seems to be the trigger. If it's Hattie, let's find out for sure. If it's someone else, we'll be able to pick them up."

"I think it is Hattie," I tell them.

"You think she can put a Molotov cocktail together?" Noah tilts his head.

Maybe not. "Someone helped her," I suggest.

Wizard rests his head back and seems to be thinking. "I'm not happy about using a civilian as bait." He opens one eye and spears me with it. "But under the circumstances, I think we need Gwen's help to draw them out. Things are definitely escalating, and we need it to stop. But we have to control the situation. They won't approach if they see we've got eyes on you."

Hawk taps his hand against his lips. His brow creases, then

he leans forward, clasping his hands between his knees. "What do we do with an unhappy woman? We put them on the back of our bikes and take them for some wind therapy."

"Unprotected while we're riding, VP." Throttle objects. "A side swipe from a truck could take us out."

"So, we plan the route. It needs to be short, maybe to one of the canyons? Brothers will head out early, take up stations along the road. If Throttle passes without incident, they'll stay put, but if someone seems to be tailing them, the first brother who sees them go pass can pass on the warning, and other brothers can get in between."

"I don't like it," Noah growls. "What about if we get to our destination before the tail is taken out?"

"Some of us will already be there waiting."

"It could work." Wizard nods his head slowly. "Get the snipers on the road. They can take out the tyres if necessary. Heart, Hound, and Cast have military experience and Shooter's a fuckin' good shot. Make sure they're spaced at intervals, with spotters in between. The rest of us will be at the end point."

It seems they have a plan, but there's one thing they seem to be missing. The stalker will have to know what we're doing. "How will they know when to follow us?"

Noah harrumphs as though I've made a good point, but Hawk doesn't seem fazed. "If Gwen agrees to call in sick at work, we could set it up first thing one morning."

"What's your reasoning, VP?" Wizard challenges.

"Gwen's lost her house, so she's here on the compound. No chance of anyone getting to her here. Her office premises are locked up tight. Her routine's predictable. If anyone's waiting to take her out, her going to and from work is their only chance of doing it."

"I agree." Noah's perked up. "They'll think we're heading to town, but we'll peel off and go to the canyon instead. They might think it's a spur-of-the-moment decision if we leave at the same time as she normally would."

"When?" I'm all for the plan. Or any plan for that matter, as long as whoever is after me is stopped. "Can it be soon?"

Wizard considers again for a moment. "Tomorrow." He leans forward. "I'll explain why. Things have happened one after the other. They didn't leave more than a day between the shooting and starting the fire at the house. Someone's frustrated as hell. Leave it any longer, and they might try for a hit on the compound, or failing that, try to get to us through another member, or heaven forbid, an old lady or one of the kids. Right now I wouldn't discount a kidnapping to draw Gwen or you out. They're desperate."

"I can call Everest. He'll get the message through I'm not going in." While right now retaining my job is the last thing on my mind, I know it should take priority. I've worked hard to get where I am.

Noah's looking torn, he stares at me for a moment, then shakes his head, grimaces and warns, "The brothers will have to get up early."

"All to the good, Brother," Hawk states with a gleam in his eye. "We can get organised under the cover of darkness. They won't be watching until it's time for you to head out."

CHAPTER THIRTY-NINE

*T*hrottle…

Gwen's a woman who, other than with sex, needs to hold the steering wheel in her life. I've been worried about her understandably downbeat mood, but immediately we decided to take a pro-active stance, she'd sparked up.

Wizard had called the brothers together, and this time Gwen wasn't to be in the room. The change in her was noticeable as I asked her to wait in the clubroom. Olivia and Amy had the babies there, and Gwen had made a beeline for them. Earlier, she'd avoided them as if she could taint them through being a victim of an arson attack.

I'd paused for a moment, seeing her cradle Hawk's newborn in her arms, realising how right she looked with a baby. *That could be ours one day.* We're both young, though, time to get to know each other better and form a solid relationship before introducing children into the mix.

Though it would be good for mine, Hawk and Wizard's kids to grow up close in age. It would be like repeating history all over again. Hmm. Maybe later could come sooner.

I'd had to leave those thoughts behind, as the summons had

been answered. As brothers headed toward the meeting room, I followed them in.

It hadn't taken long to fine tune the details of the VP's plan. That he'd come up with it cemented we were right to put him back as Prez's right-hand man. The fucker has always had a good head on his shoulders.

There's no dissent, just suggestions for how this could play out. A few expected grumbles about being up at the crack of dawn, with Marvel coming up with some half-baked excuse his vision was fuzzy first thing. Joker had just told him not to jerk off tonight.

Meeting over once all the details had been agreed, I dragged Gwen away from the babies, wanting her all to myself.

While I didn't want to express my thoughts, us taking the initiative could backfire, and rather than us getting them, they could get us instead. If I had my way, I'd wrap Gwen in cotton wool and keep her safe on the compound forever, but Prez's suggestion about someone else being taken to draw us out had been chilling.

All I could do was play my part to the letter and do all I can to keep my old lady safe.

Tonight isn't about kink, these last few hours with her are to be cherished. While I'm trying to push the thought to the back of my mind, this might be my last night on earth. I'm not being macabre, just realistic when I say, there's no way Gwen's not surviving, I'd give my life to save hers.

Back at the suite, I make love to her. Kissing, caressing, touching and memorising her body, taking time like I've done with no other before. I won't even bother with a condom. She's said it's a safe time, and even if it's not, if I die tomorrow, she'll always have something of me with her. That she doesn't remind me to take precautions leads me to believe she's thinking along the same lines.

I use my mouth, loving the feeling of her thighs clenching around my head. When she's come a couple of times, I start to situate myself, but she's got other ideas. She pulls herself into a kneeling position and pushes me down. Of course I didn't resist, I'd have been a fool to.

A thought I revisit more than once as Gwen takes my cock into her mouth and begins to work her magic.

Women have given me blowjobs more times than I can count. I thought I knew what a good mouth fuck felt like, but I was totally wrong. Gwen isn't doing this tit for tat, she isn't returning a favour, she's doing it because she wants to and is enjoying it. There's no faking her reactions. A glint in her eye as she watches me, when I suck in air, she does what she just did again. She's licking precum off the tip as though it's the tastiest delicacy.

What she can't get into her mouth, she caresses with her hands, and all the time her tongue is teasing my piercings.

I can't turn off my dominant side, but she seems to like it. When I tangle my hands into her hair, positioning and guiding her, she redoubles her efforts. My balls throb to her touch, my spine tingles and my dick swells. I can't take this sweet torture any longer however much I'd like to extend it.

She complains with a groan as I pull her away, and now it's her on her back again. I can't wait to get into that place that feels like nirvana. She's wet, I'm harder than I've ever been before.

I thrust in unable to take my time, pausing as her walls surround me. I love this woman so fucking much. I was an asshole for ever thinking there wasn't a difference between spending the night in the equivalent of a cheap, convenient hotel and enjoying the comforts of home. Being inside Gwen is so special, it's all I'll ever want and need.

"Noah," she calls out, wriggling and trying to get me moving.

I oblige, pulling out and pushing back in. My cock's primed and ready, and again that tingling begins. But I'm not letting go until I've reminded her of the heights to which I can take her.

I finger her clit, using my piercings to torture her sweet spot, being rewarded by her clenched fists, her indrawn breath and the rippling of her muscles against me.

When she screams, she takes me with her.

I groan, she cries out, and for a moment I have sympathy with Marvel, but I don't give a fuck who hears me pleasuring my woman.

Without needing words I curl up around her, just holding her tight. We doze, recover, then wake and repeat it. When morning comes, we've had fuck all rest, but I'll be as sharp as I need to. I have to be.

It's still dark when we meet at the clubhouse. Although Gwen and I won't be leaving until everyone else is in place, I want to be there to make sure there are no last minute hitches, and check that everyone knows what they're doing, and will all head to the right place.

"Hey, old-timers should get a fuckin' pass. What time d'ya call this?" Blade walks in rubbing sleep from his eyes.

"Young'uns need help from us FOGs," Wraith replies, stifling a yawn. "We've got to show them how to do things."

Drummer walks in looking bright and sharp. "You'd complain if they left us out of the party."

Prez sends them a tolerant stare and shakes his head.

Peg arrives and heads straight for me. "Don't take fuckin' risks, Throttle. Lead them to us, don't take them on yourself."

"I will. Whoever it is, I want them alive, Peg. I want to know what started all this and make sure it's ended." It was what I'd expressed last night.

"I hear you, Brother."

Yeah, today we're brothers in arms, that transcends our familial relationship. But still I add, "You keep your head down." He rolls his eyes.

"We doing this?" Rock comes up, tugging at his ear.

"Where are the others?" I glance around.

"Out with the bikes. We're ready to get rolling."

The snipers, Heart, Cast, Hound and Shooter, are holding

back, giving the others a chance to get clear before heading out to pick the best spots. Joker, Lady, Mouse and Bullet are waiting to leave with them. They'll be interspaced between the sharpshooters and able to give a prewarning for them to be ready to take a suspicious vehicle out.

"Everyone got their earpieces in?" Prez shouts.

"Yeah," comes multiple responses through the bud in my ear.

"That's all of us." Rock jerks his head to show those outside are outfitted out as well.

"Throttle, you and Gwen got body armour on?" Prez continues to check.

We have. Luckily it's lightweight and doesn't weigh Gwen down.

Hawk comes up carrying something. "Olivia got this done for you. Picked it up last night." He opens the bag allowing me to peer inside.

Whispering, I ask, "Has it got my patch on it?"

He nods, his eyes gleaming.

Without fanfare I go over to my old lady. "Seems right you wear this, Gwen."

She'd been downing a cup of coffee, and swings around. I notice for all her bravado, her hands are shaking.

"What is it?" When I pass her the leather cut, she stares at it for a moment. The seconds stretch out, and I wonder if I should have spent a few minutes talking about our meaning of property when suddenly she squeals, slips it on, and jumps into my arms.

I return the kiss she fiercely presses upon me.

"Your mine, and I'm yours," I tell her when I grab some air.

"Looks good on you, Gwen." As she turns to thank Hawk, he gives her a chin lift. "Right we're off. We'll be ready and waiting."

I raise my chin and we exchange back slaps. It's the first of many.

Going outside, everyone steps up as they pass. Drifter, Truck, Roadkill and Jekyll tell me to take fucking care. Joker and Lady pull me in for hugs and we exchange, 'love you, brothers'. Next are Marvel and Mouse. Marvel whispering, *don't fuck it up*, and they're followed by Rock, Heart, Bullet and Dollar.

Peg holds back with Drummer, Wraith and Blade, the ones who we collectively, and affectionately, call the fucking old guys. Not that there aren't others who've been with the club just as long, but these are the ex-officers and have assumed special status. While they jerk our chains regularly, kicking back their heels now their work is done, when they offer advice it would be stupid to disregard it.

"Hawk's called it right," Blade notes, as he locks thumbs with mine and pulls me in for a bear hug. "Follow his plan."

When he steps aside, Wraith takes his place. "You got this, Throttle."

I nod, full of confidence that I know I have. To be otherwise means acknowledging I might lose my old lady.

"Shiny side up, Brother," is Drummer's advice. His stern stare that can make grown men tremble, softening as he meets my eyes.

Last it's Peg, hovering between his role as a father, and as a protector of the club. He doesn't say anything, just holds me tighter and slaps my back harder than the rest.

When the last of the brothers leaves the compound, Gwen's hand slips into mine. I can feel her trembling. Swinging around, I pull her into my arms.

"We're going to be fine, Gwen."

"They might not even turn up." She raises her face to look into my eyes. "What do we do then?"

"Try tomorrow. Try the next day. Alter the plan, go for evening time." Though that's more risky, not allowing the brothers to go in with darkness on their side. "Want more coffee?" I ask, trying to take her mind off what's to come.

The clubhouse is eerily silent as I walk into the kitchen flicking the lights on. The prospects are all who's left here and quite rightly they're leaving us alone and minding their business. The old ladies and the range of grown and younger children, will no doubt emerge later. They're all aware *club business* is going down and know not to interfere in it.

Gwen starts making the coffee, sensing she needs something to do, I let her get on with it. While she does, I check my gun and the spare magazines in my pocket. Something I've already done more than once, which makes me realise I'm almost as nervous as her.

When she places a steamy cup in front of me, my eyes settle on her cut. It was given to her without ceremony. I know I'll have to make it up to her.

"Love seeing you wearing my patch." She startles, making me wonder if in the midst of everything, she's forgotten she's got it on. Grinning, I add, "I'm going to fuck you later. You wearing nothing but that."

She blows on her own coffee to cool it. "I'm scared that something's going to go wrong."

Standing, I move over to her, and put my hand around the back of her head. "Trust me. Trust my brothers. We've gone over this plan a hundred times. It will work." *It's got to.* I need her safe so we can move on and start a new life.

A voice sounds in my ear, "In position."

It's Heart confirming he's the first sniper to get set up. His call is like the damn breaking, as one after the other the rest of my brothers check in.

After the last one has spoken, Wizard's voice comes on. "Ready when you are, Throttle."

Tapping my mute button off, I respond, "Copy that."

CHAPTER FORTY

*T*hrottle...

The sun is rising behind the mountains as we head out of the clubhouse and go to my bike. The shadows are still long, the day is new as yet.

I don't need to edge my bike forward to let Gwen get on, standing as it is lonely and forlorn as though missing its companions. With everything else going on, it's still sporting the replacement tank, I vow to get that repainted soon.

First things first. Let's get this business behind us.

Of course the success of the day relies on Wizard being right that the stalker's impatient, and won't wait long to make his next move. And, that he'll also assume that will be when I'm taking Gwen to work. If that fails, as I told her, we'll try again.

For a second I debate taking an SUV, but dismiss it. Riding the bike with her is dangerous, but my brothers will have my back. For this to work, I need to be recognised. Despite the risks we're taking, I admit the thought of Gwen riding behind me, wearing her property patch is a major perk.

She gets on behind me, more confident than she did before. When she hangs on tightly I realise it's not just the thrill of the ride to come, but fear of losing me today. I pause before starting the engine, allowing myself a moment to just enjoy the feeling of her surrounding me. Once we get underway, I'll be solely focused on what's ahead, what's behind me, and whatever might be coming our way.

"I'm leaving now," I say.

It only takes a second for Wizard to acknowledge me. "Ride safe."

Then I press start, kick down into first, and ease away. Once the gates of the compound appear in my rearview, I feel Gwen tense behind me. Her tightening grip reminds me this is no pleasure ride today.

We ride a couple of miles before I see it, a black Ford Explorer coming up fast behind. *Is this the one? Should I try to outrun it?* But then it turns off into a service area. *False alarm.* Damn it, my nerves are stretched taut.

It's approaching rush hour, and there seem to be hundreds of SUVs matching the only description we've got, the make and the colour. I begin to regret riding alone. *Relax,* I instruct myself. The road is busy, they'd be fools to try something here, that was the conclusion we'd come to. At this time of the morning they wouldn't be able to get away with anything, not until I turn off into a more remote area, or into the side streets leading to her work.

Another black SUV appears in my mirror. *Is that them?* Well, I'll know soon. The turn off's coming up quickly. If it's them, I want them to know where I'm heading so they'll follow straight into the trap waiting for them. To remove doubt, I indicate early.

The SUV indicator flashes in the opposite direction and moves out into the outer lane. Just as an innocent person is prone to do when a vehicle is slowing for a turn.

Nothing. Nada. Briefly I wonder whether to keep driving, and see if I pick up a tail nearer town, then I could make a U-turn and lead them back here. But loathe as I am to give up on catching the stalker this morning, Hawk's voice rings in my head. *No improvisation. Stick to the plan.* If it doesn't work, we can try again. I'm not going to risk Gwen's safety.

The turn is one hundred feet away. Fifty. *What the fuck?* The SUV has slammed on its brakes, grit flying up and smoke billowing from the abused tyres. *It's blocked the turning.* Having already started to lean to take the exit, I wrench the bike up straight, causing it to wobble which in turn makes Gwen clutch at me.

I've no choice but to go straight ahead and carry on.

"They blocked the turning." I speak rapidly, shouting loudly to make sure the mic picks my voice up as I gun my engine. "I'm heading into Tucson." A glance in the mirror confirms my fears.

"I hear you. We're coming to join you."

But I know my brothers are a fair distance away and at the speed we're travelling will mean it will be awhile before they can catch up. Meanwhile, behind us, the SUV has pulled out, right in front of another vehicle.

Only flicking sufficient quick glances ahead of me to make sure we're safe, I watch what's happening behind me. The vehicle behind the SUV had swerved to avoid it, pushing it right into the path of an eighteen-wheeler. Car after car slams into the wreckage behind, smoke billows up, but the SUV has gotten away cleanly.

Fuck.

Sure, the other side of the road is still busy with traffic heading north, but my side is empty, except the Ford Explorer and me.

Twisting the throttle makes the bike leap ahead, a thunderous roar comes from the pipes as she gives me everything she's got.

It's not enough. The SUV is gaining.

"Crash," I gasp out, hoping they can hear me over the roar of my bike. "Road blocked. They're clear. Souped-up engine, has to be. It's fuckin' gaining on me."

"Throttle. What's happening? Throttle, repeat. What the fuck's going on?"

Prez's voice comes into my ear clearly, but it seems he can't hear me.

"Son, you take care. You hear me, Son?" Peg's voice blares.

I tune them out, not liking how close the SUV is getting. It's obvious I can't outrun it, and I don't like the thought of it running us off the road.

There's only one thing to do. A side swipe could kill or seriously injure us both. In a split second I take the only option, to stop and fight.

My next moves take longer to think about than to put into action. Braking hard, I ease onto the shoulder, coming to a stop as soon as I can. Kicking the stand down, I throw myself off, dragging Gwen with me yelling at her to get down into the drainage ditch beside us, while simultaneously taking my gun out of my cut.

Again at the risk of shredding its tyres, the SUV pulls to an abrupt halt only yards ahead.

With all southbound traffic stopped, an eerie silence surrounds us as the passenger door opens and I ready my aim. I won't be playing about. I'll shoot first and ask questions after.

Taking a deep breath, I hold it until a pregnant woman appears in my sights and begins walking toward me.

It's Hattie. *I can't shoot her.* It's not my baby, but that doesn't matter. My brain freezes until she gets close.

"I just want to talk, Throttle," she calls out when she's near enough. She holds out her hands as if to prove she's unarmed.

I might not be going to fire, but I've still kept my gun trained steadily on her. "Who's driving?" I yell in reply.

"My brother. He's just going to wait for me."

There indeed seems to be no move from the driver's side. I relax my grip on my gun and lower it.

"You haven't got anything to say that I want to hear, Hattie. It's over."

I've been crouching, I now go to stand up. Taking my lead,

Gwen stands beside me, as she does she bends to brush dirt off her knees.

"You patched her," Hattie spits out, her voice full of horror and disgust.

"Nothing the fuck to do with you, Hattie."

As she steps forward, minimising the gap between us, I throw out my arm protectively to keep Gwen back. Hattie might not be carrying a weapon, but I don't trust her.

"Go back to your brother and get out of here. We've got nothing to say to each other."

"Just a moment, Throttle, please. Just a few words." Her steps bring her too close. I hate her so much, I don't want her breathing my air.

When she's six feet away, I tell her to stop. "That's close enough."

She raises her hand, rubs at her face, then goes to lower it, but it detours around her back. In a movement that, despite myself, I have to admire, in the next instant I have a gun pointing straight at my face.

Stupid mistake. I often carry my weapon in my waistband, but I've never seen Hattie armed before. I'd miscalculated. And now I might pay for it. By the time I raise my own gun and get a shot off, I could be dead. *And Gwen?* It's her that Hattie's wants to stop breathing air.

"Behind me, Gwen," I rasp out. Hattie's got nothing to gain by killing me.

As if he'd been watching in his rearview, a man steps out of the driver's side. He, too, has a gun held in his hand, and swaggers toward us wearing a cocky smile on his face as if he holds all the cards. I've known prospects like him before, until we knock the stuffing out of them, that is, and show them their place.

"Drop the gun," he instructs. "You don't have a fuckin' chance."

I keep hold of it tight.

"She's dead if you don't." Stepping to the side puts Gwen in his sights. I notice his hand is steady.

My mind's racing, but comes up with just one option. *To buy us time.* "What do you want with us?" I ask, hoping to get them talking. Hopefully my brothers are on their way—if they can get around the roadblock that Hattie and her brother had caused.

"Get her," Hattie instructs over her shoulder, then to me, she says, "I want you dead."

"Why?" She'd wanted me alive to play happy families. Her removing her competition, that I can understand, but taking me out? That's crazy talk.

"Leave Gwen alone and I'll do whatever you want."

Hattie shrugs. "Too late, Throttle. I don't believe you. If I can't have you, I'll make sure nobody else ever will."

Gwen makes a sound behind me, then cries out, "You're insane. You can't kill a man just because you can't have him."

"Can't I?" Hattie widens her stance.

I start calculating distances, I'd rather die trying to take her out than just stand here and receive a bullet in my skull.

Hattie's brother, having waited to hear this conversation play out, and grinning widely at the death sentence his sister's just pronounced, approaches Gwen.

I want to tell her to run, but from his steady hand on the gun, she wouldn't get far. "You've got no problem with her," I growl. "Leave her the fuck alone."

Without once taking her eyes off me, Hattie smirks. "Oh but I do. She stole my man."

"I was never fuckin' yours!" I yell. I'm wavering between watching Hattie and the pressure she's got on that trigger, and the brother approaching on Gwen.

"My brothers will fuckin' hunt you down!" I roar.

"Get her. We'll take her with us," Hattie instructs. "As for you, I'll leave you here to bleed out. Hopefully you'll last long enough to consider what you've lost."

Fuck. The bitch hasn't gone for a head shot, instead she fires straight into my chest. A chest covered in body armour. Even so, it hits me like a kick from a mule and I go down.

Gwen literally roars from behind me. There's a blur of action as she throws herself forward. I'm gasping, trying to get air into my lungs, trying to get my body to move while the intense pain throbs through me.

Gwen! I scream internally. Gwen!

I cough doing anything I can to gasp oxygen, when I hear the shot. *Gwen. No!* I can't intake sufficient air to scream, though that's what internally I'm doing. *Gwen.*

It won't be the shot that kills me, it will be losing her. A pain, worse than the damage the bullet had caused surges through me, when a voice sounds through the roaring in my ears.

It's Gwen's, but not one I've heard from her before, it's deep, in control, and if I was on the receiving end, utterly chilling.

"Drop the gun or your brother is dead."

Forcing my eyes open and my head to turn, I see Gwen crouched over the brother, his gun in her hand. From how she's holding her aim, she's not going to make the same mistake as Hattie, one twitch of her finger and his brains will be all over the pavement.

"No!" Hattie cries.

I make an effort, breathing in fast and shooting out my leg, managing to topple her. Her gun goes flying. Before she can scrabble for it, I fall on top of her. I might not be as agile as normal right now, but I'm big enough to pin her to the ground, and irate enough to place my hands around her neck.

"Alive, Noah," Gwen reminds me, her tone more reasonable than expected. It gets through the murderous fog in my mind. Then she asks, "You got zip ties on you?"

What biker goes without them? Certainly not one trained by Blade. "Back... pocket." Words still prove difficult for me.

Intrigued, I watch as she inches over and all the time holding the gun unwaveringly on Hattie's brother, she gets them out.

"Turn the fuck over," she instructs. When he sneers and

refuses, she uses that cold, dominant voice again. "I don't give a damn about shooting both you and your sister." She eyes her victim for a moment. "Maybe I'll aim for your dick. I'm a good shot, I can hit a small target." To laugh would be inappropriate, but I can't help my snort.

"You wouldn't dare, bitch."

She lines up a shot. "Want to try me?"

Even I wouldn't push her at that moment. I'm not surprised when he rolls. Immediately she drops her knees into his spine, and now it's him who involuntarily exhales and loses all his breath. Expertly she takes both his hands and zip ties them quite impressively behind him.

Have I said how much I love this woman of mine?

I'm just contemplating exactly how much when I hear blessed music behind me. The roar of twenty or more motorcycles.

Wizard's first off the bike, Hawk a close second, and Peg not far behind. They stand and sum up the scene.

"You okay?"

"Bullet to the chest." I don't need to explain it just winded me, and may even have broken a rib.

"Gwen?" Prez now asks, his brow creased in concern.

She actually chuckles. "Oh I'm fine. I've had more fun than I've had for days. Best medication there is."

Peg snorts loudly, and steps forward, taking the gun out of her hands. "I don't think I've properly welcomed you to the family, yet, but darlin', you're going to fit right in."

CHAPTER FORTY-ONE

*G*wen…

"Are you sure you're okay?"

Noah's only just regained some of the colour in his face. It had killed me when I'd heard the shot. For a moment I hadn't known if he was dead or alive and a blinding rage had swept through me. On impulse I tackled the man, using all my self-defence techniques to turn the tables on him so his gun ended up in my hand. I'd had one thought in my mind, I was going to shoot them both down.

But then I remembered Noah had been wearing a Kevlar vest and was hopefully winded not dead. When he'd overpowered Hattie, my sanity kicked back in, and I knew we couldn't leave bodies scattered around.

For just a few seconds, when I thought he'd gone, I wish I'd have died. I never want to come so close to losing Noah again. *If she'd gone for a head shot…* I shake myself, trying to suppress the terror that thought causes within me. *He's alive, and so am I.*

Now we're back on the compound, and I'm hovering behind him like a mother hen, not wanting to let him out of my sight. On his part he keeps touching me, as if reassuring himself that we're both safe and alive.

Typical man, though, he brushes off my concern about how he is, asking Hawk, "What about my fuckin' bike?"

"Prospects are out there now." Hawk places his hand on Noah's shoulder. "Don't worry, Brother, we'll get it back."

"And my phone?"

Apparently that had fallen out of his pocket when we'd so hurriedly dismounted the bike. It had cut all communications between his brothers and him. Understandably they'd been out of their minds with worry.

Noah hadn't been up to riding, and someone needed to drive the SUV back, the vehicle which had two unwilling passengers trussed up inside. I'd offered, and Wizard, after a shrewd look my way, had accepted. I think that drive had been one of the strangest of my life. Hattie playing the victim in the back, her brother blaming her for fucking up. Noah, half turned in the passenger seat with his weapon trained on them. And all the time, I'd had an escort of bikes in front of me, and more behind. I'd clung to the wheel, blocked their voices out, kept one eye on Noah to make sure he was right and used the other to keep a safe distance, worried more than anything about knocking a man off his bike.

We'd made it back without incident, thank God.

Once I'd pulled up in front of the clubhouse, Butcher had run out, and had jumped into the driving seat as soon as I'd vacated it. He'd driven off up the compound. I have no idea where Hattie and her brother are now.

Inside the clubhouse brothers flood to the bar, and Nathan is run ragged getting drinks into their hands.

Hawk leans in and speaks into Noah's ear. "You gonna be okay to do this, Brother."

"Yeah." Noah caresses his chest gently. "Getting my second wind. I'm just bruised, pretty certain nothing is broken."

"Hurts like a bitch," he agrees. "I'll pass on the message." Another pat to his shoulder, then Hawk has gone.

Gently I ease myself down beside him. "Do what, Noah?"

His head had been resting back with his eyes closed. Now he opens them and turns his head to the side looking at me directly. "Never you mind."

I bristle. "You're going to question Hattie and her brother, aren't you?" I'm not stupid, nor a little woman to be pushed to one side. "You forgetting I saved your ass out there? And that I'm the one who has a major stake in this, I was the one who they beat up and who had their house burned down and car totalled?" I don't think any of us doubt the pair were behind everything now.

"Gwen…"

"Don't you dare keep me out of this, Noah."

"Fuck." His eyes flash. "Gwen, you wanna use that voice in the bedroom? Well I'm fuckin' in." My eyes go to the ceiling then come back down. Does everything come down to sex with men? "Anyway, it's not my decision." He brushes me off. "Women don't get involved in club business."

If he can't make the call, I'll find someone who can. I stand, place my hands on my hips and stare down. "I need to know *why*, Noah. And I need to hear it from the horse's mouth."

"You know why. She wanted me." His voice sounds more normal as he starts to take slightly deeper breaths.

I roll my eyes. "Sure, you're a catch, Noah. But much as I love you, I'm convinced there's more to it than that. The normal reaction is to be disappointed, not want to kill the man you want just so others can't have him."

His eyes flare. "Hattie's not fuckin' normal."

He doesn't need to tell me that. But there's more going on, I know it. Spinning on my heels my eyes search the room to find the man that I want. I spy him over at the bar, holding a beer bottle to his mouth. I head in his direction.

"Wizard." My voice is sharp, designed to get his attention. When he turns, I demand, "You're going to question Hattie, aren't you? Well, I want to be there."

He turns to me, his face impassive. "Not the way we roll, sweetheart. Members only."

I feel my cheeks begin to burn. "If it wasn't for me you'd be a member down." My breath catches, hating myself as reminding him had reminded me. "Hattie wouldn't have failed twice. She was determined to kill him, and heaven knows what they had planned for me."

His eyes soften slightly. "I know, Gwen. Noah's told me. You had his back. But leave this to us, we know what we're doing."

I won't back down. "Perhaps you don't." When he raises an eyebrow, I explain why. "I may not have been around the club for long, but you're all honourable men. You protect women, you don't hurt them. And, she's pregnant."

"You suggesting we'd pull our punches and you won't?" He seems amused.

"She tried to steal my man with lies, then when that failed, she set out to kill him. If Noah hadn't been wearing body armour, she's have succeeded." My voice is fierce.

"You're forgetting about her brother," he reminds me. "They were partners in crime.. I doubt we'll need to lay a hand on her. We'll have him singing in no time."

I don't think they've thought this through. "So he'll sing you a song, then, what? You might learn the truth about a pregnant woman. What happens next, will you just let her go?" If they do that, I'll always be looking behind me, and so will Noah.

"Throttle!" Wizard suddenly yells. "Get over here."

Turning, I watch Noah painfully get to his feet. His hand rests against his ribs as he slowly makes his way over to us.

Half expecting Wizard to tell him to get his woman under control, I'm stunned when he asks, "Got any objection to Gwen sitting in on the interrogation?"

Noah's eyes go wide. First his eyes find mine as if to check I'm serious, then he stares at his prez. They seem to have a silent conversation with grunts and gestures which go over my head.

"Blade?" Wizard again raises his voice, and the older biker

comes over, I notice grimly he's moving far easier than his younger counterpart.

The three men tower above me, and though I strain, I can't make out their fast spoken whispered conversation, except for the odd words, *Gwen, woman and pregnant.*

When they finish, Noah takes my arm. "You've got your wish, Gwen, but you might see some things you'll wish you hadn't. They'll be no going back." He pulls me slightly away from the other pair and out of their hearing. "Any blowback on the club, and it will come down on me. I've had to take responsibility for you."

"I won't say a word," I reassure him. "And just so you know, I was being serious about shooting that asshole in the dick. It was extremely tempting. I hardly think I'm an angel."

"Fuck, Gwen." his eyes soften, and he places a hand behind my head. "No wonder I fuckin' love you." He leans down and takes my lips in a kiss. A caress that becomes heated quickly.

Passing us, Blade snorts. "Think that display might be Hattie's torture in itself."

"That's an idea." Noah chuckles.

"Why stop there?" Marvel calls out. "I'm all for a bit of public sex."

I'm certainly not. My eyes widen in horror.

Wizard must have given a signal as one by one all the men start making their way out. Noah, moving stiffly and slowly, puts his hand to my back and encourages me to follow them.

"Are you up to this?" I ask Noah.

"Of course I fuckin' am." But the pain etched on his face belies him. When concern shows in mine, he adds, "I'm just bruised, I'll be fine."

Tutting under my breath, I say no more, but match my pace to his. We're heading along the track taken by the SUV earlier. A building comes into sight. Unlike the rest of the compound which is well maintained, this one is shabby and looks like a strong gust of wind might topple it.

"What is this place?"

"Our storeroom," Noah answers, but there's a glint in his eye. I shudder slightly, wondering just what they might stock in its depths.

It's also deceptively larger than it looks, big enough for all the members to disappear inside. As Noah's been walking slowly, we're the last to arrive. When we enter, I don't miss the thickness of the walls, and revise my opinion as to how sturdy it is. There's cladding which must make them close to a foot deep.

Soundproofing.

The Satan's Devils have formed a circle around something, but being so short, I can't see over their heads. As though we're guests of honour, the brothers part, allowing us to move through them.

I'd expected something like this, but the reality makes me gasp. Hattie's brother is strung up with tight ropes binding his hands to a hook in the ceiling, and his toes barely touch the ground.

Hattie, probably due to her sex and condition, is tied to a chair. Underneath the pair is a carpet of plastic sheeting. Swallowing hard, I knew this was going to be no tea party, but now question whether I really want to be here. But all I need to do is envision how I felt after my beating, and my fear when the shots were fired at my house, let alone my sadness when the fire had burned everything. As for when Noah was shot... My heart becomes stone. I want Hattie to suffer, I want her to feel the terror that I felt.

When we reach the front, my feet don't stop moving. Instead I advance, and without really knowing what I'm doing, I spit a mouthful of saliva straight at her.

She flinches, but can do nothing about the spittle sliding down her cheek.

I hear a slow handclap behind me, then Blade steps up alongside. The prospects, who had clearly been on guard duty, step away from their captives and make their way through the gap in the men still left from when Noah and I had walked through. Hearing the outer door slam makes me realise just what special consideration has been given to me, if the prospective members aren't allowed to be present.

Blade flexes his hands, or as much as he can, then steps forward. "Name," he demands of the strung up man.

Hattie's brother stays dumb. Blade kicks his legs and sends him swinging, the strain on the man's arms making him cry out.

"Name," Blade repeats. "I won't ask nicely again." He gestures toward me. "Got a woman here who's got a fondness for shooting off dicks." He makes a move toward the gun in his waistband as though he's going to pass it to me.

"Dirk. Dirk Sowerby," the man screams.

"There, that wasn't so hard, was it?" Blade grins. He checks in with Noah who's leaning against a workbench. Noah nods for him to continue. I guess as movement is painful for the enforcer, Blade's stepping up to do the physical work. From his expression, I think the older man's enjoying it.

I should find it sickening, I don't. I wish he'd hurry up and get answers.

Instead, Blade takes his time, eyeing Dirk, then switching his consideration to Hattie. After a minute, he asks, "So which of you is going to talk to me?"

Hattie cries out, "Dirk's got nothing to do with this. All I did was want Throttle to step up and be a father to my son."

"You tried to fuckin' kill me!" Noah roars, stepping forward too quickly and grimacing. At a gesture from Blade he falls back again.

"Now let's see." Blade tries to straighten a finger of one hand. "One of you beat up Gwen, stalked her, stalked Throttle, shot up Gwen's house, then set fire to it. Am I missing anything?"

"They sent anonymous gifts." I jerk his memory.

Hattie's eyes flick around the room. "I sent the gifts. I wanted Throttle to see how much he meant to me. I swear I didn't do anything else. I don't know what you're talking about."

Blade nods as though he believes her, despite her being the one who shot Noah. "So it was you, Dirk."

"No." Dirk's shaking his head frantically. "It wasn't me. You've got the wrong man."

Blade looks like he's considering his statement. Then he approaches Hattie. "See my problem here? Your brother says it was you."

"I didn't do anything," she says, sullenly.

Suddenly Blade lurches forward, his hands rest either side of the seat of her chair, his face right up into hers. "You tried to kill my brother this morning."

Taking a leaf out of my book, she spits into his face, making him leap back, and wipe his cheek.

I'm not going to be a bystander. Without asking for permission, I take the space in front of Hattie that he's just vacated. "Why, Hattie? Why did you shoot Noah? If he hadn't had been wearing body armour, you would have killed him."

"I wish I had!" she screams back.

"Blade? Give me a knife, will you?"

To my surprise, Blade does. "What are you going to do?" he asks, conversationally.

"Gut her."

"No!" Hattie's gone completely white. "She's batshit crazy!" she yells out. "I'm pregnant. You can't let her hurt me."

Hmm. Seems she's realised a woman might have more guts in this situation. I press my advantage, aided by the tip of the blade under her chin. "I suggest you don't test me." I pause for effect, then ask, "Why did you want to kill Noah? And no more bullshit about no one else having him, because as much as my man is magical in the sack, I don't believe that's the reason."

When she's reluctant to speak, I jerk the knife up, just enough to break the skin and send blood trickling. Now she knows I mean business.

"Because he wouldn't step up and be there for my baby." She comes up with another excuse.

"A baby we already know isn't his."

"We don't know that! Not yet."

I don't give an inch. "But we will, Hattie, won't we? And I'm becoming extremely interested in who exactly the father is. Why didn't you go to him to support you?"

Hattie's eyes flick wildly left and right. "Because he refused?"

The fact that her voice can't disguise it's a question strongly suggests she's fishing for a credible excuse.

Blade steps forward and touches my shoulder. "Let's see if I can help this along. I doubt much is left secret within families." As soon as he's spoken, he takes another blade out of his obviously adapted cut, and before I can register what he's doing, he's jabbed it hard into Dirk's leg. Dirk yells so loud I worry for my eardrums.

Then he steps back. "Who's the daddy, Dirk boy? I'd advise you to answer me."

Dirk's screaming in pain, but all he says is, "Throttle. That's what she told me."

"I've got years of experience questioning men," Blade speaks casually. "More than enough to know when they're lying." He pauses, then says over his shoulder. "Think Dirk here is overdressed."

He doesn't have to say anything more. Several men step forward, knives flash, within moments Dirk is as naked as the day he was born.

"Gwen?" Noah's voice comes loudly. "Don't... oh, it's okay. You can look. You'd need a magnifying glass to see that dick."

Several of the men start laughing.

I don't know if it's the insult to his manhood, or the fact that the trappings of civility have been removed, but Dirk's face glows red.

"Don't hurt him!" Hattie cries out as though realising the Devils are serious.

"You going to talk? Or are you going to see your brother chopped into pieces?" I can't believe the words that are coming out of my mouth. Especially when I follow them up with, "Once they've finished with him, I'll start on you. By the time I'm finished, you won't need to worry about any baby." *Christ is this me?*

"No, no! Not my baby. Don't hurt me. I'll talk." Tears are flooding down Hattie's face, her nose is dripping. But I feel no sympathy. *Noah could be dead.*

I return to that question. "Why did you try to kill Noah?"

She hiccups, then a look of utter defeat comes over her face. "Because the test results hadn't come back. If he wasn't around, he couldn't deny paternity. If he was dead, no one else would have cared."

Incredulously, and ignoring the holes in her plan, I ask, "You preferred a dead man to be your child's father than a real one?"

"Who is the fuckin' father?" Noah roars. Grimacing, still holding himself, he steps forward fast. "Fuckin' tell me, Hattie, else I'll gut you myself."

"No, don't!" Dirk screams. "Don't harm my sister or kid! I beg you."

My sister or kid. Not, or the kid. *Could it be?* Or has my mind gone off into la la land? Ignoring his, as Noah said, not very impressive dick, I approach Hattie's brother and voice the almost unthinkable idea that's come into my head. "It's you, isn't it? You're the baby's father."

While both cry out their denials, I turn to Wizard who's been watching proceedings. "Think about it. No one would suspect what might go on between brother and sister behind locked doors, unless there's an accident and they make a baby."

"Incest?" Hawk, at his prez's side, creases his brow.

"That's why they wanted to label someone else as the father. They probably didn't even want Throttle to step up and claim it, just for it to have a parentage that no one would question. That's why it was so important to prevent the results being revealed."

"Is she right?" Blade challenges Hattie.

But the look of defeat on her face shows everything.

The sound of jeers around the room is almost deafening. "That's fuckin' sick," Joker calls out.

"What's sick is that Throttle almost got killed for it." Truck looks furious. "All to cover their delinquencies up."

"Fuckin' perverts!" Roadkill shouts. "Your own sister, man?"

"I suppose you can't help who you love," Marvel states, while beside him Cast sticks his finger in his throat and pretends to throw up.

"Kid could be born with two fuckin' heads or something." Lady looks angry. "Why didn't you just abort it?"

"It's our *baby*," Hattie cries out.

With that I think I realise the depths of their depravity. They obviously don't care in the eyes of society and the law they've done wrong, just that someone might find out about it. The baby could be taken away, what kid should be allowed to grow up calling their uncle, daddy?

CHAPTER FORTY-TWO

Throttle…

Well if that isn't one of the most sickening things I've ever heard. I knew there had to be a reason behind the stalking and everything that had happened lately. The gifts to butter me up, then the escalation trying to split up Gwen and me. Hattie must have concocted the plan and had set her sights on me.

They must be deranged to have the relationship they have. Which might explain why they'd go to such lengths to hide it. Why she was prepared to kill me to keep their secret.

That it wouldn't have worked, that even after my death, Peg and Mom would have contested the paternity obviously hadn't occurred to them. But then, I'd never have credited Hattie with much intelligence.

A sudden burst of rage comes over me, making the ache in my ribs fade away. I get right up in Hattie's face.

"Why me, Hattie? Why not finger one of the other motherfuckers you slept with?"

Her face contorts. "I only slept with you. I'm faithful to Dirk. And you were nothing compared to him anyway."

I let the insult roll off me. Seeing his dick, I'm quite certain she's lying. It's possible he's a grower, but not to the extent to match how I'm endowed, and I very much doubt he knows as much as me to do with it.

What is clear though, is once she all but laid herself out at my feet like an all-you-can-eat buffet, she was stuck. She set both me and her up when she put all her eggs in one basket. Mine. An ignorant biker who was known as a manwhore and who'd be likely to fuck up at some point. A thug like me who she assumed wouldn't have questioned it. *Just like my own father had done.*

I've been played for a fool.

She was already pregnant when she came on to me and desperate to cover up who the true father was.

"What if I'd fallen for it, Hattie? What if I'd stepped up?"

She sneers. "You're nothing. Any court in the land would have preferred a mom and uncle parenting than an outlaw biker."

"You could just have said you didn't remember the name of the father. Why the fuck come up with this plan?"

"Because," Gwen astutely answers for her, "a name on a birth certificate would stop questions being asked. They wanted to cover all bases."

"I say we put both of them down." Jekyll sounds utterly disgusted. "Including the kid. Would be a kindness. Who knows what problems it might have?"

"Nah," Heart says. "That baby is the one innocent in this. Kill Dirk. He's probably the one who took advantage of his sister."

"Noooo," Hattie wails again. "I *love* him."

I spin and face her reading the truth on her face. She loves her brother, but certainly not in the way Lisa loves me.

"Cut off his dick at least," Rock yells out. "Stop them making more babies."

Now it's Dirk wailing, and writhing on his strung up arms.

Out of the corner of my eye I catch Hawk beckoning to me. I go over to where he's talking to Wizard.

Prez shakes his head in a tired way. "This is beyond fucked up, Brother."

I run my hands through my hair. "You're telling me."

Hawk glances behind me, settling his eyes on the weeping pair for a moment, then looks back. "If it was just the asshole, I'd put him down in an instant. Deviant fuck."

"But it's her, isn't it?" Prez clenches his jaw. "I don't pick up that she was an innocent victim."

Like Hawk, I take a look behind. "He's older, but not by much. I don't know their back story, and hell, I don't want to think about it." Thoughts of my more appropriate relationship with Lisa return to my head. "He might have coerced her, but in all of this, she's not once played on our sympathy. She's genuinely frightened for him. And don't forget it was her who came onto me, whatever his involvement in everything else."

"I don't get the innocent vibe either, Throttle. Maybe I'd buy it if she hadn't put that bullet in your chest." Prez winces, as if imagining my blossoming bruise for himself. "But I don't like the thought of executing her, not when she's carrying a baby, despite what its parentage is."

Other brothers have gathered around, from the murmurs they would also have difficulty ending her life. Even me, and I'm the one she shot.

"We can't let them go free." Peg's joined us. "Not with all that they've done. They're insane, and who knows whether they'd try to take Throttle or Gwen out again."

Mouse steps forward, speaking quietly, "You know we record confessions so we can replay them later?"

I nod, we do. It's a closed loop in here, completely unconnected to any network so no way to be accessed by the outside world. Mouse and Prez take security seriously. We make recordings as sometimes it's useful to play back a confession, for our ears only, of course.

"How about I work on the recording," he suggests, "Edit out

any of the persuasion to get them to talk, then deliver them, and it, to the cops."

I stare at Mouse, wondering whether he's on to something. Gradually I start to grin. "Cops all but refused to put effort into tracking Gwen's stalker down," I remind them. "So they can't complain that we've done their job for them."

"It will mean a court case and a trial," Hawk reminds us. "Would Gwen be up for that?"

"She works in the legal field," I tell them. "I don't see they'd be a problem. Attempted murder, arson and indiscriminately letting off firearms means they'll go away for a very long time. And the baby would need to be adopted or something."

Prez thinks for a moment. "Go talk to her Throttle. She's been the most affected out of all of us."

After pinching the bridge of my nose, trying to get my thoughts into order, I raise my chin, then turn around. Gwen's standing off to the side, her eyes glazed as if she's lost in her mind somewhere.

Approaching her, I pull her into my arms, kissing the top of her head. "It's not easy, is it?" She'd impressed the hell out of me taking over questioning as she had, her intuition speeding us getting the answers we needed.

"I'm used to liars," she says quietly. "Custody battles often mean learning to discern which parent is telling the truth. I knew there was something there if I started digging." She shivers. "Never suspected it was as bad as that. What's going to happen to them?"

"Got a proposition for you." I take a moment to explain, and what that will mean for her. Me, I'm prepared to stand up in court and tell my part in the sorry tale. But if Gwen doesn't want that, we'll think of something else. Hattie's put her through too much already.

But when I've finished speaking, Gwen sighs with relief. "I thought you were going to hurt them..." *She thought we were going to kill them.* And so we might have, had it not been for the child. If we'd just disposed of Dirk, Hattie would put the blame for his disappearance on us. This is a rare time when it's best to put it all in the hands of the cops.

"That poor kid," Gwen shudders. "That's who I feel most sorry for."

Over her head, my eyes land on Hattie. "At least it'll be out of their hands. Fuck knows how it would have been brought up."

Again Gwen shivers and wraps her hands around herself. "If it started when they were young, Dirk could be a paedophile to boot."

I close my eyes. *We've just agreed to let the cops deal with this.* It's hard to stop myself tearing him from limb to limb. *If we'd never found out… that poor kid.*

Turning away so I can not longer see him, I fix my eyes on my woman instead, making myself think of our future that is now within reach.

Hawk's already organising the prospects to firstly bandage Dirk's leg, then find some clothes for Dirk to wear. Once he's dressed, the pair are loaded into their own SUV once again, secured in yet more zip ties.

Mouse works his magic with the tape which, along with Hawk and Wizard, I listen to a few times. It's the excellent job I expect from him. It's impossible to hear a scream, or even a gap where the recording has been chopped together. It makes for even more of a compelling, chilling and decidedly sickening story.

Finally, after a call to Fontaine, Gwen and I get into the SUV, and drive down to the precinct. It's probably the first time I've driven there under my own volition.

Hattie and Dirk seem resigned to their fate as I usher them inside, or perhaps they're grateful just to be alive.

"I'm making a citizen's arrest," I inform the officer at the desk.

"On what charge?" He doesn't appear to be impressed.

"Stalking, for a start. Arson, indiscriminate use of a firearm, attempted murder… oh, and for causing a pile up on the I-10 this morning. You'll find the Ford Explorer that caused it outside."

"And incest," Gwen adds, a look of distaste in her eyes. "Which in Arizona is a class four felony."

The officer resembles a gaping fish right now. "Is this a joke?" He eyes the pair who stay silent.

"No joke." I extract a flash drive from the pocket of my jeans. "You'll find the confessions are all there."

That kicks off a buzz of activity. Gwen and I are interviewed together at first, then separated and attempts are made, on her part to trip up my story, and on mine, for exactly how the Satan's Devils extracted the information.

But when Everest Fontaine turns up, things start to settle. At his insistence, I'd bared my chest and allowed it to be photographed as evidence of the attempted murder. The cops started to become more interested, then defensive after the lawyer's observation that the cops hadn't exactly fallen over themselves to find Gwen's stalker, and that the Satan's Devils had conveniently done their work for them,. He might also have suggested the club doesn't want any of the glory, which had made the slouching cops sit back up. Closing such a case would be a good result for them.

When they revealed that someone had sadly lost their life in the pile up this morning, just another innocent victim of the Sowerby siblings, they'd decided not to question the gift we'd presented them too closely, having a reason now they can wrap everything.

At last they let us go, but with warnings our involvement might be followed up.

I call a cab to take us back to the compound and hold Gwen tight on the journey. We're both quiet as though it's only just sinking in that we can stop looking over our shoulders.

When we're dropped off at the gates, I take her hand, and

also a moment to breathe in the fresh air. *I'm home, at last, with my old lady.*

As though taking my lead, she inhales deeply. "It's really over, isn't it?" Her tone is hopeful, but tinged with disbelief.

"It is. It really is." I confirm in a voice full of as much sincerity as I can put into it. There's no need for her to worry anymore. As we walk past the auto-shop and on up to the club-house, I inject a note of optimism. "Now we can concentrate on our future, no need to keep looking behind."

"No Hattie," she replies with feeling. She tugs on my hand, pulling me to a stop. As I look down, her teeth are worrying her lip. "Is this going to change anything?"

I don't understand. Perplexed, I ask, "What do you mean?"

She glances away before meeting my eyes. "Well, you've always been rescuing or protecting me. Now it's just us, won't that get boring?"

Chuckling softly, I respond, "Somehow I don't think life with you will ever be boring, Gwen. Hell, you were the one doing the protecting today. You saved my fuckin' life. I think you'll always keep me on my toes. I do worry, though."

"You worry? About what?"

I take a moment before replying. She needs to accept what I am, and I need to know that her new knowledge won't haunt her. "You've seen the worst of the Devils now. I'm not hiding it. This is what I do. This is who I am. If I hadn't been injured, then it would have been me in Blade's place today."

She raises her hand and places it on my face. "All I saw was a family protecting family. It was terrifying, but also beautiful. You can't know how much that means to me. That's not going to scare me away. I doubt you'd hurt anyone who didn't deserve it."

"I wouldn't," I tell her sincerely, "and neither would my brothers. We protect our own, in whatever way is necessary."

When a warm smile curves her lips, we start walking again. Only a few strides later, she again stops. "Am I a bad person that

I've no sympathy for Hattie? I mean, she's younger than her brother and who knows what pressure he put her under. He might have been controlling her all the time."

"You're not a bad person, Gwen. If that was the case, she could have asked for help. Fuck, she could have asked me. My suspicions are things could be the other way around. She's pretty damn persuasive and once set on a course, doesn't deviate. It might have been her taking the initiative, and not him. He might have just gone along with it. Or, they both went into their relationship with eyes open." Raising my eyes, I stare into the distance. "Who knows how fucked their growing up was. Maybe something pushed them together. For myself, I can't have much sympathy for how their twisted relationship started. It did, and the fallout was on us."

"Do you think we'll ever know?"

"I know I don't care," I tell her sharply. "We should never have been caught up in it. We're the victims here. It might come out in court though. One of them might drop the other in it for leniency."

"I don't understand how a brother and sister can, well, you know." Her voice drips with distaste. "I mean, I've heard about some sick shit happening in foster homes, but to step into, or at least continue such a relationship voluntarily? And to think they could bring up a baby?" She shudders.

She's not the only one who can't understand it, but it's the reference to her past which worries me, and makes me feel guilty. At school, I'd thought she was living a life too perfect to be tainted by a motorcycle club. I was so fucking wrong. She'd only appeared that way because she had to. I've seen glimpses of a more spirited woman slowly emerge. Boring, she'd asked? Nah, no way. I think Gwen is going to keep me on my toes, and I'll love every fucking moment of it.

At the clubhouse, we have to retell what happened with the cops more than a few times. The general mood is a mix of pleasure that everything's over, and bewilderment at what had been at the root of it. That Hattie had wanted a legitimate father so she could keep her child was something that had never crossed any of our minds.

"She was crazy, you know?" Darcy, once home from her shift, has joined us. "I can't compute how a brother and sister can get in to such a relationship. And go so far to keep a baby that came of it."

Mouse flops down beside us. "From her background check, I know their parents are dead. Possibly they only had each other."

"Hattie was quite pretty, but he wasn't even good looking," Gwen comments, making me laugh.

"Nor had a big dick," I remind her, getting a thump on my arm for my observation.

Bikers don't need much to kick off a celebration. Drinks are flowing, music, for once not my dad's choice, is playing. Gwen's getting a kick out of brothers treating her as the hero of the hour, cementing her place in our mismatched family.

She begins to glow, the happiness radiating off her is addictive. Even the pain in my chest disappears as I get too much pleasure simply watching her, whether it's cuddling babies or talking with the other old ladies.

"She's a good one." Marvel flops down beside me, his eyes following Gwen. For once, he's not being snarky.

"She is that," I agree, content to sit back and watch her as she says goodnight to Amy and Olivia, who are taking their kids back to their homes.

"She's got hidden depths," he continues. "Hell, she saved your life today."

I wait for the punch line, something about me needing a woman to save me, but he's being genuine tonight. My eyes never leave her, needing a line of sight to bind her to me. Now it's Mom she's waving off, making me realise that most of the other old ladies have slowly taken their leave. Out of the corner of my eye I see Drummer and Sam making out in ways they really shouldn't do, not at their age. *Will Gwen and I be like that when we're old?* I'd like to think so.

Turning away from the non-PG couple, I spy Peg talking to Gwen animatedly. She'd earned his respect today. It warms me how she fits into my family. *I can give that to her.*

I'm still watching, unable to tear my eyes away, when Sable and Clover emerge. Clover makes a beeline for Marvel, offering her hand to pull him up from his seat. He chuckles and gives in quickly. Him getting up and tossing me a knowing wink, then putting his arm around her, blocks my view momentarily.

A commotion at the bar has me standing and physically moving Marvel. *What the fuck?* Sable's on her back on the floor, legs askew and Gwen pinning her down with her foot. As other conversations cease around her, I hear my old lady.

"You fucking go near my man and you're dead," she warns. "For your information, I *do* think I'm enough for him. I also know hell will freeze over before he goes near you again."

"Throttle's ol' lady's really something," Hound remarks. "You see how she took that bitch down?"

I can do nothing but stand here grinning so wide it feels like my face could split. Gwen needs no support from me, she's more than capable of dealing with a club whore. But someone else is moving past me.

Now it's Sam standing with her arm around my old lady, a tactile gesture of support.

"One chance, Sable. You know the rules. One move on a taken man and you're out of here."

Sable rubs at her eyes, tears smearing her makeup. "Throttle said he'd never settle down. I thought it was a joke when I heard."

Gwen catches my eye and grins widely, then looks down to the girl who seems too scared to move. "He was just waiting for the right woman and one who could handle him."

She's right. I raise my beer bottle in salute while thinking, *she can handle me anytime she fucking wants.*

CHAPTER FORTY-THREE

*T*hrottle...

A month ago, the arrest and detainment of the Sowerby siblings without bail had taken the pressure off not just me and Gwen, but the whole damn club. Church meetings returned to normal now we no longer had to wrack our brains to any possible enemy we could have who might be out for revenge.

I'd been genuinely worried that without the external forces pushing us together, Gwen and I might drift apart. She's grown in confidence, and it had occurred to me now she didn't need me in my role of protector anymore, would she get tired of me?

While on my part I knew I wouldn't get bored, I did have concerns whether I could totally suppress my manwhore ways having been such for so long. Whether I'd view Gwen with new eyes, fearing that my intense feelings toward her were a mix of needing to keep her safe, and leaning on her for support, tinged with more than a taste of gratefulness. If it wasn't for her, chances are, I wouldn't be alive.

I was wrong on both counts. Once the pressure had been taken away, we'd been able to relax and grow in our relationship. Instead of getting itchy feet and wanting to stray, to try something different for a change, Gwen had ensnared me. I know now I have the greenest grass my side of the fence, and no appetite for any other.

Gwen, thank fuck, seems to feel the same way.

While I'd never expected to find the perfect woman for me, had I ever been asked to describe my one, I'd have listed all the attributes she possesses, from fitting in with my family, to being admired and accepted by my brothers and the way she accepts me and my lifestyle.

I'd put behind me my guilt that previously I'd kept her away from the compound, knowing that then, I'd never have had the same relationship with her. I think we both needed time to mature into our own person. On my part to get my wild oats sowing out of my system, on hers, for her to learn to stand on her own feet.

If anything, we've grown stronger together, as slowly we've stopped rehashing the past, and instead concentrate on building the foundations of our future.

The gifts from Hattie had stayed at the back of my closet for a while. Even when a hole appeared in my left boot, I couldn't bring myself to use her offering. Instead, I purchased a new cheaper but serviceable pair. Hattie's went to Goodwill along with the gloves. I'd felt lighter when there was nothing physically left to remind me.

Proof, if I needed it, that the thrill of walking into the room and Gwen's presence immediately making my heart beat faster hasn't diminished at all comes today. I knew she'd be home from work, but not finding her in our now-adapted-suite-come-apartment, doesn't come as any surprise. I wander up to Dad and Mom's house. As expected, their daughter-in-law, treated more like a blood daughter, is there.

She looks beautiful, her face animated as she sits at the table pointing out the plans for the house we're having built. Observing, just for a moment before drawing attention to my presence, I watch as her lips press together at something

Mom's said, then nods, picks up a pen, and makes some adjustments.

Grinning, I step forward, the thump of my boots on the floor announcing my arrival. Leaning down and kissing her upturned face, I turn to my mom.

"What you got us doing now?"

"Your fire precautions are lacking."

I glance up then down. "Shooter and Bullet have followed the fire regulations to the letter. You think they wouldn't?"

Mom huffs. "Latest research has shown it's best to have fire retardant walls here and here." She points to the plan. "There's new advice coming out about the number of fire extinguishers you need, the type and their placement."

I wasn't born the last time wildfire was a serious threat to the compound, I'd come along a suspicious nine months or so after. Mom had been a firefighter then, and it was as the fire had raged that Dad and her had got together. It's down in part to her insistence that the firebreak is, even today, still well maintained. In the main though, having once skirted with losing the compound, it's a high priority of all the brothers. Hence I would never tell Mom her caution was over the top, nor disregard her suggestions.

Gwen, also admires her. If that means making changes to our new house, she complies without objection.

"I'm just making sure you won't get burned to death in your bed," Mom says, primly.

"I assure you, Mom, what goes on in our bed is sizzling hot as it is. We keep an extra fire extinguisher on hand just in case."

When Mom inhales sharply and shoots me a look, I wink at Gwen who's gone red. Bored with one person? I can't believe I ever thought that. If I run out of ideas, Gwen seems to have plenty. Her lips wrapped around my cock… *don't go there*, I lecture myself sternly, knowing my tenting pants would not be appropriate in front of my parents.

I do notice Dad's not upset at all with my comment. In fact, he smirks at Mom. Hell, I don't even want to think about what goes on in their bed, but as I see her catching his eye and blushing, I know I have to change the subject quickly unless I want to be witness to a PDA between my parents.

Will we be like that? Will we be seeing our silver anniversary on the horizon and still be as much in love as we are presently? I think there's a good chance, then cleanse my mind from that way of thinking. From the look of desire on Dad's face, and Mom's flushed with something I'm worried is arousal, it's a sign that attraction doesn't fade in the right relationship.

Was it really only a couple of months ago that I was extolling the virtues of being single to Peg? Berating him, telling him I'd never settle? I suppose I'm lucky he's refrained from telling me he told me so. But sometimes he does have a look of superiority when he's watching Gwen and me.

"Hi everyone. I'm home." A singsong voice announces the arrival of the one person who can take Gwen from me. My own fucking sister.

Lisa bounds into the room. "Gwen! I was hoping you were here. I've been shopping."

"Oh?" Gwen looks up interested and already starting to stand. "What did you buy?"

Lisa waves the bags. "I brought them to show you before taking them home. Want to come to my room?"

"Oh, it's still yours, is it?" Mom glances up. "I might have changed it into my sewing room."

"Sewing room?" Lisa's eyes grow enormous in her face. "Since when have you been into sewing?"

"I could start. I'd need a place to do it."

Lisa pouts and comes rushing over. "But you love me, Mom."

Mom can't keep it up and starts to laugh. "Go away, show Gwen your purchases."

When the girls leave the room, I smirk. "You still keep my room as it was." I've often wondered why they don't repurpose it.

Without missing a beat, Mom replies. "I'll need somewhere for the grandchildren to stay over."

"Lisa's pregnant?" I ask casually, knowing I'm stirring shit up.

Peg growls, "She better fuckin' not be."

After I laugh at his predictable response, I tell them seriously, "Gwen and I have decided to wait. We're still getting over that business with Hattie. We're both young, it could be a question of if, not when."

"Is that you speaking or her?"

"You've always known my view." But truly it's both of us. Gwen and I had had to face being parents too soon, when we'd only just started our relationship. After a couple of occasions when we took risks, we'd been more careful relying on condoms which, thank fuck, I can now trust again. We want to build the house, Gwen to get settled into her career and us both to grow in our relationship before even thinking of adding children into the mix. We'd discussed it like the adults we are and come to a joint decision. "Don't go pressuring her, Mom." I add, warningly.

As Mom holds up her hands in a *would I do that* gesture, footsteps and giggles sound on the stairs behind us.

"We're going down to the clubhouse," Lisa announces.

Gwen gifts me with a wave of her hand before the two of them disappear.

Shaking my head, happy Gwen's got friends and family around her now, I pull the house plans toward me. After discussing security with Dad for a while, I put them to one side.

"Guess I better go find my ol' lady."

"Later, Son," Dad waves me off, while Mom has a kiss for me.

In the clubhouse, all the women are around, and so are the babies. Even the screaming doesn't bother me so much as it used to, though I still grimace when I see Hawk trying to pacify Layla. I grin when with a roll of his eyes he gives up, and she settles immediately she's put into the crib beside Calvin. When Hawk sees my smirk, he shows me his finger.

The doting grandparents are there. Heart and Marcia, Sam and Drummer, Wraith and Sophie as well as Mouse and Mariana. Lisa and Gwen are sitting by the bar and have their heads bowed together. They're laughing. I have a quick word with Blade, then approach my old lady.

Looping my arm around her shoulder I ask, "What's so fuckin' funny?"

For some reason that starts them giggling again.

Lisa gives a wicked grin only a sister can. "I might have shared some things."

Gwen pats my arm, and says condescendingly, "I don't mind that you used steal her Barbies."

I huff. "Only to go on Action Man's bike."

"Naked," Lisa adds, her head nodding in emphasis.

"I was six, Lisa. What's wrong with a kid wanting to see what a woman was like under her clothes."

Gwen peels with laughter. "As Action Man doesn't have a dick, I suspect you were confused."

"Nah," Lisa refutes straight-faced. "Noah thought it was normal." She leans in, and stage whispers, "His was so small he didn't know it was there."

Grabbing her wrist I give her a Chinese burn. Only lightly, of course.

"Can I get you anything?" Rascal's head pops up from behind the bar.

"I'll take a beer," I tell him, ceasing the abuse of my sister.

"Coffee for me," Lisa requests.

"And me," Gwen responds.

"Bloody heathens. Tea for me, please, Razza."

Spinning around, I chuckle at Sophie who's appeared. While the prospect puts our order together, she carefully watches him placing a tea bag in the cup, and then drowning it in boiling water. She tuts when he takes the bag out immediately, so loudly, he hurriedly puts it back in, and leaves it while he gets my beer and the girl's coffees. Then, with a worried glance her way, he fishes the bag out with a spoon, and tops the cup up with milk.

When he passes it to Sophie, she examines it with narrowed eyes, then pronounces, "That's great. That will put hairs on your chest."

What the fuck is that all about?

"It's a proper builder's brew that," Sophie continues, equally mysteriously. "Carry on like that, Razza, and you've got my vote."

I'm just about to point out he'll be voted in on his loyalty to the club, not how he can make a drink for a fucking old lady, when Gwen suddenly makes a strangled sound. Turning, I see her rapidly replacing her coffee on the bar top, covering her mouth with her hand and rushing in the direction of the bathrooms.

"And another one bites the dust. I thought we warned her not to drink the water." Olivia has come up to her mom and, taking her cup out of her hands, steals a sip of her tea.

Water? What the fuck?

Worried about Gwen clearly being ill and wondering why the others aren't concerned, I start to go after her. Then pause my steps. *Water?* It hits me so fast I stagger.

There's an ongoing rumour about the Tucson club and the number of babies we produce. I put it down to the compound which is a conducive environment to raising a family myself, but all the other chapters warn about drinking the fucking water.

Gwen can't be pregnant. That wasn't in our plan. We'd agreed to wait. *I'm not ready.* The relief I felt knowing Hattie's baby wasn't mine gave us both a new freedom that we were determined to enjoy. Sure, one day I'd like her pregnant with my baby, it's just not now.

But whether or not I can deal with the outcome, my old lady's probably throwing up. It's more likely to be an upset stomach, we've been careful. But whatever, she needs me.

They're wrong. They have to be.

I take a step, then another. *Could she be?* Now I take the third more lightly. To my surprise, a grin splits my face, and I cover the rest of the distance quickly.

If Olivia's right, even now, Gwen's carrying my baby.

I could be a fuckin' daddy in a few months' time, surrounded by dirty diapers and trying to soothe a crying baby.

I'll be fucked, if that doesn't feel right.

Niran

When Grumbler was held up by a flat, he asked me to accompany his wife, Mary, to her prenatal appointment. Due to their ages, he's always prepared for bad news and didn't want her to go alone. Of course, I said yes and went along.

Would I have been so eager if I'd known the consequences? I met a woman who pulled at all my heartstrings, who was asked to make a decision no woman should have to face.

I'm a protector, so I got involved. I couldn't leave her to face what was ahead all alone, but just as a friend. Being anything more was the last thing on my mind. I didn't expect to put my life and those of my brothers in danger.

Saffie

I liked Niran when I met him. He was there when I needed a friend. But when I discovered he rode with a motorcycle club, I was scared and told him to go.

I've met bikers before. I know what to expect of them, and none of it is good. Even in the depths of my despair, my innate urge for self-preservation is strong.

But Niran won't take no for an answer. He's intent on invading my life. Why? Is he going to betray me?

I'd rather be scared and alone than hitch my wagon to another biker. That is, until I'm facing danger, and Niran is the only one there.

Is Niran the good man he pretends to be? Or is he something darker?

OTHER WORKS BY MANDA MELLETT

Blood Brothers – A series about sexy dominant sheikhs and their bodyguards

Stolen Lives (#1) Nijad and Cara

Close Protection (#2) Jon and Mia

Second Chances (#3) Kadar and Zoe

Identity Crisis (#4) Sean and Vanessa

Dark Horses (#5) Jasim and Janna

Hard Choices (#6) Aiza

Satan's Devils MC - Arizona Chapter

Turning Wheels (Blood Brothers #3.5, Satan's Devils #1) Wraith and Sophie

Drummer's Beat (#2) Drummer and Sam

Slick Running (#3) Slick and Ella

Targeting Dart (#4) Dart and Alex

Heart Broken (#5) Heart and Marc

Peg's Stand (#6) Peg and Darcy

Rock Bottom (#7) Rock and Becca

Joker's Fool (#8) Joker and Lady

Mouse Trapped (#9) Mouse and Mariana

Blade's Edge (#10) Blade and Tash

Heart Mended: A Satan's Devils MC Novella

Truck Stopped (#11) Truck & Allie

Satan's Devils MC Boxset 1 Books 1-5

Satan's Devils MC Boxset 2 Books 6-8

Satan's Devils MC Boxset 3 Books 9-11

Satan's Devils MC - Colorado Chapter

Paladin's Hell (#1) Paladin and Jayden

Demon's Angel (#2) Demon and Violet

Devil's Due (#3) Beef and Steph

Devil's Dilemma (#4) Pyro and Mel

Ink's Devil (#5) Ink and Beth

Devil's Spawn (#6)

Satan's Devils MC - Next Generation

Amy's Santa (#1) Wizard and Amy

Hawk's Cry (#2) Hawk and Olivia

Satan's Devils MC - San Diego Chapter

Being Lost (#1)

Grumbler's Ride (#2)

Satan's Devils MC - Utah Chapter

Road Tripped (#1)

Stormy's Thunder (#2)

ACKNOWLEDGMENTS AND AUTHOR'S NOTE

People often ask me where I get my ideas from, and it's hard to pinpoint any particular source. For this book, though, it was a question in a group on Facebook, where a reader was asking if there have been any books where the H got stalked. I didn't even see the answers, but my mind took off at full pelt, and Twisted Throttle's story is the result.

I hope, like me, you've enjoyed catching up with the FOGs and revisiting Tucson again. Secretly, I think Drummer enjoyed his brief spell back at the head of the table.

As always, a massive thank you to my beta readers, with particular mention to Sheri and Danena, who both have a large input to my books. Honestly ladies, I couldn't do without you. Mention, of course, to the other betas, Jo, Tami, Alex, Nicole, Terra and Zoe. It's so encouraging to know at an early stage that the plot works and that you enjoy the book.

Maggie Kern, you are an amazing friend as well as a brilliant editor, and I can't wait to meet you in person again. Once more, you have my grateful thanks and appreciation.

Melanie Darrow has once again been my proofreader. Thank you so much for meeting my timescales and the work you put in to giving the book a final polish.

The cover image was provided by Golden Czermak of Furious Fotog. As before, he had the perfect model, Dylan Horsch, who was a perfect muse for Throttle and he looks so much like a younger Peg. The cover was again brought to life by Dar Dixon of Wicked Smart Designs. Thank you all.

Finally, last as always, but definitely not least, thanks to all of you, my wonderful readers who've taken a chance on this book. If it wasn't for your encouragement, I wouldn't keep writing. I have recently received messages and emails telling me how much you like my books, and I love reading every one. A positive message inspires me to write more.

This book, like all of my works, has been to beta readers, through editing twice, to a proofreader and then to ARC readers, but there could still be the odd typo that's crept through. Please message me if you've found anything, so I have a chance to correct the book. I love to hear from readers, even if you're pointing out something I've got wrong.

If you've enjoyed this book, please consider writing a review. Reviews are essential to us authors, and I appreciate and read them all.

This book may be done, but don't worry. There'll be another Satan's Devil coming along very soon.

STAY IN TOUCH

Email: manda@mandamellett.com

Website: www.mandamellett.com

Sign up for my newsletter to hear about new releases in the Satan's Devils and Blood Brothers series.

Facebook reader group: https://www.facebook.com/groups/mandasbadboys/

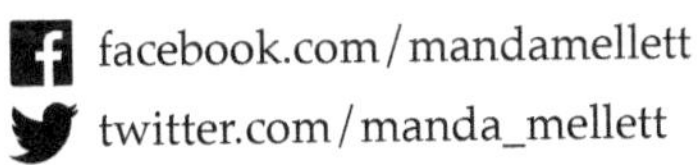

facebook.com/mandamellett
twitter.com/manda_mellett

Manda's life's always seemed a bit weird, starting with a childhood that even today she's still trying to make sense of, then losing her parents in the late teens. Going from the tragic to the bizarre, who else could be unlucky enough to have had two car accidents, neither her fault, one involving a nun, and another involving a police woman?

There isn't enough space to list everything that's happened to Manda, or what she's learned from it. But by using the rich fabric of her personal life, psychology degree, varied work experiences, and amazing characters she's met, Manda is able to populate her books with believable in-depth characters and enjoys pitting them against situations which challenge them. Her books are full of suspense, twists and turns and the unexpected.

Manda lives in the beautiful countryside of Essex in the UK, the area's claim to fame being the Wilkin's Jam Factory at nearby Tiptree. She can usually find jars of jam which remind her of home wherever she goes. As well as writing books and reading, Manda loves walking her dogs and keeping fit. She lives with her husband of over 30 years, who, along with her son, is her greatest fan and supporter.

Manda is thankful that one of the more unusual, and at the time unpleasant, turns her life took, now enables her to spend her time writing. Confirming, in her view, every cloud has a silver lining.

Photo by Carmel Jane Photography